Emily Calby Book 2

THE GIRL IN CELL 49B

DORIAN BOX

FRICTION
PRESS

THE GIRL IN CELL 49B

Copyright 2021 by Dorian Box.

This book is a work of fiction. Any references to historical events, real people, or real places are used fictitiously. Other names, characters, places, and events are products of the author's imagination, and any resemblance to actual events or places or persons, living or dead, is purely coincidental.

ISBN 978-1-7346399-2-6

Also by Dorian Box

Psycho-Tropics

The Hiding Girl

For Mary Pat Treuthart

Prologue

IT BEGINS at the end. I'm running through the backyard, past the clothesline and swing set. The stocky man is shouting from behind me, out the bathroom window, "I'm coming to cut you into pieces."

I'm not even into the woods before I'm swallowed by guilt. *Mom.* The gunshot. *And Becky.* Where's my baby sister? *Take care of your Mom and Becky.* I promised Dad.

Have to go back ... but I barely made it out the window, stocky man grabbing at my legs, trying to see through the bleach I sprayed in his eyes.

You have to go back ... but I can't. My legs won't turn. He's coming after me. I hear his footsteps pounding through the leaves. I run faster. *Coward.*

I dive into the shallow ravine I know so well and bury myself in the leaves just before he arrives. He stops, feet shuffling in the underbrush. The crunchy leaves tickle my face and I have to hold my breath to keep them from rattling.

He's muttering curse words. In the distance, the tall man is yelling. "Boss man. Place about to blow to Kingdom Come. Got to go."

In a regular voice, like he knows I'm there, "Little girl, if I ever get my hands on you, you're gonna wish you died with your mama and sister."

I already wish it. A whimper as soft as a cricket chirp. If Mom and Becky are already dead, *this will be my grave.*

All I have to do is move. He'll see me and it will be all over. I let my breath out and will my trembling arm upward through the leaves. I keep my hand poised, flat and straight, like I'm raising it in Mrs. Bianchi's math class.

A spooky silence makes me grab onto the fantasy that he's gone. Then I hear snarky laughter. "Thank you for your cooperation, blondie. Your mama was right. You are a good girl."

One click and the gun starts firing. Everything slows down. The first two bullets miss. They zip through the top layers of leaves and halt with a thud when they hit the damp decaying mat that gathered last winter. Two more shots miss. Maybe he'll run out of bullets.

But the fifth shot is a direct hit, right through the center of my chest, straight into my broken heart. Bullseye.

It hurts and I know I'm dying, but I'm not afraid. I was raised to believe. I wait for the bright light, to be lifted up and join the angels. I can already picture sweet little Becky, an angel even on earth.

... but something's not working right. The blood pumping out of the hole in my heart is being replaced just as fast with an inky black liquid, thick and gooey, like oil. It's heavy and weighs me down, pulling me farther into the ground, filling my heart and veins before overflowing from my mouth and nose and finally eyes ...

Choking, gasping ... My eyes snap open. *Just a dream. Not real, not real.*

I lie under the covers shivering as my heart rate slows and breathing returns to normal, but there's no sense of relief. Because real is worse than the dream. In the actual record of events, I didn't raise my hand through the leaves that day and die with my mother and sister. I stayed frozen as a log until the stocky man left, committing a sin I can never forgive.

I survived.

For an extra eleven hundred and forty-six days I've been able to laugh and cry and read books and see sunrises ... and breathe. Eleven hundred and forty-seven if I count today. My sixteenth birthday.

1

"HAPPY BIRTHDAY," Lucas says. "Hope you like it."

"I'm so excited," I say lethargically, the nightmare still weighing on me. I tear off the Sweet Sixteen wrapping paper, bursting with luminous gold stars and pink balloons. In my hands is a compact Sig Sauer nine-millimeter semiautomatic pistol, no box.

Lucas says. "*Sweet? I wish.*"

I force a laugh.

We're in the front lounge of the bus we've been living in and out of for three years, parked at Zinnie's Paradise Campground in the Ozark Mountains in northwest Arkansas. The air conditioner is going full blast.

"What's wrong? That's what you wanted, ain't it?"

"Uh-huh. Exactly." Right down to the black anodized finish. "You shouldn't have done it though. These things cost a thousand bucks."

"Not the way I get 'em. That gun was stolen six hundred miles from here. Got an obliterated serial number. Untraceable."

"Oh."

Birthdays have definitely changed since my twelfth, the last one I spent with my family. That day I wore a glittering tiara over my sheeny blonde hair. I got a softball glove and a pair of rubber cleats from Mom and a picture Becky colored that said *I LOVE U, LUV.* She was dancing around the living room in the cleats, way too big for her, slipping and sliding on the wood floor. We were all laughing.

For my thirteenth birthday, I got a thirty-eight caliber pocket-rocket from Lucas in a brown paper sack. No tiara. I'd already torn my golden locks to shreds.

I don't know why I'm not happier. Maybe it was the gun in my dream. Maybe because birthdays always remind me of my family.

"Thank you, Lucas." I lean to give him a hug. I'm five-seven now, same height as Mom, but the top of my head barely grazes the chin of his massive body.

"No problem," he says. "Remind me. This your real birthday or fake birthday?"

I'm counterfeit in just about every way imaginable. I live under a false identity: *Alice Black*, Joseph Black's fake adopted daughter. Joseph Black—real name Lucas Ellington Jackson—is an expert document forger. That's how we met in South Memphis, when I was on the run and looking for a driver's license. He's also a former gang member and drug dealer smart enough to have invested his profits in mutual funds.

I frown. Another punctured moment. "*Mi-ine*. Emily's. You don't even know that?"

"Hard to keep track of dates when you forge documents for a livin'." He hands me another wrapped package. "These from Kiona."

Kiona is his wife, a boxing trainer who found her dream job in Las Vegas as a result of my effed-up life. Haha, at least it's good for something!

We'd been on the run for a long time, living out of the bus. *The Calby Murders* were still in the news and Lucas had faked his death in Memphis. We took a break and rented a house in Vegas so I could go back to school. With Alice Black's identity and forged academic records, I attended ninth grade, having missed seventh and eighth.

Things were going fine until a social worker showed up at our house with a cop saying they received a welfare complaint *about a white girl living here*. They asked to look around. After all his lectures about not antagonizing the authorities, Lucas told them to shove it and get a warrant. Worried they might, we left town the same night. Kiona refused to get back on the bus. I don't get it, but living apart seems to work for them.

Inside her package are a box of nine-millimeter cartridges and a black belly-band holster.

"Kiona got me these?" Kiona hates guns and can't understand why we don't, especially us. I still remember her walking out in disgust when Lucas gave me the pocket-rocket, number 13 candles melting all over the cake.

"Don't say nothin'. She insisted on sending money to buy a present. Just thank her for the Amazon card."

I nod. "I'll say I spent it on creatine and protein powder." I still make her custom shakes. It's harder on a bus, but I've never stopped training.

We arrived at Zinnie's last night after spending a week in Little Rock with Darla and Peggy, my other two saviors. I met them at a campground in Louisiana three years ago. They've retired from RV life, even sold the cute pink trailer. Seems impossible it's been so long since Darla, a psychologist, worked to keep me from having to be recommitted to a mental hospital.

Lucas and I drove all the way from Wyoming to see them. He said it was just to visit but I knew he was lying. He thinks I'm losing it again and wanted Darla's professional opinion. I spilled everything to her, about all the bad stuff returning. The impulsive anger, seeing threats everywhere ... the nightmares. *PTSD*, Darla said, same as always.

The latest episode happened on our way here, at an RV park in Kansas. Someone pulled on the bus door in the middle of the night. I kicked it open, neck knife in hand. If Lucas hadn't held me back, a drunk guy who wandered home to the wrong bus might be dead.

Darla and I worked on *taking a break from anger* and reversing my *act first, think later* pattern. She was encouraging, gave me a pep-talk about *the bright side*, that at least I'm not dissociating again, but when we hugged goodbye, her eyes said she was just as worried as Lucas.

"Turn around so I can try on the holster," I say.

I tighten it under my jeans and pull my shirts down. I always wear double shirts and long pants, even in summer.

"Alright, you can look. Not bad. Only a little bump."

"Be better if you wasn't so skinny."

I'm Mom's twin, including the same long straight body—except mine is solid muscle from three years of brutal training under Lucas and Kiona.

I pull out the Sig and aim it out the dark-tinted windows at a bald guy reading a book on a lawn chair at the next campsite. The tritium sights glow like cat eyes.

Lucas wags a finger. "Don't go taking that gun nowhere without my permission. It's illegal. Got to be twenty-one to get a carry permit."

"Just forge one for me."

"*Pfft*, you ain't passing for twenty-one. You just a kid."

"I am not," I protest like a whiny kid. "I passed for sixteen when I was twelve, and I'm already taller than most women. I can do the rest with makeup and attitude."

"We ain't ever gonna find out."

"Why not?"

"'Cause I ain't doing it. You already grew up too fast. Time to be your own age."

"I'll never be my age again. You know that. You helped make me that way."

It comes out like an accusation, and for some reason I'm not understanding, I intend it to. Lucas did help make me this way—but only because I badgered him into it.

I was twelve when I persuaded him to teach me *self-defense*. He still insists on calling it that, doesn't like to admit he trained a killer. I was a highly motivated student. Even Kiona couldn't break me, and she tried. Whenever she brought me to my knees during a workout, dizzy and throwing up, I'd think about the red-tailed hawk circling our front yard the day the two men came. *Predator, not prey. Never again.*

Lucas is rubbing his eyes with his fists. "Look, I didn't even wanna give you the damn gun. Way you been acting, might shoot me in one of your little fits."

"Well, I guess you'd better be nice to me then." I mean it as a joke, but his nostrils flare.

This is a big reason we came to see Darla: I've been acting like a total bitch lately, which is not me. Annoying, yes. Bitch, no.

"Gimme," he says, grabbing for the gun.

I pull it away. "No. You gave it to me."

Simmering, "I've been trying to be patient 'cause I know you're struggling, but you know patience ain't my strength. It's time for you to get it together and fly right."

"*Fly right?* Are you going to send me to my room?"

He locks his thick fingers together, possibly to resist strangling me, which I probably deserve. "I'm trying to help, Emily. That's all."

"Then quit trying to be my dad. We're just a bunch of forged documents. Nothing about us is real. You didn't even know it was my real birthday."

I push open the bus door and jump out, the stippled gun grip abrading my skin when I hit the concrete RV pad.

"Get back here," Lucas says.

I put my hands over my ears and start walking to the campground exit, trying not to fall over from the knife in my heart. Not my neck knife, which is tucked safely behind my bra. This is the stab that comes from knowing you're worthless, worse than worthless. *Horrible*, someone who hurts the person she loves most.

At the guard station I fake a smile and wave, tugging down my shirts.

Two miles to the nearest town. The road is empty, everyone chased inside by the heat.

* * *

I buy a bottle of Gatorade at a convenience store, dawdling inside to enjoy the chilled air before heading back into the steam bath. Walking always clears my head. I even had an epiphany on the way.

Maybe I've been treating Lucas bad because I'm afraid of losing him. It doesn't make sense, but in a weird way it does. Everyone else is gone. It's only a matter of time before I lose Lucas. That feeling is always there. So I push and push, expecting the point to come where he gets fed up and says, *That's it, you're out of here,* and I can think, *I knew it!*

I said nothing about us is real. A big fat lie, and a cruel one. *Love, loyalty, trust.* Nothing is more real about me and Lucas. I get a lump in my throat.

My regret is interrupted by the distinctive syncopated popping of a Harley Davidson. Dad had one. I helped him work on it every week.

Two Harleys roar up to the gas pumps. Both drivers are men, but there's a woman passenger on the back of one. She hardly fits because the driver is a tub, wearing an open vest with an ink-stained belly hanging out. Front and center is a tattoo of a revolver-shaped American flag. The other guy has the cadaverous face of someone who's lived a hard life. A fringe of black hair hangs below a red bandanna wrapped tightly around his head.

I avoid eye contact. I've learned a lot about men since the day everything ended. One day I was innocent, the good daughter of a good family in rural Georgia. The next day I wasn't.

The men lean the bikes on the side stands—the big guy's is made in the shape of a serpent—and start filling the tanks. The woman stands off by herself next to the pumps. She's thin, almost malnourished, dressed in torn blue jeans and a sleeveless top, arms and neck badly sunburned. A pile of bleached blonde hair falls out when she removes her helmet, the only one of them with the good sense to wear one.

Gas nozzle rattling around in his tank, the tatt-man turns to her. "Get me the tire gauge." An order, not a request.

"Um, where is it?" she says.

"Where do you think it is? In the saddle-bag, dumbass."

She unbuckles a black bag and rummages through it. "I don't see it."

"Jesus Christ. Can't you do anything? It's on the other side."

My dad didn't have a lot in common with Lucas Jackson, but one thing they both taught me is that any man who abuses a woman deserves a good beating.

I add the biker to my *deserves-to-die* list. It's long, already has like a hundred people on it. I learned the code from Lucas. Zen-like in its simplicity, a person either deserves to die or doesn't. The surprising part is how easy it is to tell the difference. That doesn't mean I go around killing everyone. I just like to keep notes.

He's still berating her when the gasoline overflows all over his glossy airbrushed tank, a skull with flames coming out the back. I barely stifle my laugh.

"Fuck!" he says. The woman shrinks. "Now look what you did. Grab some paper towels and clean this tank—and hurry. I'll find the damn tire gauge myself."

I wish Lucas were here ... to put a piece of tape over my mouth. I know I should keep it shut, but of course I can't.

"It wasn't her fault," I say.

Both men wheel at the same time. Tatt-man takes a step toward me. "What did you say?"

"You heard me. You blamed her, but you're the dumbass who overfilled the tank."

Face blotching, hands tightening into fists.

"Ooh, big tough man. What now? Are you going to beat up a teenage girl? Impressive."

He looks *very* tempted, but do-rag man quickly sidles up and grabs his arm, saying, "What's your problem, Goldilocks? Ain't no one ever teach you to be polite?"

I almost laugh. I spent my entire life being polite. *Goldilocks.* Growing my hair back was probably was a mistake. *That blonde hair shines like a fuckin' beacon,* Lucas complained the day I met him. I cut it short and dyed it black, but let it grow out again, worried I was losing Emily Calby completely.

"Why don't you ask your rude friend that question?"

The tatt-man is barely under control, breathing heavily between clenched teeth. *Think, then act.* Darla was right. Need to let these things go.

I toss the Gatorade bottle in a recycling bin, wave goodbye and circle around them. I make it three steps before a hand lands on my shoulder, causing all the triggers to fire at once.

I turn and deliver a short quick punch to the throat. Dad always said go for the balls, but Lucas taught me that crushing a man's trachea is more reliable. Tatt-man drops to his knees clutching his neck. The American flag on his stomach flutters as he sucks for air, sputtering curse words and staring at me in disbelief.

Element of surprise. That was the foundation of my entire training. *Bein' young and a girl, you gonna have the element of surprise every time unless you fuck up. If Lucas walks up to a man, that man's gonna be grabbin' for a bazooka, but no one's gonna expect you to fight.*

I lift my knee to sweep it into his head before he can react. Kiona trained me to box with fists, but Lucas prefers knees and elbows. Standing on one leg like the Karate Kid, I hear Darla's scolding: *Take a break from anger.*

I replant my foot and step back, holding my palms up as a peace offering, but do-rag makes the same stupid miscalculation and lurches toward me. I pull my birthday present from the holster and aim it at his pockmarked, wide-eyed face. He stops and raises his hands like he's being robbed as I instantly regret my latest huge blunder.

It's not that the gun is unloaded. I wasn't planning to shoot him. *Fear is a powerful weapon. Stronger than bullets. Can get people to do anything if they afraid enough—and they a lot more afraid before they dead, than after.* Another of my first lessons.

The problem is I'm standing in a public place in broad daylight threatening to shoot a man with an illegal handgun. To my right, the woman is tending to tatt-man, trying to, but he pushes her away. I re-holster the gun and backpedal. When it's clear they're not coming after me, I turn and run like fire down the road that brought me here.

Halfway back to the campground, cresting an asphalt hill with an incline that seemed a mile long, a wave of dizziness hits me. Could be the heat, but I think it's more than that. In Nevada, Kiona made me train in the desert. I veer off the road, under the shade of a row of mossy trees, and slow my pace.

A little girl with pigtails is playing in her front yard. She smiles with missing front teeth and points a plastic assault rifle at me. I give her a thumbs-up.

My skull is burning ... it's my hair, stretched tight around my finger. I unwind it and shake the loose pale strands onto the ground. Not a good sign. My *trichotillomania*—obsessive hair-pulling—has been under control.

I messed up *so* frigging bad and the worst part is I *knew* it the whole time, with every word, every action. I told Darla the night we left Little Rock that sometimes I feel like a runaway train steaming down a dark tunnel that never ends.

"Sometimes you have to hit bottom before you can look up and see sky," she said.

I hit it. I risked everything, even Lucas. *Of course* it's time for me to get it together and fly right. When I get home, he's getting the biggest hug and apology in the world.

A mockingbird whistles excitedly in the trees. I look up. Patches of blue play hide and seek in the branches. *I can see sky, Darla.*

I lower my head. *Thank you, Lord, for giving me this chance to save me from myself before it was too late.*

I say *Amen* as a police car revs over the hill, blue lights flashing.

2

STAY OR RUN? It's a question I face more often than the average teen. The cops could be rushing to an accident scene, but I can't take a chance.

I dash through a yard and hop the back fence, only to see more bursts of blue light reflecting off the houses from the next street over. I stop to consider my limited options and decide on old reliable: *fake it*. I climb back over the fence and stash the gun and neck knife in a garbage can.

The police car is parked on the side of the road. The officers are already out, a tall male driver and a short woman passenger with dark curls flaring from under her cap. They both have their guns drawn. I run to them waving my arms.

"*Omigod*, I'm so glad you're here!"

The woman says something into a microphone clipped to her shirt. The man is yelling at me.

"On the ground! Face down, arms and legs apart. Now!"

I could probably get a patent on manufactured looks of bewildered innocence. "Huh? What are you talking about?"

"You heard him. On the ground. Now." The woman.

I kneel and start crying. For the longest time I couldn't cry even when I desperately needed to. Now I just let one of the images of that day slip from the black boxes in my brain. There's Becky's stuffed dog, Pooky, on fire in our backyard, plastic eyes melting onto the grass.

"I don't understand. I thought you were here to help me. I just got attacked by two men at a gas station."

The woman holsters her gun and motions for the man to lower his. I sniffle as she helps me to my feet. Another cop car pulls up, maybe the one from the other street. Two more men get out. "Settle down," the woman says more gently. I see her name tag. *Russo.* "I want to hear your story, but I need to search you first." "Seriously?"

"Seriously. We had a report of a girl who looks like you threatening someone with a gun. Arms up."

The man-cop pulls handcuffs from his belt when I hesitate.

"Okay, fine," I say.

She pats me down. "No gun," she reports. "Empty your pockets.

"Is this legal? Don't I have rights?"

"Empty your pockets or I'll do it for you." All I have is my fake driver's license and a few dollars. I stormed out of the bus so fast I didn't even grab my phone.

"Alice Black," she reads off the license, checking my face against the picture. "Fresno, California. You're a long way from home, Alice. What are you doing out here?"

"Just, you know, passing through." I can't lead them back to Lucas. He's got weed, illegal guns and a busload of document-forging equipment.

"In the middle of the Ozarks? On foot?"

"I had a car, but my boyfriend took it. We got in a fight and he drove off and left me. He'll probably come back. He's done it before."

"Sounds like you need a new boyfriend. What happened at the gas station?"

"I was standing out front minding my own business when two men on motorcycles pulled up and started saying nasty things to me. Then one of them grabbed me. They're the ones you should be looking for."

"We will." She opens her phone and starts typing. "Give me a description."

I hesitate. I might be able to justify the punch as self-defense, but not pulling out a gun and definitely not having one. Accurate descriptions would just lead to eyewitnesses.

"I was so scared, the whole thing is kind of a blur." Qualifying everything with *I'm not completely sure*, I spin vague details, keeping an eye on the three man-cops clustered together talking.

"Why did you run when you saw us?"

They break huddle and spread out into the yard. "Um, I wasn't running from you." On-demand blushing. "I drank a whole quart of Gatorade at the gas station and had to pee super-bad. Couldn't hold it."

"What about the gun? They say you pulled a gun."

"A gun? Me?" I laugh. "I've never even seen a real gun." Something's not computing. "Who is *they*? I thought you said you hadn't found the bikers."

"The store clerks. They saw everything and called it in. They said it's all on security video."

While I grasp for a response to that, her partner moots the point, strutting from the backyard holding up the holster and neck knife like trophies.

Russo nods. "You wanted rights? Congratulations. You got 'em, kid. You're under arrest." She pulls a card from her shirt pocket. *"You have the right to remain silent. Anything you say can and will be used against you . . ."*

I never should have opened my mouth. Lucas told me that a dozen times.

They roll my fingertips on a scanner, cuff my hands and lower me into the backseat, Russo apologizing for the handcuffs. Department policy, she says. Probably a mom.

Russo and the man-cop talk back and forth in low voices. His name is Bates. His overpowering cologne smells like licorice. He guns the motor and we squeal back onto the road. Russo is talking into her radio, requesting someone go interview the gas station clerks and put out a BOLO for the bikers. It's a comment on my life that I know what a BOLO is. *Be On the Lookout.*

We're coming up to Zinnie's. If I hadn't self-destructed, Lucas and I would be outside getting ready to fire up the grill for dinner. He's going to be worried sick when I don't come back. My heart hurts as I watch the campground disappear behind us. I paw at my eyes, handcuffs clinking.

"Where are you taking me?"

"Police station," Russo says.

My mind races to reprogram my story as the car whooshes up and around the winding mountain roads like we're on a roller coaster. Russo is typing on a tablet.

The driver's license should stand up. Lucas only uses real driver's licenses to make fake ones. There really is a sixteen-year-old girl named Alice Black in Fresno, California.

Sell it. You're *Alice Black.* The gun belonged to my boyfriend. Plausible. Lucas said some gang members get their girlfriends to carry their guns because they're convicted felons and felon-in-possession is a five-year gun crime. The video will show the belly-hanger grabbing my shoulder from behind. I've talked my way out of worse. *Buck up.*

Russo interrupts my motivational speech by suddenly jerking her head around and saying, "No way. Cannot be."

Gawking, holding up her tablet, eyes flitting back and forth between me and the screen.

I force a smile, cuffed hands folded on my lap.

"What's wrong?" Bates says.

"You remember that home invasion case in Georgia a few years ago?" she says.

And I know I'm dead.

"Which one?"

"The *Calby Murders.* Two men killed the family and blew up the house. One girl escaped."

"How could I forget? It was in the news for months. Everyone thought the girl burned up in the fire, but the forensics showed no trace. I wonder whatever happened to her."

"She's sitting in the backseat."

He cranes his neck. "You are kidding me."

"I'm not. The fingerprints came up a match. And that's not all. Hold onto the steering wheel because you're not going to believe this one. There's an outstanding arrest warrant for her in another state."

"Arrest warrant? I thought she was the victim. For what?"

"Murder."

3

"HEY-UH, JULIO," I say.

Officer Russo is standing a few feet away, leaned against the pea-green wall, picking at her red nail polish and pretending not to listen.

When we got to the station she said juveniles have a right to call their parents, but must have remembered Emily Calby's story because she looked embarrassed and said I could call anyone I want. I said I needed to talk to my boyfriend. She frowned, but let me. I called Lucas on his burner. He makes me memorize the number each time he gets a new one.

"Julio? What the fuck? You still playin' games? Where you been, Em—"

"That's right. It's me. *Alice.* Your abandoned girlfriend. Bet you didn't expect to be hearing from me so soon." I smile at Russo as Lucas rants about whether I've lost my mind.

I turn my back to her and whisper. "Don't say anything. I'm in a jail standing next to a sign that says *All Calls May Be Monitored and Recorded.*"

A groan. "Go on," he says in a voice so heavy it could sink a ship.

"I'm in a lot of trouble. I don't understand it all, but wanted you to know I'm alive and okay. Don't try to come visit me. It's too dangerous. There's nothing you can do right now."

A murder warrant from another state can mean only one thing. Either the FBI or the Florida state police found evidence

24

linking me to the deaths of tall man and stocky man, my family's killers, in Pensacola. Some of them always suspected I was involved. That means Lucas could be in trouble too. He left a pint of blood behind at the scene.

"You should ditch this burner after we hang up. They might be tracking my calls. They figured out ... um"—I don't know how to explain it in code—"that my name hasn't always been Alice. We'll figure out a way to hook up later."

Lucas curses while Russo points at the clock.

"I have to go. I'm sorry for saying that stupid stuff ... and for ruining everything. I love you."

*   *   *

Russo put me in a small, locked room. I know because I tried the door, ignoring the video cameras mounted in the corners.

I pace in circles around a metal table bolted to the floor before taking a seat in a white plastic bucket chair, the kind you buy at Walmart in the garden department. My only company is a moth battering itself silly inside one of the light fixtures. I stand on the table and set it free.

Russo finally returns. Tagging behind her is a trim, balding man in a blue suit carrying a yellow pad. He introduces himself as a detective and starts reading me my rights. I cut him off.

"I know my rights. I don't want to talk."

"Do I understand you to say you are invoking your right to remain silent?"

"Was I unclear? I can rephrase it if you need help. I invoke my right to remain noiseless, soundless, wordless, mute *and* silent. Don't try to play me. Go bully someone your own age."

Russo scowls.

The detective snatches up his pad, gives Russo a pissed-off look and walks out. She wastes no time getting in my face.

"Let me explain a few things, *Alice*, and since you've invoked your right to remain silent, I don't want to hear even one peep out of you. Not one peep. Understand?"

Her olive skin and dark hair and eyes, even her hectoring tone, remind me of Mrs. Bianchi, from sixth-grade, back in Georgia.

"First, you're going to be spending the night in a holding cell. In the morning you'll see a judge for your first detention hearing."

"The whole night? Seriously? Can't I get out on bail or something?"

She raises a finger to her lips. "Remember? No peeps? I can rephrase it for you if you need help. There is no bail for juveniles and the judge only holds detention hearings in the morning. This isn't a game. What's wrong with you?"

I almost answer honestly. *I don't know.*

"Your charges are serious. Felony assault and illegal gun possession. For some crazy reason, judges are not fond of kids carrying around guns and threatening to shoot people. Go figure. Then of course we have the icing on the cake, a murder warrant from another state."

Doors bang outside, a man yelling, "But I already tol' ya. I ain't drunk. It's just my medication."

"Sweetheart, I'll be honest. I'm guessing you're going to be spending a lot of nights in custody. Not here. Tomorrow you'll be taken to a juvenile detention center. If an extradition order comes through on your outstanding warrant, then ..." She doesn't finish.

"Then what?"

"I'll let the judge explain it tomorrow. In the meantime, here's some advice. I have a daughter about your age. I'd give her the same advice."

I knew she was a mom.

"You're going to be interacting with a lot of people in the criminal justice system. They can help or hurt you. Guards, cops, judges, other prisoners. Some of them are dangerous."

I'm not sure if she means prisoners or the whole lot.

"How you get treated is going to depend on how you act.

Keep insulting people and your life is going to be much harder. You have to go along to get along."

Ironically, that's how I survived my entire time on the run way back when, forcing myself to stay courteous always. All *Yes, ma'ams* and *No, sirs*, even to people who didn't deserve it.

After the lecture, she took me to get *processed*: booked, searched and issued a men's size sky-blue uniform and a small bag of hygiene stuff.

They entered me in the system as Alice Black. Maybe they haven't confirmed I'm Emily Calby yet, but it won't take long. Fingerprints don't lie. That's how the FBI found tall man, aka *Ronnie*, from his fingerprints on the gas can they used to burn down our house.

The FBI took my fingerprints and DNA the day they snatched me from the Mexican restaurant in Atlanta and put me in the hospital. Said they needed to verify my identity, didn't bother to mention my data would stay in the system for three years and get sent to Arkansas.

I spend the night in a closet-size cell on a thin mattress pad that smells of urine. The minutes and hours tick by like a slow water drip in the basement. The more I want to fall asleep and make everything disappear, the more I can't. Too many thoughts swirling in my tornado brain. I latch onto one and try to focus. *How do I fix this?*

... No clue. Even if I could talk my way around the gun charge, the murder warrant is, what did Russo call it, the *icing on the cake*? More like the world collapsing on my head.

I know what *extradite* means. They can send me to Florida to stand trial. It scares me, but also pisses me off. The whole time they interrogated me about tall man and stocky man, I only had one thought: *Why the eff do you care?* How can it *not* be okay to kill people who slaughter innocent mothers and daughters?

It never made sense to me. Never will.

4

THE COURTROOM is a large windowless rectangle with off-white walls, path-worn industrial carpet and an oppressively low ceiling, nothing like in the movies. Florescent bulbs cast mood lighting appropriate for the occasion: gray dimness.

The judge is a black man in a black robe with white hair and horn-rimmed glasses, sitting behind a huge desk-thingy on a raised platform. Set up that way on purpose, I'm sure, so they can look down at you, make you feel small.

I'm standing in front of it, wrists and ankles shackled to a chain around my waist. I jangle every time I move. Russo's here, in uniform, along with a handful of people in business clothes and a cop guarding the door.

"Good morning," the judge says in a friendly voice that surprises me. "I'm Judge Reed. And you're Ms. ..."

"Black. Alice Black."

"I see," he says. I can't tell if he already knows I'm Emily Calby.

"Wait, I retract that," I say. "I mean, if it's okay with you." Tossing and turning all night on the pee-stained mattress made Russo's words sink in. *Go along to get along.* They control me. *BE NICE.*

"You retract your name?"

"Yes sir, I mean, your, um, lordship."

A laugh from behind me. It's a guy with round wire glasses, long hair and a scruffy beard, wearing a brown suit that's at least a size too big. He's sitting alone at a large rectangular table, strips of plastic wood laminate peeling from the edges.

"The appropriate term is *Your Honor*, but you can just call me Judge."

"Thank you, Judge!" Effervescence was key to my survival when I was on the run. Works on almost everyone. Men and women.

"Why do you want to retract your name?"

"On the ground it might incriminate me."

He nods like it's actually not a stupid point, which means he must know I'm Emily Calby. "Okay. What should I call you? How about *Defendant*? Will that work?"

"Sure, and thanks for asking!" Don't overdo it.

"This gentleman is an attorney for the county," he says, motioning to a cherub-faced guy with curly brown hair who looks like he could still be in high school.

"Please read the petition," the judge says.

Baby-lawyer reads a document outlining the charges: aggravated assault, minor in possession of a firearm, and an extra felony tacked on because of the obliterated serial number on the gun. But good news! Carrying a concealed knife apparently isn't a crime in Arkansas.

"Do you admit or deny these charges?" the judge says.

"I plead not guilty."

"We don't use that term in juvenile proceedings, but I'll put you down for a *deny*. How about that?"

I nod.

He shifts uncomfortably. "I understand your parents are not here today."

"Correct."

"Is there any way we can contact them?"

"No way I know of, Judge."

"Do you have another legal guardian?"

I have an illegal guardian. "No, sir."

"I take it you do not have an attorney."

I shake my head.

"Do you have any financial resources?"

"I had a few dollars when they arrested me, but they took it."

"Very well. I hereby appoint the public defender, Andy Ball, to serve as your counsel." He points to the guy with the long hair and scruffy beard, who looks half-asleep, tie tilted sideways, brown shoes scuffed to a light tan.

"*Him?*" What kind of lawyer is named *Andy*?

"Mr. Ball is an experienced public defender."

He directs me to go sit with him and calls Russo up to explain what happened. Every word makes me sound guilty as sin. I nudge my lawyer but he doesn't move.

When she finishes, the judge doesn't hesitate before declaring there is probable cause to believe I've committed serious crimes and am a threat to public safety. He orders me transferred to a juvenile center for detention pending further proceedings.

Andy the Lawyer yawns.

The judge cleans his glasses with his robe and scans the courtroom. "I don't need to remind everyone that juvenile proceedings are confidential, but I'm doing it anyway. This is an especially sensitive case."

I can think of only one reason it would be especially sensitive. He definitely knows it's me.

"If one word of these proceedings leaves this courtroom, I will hold whoever is responsible in contempt."

He excuses everyone except me and the two lawyers, asking us to *approach the bench*, the big wood desk. We do, with me sandwiched between them.

"We have one more matter to address, which is the unusual circumstance that based on a fingerprint match, there appears to be an outstanding arrest warrant for the defendant from another state. Gentlemen, I assume you are both aware of the situation?"

"Yes, Your Honor," the county attorney says.

"No clue, Judge," says Andy the Lawyer.

Of course not.

"The fingerprints match the prints for a girl named Emily Calby. Does the name ring a bell, Mr. Ball?"

Andy shrugs.

"She was, or *is* ... a ..." He gives me a pained look and stops, like he can't spit it out.

"She was a twelve-year-old girl from Dilfer County, Georgia," I say. "One day two psychopaths came to her house and raped and killed her mother and sister. Emily, the oldest child, ran—"

"That's enough," the judge says, holding up a hand. "You were right before to not want to incriminate yourself. There's still no verification that you are ... aren't Alice Black."

"Oh, I wasn't saying that was about me, Judge. I just remember reading about it and wanted to help out my lawyer," barely managing to hold back *who apparently hasn't seen the news in three years.*

"In any event," the judge continues. "If and when your identity is confirmed, it will be up to the State of Louisiana to decide whether to pursue your extradition."

I nod along until ... hold on. "State of Louisiana? You mean Florida."

"Excuse me?" he says.

"You said Louisiana, but you meant Florida, right?"

"What are you talking about? This warrant comes from Louisiana."

"Are you absolutely sure?"

He pulls a document close, looking over his glasses. "Yes. It says right here, *State of Louisiana, Saint Landry Parish.*"

Saint Landry. I can see the green sign at the interstate exit. *Homemade apple pie to die for. ... Is this where the restaurant is? ... We're almost there.*

It's not about tall man and stocky man.

The judge reads my confusion. "I have limited information, but the charge apparently involves a deceased by the name of ..."

Scott Brooker.

"Scott Brooker," he says.

He continues, but I'm not listening, lost in clouded memories. Taylor Swift singing on the CD player, Brooker talking about his daughter and boring job selling business software, then taking us off the interstate, out to the bayou, to the middle of nowhere.

When I snap out of the fog, the judge is ordering my records sealed.

"The defendant will retain the identity of Alice Black until such time as I order otherwise."

Court adjourns and my lawyer takes me to a small adjoining room. A guard stands outside. I suppress my instinct to light into him.

"Um, Mr. Ball—"

"You can call me Andy."

"Yes, well, *Andy*, I was just wondering why you ..." *Didn't eff-ing do something.*

He cuts me off and explains almost serenely: Juvenile court is a lot less formal than regular court. Pray I don't get transferred to adult court in Louisiana. It was obvious Russo was telling the truth. Asking questions would have just pissed off the judge. I had no chance in a million years of getting released, especially with no legal guardian to take custody of me. Add in the fact that I'm a proven flight risk, having gone missing for three years.

It makes too much sense to argue with. "So what do I do now?"

Like he rehearsed it with Russo, "Try to get along with people. That's the best way to help yourself while things get sorted out."

"I'm sorry I reacted that way when the judge made you my lawyer. I didn't mean to hurt your feelings. You're probably, I mean I'm *sure* you're a good lawyer."

"Apology accepted."

"Tell me about extradition. I want to fight it."

"You haven't got a prayer."

5

ANDY THE LAWYER was right. Grabbing someone in one state and shipping them to another should be kidnapping, but it's in the freaking constitution of the United States of America. A person charged with a crime in one state *who shall flee from Justice* and be found in another state shall be *delivered up*—just like that.

I argued I didn't flee from Justice, but nobody listened. Inside, my head screamed, *I'm the one who MADE Justice.*

The Law. It can save or destroy you. As far I can tell, it can do anything it wants. For extradition, all they have to do is get the paperwork right, confirm your identity and poof, you get *delivered up.*

One morning two state troopers showed up at the juvenile center with an extradition order. They loaded me in the back of a van and we left on a seven-hour trip for Louisiana. They wouldn't even stop to let me pee because there was no female guard to go in the restroom with me.

Arkansas must have been eager to get rid of me because they waived my charges. I overheard the judge's clerk talking about the media circus that would ensue if word got out they were holding the *missing Calby girl* on a murder charge. "The security costs alone would swallow the county's budget," she said. "Let her be Louisiana's problem."

So now I am. I didn't think it was possible, but knew my life had changed for the worse the second the van emerged from the winding backcountry roads and I laid eyes on the Pochachant Detention Center for Juveniles, a sprawl of gray buildings protected by high concrete walls surrounded by a tall perimeter fence, all topped with spiraling rows of shiny razor wire. Completely isolated, nothing but woods and bayou in every direction.

More than five hundred juveniles, boys and girls in separate units divided by double fences and more razor wire. They call it a detention center, but it's a prison.

I've been here a week.

I live with another girl in Cell 49B, an eight-by-ten concrete box. The only furnishings are a pair of adjacent bunks bolted to the floor, a stainless steel sink and toilet and two cabinet-size lockers painted gunmetal gray.

The paint on the lockers is fresh. Etched into the door of mine is *Welcome to Hell*. It contains only what they issued me the first day: evergreen polyester uniforms, scratchy underwear and sports bras, a single roll of toilet paper, a short-handled toothbrush and a crummy hairbrush that won't go through even my straight hair. Everything came in a bag labeled *Courtesy of the Draxon Corporation*. I asked about it and found out Pochachant is a for-profit prison. Bizarre. The government pays strangers to lock up kids.

At least the cell has a window. Just a slug of plastic covered by wire mesh, so filthy I can barely make out the hulking HVAC units on the other side, but it lets in light so I'm grateful to have it.

Be thankful for even the smallest blessings in life. One of my old preacher's favorite sayings. It hasn't been easy, but I've held onto my faith. Lucas calls it *magical thinking*. I don't claim to know the answers, but one thing is for sure. Without it, I would have given up a long time ago.

Everything here is on a schedule. You get up at seven, lights out at ten. The hours in between are filled with showers, meals, yard time and a lot of boredom sitting around in your cell. At some point you get a job and start GED classes.

Showers are the worst. I hate taking my clothes off, period. To do it in a group freaks me out. And the floors are one big fungi pit. I'm the only girl without shower slippers. The hot water runs out in ten minutes, but at least it keeps everyone moving. I've already heard stories about bad things happening in the showers.

The whole system seems designed to degrade and humiliate. Getting processed, I not only had to strip, but squat and cough. The correctional officers—COs—yell constantly, dogs bark at you, inmates taunt each other. Gang signs are everywhere.

I'm trying harder than ever to be nice. Go along to get along. Everything is about rewards and punishments. Do what they say and you get privilege points. Don't and you lose them, or worse, get sent to solitary. Polly want a cracker? Walk in a straight line, hands on the shoulders of the girl in front of you, don't talk.

Twilight surrendered to darkness about an hour ago. I just finished my cell workout: push-ups, crunches, burpees, anything I can do in a small space without equipment. I figured out a way to do pull-ups on the window ledge with my stomach flat against the wall. No better exercise to change body composition. One of Kiona's first training lessons.

We get an hour of outdoor time each weekday that I split between weights and cardio, running laps around the quarter-mile track that circles the yard, but I always want more. I've spent three years in hard training and have no intention of stopping now. It's already saved my life more than once.

I fall back in the bunk and open a book. I gained enough privilege points my first week to check it out of the prison library. *Crime and Punishment*. The title got my attention.

They put me through a bunch of tests the day I got here. The counselor was surprised I read at a college level, gave me another test to make sure. All Mom's books paid off.

I'm at the part where Raskolnikov says, *I maintain that all great men ... must from their very nature be criminals—more or less.* It makes me think of Lucas, a great man and a great criminal.

I haven't talked to him since that first phone call from the Arkansas jail. I called back, but he must have ditched the burner. I have no idea where he is or how to contact him, which means I'm an orphan again.

Clomping boots outside and the steel door rattles. A thick-necked CO with a puffy face appears behind the small cell-door window. It's the same guard who came to take my cellmate an hour ago.

Rebecca Seyere. What are the odds? Rebecca was Becky's given name. She even looks a little like Becky, with dark brown hair and eyes too big for her face. She's fifteen, just a year younger than me, but barely five feet of skin and bones.

I heard a rumor she's here for drugs. That's what I'm going to say if anyone asks. Even the warden said I should lie to keep my identity secret. I'm still Alice Black in the system. Louisiana agreed with Arkansas it would be bad for everyone if my name got out.

The door screeches open. The guard is so big and Rebecca so small she looks like a child standing next to an adult. He stays outside, slitted eyes following her to her bunk. Neither of them say a word before the door bangs shut again. He didn't talk when he came to get her either so she must have known he was coming.

Her face is tilted at the floor, obscured by her long bangs, like always. Next to her is a teddy bear missing an eye.

"Hi, Rebecca."

She never talks unless I talk first. I stay to myself, but some-thing about Rebecca makes me want to talk to her. Maybe her name or maybe I'm just lonely. After all, she is my *cellie.*

"Hi," she says dully.

"Everything alright?"

"Mm-hm."

"Are you sick?" Maybe the CO took her to a doctor appointment.

Her dark eyes flash. "*No.* What's wrong with you? Why do you ask so many questions?"

If I thought I could make her smile, I'd tell her about Lucas describing me to Kiona. *I swear, that little girl's worse than the fuckin' District Attorney.*

"Just wondering why a guard would come get a prisoner at night."

"Mind your own fucking business." She flops on the mattress pad and rolls her back to me.

6

THE GIRLS from Cellblock B inch forward in a zig-zaggy line, snatching up yellow plastic trays along the way. The cafeteria is a tile and metal cavern that reeks of bleach. Always loud, it pulsates with more energy than usual, maybe because it's Saturday night.

I slide my tray along the stainless steel shelf, watching the people at the front peel off and go to their tables. It's always good to know who's with who. Lucas taught me to study my surroundings, predict danger before it happens. Everyone's part of a clique. Except for the evergreen jumpsuits and tattoos, I'd swear I was in a high school cafeteria. A brawny black girl with a skull on her arm sits down at a table where every girl has the same skull.

I'm probably the only girl at Pochachant without ink. Rebecca has a tattoo on the small of her back. I saw it when she was changing. *We Live as We Dream. Alone.* I don't know how she got it since she's only fifteen. I told Lucas once I wanted to get a tattoo and he threatened to cut it out of me with a knife.

Women behind the glass in hairnets and gloves dole out the night's feast: spaghetti, green beans, one slice of white bread, green Jell-O cubes and a small carton of milk. Glue must be the special ingredient in the spaghetti recipe because the lady has to bang her spoon on my tray three times to empty it. At the end of the line I grab my plastic utensils and walk to an empty table in the far corner.

I instinctively try to pull the seat closer, still not used to everything being bolted down.

The food tastes about how it looks. You can buy better stuff, at least better-tasting, at the commissary if you have money in your account. I need to find a way to get some. The jail runs on a barter system. I learned that the first day when a girl offered me her dessert for my roll of toilet paper. With money you can buy things you need or stuff people want to trade for.

Rumor says you can buy or trade for almost anything. Some kids supposedly have smuggled-in phones. That's what I need most. A weapon would be nice too. I've heard they're available. Drugs are around for sure. I smelled pot my first night here. I don't know where people hide everything because the guards search the cells constantly.

Here comes Rebecca, prowling my way with her hair shield in place, tray tugging on her broomstick arms.

I smile and wave but she ignores me, or maybe her hair blocks the view. She takes her usual spot, at the table next to mine, the only other empty one. Could there be two more antisocial cellmates?

I force myself to eat slowly. As bad as the food is, I'm always hungry. When I trained, I ate five times a day.

Animated conversation and girl-energy pulsate all around me. I can already recognize some of the girls by their voices, laughs, even favorite profanities. "Puta, puta, puta!" Carolina, a girl I met in the yard when we were both running the track, is having a disagreement with the detainee sitting across from her.

I pass time guessing what everyone did to end up here. *She* looks like a car thief. *She* looks like an innocent, someone who got caught up with the wrong people. I could see *her* killing someone. When that gets boring, I go deeper and imagine where their lives turned wrong.

Midway down the aisle, four girls stand up simultaneously. I know who they are. Everyone does. They're always together. The leader is Lola, a loudmouth with a shaved head and

F-U-C-K L-I-F-E tattooed across her hands, one letter per finger. She's strong. I saw her bench press a hundred and fifty pounds in the yard.

They're laughing and glancing in my direction. I look away. Nothing to gain by provoking them. I've been lucky so far. Except for some taunts about my blonde hair, people have left me alone.

It looks like that's about to change because they're marching in my direction with purpose. A girl named Tamika, second in command, walks alongside Lola. The other two follow behind. When they pass the last group table, I know they're coming for me.

Tactically, it makes sense to stand but that could be interpreted as aggression. Stay cool. *Think first, act later.*

I overanalyze for nothing because at the last second they veer off to Rebecca's table.

"*Becky-bee, Becky-bee, such a little worthless she,*" they chant.

Hearing the name *Becky* mocked sets my teeth grinding.

Lola picks up a green bean and grinds it into Rebecca's hand like she's stubbing out a cigarette. Rebecca doesn't even look up.

"You didn't do our laundry this week," Lola says. "Bad pet. What should we do with you?"

"I couldn't get to it. I'll do it this week," she says into her hair.

My fork snaps. I hate bullies. Three years ago they put me in a group home. An older girl bullied me the first day and I knocked her out. All it got me was kicked out of the home. Here, they tell us over and over: fighting results in solitary confinement with no privileges. It can even add to your time.

Lola's harassing Rebecca about not folding their underwear right. "It's because she spends all her time sniffing it," says a red-haired girl with a patch over one eye. She looks like a pirate.

Rebecca remains frozen, trance-like.

"Bitch, you in there? Wake up," Lola says, slapping her cheeks.

My hands grip the rolled edges of the metal seat like clamps holding down a rocket. *Not your fight. Not your fight.*

But then Lola shoves Rebecca's face into the spaghetti and pulls her up by the hair, red sauce dripping from her chin, noodles pasted to her forehead.

I stand up. "Hey, leave her alone."

Lola lets go as they all turn to me.

"Well, look at this," she says. "How cute. It's our new blonde-haired, blue-eyed princess. Poor baby, what got you sent here? Take daddy's Mercedes without permission?"

Actually, I rammed a knife four inches up Scott Brooker's large intestine before slashing his carotid artery.

I say, "She's not bothering you." A guard in the corner is watching, a wiry Hispanic guy with a mustache. Why isn't he doing something?

Lola glares and I glare back. I can outstare anyone in the world. Dad said I was born with motor oil in my eyes. Tamika summons the troops to form a wall screening out the CO.

Lola leans in. We're about the same height, but she's twice as thick. "You got a problem with me, bitch?"

"No problem. Just leave Rebecca alone."

"Is that a request or an order?"

"Request."

"Say it nicely."

"Could you please leave Rebecca alone?"

"Fuck you." She pokes me hard with a finger. "Now what are you gonna do? Wanna try and make me?"

I catch a peek of the CO in the corner. Another one has joined him, the same thick-necked guard who took Rebecca from our cell. Surely they can see something's going on. What are they waiting for?

"I don't want to fight you," I say. There are lies and there are *LIES.*

"Fucking coward."

"If you want to think that, fine. I just don't want to fight. Could you please just leave us alone?" I look at Rebecca, still staring into her hair. A spaghetti noodle breaks loose from the bridge of her nose and falls into her Jell-O.

"It'll cost you."

"How much?"

"Start by helping Becky-bee here with our laundry. We'll come up with more chores real soon. Consider yourself our new pet."

Yeah, that's going to happen. "How about I pay with money instead?"

She laughs. "Money? Okay. Hundred dollars. Hand it over." We're the Saturday night entertainment. Some girls laugh and high-five each other. Others talk in excited whispers. Some look on wide-eyed, like they're just glad it's not them. The pair of COs are watching too, thick-neck saying something to mustache-man.

"A hundred is too much."

"That's the price," she says. "Take it or leave it."

When I hesitate, the four of them close in and form a circle around me. "Alright," I say. "But I've only been here a week and don't have any money yet. I'll be getting some soon. In the meantime, you have to agree to leave us alone."

"You have one week," she says, spearing my chest again.

Only by shutting my eyes am I able to resist executing a finger-lock that would entail torn tendons and broken bones. But closing your eyes in a fight is stupid, pure and simple. Lucas would bitch a blue streak about it. I don't see the sucker punch coming that wallops my stomach, taking my breath away and buckling my knees.

"One hundred dollars," Lola repeats. "One week." She spits on me and they walk away.

I pick myself off the floor, trying to disguise that I'm sucking for air. I wipe the spit off with my dinner napkin. The guards are looking the other way like nothing happened. What is going on in this place? If there was any doubt before, punching someone in the stomach is *fighting*. Even if they didn't see it happen, they had to see me on the floor.

I can't believe how bad I just effed up my prison life. It wasn't even my fight.

You got a major flaw for a killer.

I know, I froze. I didn't seize the advantage.

Worse. You got a heart.

But you can't ignore four against one, especially a defenseless one like Rebecca. I'll bet Lucas would have done something too. *I did the right thing.*

That's what I'm telling myself when I turn to Rebecca, who says, "I told you to mind your own business."

7

THE SAINT LANDRY PARISH courthouse is in Opelousas. I remember stopping here at a drugstore three years ago after fleeing the crime scene in Brooker's silver Lexus. I sideswiped a Toyota pulling into a parking spot and bought my first hair dye. *Pecan Brown.* Ah, the good old days. Haha.

The trip from Pochachant took an hour. We left before I could take a shower and the air-conditioning didn't reach the back of the van. I'm a greasy-haired wreck when the guards lead me into the courthouse. So much for impressing the new judge.

A frail fortyish woman intercepts me on my way in. She's wearing a loose print dress, tiny faded roses over gray, that hangs from her stooped shoulders like a tent.

"Hi. I'm Paula Dunwoody, your public defender," she says warmly, holding out a bony hand with knuckles that protrude like rivets. I shake it gently. "And you're Emily."

Am I? I'm not sure I'm ready for that. "Maybe," I say.

"Of course. I understand."

I doubt it. With a guard following, she leads me to a small white-walled room devoid of decoration. She asks the guard to remove my shackles, which I appreciate. We sit across from each other at a small round table.

"First, let me say how very sorry I am about what happened to you and your family."

She reaches across the table and lays her hand on my arm. I jerk away.

"Oh, I'm sorry," she says, recoiling.

"No biggie. Just a reflex. I don't like to be touched."

Her right eyebrow starts twitching. "I'm so, so sorry. I was just trying ..."

"It's fine, really."

She explains I'm here for a probable cause hearing. The state has to say what evidence they have against me. About time. I have no idea how they connected me to Brooker. After he picked me up hitchhiking, we didn't stop until we got out into the bayou where there was no one around, and I used wipes with bleach to clean the Lexus before abandoning it in Lafayette. The only person I ever told was Lucas.

"Just so you know, I'm not going to be asking questions to-day," Paula says. "This isn't a trial, just an opportunity to learn about the state's case."

"Okay," I say. "I have a question. Are they going to transfer me to adult court?"

From what I've heard, being transferred to adult court is the worst thing that can happen. Adult court means adult prison, full of adult criminals. And adult sentences. For first-degree murder, it's automatic life in Louisiana.

"I don't want to worry you," Paula says before proceeding to scare the crap out of me. "The prosecutor would if she could. Her name is Leslie Tierney. She's running for election as a judge on a law and order platform. Her claim to fame is she's sent more violent juveniles to adult prison than any prosecutor in the state. But you're lucky."

That's me, one lucky girl. "How so?"

"Louisiana law protects you. You have to be fourteen at the time of the crime to be transferred to adult court, even for mur-der. Now, the way I've calculated it—"

"I was only thirteen," I gush. "In fact, I just turned thirteen, so if you think about it, I was really like only twelve." *Think first.* "I mean, if everything happened like they say, which it didn't."

She sucks in her bottom lip. "Alright then. Now, you have to be very careful what you say out there and how you say it. And you want to be sure to be courteous to everyone. It can make a big difference."

"Go along to get along."

"Exactly. Meanwhile, we—I mean *I*—have to keep an eye on Leslie. She can be dangerous. Not only is she smart, she's known to play fast and loose with the rules to get what she wants."

"Who's the judge?"

"The Honorable William R. Hanks."

"What's he like?" The judge in Arkansas was nice.

"Fair, but by the book. Trials in juvenile court are usually informal, but Judge Hanks runs a tight ship. With such a serious charge and a, um, *unique* defendant, I suspect he's going to go the extra mile to ensure a clean, formal record."

When a guard knocks and says it's time, Paula jumps up. "I'll see you in the courtroom. I have to go to the bathroom. I have irritable bowel syndrome and it acts up under stress. I get cramps and terrible diarrhea."

TMI! "What gets you stressed?"

A yippy laugh. "Oh, goodness. Lots of things, like going to court."

Beautiful.

* * *

The bailiff's booming voice fills the courtroom. *All rise. Oyez, Oyez, this Juvenile Court of the State of Louisiana, in and for the Parish of Saint Landry, is now in session. The Honorable Judge William R. Hanks presiding. God save the State and this Honorable Court.*

Everything's more formal here than back in Arkansas, including the courtroom, which has a tall majestic ceiling and glossy wood walls. The prosecution and defense tables are longer and wider and made of real oak. Even the judge's chair is taller.

I stand beside Paula, trying to comb out my tangled hair with my fingers.

Judge Hanks enters from a door behind the bench. Mounted on the wall above his head is the state seal of Louisiana, a pelican and her babies nested over the word CONFIDENCE.

No smiles from this guy. His face is somehow twisted in a scowl even though the corners of his mouth are turned upward. Never seen that before. Turning hooded eyes on me, his square jaw tightens, like he's pissed off at me just for being here. This all occurs under a thick helmet of black hair that looks dyed.

"You may sit," he says. "We are here this morning for a probable cause hearing in the matter of *State of Louisiana v. Emily Blair Calby aka Alice Black*. Let's get right to work. Ms. Tierney, what does the state have for probable cause?"

Like Paula said, all business.

Leslie Tierney struts to a lectern and adjusts a snaky cable microphone with perfectly manicured fingers.

"May it please the court, what we have is evidence the defendant brutally murdered Mr. Scott Brooker, a forty-two-year-old husband and father traveling by automobile from Illinois, a salesman on his way to Lafayette. Somewhere along the way, he apparently decided to give the defendant a ride."

Leslie is the anti-Paula, her words and moves as smooth and confident as Paula's are awkward and self-conscious. Paula is plain, drab. Becky would have called her *frumpy*. She loved that word.

Leslie's pretty, glamorous even, her highlighted hair cut in a smart, layered bob that curls up at the ends. She's dressed in a silvery blouse under a black suit jacket with large pearly buttons. Her teeth gleam as white as a barracuda's. Sharp eyebrows point like arrows above intense green eyes.

I feel her aggression as she stalks her space behind the microphone in black velvet heels, like something caged inside is trying to bust out. *She can be dangerous*, Paula said. That's the kind of lawyer I want. A dangerous one.

She points a clicker at a screen, cloud-colored nail polish shining under the ceiling lights.

An image bursts onto the screen. A car on a highway. Silver. Two passengers in front, one a young girl with blonde hair.

"We begin with this picture taken by a state highway camera on I-49."

Highway camera? *WTF?*

"This is the victim's silver Lexus automobile. The image was captured between Alexandria and Saint Landry on the day of his death. In the passenger seat we see a blonde girl who looks remarkably like the defendant. The driver is Mr. Brooker, the victim."

Victim! Whatever.

She thumbs the clicker. "This photo is from another highway camera, time-stamped approximately one hour later, farther down the interstate, just outside of Lafayette. We see the same car, but now it has a new driver. The defendant. We also see an empty passenger seat. That's because the victim is now floating in the bayou near Chicot State Park with fatal stab wounds to his neck and groin."

The scene changes again. A picture of the crime scene appears, Brooker's bloated body, clotted with blood and algae, pulled onto the bank of the marsh.

A gasp from somewhere behind me.

"And this, Your Honor, is the victim."

Part of me is saying *Don't, Don't.* The losing part, as usual. I leap to my feet. "I object to that pig being called a victim!"

"Sit," the judge orders.

I don't like being talked to like a dog, but Paula is tugging me down by the sleeve.

Judge Hanks says, "You are not permitted to speak. Your lawyer is the one who speaks for you. Do you understand?"

"But Judge—"

"I said, do you understand? Yes or no."

I nod.

"Yes or no. The court reporter can't record a nod."

"Yes."

"Yes, what?"

"Yes, Your Honor."

Paula is frantic. "What's wrong? What's wrong?"

I just shake my head.

Leslie turns to me with a smug smile. "Are we to take from your remark that you knew *the victim?*"

The judge cuts her off. "Eh, eh, eh. You know better than that, Ms. Tierney."

I stay in my seat, but my mouth hole opens again. "What would *you* know about victims? You're just a stuck-up rich b— … person. You want to see real victims? Go look at pictures of my mother and sister. Go find …"

I'm about to unleash *all the other girls that pig picked up hitchhiking* but Paula is digging her nails into my thigh under the table. She's stronger than she looks.

Leslie takes a step toward me. "Listen to me, you little gutter rat."

Judge Hanks bangs his gavel. "That's enough. All of you. Step back, Ms. Tierney. Guards, put the restraints back on the defendant. Ms. Dunwoody, if you are unable to control your client, I will order her mouth taped shut. Do you hear me?"

Paula stands, wringing her hands. "I'm so sorry, judge."

From Andy the Lawyer to Paula the Apologizer.

Everyone watches as the guards reattach the chains to my wrists and ankles: Judge Hanks, looking pissed, Leslie Tierney, smirking, and Paula? Fretting, what else? Then there's the bailiff, court reporter, juvenile case coordinator, court clerk … and two strangers behind the prosecutor's table. A lady and a girl a few years older than me. Definitely not court people.

Paula begs in my ear. "Please do not say another word or you will get us both in trouble."

"Ms. Tierney, move on," the judge barks.

"Next up we have a video, security footage from a shopping

center in Lafayette. What we are seeing is the defendant thoroughly cleaning *the victim's* automobile. Either she's a very considerate murderer and car thief or trying to destroy evidence. The state's bet is on the latter."

I seethe. Cameras everywhere. There is no privacy anymore. The only place there wasn't a camera was out in the swamp, where Brooker demanded I do him a *favor*—or else. But all the images are low-resolution, fuzzy. Could be any blonde girl.

"Additionally," Tierney says, "we have sworn statements from several witnesses who identified the defendant from a photograph as being present in Lafayette shortly after the murder." She goes on to list Officer Talley, the parish parks cop who almost arrested me at Acadiana Park, a librarian at the public library, and a girl who claims to have sold me pizza.

"Is that it?" Hanks says.

"We believe it's sufficient to establish probable cause," Leslie says. "With all due respect, the state's not required to divulge all its evidence at the probable cause hearing. We're also continuing to gather additional evidence."

"What's the basis for charging the defendant with murder in the first degree?"

"The Louisiana code includes within the definition of first-degree murder intentionally killing a person while engaged in the perpetration of an armed robbery. The defendant stole Mr. Brooker's automobile. We've already seen photographic evidence of that. We also located Mr. Brooker's wallet, empty."

I wonder how they found that. I sunk it in the bayou.

"It is the state's theory that the defendant rendered a kind gesture by giving the defendant a ride and she returned the favor by fatally stabbing him and stealing his property."

"What about the fact that the defendant was herself the victim of a terrible crime?"

"Judge, please tell me we're not going to indulge the defendant with a *poor, poor me* defense."

Paula is whispering, "Easy, easy."

Hanks says, "Let's assume hypothetical'
what you're alleging. Surely there are men
from the defendant's prior traumatic ex
    "If diminished capacity is an issue,
raised and proved by the defendant at trial.
    I can't tell if the judge was trying to help me by sugg
defense or is already convinced I'm nuts because I jumped up
yelling in his courtroom.

At the end of the hearing, he finds there's probable cause. No surprise. Paula makes a motion for my pretrial release, which Hanks rejects matter-of-factly, ordering I remain in detention at Pochachant pending trial.

"This court is adjourned," he says, banging his gavel.

At the bailiff's command, we all rise and watch the judge exit through the back door. The guards waste no time coming to fetch me.

They lead me down the aisle in my full-harness transport restraints. Paula walks ahead like the flower girl in a wedding processional.

Words suddenly attack me from the side. "You will burn in a pit of fire forever."

Startled, I turn to see the older woman snarling at me, eyes shooting lasers. The girl next to her gazes straight ahead with a blank face.

"That's right. I'm talking to you, devil child."

And it comes back to me. The picture in Brooker's wallet, the one I held in my blood-soaked hands before I rolled his body into the bayou. His wife and daughter. The daughter still looks just like him.

Paula waits with me in the hall as the guards retrieve the van to take me back to Pochachant. "Paula," I say. "Is it okay to call you Paula?"

"Of course."

"First, I'm really sorry for my outburst in court."

"I'm sorry I didn't make it clearer that you needed to stay quiet."

oll my eyes. "You made it clear. It was my bad, and I'm smart enough to know I hurt my case. I have a bad habit with impulse control. I'll try not to do it again. I have a question. Did you see those two women we passed? I thought no one was allowed in juvenile proceedings except for the court people. That's the law, isn't it?"

"Well, the law is full of exceptions. Family members of the ... family members are allowed. I can check, but I assume that's who they are."

No need to check. "So what happens now?"

"Here's the deal. To defend you, I need information. We basically have two choices. Deny you killed the man or assert a legally sufficient reason for doing it."

"What's a legally sufficient reason for killing a man?"

"There aren't many. Self-defense is one ... insanity may be another. With your traumatic history—"

"I'm not insane," I say flatly. Maybe I am, or was, but I'm not admitting it in court. Even Lucas and Darla don't know about the three girls who lived in my head.

Self-defense is the obvious choice, because it's true. But would anyone believe me? If it was self-defense, why did I try to cover it up? Why did I steal Brooker's money and car? Why did I flee? Why was I carrying a neck knife in the first place, and how could a regular girl have executed him so expertly? Lucas taught me that up-the-groin move, but even he never knew anyone who actually did it.

Paula says, "I'd like to request a full psychiatric examination, with your permission. It could help your case."

"I don't want one."

"The judge might order it anyway."

"Seems like it should be my decision. It's my psyche. You want to talk insanity? This whole thing is insane. I'm the girl who *ran* from murder. Isn't that important?"

"Actually, it could be very important to a diminished capacity defense. And in the court of public opinion, it could count for a lot. But the fact that you were a victim of a different crime isn't directly relevant to this case and since juvenile proceedings are confidential by law, you won't have a court of public opinion unless someone leaks information to the media."

I've been wondering about that. "Do you think that will happen?"

"I hope not, but can't rule it out. You are a ..."

"Juicy story?"

Another yippy laugh. "I was going to say *unusual case*, but you captured it better. If that happens the media are going to descend on this place like hungry wolves. The story of the mysterious surviving Calby girl being charged with murder is like something Hollywood would make up."

Leaking it would let Lucas know where I am, but the attention could only lead to bad things. I'd lose my cherished anonymity and there are too many secrets that need to stay buried. It would also make me a target at Pochachant. People would hate me just for being special.

"How about we do this?" she says. "You think about which way you want to go and I'll come visit you at Pochachant next week so we can talk. Have you got your phone and visitor privileges set up yet?"

"Um, no. I don't have any people," I say, voice trailing off.

She hands me a card, clinging to my hand too long. "Get me on your list. You have a right to talk to your lawyer on the phone and I'm allowed to visit you."

"Okay."

"Alright then," she says with a big smile, like she wants to wrap up the terrible day with a big happy bow. "Is there anything I can get you in the meantime?"

A hundred dollars in extortion money would be helpful. "No, but thanks."

I watch her walk down the hall toward the automatic doors that open into the bright sunshine of freedom, but she hangs a right at the bathroom.

The guards shuffle me through a side door down a back hallway.

Well, look who's here. It's Leslie Tierney, blocking the path, hands on her hips. She pulls one of the guards aside and whispers something to him, then turns to me.

"Such a shame that man's poor daughter had to sit there looking at those terrible pictures of her dead daddy. Sure would be nice if she could know the truth and get some peace."

If she knew the truth, she'd never find peace. I elbow past her and keep walking.

8

MAVA DIXON, the old black woman who runs the prison library, requested I be assigned there for my job. I guess she was impressed I checked out *Crime and Punishment*, which I returned for *Alice in Wonderland*, Mom's favorite book of all time.

For my interview, she asked if I believe in God while stroking a cross hanging from her neck on a braided silver chain. "Oh, yes, ma'am! I went to church almost every Sunday of my whole life until I, um, moved from Georgia. And the only time I miss my prayers at night is when I accidentally fall asleep first."

Her only other question was whether I like books. I told her Mom was a teacher who read to us every night and that I had more books than toys growing up.

The library is on the girls' side of the double fences. Boys can visit, but a CO has to bring and stay with them. I've only seen one boy so far, but not many girls either. It's a two-story building of crumbling brick, painted gray like everything else. Two second-floor windows wink like cat eyes when the afternoon sun hits them. Once upon a time the bottom floor had windows, but they've been filled in with cinder blocks.

It's a cake job. Rebecca works in the steaming laundry room. I see Lola digging ditches in the baking sun as part of her job in the dubiously named *Landscaping Division*. I'm surprised they trust her with picks and shovels. Other girls work in the cafeteria. You can spot them by their bleached-out hands.

The library is cool and quiet. OMG, jails are noisy. Shouting, laughing, crying, everyone trying to out-talk everyone else.

And I love the old-coffee smell of the books. It brings back memories of Mom taking me and Becky to the library, a Saturday morning ritual. Each week she made me pick out one shelf and look through every book on it, ignoring my whining and eye-rolling. *Every one? Mom, seriously? Why not just the ones I want?* She never told me, just smiled with her all-knowing eyes.

The job only pays eighteen cents an hour, but at least it's something going into my account at the commissary, the *store* as everyone calls it. I've amassed a fortune of $5.40, leaving me only $94.60 short of the one hundred dollars I need to pay off my *peer*, Lola. That's how we're supposed to refer to each other according to our *Unity Matters* workshop.

When I ran into my peer this morning, she helpfully taught me how to count. "It's Wednesday. That's *one two three* days 'til Saturday. One hundred dollars," she said, sandpapering imaginary bills between her fingers.

Whatever. I wouldn't pay her even if I had the money. I'm saving for shower slippers and instant coffee, then an art pad and pencils. I got addicted to coffee when I was twelve.

"How's everything going out there?" echoes a disembodied voice from down the hall.

It's Mava, calling from her office. She spends most of her time there, another thing I love about this job. I get left alone.

"Just fine, Miss Mava!" I started out calling her Mrs. Dixon, but she corrected me, saying she's been Miss Mava, "like the month of May," to the girls at Pochachant for twenty years.

I'm on a stepladder, rearranging the books in the display stack. They're the first books people see when they enter the library. Mava likes things clean, so I spend most of my time sweeping and dusting, but the display stack has been bugging me. The books were completely in the wrong places.

It took a couple of hours, but I reorganized them all by subject and labeled the shelves with sticky notes. I need to find a way to make permanent signs or talk Mava into ordering some. I'm planning to surprise her.

Admiring my work, I hear my dad's voice. *Initiative, Em. That's how you get ahead in the world.*

Thuds coming down the hallway. Mava's block heels. I know all her shoes. She has three pairs. Brown ones that look like orthopedics and barely make a sound. You have to tune your ears to their soft squish. Black flats that slap like a tack hammer driving nails, and the ones she's wearing now, white with thick square heels, thudding bullets.

"Hi, Miss Mava!" She's dressed in her usual attire, a mid-calf skirt and long-sleeve blouse buttoned all the way to the neck.

She looks at the display stack and clutches her cross with both hands. Behind the thick lenses of her wire-framed glasses, her veined gray eyes are stretched wide. I definitely succeeded in surprising her.

"What on God's green earth have you done, child?" she says.

"I reorganized these books, by category, to make it easier for people to find ones they like right when they come in. See my labels? I have *Adventure, History, Science,* some of almost everything."

"Did I tell you to do this?"

"No, ma'am. I was showing initiative. I admit my system will take some tweaking. Some of the books fit in more than one category. But I'll get them right. You don't have to worry about that. I'm going to do a good job for you."

She rubs her temples. "You got *Literature* right here in the middle. This is the first shelf anyone lays eyes on."

"Yes, ma'am. I figured it's always best to lead with your best products."

"And you got *Children's Books* on the top where no one can reach 'em."

"Well, since there aren't any children here, I thought it would be the best place."

She yanks *Crime and Punishment* from its prime position in the center of the *Literature* shelf and shoves it in my hands.

"Girl, don't you understand? Half these kids can barely read

Judy Blume. Some of them saw more guns and drugs in their homes than books. They didn't grow up with mamas reading to them every night. They weren't privileged like you."

I feel my face flush.

"We want them to read—*anything*. They were organized by grade level, easy books in the middle, hardest on top. Put them back exactly like you found them and stow that ladder when you're done. The storage closet is over there."

"Yes, ma'am."

She thuds back to her office. Her words still stinging, I set about un-reorganizing. *Crime and Punishment* goes back on top, Judy Blume in the middle.

The wall clock says I only have fifteen minutes to get back in time for cell count. It's going to take a whole afternoon to get the books back in place.

I fold the stepladder and search for the storage room. Shouldering my way down a narrow corridor behind the tall stacks, I twist ancient doorknobs. One comes off in my hand. I glance around guiltily and slide it back in place. None of the doors budge.

Then I come to a different kind of door, metal with fresh paint and a modern handle. I twist the lever and it glides open. The first thing I notice is the smell, fresh, but in a chemical way. The room is dark as coal. I flip a light switch and like it's built into the wiring, a loud *Hey!* shatters the silence.

"*Now* what do you think you're doing?" It's Mava, spying on me from behind the stacks through a slit in the shelves.

"Um, just storing the ladder like you told me." But the bright lights show the room is no storage closet. A plaque next to the door says *Catlett Foundation Law Library*.

Mava makes her way around the stacks as I take it all in. Four entire walls lined with rows of shiny hard-bound books on metal shelving stretching all the way from the floor to the ceiling. Two rectangular wood tables, bigger than ping-pong tables, fill the space in between. The burgundy carpeting, the only carpeting I've seen at Pochachant, looks like it's never been stepped on.

"Wow," I say in awe. "What are all these books? They look so *important*." They're in magnificent matching sets of different colors. Each book has a bold number on the spine.

The pleats in Mava's forehead smooth out. "This here is the law library. Some damn fool donated a truckload of money to buy all these expensive books in the name of *access to the courts*. Law books, to kids who can barely read. Every penny wasted."

An imposing edifice of tan books towers next to me, hundreds of volumes, each one with *Federal Reporter, 3d Series* emblazoned in red across the binding.

"These kids got enough access to courts. That's their problem. What they need are more teachers, job training, oh, don't even get me started."

She pounds the light switch with her fist. "Git. You don't want to be late for count. Fix those books tomorrow, hear?"

"Yes, ma'am."

She shoos me out the front. I go three steps before turning back. The door's already locked. I rap on the wood. I don't think I've seen another wood door at Pochachant. I guess the library is the only place the guards aren't afraid people will try to break into.

Mava pulls it open with a frown. "The library's closed. Oh, it's you. Forget something?"

"Miss Mava, can anyone use those books?"

"What books?"

"The law books."

"Nobody ever asked. Anyone with library privileges, I suppose."

"Can I use them?"

* * *

It's after dinner and I'm in the cell envying Rebecca, sitting cross-legged on her bunk painting with watercolors on an art pad, hair hiding her face and thoughts. I don't know where she got it, but her paint set is awesome, a sleek silver box with eight rows of half-pans. So is her art pad, jumbo-sized with a wire-bound top. I want one just like it.

She loves painting animals. The wall above her bunk looks like a petting zoo. From left to right: a cat, rabbit, lamb and deer. They all look real and each one has a personality, which makes them super-cute. The rabbit is holding a carrot and flashing a thumbs-up. She keeps her work-in-progress hidden, but I caught a glimpse of a yellow mane. Maybe a lion.

"You're a fantastic painter, Rebecca."

"Thanks."

"I like art too. I've done some painting, but mostly I like to draw. I really miss it. I'm saving money at the commissary to buy pencils and an art pad like yours. Did you learn to paint in school?"

She shakes her head.

"I had an awesome art teacher in elementary school, Mr. McKenzie, but my mom helped a lot too. She had an artistic soul. She could do almost anything creative. Did your mom teach you?"

"No," she snaps.

Footsteps in the hall and the door rattles. You never know who it's going to be. Sometimes they warn you, sometimes it's a surprise. A suntanned face with chemically damaged blonde hair appears in the window square. It's Longmont, one of the nice COs. She helped me get tampons when I got here and didn't have any money.

"Knock, knock, just me. Rebecca, it's visiting hours and your mother is here."

Without looking up from her painting, "I don't want to talk to her."

"Ah, come on. This is the third time. She drove all the way from New Orleans."

She rinses her brush in a plastic cup. "I said I don't want to see her."

Longmont looks at me and shrugs. "Okay, I'll tell her," she says and leaves.

I can't *not* ask. Not about this. "Rebecca, why don't you want to talk to your mom?"

"Why is that any of your business?" she says.

"It's not. It's just that … my mom died and I'd give my life to see her for even a minute."

"Well, aren't you and your mom special?"

"I didn't mean it like that. I just—"

"Did your mom prostitute you?"

"I, huh? What?"

"Did she give you to men so they could have sex with you?"

"I–I … no."

Rebecca parts her hair and leans in close. I never noticed how pretty she is. Her pale skin is as smooth as ice cream, brown eyes deep and lustrous, like pods from an exotic tree.

"Mine did, starting when I was eight, with her boyfriend. *There.* Are you glad to finally get to know me?" A sardonic laugh.

I think about Mom, pleading with the two men to do what they wanted to her, but please don't hurt Becky and me. For the first time in my life, I lose a staring match, breaking away out of respect.

Silence. When I look back up, she saves me. "It was stupid to promise a hundred dollars to that bitch Lola."

"I know. I didn't know what to do."

"You can't even have cash in this place. The only money you're allowed is what's in your commissary account."

"I wasn't thinking, but I'd kill myself before …"

She must read my mind. "Do you wonder why I'm such a sickening loser that I do their laundry? Because they leave me alone and protect me from other prisoners. I'm small, people pick on me."

"It didn't look like they were leaving you alone Saturday night," I say.

"Well," she shrugs. "I didn't do their laundry last week. That's just the way this place works."

"You can't accept that."

"Yeah, like there's a choice."

When I was weak, Lucas risked everything for me. Took four bullets for it and almost died. *The strong must bear the weaknesses of those without strength.* Romans, Chapter Fifteen. My preacher back in Georgia gave a whole sermon about it.

Nonchalantly, "How about if I protect you from now on?"

At least I found something to make her laugh.

"Get real." I'm sure she's picturing me on the cafeteria floor gasping for breath. Then she turns serious. "You're not mental, are you?" Like she'd feel bad if she was laughing at the mentally disabled.

"Well, you know, everything depends on definitions, but no, not the way you're thinking."

"Look, it was nice of you to try to help me. Don't do it again." She twists her body to face the other way.

I watch as she dips her thinnest brush into a blue paint pot. She floats it above the paper, hesitates and sets the brush down. She tears a blank page from the pad and hands it to me with a pen.

"Here," she says. "You can't have pencils here. They make good weapons."

"Count, count, count," resounds down the hall. "Lights out in five, ladies. Lights out in five. Stand up for count."

9

MY FIRST GED class is math. They gave us a workbook and even a pencil. I'd steal it except that every class ends with a pencil count. If one is missing, no one can leave until it's found. Like Rebecca said, they make good weapons, but I just want one for drawing ... okay, maybe a weapon too.

Like everything at Pochachant, the classroom is ancient. The vinyl flooring is scuffed and scratched. Rafters show through the patchy ceiling. An old-fashioned green chalkboard covers the front wall, dwarfing a sad teacher's desk, covered with graffiti and propped up by dusty books where it's missing a leg.

We sit on plastic chairs at folding tables strung together in rows, about fifty of us, one of four GED sections. With everyone wearing the same evergreen uniforms, it looks like some kind of a convention.

My biggest surprise is that the classes are co-ed. For no good reason except government, they make us sit alphabetically, leaving me wedged between a black guy who looks more like a man and a white kid with shiny brown hair tucked behind his ears and weirdly long eyelashes.

The teacher is Mr. Medillo. Bald and bearded with a belly that untucks his wrinkled dress shirt another half-inch each time he turns, he's been writing problems on the board in a cloud of chalk dust, asking for volunteers but getting none.

The questions are easy, despite my missing two grades. Lucas made me take online courses from the beginning. Hard ones.

Chemistry, Geometry, Computer Science. For someone who dropped out of school in the tenth grade, he's big on education, always bragging about his little man James, a genius hacker from South Memphis who got a full scholarship to Stanford.

"Chop, chop, people," Medillo says. "Pay attention. Look at this problem. The shoes you want to buy are on sale for fifteen percent off. The original price is forty-two dollars. How much will the shoes cost? Here are your choices." He lists them on the board.

"Come on, help me out. Don't worry about giving a wrong answer."

Maybe because Mom was a teacher, I feel sorry for him and raise my hand. He points at me with surprise. "You."

"The answer's C, thirty-five dollars and seventy cents."

"That is correct. How did you know that?" he says with narrowed eyes, like I must have cheated.

"Um, I multiplied forty-two by point eight five."

His face lights up. "You hear that? She multiplied ..."

He gives us another problem, gets no volunteers and looks at me again. I give the right answer and hear hisses.

"What is your name?"

"Alice Black," I murmur, not wanting anyone to hear it.

He announces, "Welcome to GED class, Alice Black." With new pep in his step, he prints on the board in big, bold script.

Solve: (10 - 5) + 4 x 11
A. 99
B. 49
C. 59
D. 109

Maybe I kindled a competitive spirit, even a war of the sexes, because a boy behind me shouts, "Ninety-nine."

"Very good try," Medillo says.

The problem's about ordering. The kid added five plus four before multiplying four times eleven. The answer's forty-nine.

"Anyone else?" His eyes scan rows of blank faces and I know they're coming back to land on me. "Ms. Black?"

The kid on my left with the long eyelashes is scribbling on my workbook. *Wrong answer!*

I look at him, annoyed. I know it was the wrong answer. Below table level he's poking a finger, mouthing: *You. Wrong answer.*

"Ms. Black? How about it?"

"Uh, one-o-nine?"

"No, I'm afraid the answer is forty-nine," Medillo says dispiritedly.

I figured out the note. Like Mava said. Privileged. People in this place didn't grow up taking advanced math and getting tutored at night by their own teacher-mom. The last thing I need is to be is the teacher's pet.

I jot, *Thanks.*

No problem.

I'm Alice.

Ben.

The contrast in his hands stands out. His fingers are long and delicate, like someone who plays piano or violin, but they're red and rough, covered with nicks and calluses.

Here long you here for? he writes.

From what I've figured out, the etiquette is you don't ask someone *why* they're here but it's okay to ask how long. Still, it's personal.

I write, *How long for you?*

He turns away. Fine, *Ben.* Ask me a question then get offended and snub me when I ask the same question back.

Mr. Medillo is posing a ridiculous problem about two snails racing toward each other from exactly one mile apart at three feet per hour. How many hours will it take before they hook up?

Why didn't I just answer the question? Ben's, not Medillo's. The honest answer is I don't know how long. I don't even know when my trial is. I should have just said that. Why didn't I?

Because I don't trust anyone ... and have no clue how to talk to a boy. In the past three years I've spent hundreds of hours practicing with guns and knives and probably thirty minutes talking to boys. Overprotective Lucas scared off the few I met. I've never even had a boyfriend. Embarrassing! When I was twelve, before everything happened, there was a boy I really liked at school, but I don't think it was real love. We never even kissed.

"Let's start this way," Medillo says. "At three feet per hour, how long will it take one snail to go ten yards?" He picks up a clipboard. "*Lola Grimes.*"

Lola? I twist my neck. She's just a few rows behind me.

"What?" she says.

"What what?" Medillo says. "Answer the question. *Try* to answer the question."

"Could you repeat it?"

"Never mind," he sighs, and proceeds to explain the mathematical journey of the snails.

Something about the exchange with Lola registers. Medillo took Lola's answer like anyone would, her being obnoxious, too cool for school, but I saw something else.

Ben's still ignoring me, like I disappeared. Fine with me ... then why am I thinking about it and stealing glances at him? His skin is smooth, almost pearly, his features fine, except for his mouth, which is wide with generous lips. Add in the eyelashes and he's almost pretty, like a girl.

The math lesson is stuff I already know. I tune it out to free up brain space. What should I tell Paula about my case? I talked to her last night and she's still planning to come to Pochachant this afternoon. My first visitor.

Something's poking my elbow. It's the edge of Ben's workbook. Etched across the page in deep strokes that tear through the paper is *LIFE.*

I smile at him. A boy tells me he's in prison for life and I smile! That's what an idiot I am. I don't know how to act. Darla once said I needed to be more *socialized*. I thought she meant be more social, go out more and stuff like that, until I looked it up and learned it means *trained to fit into normal society*.

Life? What's the comeback to that? *Sorry. Really? Wow!* I default to an oversized question mark.

Medillo declares class is over, telling us to do our homework while reminding us to turn in our pencils on the way out. His resigned look says he knows the contradictory instructions defy logic, but also that he can't change the rules.

I introduce myself to the man-child on the right, who says his name is Jermaine, and turn to Ben.

"Life?" I whisper. "But how ... what did you do? Sorry, I guess we're not supposed to ask that."

"Second-degree murder."

"Really?"

"Broke into a house with a friend to steal money from a guy who was supposed to be a drug dealer. We thought it was empty, but the guy was there and started shooting. So did my friend. They both died."

"And you got life? But you didn't shoot anyone. How can that be murder?"

The guards are moving everyone out. A burly CO who looks like he could have played pro football shouts, "Line up, kiddies, line up." It must be his favorite line because I heard it on the way in too.

"What about you?" he says.

"Waiting for trial."

"Must be something serious if they're keeping you in detention."

"Don't tell anyone. Promise? First-degree murder. Beat you by one degree."

"Yeah, right," he laughs.

The CO butts in and funnels us into separate boy-girl lines where another guard collects our pencils.

* * *

It's my first time sitting in the visiting room, a former gym filled with folding tables and chairs arrayed on a dull wood floor that still shows signs of free throw circles and lane lines. I'm sitting across from Paula. There are about a dozen other kids here. Guards watch every move.

"How have they been treating you?" Paula says. "The guards and other detainees."

Detainees. Everyone likes to call us that, instead of prisoners. Makes them feel better, I guess. The whole system is built on euphemisms. Juveniles aren't *convicted*, but *adjudicated*. We don't get *sentenced*. We get a *disposition*.

"Fine."

"Any problems."

"Not really." Unless you count assault and extortion as problems.

"It has a reputation for being a pretty rough place," she says, giving me permission to open up.

It doesn't take long to learn that snitching is the most dangerous thing a person can do in a prison. *Snitches get stitches.* Doesn't matter. I handle my own problems. I change the subject.

"About my case," I say. "I deny everything."

I agonized over it and decided denial was the best way to go. I can't see anyone believing my self-defense story. "I don't know who that girl is in those pictures and video. I admit she looks a little like me, but I can't even make out a face."

"Okay," she says uncertainly. "But they could have other evidence and they're still searching for more."

It's a risk, but I retraced every step of that day and can't think of any other evidence that could tie me to Brooker. I not only wiped down his car, I checked every inch of it for strands of blonde hair. The knife is somewhere in Pensacola Bay.

"How long do they have to find more evidence? I mean, not that there is any."

"Technically, until your trial."

"When is that?"

"Under the juvenile code, a disposition is supposed to happen in thirty days, but the time can be extended for good cause. Yesterday the judge granted Leslie's motion for a thirty-day extension."

Just like I thought: the law does whatever it wants to do. The law says trial in thirty days, but no problem. Make it sixty, make it a thousand, whatever the government wants.

"She probably did it just to keep me in jail. She doesn't like me. That's obvious."

"You didn't seem to be a big fan of hers either. What was it you called her in court?"

"Stuck-up rich person, but at least I didn't say the b-word like I started to."

"Thank you for small favors. In any event, extensions are common in complex cases involving serious charges."

"Did you fight it?"

She bites the corner of her lip. "To be honest, no. I'm sorry, but we need time to prepare too."

It's hard to get mad at Paula because she's so nice. Too nice. I ask how her IBS is doing and she says fine, thanks.

"Paula, can someone be convicted of second-degree murder if they never hurt anyone, but someone else did?"

Alarmed, "Why do you ask?"

"Just curious."

Why is Ben stuck in my head? Maybe it's the eyelashes, but I hope I'm deeper than that. I sensed something gentle in him, something I don't have anymore, something I don't even know anymore.

"A person can be found guilty of second-degree murder if they participate in a serious crime where someone gets killed."

"Like breaking into a house to steal money and someone gets shot?"

She cradles her abdomen. "Exactly like that. Please don't tell me you did that too, I mean, did that. I'm sorry, do tell me."

"No, no. Just a hypothetical. It doesn't seem fair."

"I agree, especially when the automatic sentence here is life in prison without parole."

I shake my head. "The law is weird."

She smiles. "That's a good word for it."

"Can I ask you a favor? A really big one. I know you're super-busy, but do you think you could teach me how to use law books? They assigned me to work in the jail library and I found a whole separate law library."

"Whoo, now that's ambitious. The law is complicated, even for people who went to law school. It takes a long time to learn."

"How long is law school?"

"Three years."

"I'm a fast learner, especially when I'm dedicated to something. I'll try really hard."

"I'm sure you will, but why do you want to learn law? Don't trust me?" she says.

Some of that, but it's not the main reason. "From what I've seen, all the real power in the world comes down to the law. You can be the strongest person, the toughest, have the most guns or knives or whatever, but the law is always going to win."

"Very astute. Just for that, I'll make it a point to come back and show you some legal research basics. Don't expect too much."

10

SATURDAY, late afternoon, almost dinnertime. I'm in my cell reading a thick green book I checked out of the law library. *Criminal Law,* by some guy named LaFave. Thirteen hundred pages that cover everything. I'm finishing up the chapter on self-defense. Competing for my concentration is the question of what's going to happen when I show up in the cafeteria without Lola's hundred dollars. It's been a week.

Rebecca turned quiet on me again after our conversation about her mom. Right now she's on her back, eyes closed, black hair draping the pillow like fine silk. Her skin is so pale her veins show through. I'll bet just touching it would leave a red mark. She looks like a sleeping princess, or a corpse. I shake off the thought and go back to reading.

The text is dense but the basic points seem pretty simple. Everything's about reasonableness. If you *reasonably* believe you're threatened with unlawful force, you can respond with *reasonable* force. For sexual assault that can include force likely to cause death or serious bodily injury. Fits my case. If I could only prove it.

When Lola's not invading my thoughts, Ben slips in to take her place. We didn't get a chance to talk yesterday in class, but he saw me drawing in the margin of my workbook, a bird on a leafy branch with musical notes floating from her beak.

What kind bird? he wrote.

I don't know. A free one.

Only a few minutes until dinner lineup. I fold up the book. Even Lola's not stupid enough to think I could come up with a hundred dollars in a week. I'm sure she has something planned. Not afraid, just apprehensive. There's a difference. One of the best lessons Lucas ever taught me was about fear.

Fear is bigger than your enemy. It will lock you up inside. Since you gonna be in the same situation anyway, might as well make the choice not to be afraid. You always got a choice. You'll come out better for it.

I spent yesterday reorganizing the library books with Mava keeping a watchful eye. Whenever she went back to her office, I snuck peeks inside the law library.

Racket in the corridor means it's time to line up. Rebecca always goes in front of me with my hands on her shoulders. This time she snaps at me to quit squeezing so hard.

Fish-sticks, coleslaw and cornbread. My mouth waters as I wait in line. The cornbread is awesome, as extra-good as everything else is bad. It's easy to trade. I saw a girl give up a nice necklace for a two-inch square.

I spot Lola, already seated with her toadies. In the corner are the same two guards from last week: thick-neck—the one who came to get Rebecca from her cell—and the Hispanic guy with the mustache. I still don't understand why they just stood there. Maybe they really didn't see what happened. Nothing else makes sense.

Rebecca and I sit at our usual tables. They're the only spares so if anyone else decides to be a loner something will have to give. Girls keep looking my way, except for Lola, who ignores me completely. Maybe it was all a bluff and nothing's going to happen.

I ratchet my hypervigilance down a notch and take a bite of the cornbread. *Umm.* Delish. Too delish. I scarf it down and have to face the fish-sticks without anything to look forward to as a reward. Even drenched in ketchup, the soggy rods are barely edible.

I'm washing them down with milk when Lola and her soldiers stand up, just like last week. And just like last week, they turn and file down the aisle in my direction. But I know the ending will be different. They're not going to veer off to Rebecca.

I'm already standing when they get close. Everyone's watching, including the two guards.

"Hello, Lola," I say.

"Been a week. I'm here to collect my hundred dollars."

"Oh, right, the hundred dollars," like it slipped my mind. I move as they move, keeping the table between us so they can't surround me again.

"Well, first, I want you to know that when I made that agreement I had every intention of honoring it. *Bu-ut*, since I just got to Pochachant, I didn't know we aren't allowed to have cash. I asked my dad to send me the money, but they sent it back to him. Sorry." I turn my palms up.

"In that case, you start working for us, right now. Clean up them dinner trays," she points. "Tomorrow's laundry day." She nods to the red-headed girl with the eye patch. "Claire here's got a hole in her uniform. Fix it."

"Actually, sewing is one thing I always wanted to learn but never did, and I've had an allergy to laundry detergent forever, since I was little. As for the trays,"—I dangle a limp wrist—"carpel-tunnel syndrome. So, you know, I don't think I'm going to be much help."

This monologue triggers laughs all around. People can't tell if I'm a dumb blonde who doesn't get it or playing Lola.

Lola gets it, face blotching with rage. "Only one other way then," she says.

A murmur starts and spreads. I can't make it out, not until Lola adds her voice. "Fight club," she says.

"Seriously? You're willing to go to solitary just for the pleasure of fighting me?"

"Ain't no one going to solitary," she says. "Hospital, maybe."

Rebecca surprises all of us by standing up. "This all started because of me. Can you let her go this time? She's new and not very smart."

"What?" I say.

"I'll do your chores extra-good this week," she says.

The guards are shoving their way through the crowd. Finally, some sanity. Thick-neck is in the lead. I see his name tag as he gets close. *Twiggs, Correctional Officer.*

"Grimes, Black. Come with me." He points a fat finger at Rebecca. "You too, and you three," rounding up Lola's posse. "Gonzalez, watch my back."

Now we're all in trouble and I didn't even do anything. With Gonzalez bringing up the rear, Twiggs leads us out of the cafeteria into the main hallway. We stop at a metal door and wait while he unspools the retractable keyring attached to his belt and unlocks it.

We proceed down a set of stairs, landing in a damp, moldy place I didn't know existed, an entire basement level with a dirt floor, clanking pipes and humming machinery. The bowels of the prison.

We travel along a dark corridor that ends at a windowless steel door framed with rivets. Is this solitary? Are we all getting put in there?

Twiggs tugs on the handle and the door groans open. He waves us in. Lola, me, then the rest. *Clank.* Gonzalez reseals the door behind us. We're in a concrete bunker, already occupied, I'm surprised to see, by six other COs. All men.

"What is this?" I whisper to Rebecca.

She shrugs. "Fight club?"

Twiggs barks, "No talking. The reason we are gathered here is to settle this feud y'all are having. Grimes, Black, front and center."

Lola steps forward. I stay planted. "What's this all about?" I say.

"You deaf? You two are gonna resolve this right here and now, man to man." The other guards laugh.

"A fight? This is insane. What about the rules against fighting?"

"In our experience these kinds of disputes fester until they're put to bed for good."

"Does the warden know about this?"

"Know about what? All we did is respond to the scene of a fight that broke out between rivals. Anyone ends up injured, praise the lord we arrived before it got worse. Ain't that right, gentlemen?"

The COs nod as one. Gonzalez says, "Amen."

"What if I refuse?"

"Then you're gonna get the shit kicked outta you even worse 'cause Grimes here is ready to fight. Ain't that right, Grimes?"

Breathing heavy with balled fists, Lola nods.

"What are the rules?"

"No rules. Winner gets extra privileges. Loser does the winner's chores for one month, no complaints."

"What kind of extra privileges?"

Snickering filters through the putrid air.

"Why is that funny?"

"The man said the *winner* gets extra privileges. The odds are twenty-to-one against you," Gonzalez says.

"Don't discourage the girl," Twiggs says. "Hope always makes for a more spirited effort. What kinda privileges you want?"

"Extra time in the library and everybody leaves us alone. Me and Rebecca. Those are my conditions. That or I don't fight."

"Awfully demanding for someone about to get her ass kicked," Gonzalez says.

Twiggs says, "Let her have 'em. She ain't gonna win anyway. We're wasting time. Mr. Gonzalez, open the betting."

I watch in disbelief as the COs gather around Gonzalez, handing him cash while he makes notes on a spiral pad.

"I want to make a bet," I say. "On me. Nine dollars and sixty-four cents from my commissary account." It's taken forever to save that much but at twenty to one odds I'll be rich if I win.

Twiggs ignores me. "Let's get this show on the road." He holds up a silver whistle. "When you hear this, you go. Fight continues until there's a winner. *Ready. Set.*"

The best way to fight is preemptively. Lucas taught me that at the beginning. *Don't think. Attack. Seize the advantage while the other motherfucker's thinkin'. Don't stop 'til the end. Finish the job.*

"This one's gonna be over in a hurry," jokes a huckleberry CO with an Adam's apple the size of a golf ball.

It could be. An upward elbow under Lola's chin would end it quickly, but could hurt her, maybe cause brain or spinal damage. She's not my real enemy, whatever she thinks. I add every guard in the room to the deserves-to-die list.

Twiggs raises the whistle.

"Hold on," I say. I roll off the elastic band holding my ponytail and wrap my hair in a bun. Hair-grabbing is an easy way to control an opponent in a fight.

The whistle blows and Lola lunges at me with a windmill punch. Good strategy, but I head-slip it and start circling to my right. Everyone backs up.

She outweighs me by probably fifty pounds, which is good and bad. Power is proportionate to weight. I need to avoid a lucky punch or letting her get me on the ground. Wrestling is the absolute worst strategy against someone bigger. But the weight will also slow her down and tire her out faster.

She launches a couple more punches that I easily dodge. We reach a corner and she moves in to trap me, but I drive her back with three sharp jabs. *It's not the number of punches. It's where they land.* Kiona said it so often she should put it on a t-shirt. One of her favorite boxing drills was to bounce a tennis ball at me, faster and faster each time. I had to grab it with a simulated jab. If I missed one, I had to do ten more.

Hitting Lola is a whole lot easier than catching the tennis ball because she fights standing still. Her left eye is already puffy.

I shut out the jeers around me as I continue to circle and

launch jabs. A cut opens above the puffy eye, sending a dribble of blood down the slope of her nose.

When she attempts a kick, I grab her foot and up-end her. She lands hard on the dank dirt, getting up panting and frustrated.

Kiona always split my training fifty-fifty between strength and cardio. Back when I was young and stupid, I used to think the cardio was a waste of time, all I wanted was more muscle. I still train fifty-fifty in the yard, but I've never seen Lola lift her butt off the weight benches. I keep moving.

"Come on, bitch. Fight!" she says.

The guards are getting impatient too, chanting *fight fight fight*. We're like dogs or chickens to them, nothing but pieces of meat. It's all I can do to not forget about Lola and go loosen some teeth in one of their gaping mouths.

The trickle of blood from Lola's cut has turned into a steady stream. She paws at it, smearing her face in red. This has to end.

"You want to call it even?" I say, dropping my hands to declare a truce.

She rushes me instead. Bad choice. I hammer her. Cross, cross, uppercut and it's over. She collapses on the floor.

The chamber is so quiet I hear a toilet flush from somewhere above. Lola struggles to get back on her feet.

"Come on, Lola. You can do it," Claire says, adjusting her eye patch.

Shut the hell up! ... This is so wrong. How can I be enemies with a girl with one eye?

Lola's teetering, but has her hands up again. "Let's go," she says, spitting blood, eye now swelled completely shut. I can't bear it anymore, not just Lola, but Claire, the guards, the blood, the whole spectacle.

I turn to Twiggs. "She can't even see. This fight is over. I won."

"No it ain't."

"Yes it—"

I land on my side, Lola's weight crushing the breath out of me to raucous hoots and applause. I did it *again*, took my eyes off the fight. She rains punches that I mostly deflect, but one lands square on my temple. My thoughts go woozy as she grabs my hair bun and wrenches my head back and forth. *You know who's nice in a fight?* Lucas once taunted me during training. *The fucking loser.* My vision clears in time to see Lola's bared teeth plunging toward my cheek. *Effing cannibal!* No more nice. *Don't stop 'til the end. Finish the job.*

An elbow to the chops busts her lip and loosens her grip long enough for me to get my hands on her throat. I seal her windpipe with my thumbs, forearms tight as steel rods. The more she fights, the harder I squeeze. Her face flames red before tinting blue. I count seconds until her arms drop and she becomes dead weight.

I push her off and get up massaging the throb in my temple. Everyone is quiet and still, staring at Lola's limp form, until Twiggs leans in with his phone and takes a picture of her face. *Come on, Lola.* Get up. She can't be dead. Impossible ... I hope. When her chest heaves and color returns, I breathe relief.

The guards huddle and argue about their bets. A dumpy guy with red hair and a round head is dancing around with his hands in the air, snapping his fingers. Must have bet on the longshot.

I kneel and offer a hand to Lola. She slaps it away. "Go fuck yourself."

"It doesn't have to be this way, Lola. *They're* the real enemy. They're using us. We should be fighting them."

Her friends rush in and crowd me out. "She just got lucky, that's all," Tamika says as they pull her upright.

Adrenalin pumping, I stroll over to Twiggs, still rubbing my head. "Hey CO. Remember our deal. Extra library hours and everyone leaves me and Rebecca alone."

He gives me a miserable look.

"Oh, and do you want to give me my money now or deposit it in my commissary account?"

"What money?"

"My bet. I bet nine dollars and sixty-four cents at twenty to one."

"The fuck ever. You just cost me fifty bucks. Be careful or I'll report you for fightin'." He holds up his phone. "Look what you just did to that poor girl. I could probably get a year added to your time. Gonzalez, get these bitches back to their cells."

11

THE BEST THING to come out of the fiasco in the basement happened the next night at dinner. I was in my usual spot when Rebecca came down the aisle, hair swish-swashing her face like a windshield wiper, but instead of branching off to her table, she came to mine.

"Can I sit here?" she said.

"Yeah, sure."

She stabbed violently in silence at the brownish-green orbs on her tray, breaking off one of the prongs on her fork. I waited to let her talk. It took a while before, "What are these things, sogballs?"

"I think they're brussels sprouts."

"Gross."

They were gross, but Rebecca doesn't eat enough of anything. You can't be too picky about food in this place or you'll starve.

She caught me looking over her shoulder. "I know what you're staring at," she said. "Lola's empty seat."

"Yep. Maybe you should change your name from Rebecca Seyere to *Rebecca the Seer.* So where is she? All her soldiers are here."

"There's a rumor she's in solitary for fighting, but I'll bet they put her there so no one can see her all busted up."

"How long has this crazy fight club thing been going on?"

"I don't know. I heard about it when I first got here. I never knew if it was true until last night."

"I can't believe they get away with it."

"They lie and stick together. Fights happen all the time. A group of COs say they responded to a call where one girl beat another girl half to death. They even have pictures to prove it. What can you do?"

Something.

* * *

A week later I'm in the law library with Paula. Twiggs didn't pay my bet, but came through with the extra library time. Paula's wearing a dowdy black dress that's about as flattering as a nun's habit.

She just completed a shelf-by-shelf lecture about the different sets of law books. Each one occupies yards of shelf space. The green and gold *Louisiana Statutes Annotated* is the smallest set and it has more than two hundred volumes.

She sweeps her skeletal hand across the library. "So that's pretty much it. Those are the three basic types of law books. Cases, statutes and secondary authorities."

"Cases and statutes are *binding* law," I brag.

She sent me an awesome book that arrived yesterday. *How to Do Legal Research Like a Pro (Without Going to Law School).* I read it last night until the lights went out, which is why I started my day at the commissary, emptying my account to buy a clip-on book-light and batteries. The batteries cost as much as the light. I had just enough left to get a small jar of instant coffee. I traded two desserts to a girl for her old pair of shower slippers with torn straps. An art pad will have to wait.

"Well, it depends," she says.

I've already learned that *It depends* is the answer to every legal question. Every rule has exceptions and the exceptions have families of baby exceptions and they all depend on the facts of each case.

"For example," she says, "Louisiana cases are binding on the whole state only if they come from the Louisiana Supreme

Court. Federal cases are binding only as to federal law and that depends on the jurisdiction ..."

My head is spinning.

"But cases from the U.S. Supreme Court are binding everywhere."

"Everywhere? Including Louisiana?"

"In every state, in every court. They're what we call *the law of the land.*"

"No exceptions?"

"Nope."

Sweet. I write it down. *Supreme Court beats everything.*

"I think that's enough for today," she says.

I don't argue. My brain can't absorb any more.

"Remember, we're due back in court on Monday."

"How could I forget? Can't wait to see my old friend Leslie. What exactly is going to happen?"

"It's called a discovery conference. Each side has to disclose its witnesses and evidence to the other. We'll get to learn more about what your old friend has come up with."

"Do we have any witnesses or evidence?"

"Well, just you. That is, if you choose to testify."

"That's it?"

Her face flushes. "It's because you chose to deny everything and not put on a defense ... I'm sorry. I said that defensively."

"Do you think I should testify?"

She rips off a piece of a fingernail she's been picking at. "It's risky. Leslie will try to trap you, catch you in lies. I agree those images are fuzzy, but if they have other evidence to prove it was you in the car before and after Brooker was killed ... well, I just worry."

"Don't worry." Isn't it supposed to be the other way around, the lawyer reassuring the client?

She explains we don't have to decide now because defendants don't have to prove anything in a criminal case. "Leslie can't call you as a witness. Forcing the state to prove guilt beyond a reasonable doubt can be a good defense strategy unless ..."

"Unless they have more evidence than we know. I get it. Well, thanks again for coming up here and for the research book." I pat her hand, which seems to make her happy, like she's still recovering from the trauma of me jerking away from her the day we met.

"I have something else for you." She pulls three yellow pads and a bundle of pens from her briefcase. "I got Judge Hanks to order that you're allowed to have these since you're doing legal research on your case."

"Cool, thanks."

"I should get going. It's a long drive back to Opelousas. I'll see you Monday at the courthouse. Meanwhile, it would be very helpful if you could work on, um, preparing yourself to ..."

"Keep my trap shut?"

She nods.

12

MATH LESSONS ended and our first social studies class is starting. Medillo's still the teacher. "Alright, boys and girls," he says, flipping a wide tie that reaches only halfway to his belt. Smack in the center is a spot that looks like mustard. "Today we begin our exploration of government, economics and history. And I know what you're thinking. Sounds like more fun than a barrel of monkeys."

His joke gets a decent audience response, but I'm barely listening. Ben's seat is empty. To my right, Jermaine's gone too, replaced by a girl with a bumpy nose.

Medillo is asking a slack-jawed kid in the front row about the Norman Conquest. It was in the workbook. "Norman who?" he says.

A door bangs at the back of the room. "Well, good day, Mr. Breyer. Nice of you to finally join us."

It's Ben, hurrying down the aisle. Didn't know his last name. *Emily Calby Breyer.* Has a nice sound.

"They kept me late in the shop," he says.

Relieved, I flash him a smile and turn my attention to Medillo. This whole subject is new to me. Maybe they covered it in my missing school years.

I'm taking notes about something called the Battle of Hastings when Ben's hand touches my thigh under the table. I practically launch through the ceiling.

What in the world? We just met and I am *not* that kind of a girl ... or maybe I am because his touch is sending shock waves up my leg. But he has no business *thinking* I am and he must be thinking that or he wouldn't be ... passing me something?

What is it? About the size of a baseball, solid and rough. I wait until Medillo turns to write *PAY ATTENTION* on the board before looking down. *Aw, it's a bird.*

I scribble on my workbook. *It's so cute! What kind bird?*

A free one. Like in your picture. I made it for you.

Something's moving in my gut. It feels like worms. I hope it's not IBS. Can that be contagious?

"Mr. Breyer," Medillo says. "To compensate for being late, tell us which of the six names I have written on the board was present at the Yalta Conference that divided up the world after World War II?"

Ben shrugs.

I butt in. "With all due respect, sir, is that really important to know?" *With all due respect* is what lawyers say before they disagree with someone. I got it from Leslie Tierney.

Medillo scowls. "Did I call on you?"

"No, sir."

"Fine, then I call on you now. Which of the names on the board was present at the Yalta Conference?"

"Roosevelt," Ben interrupts. "And his pals, Churchill and Stalin."

Medillo's bushy eyebrows stitch together like the tail of a baby squirrel. "Congratulations, Mr. Breyer," he says. "That's the first correct answer you've given all year."

I turn to Ben when class ends. "Yalta Conference? How did you know that? I never even heard of it."

"Just remembered it from somewhere. I read a lot."

"Really? Me too. I work in the library ... I love my bird," I say.

He laughs. "Sorry it's so rough. I made it in the shop, where I work. Had to use an angle grinder to carve it. It has a hump on its back."

"It's perfect."

"Were you joking last week, about first-degree murder?"

"I wish. But not convicted—yet." I cross my fingers on both hands. "How about you? Are you really here for life?"

A grim nod. "Not *here*-here. When I turn eighteen, they transfer me to adult prison."

"You're kidding. How old are you?"

"Seventeen."

"I can't even imagine you in an adult prison."

"Me either."

"How do you deal with it?"

"I don't. I shut it out, pretend it's all a bad dream."

I can relate to that. "You don't look like a murderer," I say.

"Thanks. You either."

My insides are still churning. These must be the moments love is made of. That, or I really am coming down with something.

His delicious lips ask, "Do they have a good case against you?"

"I'm not really sure yet. How about you?"

"They didn't have any case until they tricked me into confessing."

"Tricked? How?"

"Long story."

"You know, it can be illegal to trick a confession. I'm studying law."

The linebacker CO barrels in. "Line up, kiddies. This ain't the Love Boat."

I stuff the bird inside my uniform. "I wish we could both be free birds. I'd be a hawk. How about you?"

"An Arctic tern. They can fly the farthest."

"Yalta Conference? Arctic tern? How does someone so smart end up in a place like this?"

"I could ask you the same question."

The CO picks Ben up by the shoulders and practically throws him into the boys' line. "It's gonna to have to wait for another time, Romeo. Line up, kiddies. Line up."

"Come visit the library sometime," I shout after him. "We have law books. I can help research your case."

My outburst silences the circle of girls around me. I expect taunts, but the first thing I hear is, "You know about law?" It's a heavy-set girl with a fro. Another girl: "Hey, I got a question about law. Can the cops search your car without a warrant?"

* * *

Rebecca sits across from me at dinner configuring her lima beans into the shape of a heart and asking about my new cell decoration, the hump-backed bird. I set it on the window ledge facing outside, pointed at freedom.

Lola is finally back and I'm glad to see it. She's dictating to her crew about something. Hopefully it doesn't involve stabbing me in the back with a pitchfork. I saw her digging with one out in the yard today.

"A boy in class gave it to me," I say. Rebecca's in a different GED section.

"You like him," she says. A statement.

"How do you know that? I haven't said one word about him."

"I just know. He likes you too."

My shoulders straighten. "Do you know him? Ben?"

She shakes her head.

"So, what, are you like psychic or something?"

"Maybe, but I don't have to be for this. Who carves a bird for someone they don't like?"

I'm mulling over that logic when Lola gets up and heads our way, but this time she does it alone. Episode three of *The Adventures of Alice and Lola* has begun and all eyes are glued to it.

The only person not paying attention is the guard, a CO I haven't seen before, tall and thin with a triangle face. No sign of Twiggs or Gonzalez since fight club. Someone said the guards rotate between the boys' and girls' units.

"Hi, Lola," I say nicely, but I'm wary. A hothead with wounded pride is always dangerous. Haha, I should know. "Would you like to join us?"

"Fuck no."

Up close her face is creepy-looking. The neck bruises have faded and her fat lip has gone down, but they shaved off her left eyebrow to stitch the cut above her eye. If we were friends I'd suggest she pencil it in or at least shave the other one off for balance.

"Twiggs said I gotta do your chores for thirty days or rot in solitary. Fight club rules. Gonzalez said the same thing. So tell me, what are they?"

"Disgusting cretins."

"What's cretin? I don't do no cretin."

"*They*. The COs. They're pigs."

"Don't you think I know that? I'm asking what the chores are. What the fuck you looking at, Becky-bee?"

"You know," I say. "I don't think she likes being called that. Could you please call her Rebecca from now on?"

Eyes on fire, "Last time. What are your chores?"

"I'm not going to make you do my chores, Lola. That whole thing is stupid. I do my own chores, just like you should do yours."

"You beat me … fair. I ain't no pity case. I pay my debts."

I tell her again to forget about it and she stomps back to her seat, mumbling, "Then it's not over."

13

I'M SOAKED in sweat when I greet Mava, having just finished twenty laps around the track. Yard time got delayed because of a cellblock search, for a phone, someone said. I don't know if they ever found one, but the holdup left me running to the library without a chance to cool down or clean up. Mava's chill about most things, but not being late.

She's waiting at the door, arms crossed, drilling nails in the floor with a steady *tap tap tap* of her tack hammer flat.

I huff and puff, "You look so pretty today, Miss Mava." Her hair is in waves and she's wearing classic red lipstick. "I love your dress!" It's a floral pattern that looks like some curtains we had in our living room that got burned up in the fire. "Do you have a date?"

She frowns. *Tap tap tap.* "You're late."

"*Sor-ry.* It won't happen again. I'll get right to work. ... Well, guess I'll start in the law library," I say and trundle off.

She follows me. At first she mocked the law books, but lately she's been asking questions about legal research. I've read the book Paula sent me three times. Unfortunately, one of the first things I learned was that most legal research these days is done on a computer, which I'm not allowed to use.

"What's this row of books right here?" Mava says. "Why are they different colors, not in sets like the other ones?"

"These are called secondary authorities. They're the best books really, because they explain the law. The cases and statutes don't make any sense until you find the ones you need, but to do that you have to know what you're looking for. I organized them by subject. I, um, hope that's okay."

She ponders it and nods.

"Most of them are criminal law books, which makes sense in a prison, right? But there's a little bit of everything here. This one's about contracts, and here's a book on wills and trusts, for when old people die ... I mean, like really old, not like you. This green one is about something called torts."

"You understand all that? You some kind of freak of nature?"

"Ha, I'm a freak, but not that way. No, I don't understand hardly anything yet, but I'm determined to learn."

"How come?"

I've thought a lot about it since Paula asked the same question and keep coming back to the same answer. "Why are all these kids in this place?"

"You playing games with Miss Mava?"

"No, ma'am. I would never do that."

"Because they broke the law."

"What happens if a person doesn't pay their rent?"

"They get kicked out of their house."

"What if you park your car in the wrong space?"

"You get a ticket, or they tow you."

"*Right right right.* All because of the law. It controls everything, moves us around like chess pieces. Do this, don't do that. And the law *never* loses. Everyone loses sometimes, every single thing in the world loses, but not the law. I decided the only way to stand a chance is—"

"Know the law," she says with the slightest curl of a smile, made noticeable only by the clean line of her red lipstick.

"Exactly. Because then you have power. For example, if a kid in here was illegally convicted, the law says they can get out on what's called *habeas corpus.*"

"Habeas corpus," she repeats.

"*Bring me the body.* That's what it means."

She pats my cheek. "You somethin' else, child."

When she leaves, I pull out a book called *Essential Contract Forms*. At breakfast I said hi to Lola. She returned the greeting with, *You don't own me, bitch.* I decided we needed to end things once and for all, *legally.*

I print CONTRACT across the top of a fresh legal pad and spend the next two hours copying and then crossing out five pages of random legal clauses before cutting everything down to one page:

THIS AGREEMENT is made between Lola Grimes and Alice Black, whose addresses are Cell 23A and Cell 49B, Pochachant Detention Center for Juveniles, somewhere north of Opelousas, Louisiana.

Lola Grimes and her representatives hereby agree to refrain from annoying, harassing, verbally abusing, injuring or killing Alice Black or Rebecca Seyere and to treat them nice at all times.

In consideration of the foregoing, Alice Black and Rebecca Seyere hereby agree to do the same and be nice back.

All preexisting claims or demands for the performance of labor between the parties are hereby discharged and released, including, but not limited to, laundry, janitorial and food services.

I remember Lola ordering me to repair one-eyed Claire's uniform and add *or personal services such as apparel repair.*

This contract shall remain in full force and effect until the end of the world.

The last line sounds like something a kid would make up, but it's real legal language from one of the forms.

* * *

At dinner, icy silence descends as I approach Lola's table for the first time. She has a new eyebrow penciled in, but it peaks in the middle, making half of her face look surprised.

I reach for my pocket and Claire snatches up her cafeteria knife, plastic with a rounded tip. Bless her heart, but I do respect loyalty.

My hand comes out holding the folded-up contract with a pen clipped to it. "Read this. Sign it and we're square."

She takes it and unfolds the paper. At least she didn't try to stab me with the pen. Maybe that's a good sign.

She glances at it and shakes her head. "I can't," she says. It comes out *cain't*.

"Yes, you *can*. There's no honor lost. No anything lost. We both win. At least read it. Please."

She scans the paper, but shakes her head and hands it back. Something different in her eyes ... yet familiar. The same look I saw in class when Medillo called on her. There wasn't a speck of fear on her face during our fight, not even when I was choking her out, but I see it now.

I stick my hand out.

"How about a handshake deal? We promise to be nice to each other, Rebecca too, and nobody has to do anybody's chores."

Awkward seconds tick by before she grabs it.

She can't read.

14

MONDAY CAME FAST. I'm back in Opelousas for the discovery conference, this time in Judge Hanks' chambers, which are ornate but old, with worn leather chairs held together by fancy metal studs and faded burgundy drapes with unraveling gold fringes.

We're sitting at a long mahogany conference table covered by a sheet of thick glass, me and Paula on one side, Leslie Tierney and her assistant on the other. Hanks is parked at the end. I recognize the green and gold of the *Louisiana Code Annotated* on the shelves behind him.

His first order of business was to extract my promise to keep my mouth sealed. I've complied so far, but he just ordered that I undergo a psych exam. I bang my knee against Paula's.

"Your Honor, my client would prefer not to undergo a psychological examination." If she said it with any less enthusiasm, no sound would come out. She obviously thinks I need one.

"It's not her option," Hanks says. "Set up an appointment with the examining psychologist. Where do we stand on witnesses? Ms. Tierney? How many witnesses does the state have at this point?"

"Eight."

"That many? Ms. Dunwoody, how many witnesses does the defense intend to call?"

She rapidly clicks her one fingernail that hasn't been chewed to the quick against the glass tabletop. "At this time, Your Honor, we intend to make the state prove its case."

"So no witnesses?"

"One. If my client decides to testify."

"Will she?" Leslie asks.

"We have no obligation to disclose that and you know it."

Go Paula! She even put some bite into it.

"Ms. Dunwoody is correct," Hanks says. "The question was improper. What about the state's witnesses? Who are we looking at?"

Leslie ticks off names from a printed list: a crime scene investigator, the coroner, people who run the highway and mall security cameras, and witnesses who saw me in Lafayette after Brooker got killed.

"Do you need all of them?" Judge Hanks says.

"We do ... and oops, one more we don't have listed yet. A DNA expert, to be determined."

"Why the hell—excuse me Ms. Calby—why the heck do you need a DNA expert if you're already calling the crime scene investigator and coroner?"

"To identify the DNA of the defendant that was found inside the victim's car."

"The *what* found *where*?" Paula says, wheeling on me, right eyebrow spasming.

It's impossible. I cleaned that car inside and out ... except ... that must be it. The first time I self-cut, after I killed Brooker, when my head felt like it was going to pop open. I dragged the neck knife across my arm and felt instant relief. A single droplet of blood fell on the floorboard of the Lexus. The carpet was black so I didn't think anything of it.

I feel like a monkey in the center of a circus ring with everyone staring at me. DNA doesn't lie. Better to cut my losses than dig the hole deeper.

I raise my hand. "Judge?"

"Not again. Remember? Your lawyer speaks. You sit. You gave me your promise."

"This is really, really important."

"Let your lawyer explain it."

"Well, she doesn't know about it."

"All the more reason to speak with her first and let her get back to me."

"It can't wait."

He exhales like a punctured balloon. "What is it? Make it quick."

"I just wanted to let everyone know I'm changing my defense." Paula is saying *Do-on't* like a slow-motion scene from a movie. "I killed Scott Brooker."

She drops her pen, which bounces off the table and lands on the carpet. I pick it up and hand it back, try to, but she's staring at the table, frozen except for a slight trembling. I set the pen in front of her, catching a glimpse of Leslie, face aglow.

Keeping an eye on Paula in case she starts to faint, I say, "But it was self-defense. He tried to rape me."

"Oh, *puh-leese*," Leslie says.

Hanks squeezes his head, leaving divots in his jet-black coif. "Bailiff, take the defendant somewhere."

"Where to, Judge?" he says.

"Anywhere. Just out of my sight, so her lawyer—God help her—can *confer* with her."

Confer comes out like *give her a good whipping*. The bailiff leads us to another small interview room, this one spruced up by a dead fern hanging from a chain. Paula says she'll be back and trots down the hall.

I don't waste time when she returns. "I'm sorry I didn't tell you before. I didn't think anyone would believe me. But it's true. He picked me up hitchhiking, took me out into the bayou and tried to make me …" I can't say it.

"But you said none of it ever happened."

"I know. I lied. I'm really sorry, but this is the real truth. Please believe me."

She pulls a tissue from her purse and dabs sweat from her forehead. "This changes a lot. Self-defense is an affirmative defense that we have the burden of proving. And we don't have any evidence."

"Isn't my story evidence?"

"It sure is, and you just gave up any option of not testifying. You can bet Leslie is already licking her chops waiting to cross-examine you. So many questions, I'll start with this one. I read the coroner's report. How did you become so ... proficient with a knife?"

"Um ... practice?" I have to be careful not to drag Lucas into this mess. "I was running from the men who killed my family. I bought a neck knife to protect myself and made myself practice with it."

"Neck knife?"

"It hangs upside down around your neck. You wear it under your shirt."

"How did you come to know about neck knives?"

"Does it matter?"

"You'd better believe it. Leslie is going to tear apart every word you say. Every single word."

Because I was trained by an expert killer. "I'm not really sure. My dad was a hunter. He had guns and knives and taught me a lot. He must have mentioned them."

The questions get harder from there. Why did I take Brooker's car? Why did I drag a branch to cover his body? Why didn't I call the police? *Why why why?* I start with the story in Shreveport, when my backpack with all the money got stolen and I had to hitchhike.

"I didn't go to the police because I was scared no one would believe me, like now. And the two men were still out there. If they found out where I was, they would have come to kill me. So I ran."

"And this is the truth?"

"Yes." Most of it.

"Okay," she says, clicking her pen while I twist my hair. "I'll be honest. There are just so many ways to attack your testimony.

We need more evidence. You said a minute ago he did this to other girls. How do you know that? Did he tell you that?"

"Yes! I mean, basically. He said he'd met lots of runaways and knew we were all sluts who needed money. When I asked what would happen if I said no, he said there was another girl who said no a couple months earlier, but I'd have to dig her up to ask her."

"Okay, that's good." She starts writing on her legal pad, stops and winces. "I mean, it's *horrible*, but it's good for your case. If we could track down one of those girls ... I'm not sure how though. The police have already made up their mind and the PD office only has one investigator for hundreds of cases."

"Maybe Brooker had a record, like being arrested for something like this before." That's how the FBI tracked down tall man.

"Look at you, thinking like a lawyer," she says with strained good cheer. "We'll definitely run a records check on him."

A knock on the door. It's the bailiff, saying Hanks wants us back in chambers.

He looks tired when we return, gazing at the back wall, every inch of which is covered with framed pictures of people playing golf. He's probably wishing he could join them.

"I'm not quite sure how to handle this new development," he says.

"Simple. It's evidence, Judge," Leslie says. "A confession made right here in chambers in front of several witnesses."

"Yes, but the circumstances ..." He looks at me.

"That's okay, Judge. It is a confession. *And* a *perfect* defense." I pause to sneer at Leslie. Literally, that's what self-defense is called, a *perfect* defense because it eliminates responsibility, much better than an *imperfect* defense that only mitigates it. I read all about it in LaFave.

"Ms. Calby, I order you to button your lips. One more word and I will have you removed from this proceeding for your own good."

"Sorry, judge ... but I do stand behind my statements."

He raises a hand. "Ah-ah. Buttoned."

I make a zipper-lip slash and give him a thumbs-up.

"Ms. Dunwoody, I'm beginning to appreciate your predicament in representing this client. Are you comfortable with this development?"

"I am. I believe her."

A snarky laugh from Leslie. "How convenient for her that dead men can't talk."

"Ms. Tierney, dispense with the editorial comments. How does counsel suggest we proceed?"

Leslie is well into her argument by the time Paula's lips part. "Obviously, this changes everything. The state will need extra time to line up character witnesses to defend Mr. Brooker's reputation, since he can't be here to do it himself."

"Ms. Dunwoody?"

Paula leans over. "I'm sorry, Emily, but we'll need more time too."

I nod.

"Judge, a two-week extension makes sense under the circumstances," she says.

"Is there any possibility of a plea agreement?" he asks.

"What's that?" I whisper.

"You plead guilty for a lighter sentence," she whispers back.

"No way. I'm innocent."

"Judge, we've ruled that out for now," she says.

"Who cares?" Leslie spits. "We're not offering any plea deal. I'm prosecuting this case to the max. My only regret is that your little slasher can't be transferred to adult court."

15

THE BOY in front of me scratches a zit on his forehead like he's thinking hard. "They're bad news, without a doubt. My granddaddy said they ate up his whole cotton crop."

"*No no no*," Medillo says, pinching the bridge of his nose. "Not boll weevils. *Bolsheviks*. Did you read the assignment?"

I sigh. Every day brings me another day closer to being a convicted murderer and here I sit learning more useless history trivia. But the reality is that without more resources I've run out of things to do on my case.

I've learned enough about self-defense law to know my fate is going to depend on facts, not law. I need more evidence. All I have is my testimony, full of holes. There *has* to be a way to track down another girl, but stuck in this place, I'd need a computer to have any chance.

I give up even pretending to concentrate on the Russian Revolution, my attention piqued only when Medillo calls on Lola again. She gets the same deer in the headlights look as before.

Medillo moves on, but I stay on Lola. What makes *her* so angry? We all have our reasons. I'm not sure why I feel sorry for someone who sucker-punched me and tried to bite a chunk out of my face, but I do.

She's actually not as hideous-looking as she presents. She could even be kind of cute—after her eyebrow grows back—if she let her shaved head grow out a little and smiled once in a while, although the F-U-C-K L-I-F-E tattoos would be hard to overlook.

Even Ben doesn't occupy his usual headspace. At end of class we hurry through our little one-minute conversation before the COs round us up. I'm tempted to invite him to the library again as he walks away, but I already asked once. I'm not going to beg.

The girls' CO today is Longmont, the nice one who spends too much time in a tanning bed. I tell her I need to ask the teacher a question. "Make it quick," she says.

"Mr. Medillo?" I say.

"Yes, Ms. ..."

"Black."

"Of course. Alice Black. The girl who mysteriously loses her ability to think after two questions."

"Well, about that ..."

"Oh, I know all about *that*. You don't want to answer correctly because you'll be a target of derision. I believe your seat neighbor, Mr. Breyer, suffers the same affliction. What do you want?"

"I was wondering how a person would go about tutoring someone here."

"Are you wanting a tutor or wanting to be a tutor?"

"Be a tutor. I heard you hire inmates, I mean, detainees, to do tutoring."

"Six to be exact, which isn't nearly enough. The job is a good one by Pochachant standards. Thirty-two cents an hour. But we don't have any openings."

"That's okay. I already have a job I really like, in the library. I'd be willing to do it without pay, in my free time."

"Commendable, but there's nothing to stop you from doing that now. You don't need to be appointed as a tutor to help a friend."

Friend may be a little strong. "Well, there is, actually, because I'm pretty sure the person I want to help will say she doesn't want or need a tutor." Especially me. "In fact, I'm one-hundred percent positive. So I'd need you to require it. Is that possible?"

"Who is this person?"

"Lola Grimes."

"Ah, Lola. A tough case. You're right, she wouldn't go for it voluntarily, but she needs tutoring as much as anyone in here. I could probably arrange it, if you're committed to seeing it through. Tutoring isn't easy, and, of course, you'd have to prove to me you're qualified to be a tutor."

"Like how?"

The bushy eyebrows join forces again. "Like by not intentionally giving wrong answers when I ask questions in class."

"Deal. But please don't call on me all the time. Like you said, derision. Also, I'm not good at social studies, so I might get the answers wrong accidentally."

"Let's go, Alice," CO Longmont says. "We're holding everyone up."

"I'll see what I can do," Medillo says.

* * *

By the time the front door to the library snaps shut behind me, I'm halfway down the hall to Mava's office. Stuck to her door with clear tape is a cracked plastic nameplate announcing *Mava Dixon, Library Director*. She's doing paperwork and doesn't look up.

A silver frame perched on the corner of her desk shows off a faded picture of a distinguished man in a black robe with gold piping. On the other corner is an oversized bible with a carved wooden cross on top.

She looks up. "Yes?"

"Hi, Miss Mava!" I point to the picture. "Is that your husband?"

She nods. "That's Jeremiah."

"He's very handsome."

"Don't think he didn't know it. I had to the fight the ladies off with a stick ... but he passed, three years now."

"I'm sorry. Was he a preacher?"

"Indeed he was, spread the gospel for forty years. That's him in his first robe after graduating from seminary school. He was so proud of it."

Her sadness weighs down the room. Grief, loss, they never go away. Need to lighten things up. "Do you have kids?" I saw their pictures on the bookshelves on the way in. No better way to cheer up a parent than get them talking about their kids.

She rolls her chair back. "I certainly do."

She dusts picture frames with a blossomy sleeve of her silky blouse, held at the neck with a beautiful cameo pin, and hands them to me one by one. Three sons, a daughter and six grandchildren.

"Do you get to see them much?"

"Not as much as I'd like. They're all in other places. That one, my youngest, he's in the Navy, lives all the way in Hawaii. What about your family?"

"Um, they're in other places too." I change the subject. "I would love to live in Hawaii. I'd give anything to live on the beach."

"Maybe you will someday, honey."

"Miss Mava, I came to ask a question. Would it be possible to get a computer for the law library, with internet? I've learned that most legal research is done on computers now."

I leave out that a computer is my only hope for digging up something on Brooker. Mava's never asked about my case and I don't volunteer things. People think differently about you when they find out you killed someone with a knife.

"Sorry, but detainees aren't allowed access to the internet. It's a strict rule."

"Is it one of those strict rules that people ignore"—like fight-ing—"or a strict rule that's followed?"

She knows what I'm talking about. "Followed," she says. "They monitor every computer, at least they say they do. I could look something up for you."

"That's okay. Thanks anyway."

I drag myself to the law library and collapse in one of the work chairs, smacking my palms against the hardwood armrests. There's *nothing* I can do to help my case without a computer. Beyond frustrating. Maddening.

I open a tome called *Constitutional Criminal Procedure* to a bookmark of folded toilet paper. Hands tied on my own case, I've been studying confession law for Ben. Wouldn't it be awesome if I could help him get out? He'd love me forever. How could he not? I need to know the facts though. All he said was they tricked him into confessing.

The law of confessions is a lot more complicated than self-defense. A lot of it leads back to *Miranda*. The cops have to read the *Miranda* rights to anyone in *custodial interrogation*. Was Ben in custody? Did he invoke his rights? Once a person does that, the cops can't ask any questions without a lawyer present. If they do, nothing the defendant says can be used as evidence. The *exclusionary rule*.

I love that rule! The book says it's controversial, but it makes perfect sense to me. If the cops get evidence by violating your rights, they shouldn't be allowed to use it.

I understand most of the substance, but not the legalese. I'm looking up *writ of certiorari* in a monstrous blue dictionary named after me, well, the latest fake me—*Black's Law Dictionary*—when the bell above the front door announces a visitor.

Time to go to work. I smooth out my uniform and put on my best customer-service smile. Kids come here so infrequently I've assumed the role of promotional spokesperson. *Here's a really great book. I guarantee you'll like it. If you don't, you can have a bite of my cornbread.*

Behind the bookcases, the sound of men talking. That's weird.

"May I help you?" Mava.

Uh-oh. She's not a fan of greeting people. That's my job. I burst around the bookcases. "Hi, can I help you find any … Ben!"

"Hi, Alice."

The CO says in a thick Southern accent, "This boy said he wants to research some law, says you got a law library in here." *Li-berry in he-year.*

Mava clicks her tongue. "He said that, did he?"

I'm kneading my hands, hoping she doesn't throw Ben out. She lowers her glasses and steps closer for inspection. "Sounds like you two know each other."

"Yes, ma'am," I say. "We're in GED class together."

"Do I look like I'm talking to you? I'm talking to the boy. What's your name?"

"Ben Breyer. Like Alice said, we know each other from class."

"We sit next to each other," I say.

"The boy has a mouth. Let him talk."

"Alice told me there's a law library in here and that she might be able to help me research my case."

"I see. Well, Miss Alice here is one fine researcher of the law. I suppose it will be alright. CO, you can take the shackles off this boy."

"Not allowed," he says. "And I have to stay with him the entire time."

I groan.

"Are you new around here, CO?" Mava asks.

"This is my second week."

"Get something straight. This here is Miss Mava's library. Has been for twenty years and, God willing, will be for twenty more. Kids don't wear shackles in my library. These two aren't going to cause any trouble. Isn't that right, Alice?"

"No trouble at all. And you can count on me to keep an eye on Ben."

"I'll bet," she says.

The CO hesitates, but undoes Ben's restraints.

"CO, have you ever heard about Miss Mava's butter biscuits? World famous. I happen to have a couple left over from breakfast in my office. Come with me."

He follows her down the hall, Miss Mava talking the whole

time. "The secret to making a perfect biscuit is in how you snap the lard to the flour ..."

Ben and I stand facing each other in silence. "So, um, how's everything in the shop?" I say.

"Not bad. We're repainting the rusted fences around the boys' unit."

"That's good ... do they let girls work there? I love working with tools. My dad and I were always building and fixing things."

"No way. They guard the fences between the boys and girls better than the perimeter walls. They'd rather risk escape than any comingling of the sexes. I'm surprised the CO left us alone."

"No one questions Miss Mava. She probably has more authority than the warden. So let me show you my law library. Well, it's not mine."

I lead him around the bookcases and through the door.

"Here it is," I say. "Amazing, isn't it? All this law in one room."

"Pretty cool," he agrees. "Kind of intimidating. Where do we start?"

I motion him to my work table and take the chair next to him. It feels oddly illicit to be sitting next to him with no guards or teachers around. I love it! I pick up my legal pad and pen.

"Tell me about your case. You said they tricked you into confessing. What did you mean?"

"You said I'm smart, but I'm not. Everything I did that night was stupid. I let my friend, Jeff, talk me into breaking into a house. He said the guy who lived there was a drug dealer who kept lots of cash. Easy money, he said, and just drug money, not like real stealing."

He's staring at the wall of law books, avoiding eye contact.

"It was night. We waited until the car drove away, thinking the house was empty. Got in by breaking a window on the back door. We wore gloves so we wouldn't leave fingerprints. Mastermind criminals, right?" Nervous laugh.

"We were in the kitchen. The light went on and a guy in his

underwear was holding a gun on us. He said to raise our hands and not move. I raised mine. Jeff pulled out a gun. I didn't know he had it. I found out later he stole it from his dad. They both started shooting."

His voice is soft but intense. "It was like a dream. When the shooting stopped, they were both on the floor. I checked their pulses. They were dead."

"Oh, jeez."

"That's when I heard it," he says.

"Sirens?"

"The baby crying."

I put my hand to my mouth.

The man was married, a computer programmer, not a drug dealer. He had a four-month-old baby in a crib. The person who drove away in the car was his wife on her way to buy diapers.

"I didn't know what to do, so I ran."

"How did the police find you?"

"There was a camera on the back porch. The light was out so it didn't show much, but you could see it was two people. Everyone in town knew Jeff and I were best friends. The police came straight to my house."

"Did they read you the *Miranda* rights?"

"Um-hm. I said I didn't want to talk."

"You did one smart thing. Most people talk."

"I wish I could claim credit, but I didn't want to talk to anyone, not even my parents. I think I was in shock."

"Did they stop questioning you?"

"Yeah, but they weren't happy about it. When the detective took me to the holding cell, he said something like, *I just want you to think about one thing. That innocent man was the father of a little baby. Now that baby won't ever know her daddy.*"

Sounds familiar for some reason. "Did he ask any actual questions?"

Ben shakes his head. "He left me in the cell, but a couple hours later I heard a baby crying. At first I thought I was losing it, being haunted or something, but there she was, standing outside my cell. A woman holding a crying baby."

"The mother?"

"She just stood there, didn't say a word. But seeing her and that baby, listening to it cry and thinking about what the detective said ... I just lost it. I broke down and confessed to everything."

"I don't blame you. I would have confessed too if they brought in the mother with that poor little baby."

"That's the thing. She wasn't the real mother. It was the prosecutor pretending to be the mother."

"You're kidding."

"It wasn't the real baby either. Someone else's."

"That's a dirty trick."

"What do you think? Do you really know a lot about the law?"

My face blooms. "Um, not really that much. I exaggerated because I wanted to meet you for, you know, more than a minute a day, but I'm working really hard to learn it. When you got here I was reading about an important confession case from the Supreme Court. If you say you don't want to talk, the cops can't question you."

I stroke my chin. "But it sounds like they didn't technically ask any questions. Seems fishy though, like they were trying to get you to talk without putting a question mark on anything. What else would be the point? I'm going to research it."

He smiles with his wide luscious lips that look like they were made to be kissed. "I appreciate it, but don't waste too much time. I doubt there's anything there. I came because I wanted to see you too." He squirms. "You know, I'm not very good at this, so I'll just say it. I like you."

"Really? How come? I mean ... um, this is *Black's Law Dictionary*," I say nonsensically, pointing to the heavy blue book. "It's awesome."

We reach for it at the same time, his hand landing on mine. Neither of us pull away. I swear I feel his heartbeat.

A noise from behind and we pull back like the Red Sea being parted by Moses. It's Mava, in the doorway. Our faces broadcast we're guilty of something.

"Did I interrupt the boy's legal lesson, counselor?"

"We were just finishing up."

"End it. Pronto." She turns her back, blocking out the CO. I say, "It was really nice to talk to you. Thanks for coming."

"Can I come back?"

"For sure."

"You tell me your story next time, fair?"

"Fair."

"Okay, cool."

The guard is complaining to Mava that he's going to be in trouble if he doesn't get Ben back to the boys' unit on time.

We stroll side by side into the main library. I have an urge to hold his hand. I say, "I wish we had more time to get to know each other. I don't even know where you're from."

"Here in Louisiana. Saint Landry Parish."

"Really? My case is in Saint Landry. That's a coincidence." Most of the kids here are from the big cities. New Orleans, Shreveport, Baton Rouge.

He smiles sweetly. "Maybe we were meant to meet."

Mava wedges between us like she's separating two dogs in heat. "Time's up, you two. *Out.*"

The guard takes Ben to the front door and begins reattaching his chains.

His wrists and ankles are almost as thin as mine. Life in prison? That's crazy. *Prosecutors.* Ugh. You can't trust them for anything ... and like a jolt of lightning, I know why Ben's story sounded familiar.

Such a shame that man's poor daughter had to sit there looking at those pictures of her dead daddy. Sure would be nice if she could know the truth and get some peace.

"Miss Mava, I need to ask Ben one more question. Last one, I promise."

I run to him without waiting for her response. "Ben, who was the prosecutor, the one holding the baby?"

"I've tried to block her out. I think her last name was Tierney. I don't remember her first name."

"Move," the guard says.

"Leslie," I murmur between gritted teeth as Ben disappears out the door.

16

LONGMONT LEADS me to the visiting room after dinner to take a scheduled call from Paula. I'm wearing a phone pass around my neck. Every day I feel less like a person and more like a pet. The gym is empty. Our steps slapping against the basketball floor rebound off the high corrugated metal roof. The phone stalls are on the other side in what used to be the locker room.

Like every time I come here, I imagine Lucas waiting for me at one of the folding tables. Longmont must read my mind.

"How come you never get visitors, Alice, other than your lawyer?"

I'm spared from answering when her radio burps. Trouble somewhere.

"I gotta run," she says, pointing to the door straight ahead. "You know the way. Take your call and wait for me to come back and get you. Don't let me down."

"I won't."

She talks into the radio and runs out. I've never been here when it's empty and have an urge to scream to hear what it sounds like, or maybe because I just want to scream.

Exiting the gym, the door shuts behind me with a vacuum-sealed *schlumpf.* A narrow hallway leads to another door. The only sounds are my rubber soles squeaking against the beige industrial tile.

I'm reaching for the door when it bursts open, so fast I have to dodge it. It practically gives me heart failure, then it gets worse.

It's Twiggs. First time I've seen him face to face since fight club.

"The fuck you doing out here?"

"Phone call with my lawyer. I have a phone pass." It's plain to see, but I hold it up anyway.

"Who's your CO?"

"Longmont. She got called away."

"Got to have a CO with you. Prisoners can't go wandering around at night like they own the place. Tell you what, I'll be your CO tonight."

His words are slurred. He steps toward me and I back up, scanning the ceiling. No cameras.

"I don't want to be a bother. Longmont's coming back to get me. I'm just going to run in and take my call."

"Ain't no bother. You know, I bet against you in that fight, but you're one helluva little tomcat."

He keeps moving closer and I keep backing up, until I hit the door I came in from. He stops close enough for me to get a whiff of alcohol.

"You and your roomie miss me? They had me over on the boys' side. Have to say, I like the girls a lot better."

I fake a smile. "Welcome back. Anyway, I can't miss my lawyer's call. It's really important." I point to a nonexistent wristwatch.

"Where'd you learn to fight like that?"

"Just got lucky." I try to sidestep him, but he blocks my path.

"Don't run away. Let's get to know each other. I got to tell you, you're the prettiest girl in this whole damn place."

The door opens behind him and a woman comes out waving a sheet of paper. "Alice Black."

"Right here." I stick my arm in the air so she can see me over Twiggs.

"Your lawyer's on the phone. Let's go. We're on a schedule."

I scoot around Twiggs without looking back.

She leads me to a stall. I pick up the old-fashioned phone,

untangling the coiled cord. "Hi, Paula," I say. "Sorry for the wait."

"That's no problem. How are you?"

"Good." Except I just ran into the creepy guard who stages fights between prisoners. "Anything new with my case?"

She explains that Hanks set my psychological examination for two weeks before trial. "Here's what you can expect ..."

I could probably write a book about psych evaluations, but try to listen patiently. "Mm-hm, mm-hm. Fine, fine," I say. "I'll be ready. So what have you found out about Brooker?"

"Well, nothing good."

"Bad stuff? Alright!"

"I'm sorry, no, I meant nothing good for your case. Our investigator talked to his boss who said he was a model employee, and I talked to two of his friends. Get ready. They described him as, I'll read you the list, *dependable, hard-working* and *kind*."

"Of course his friends are going to lie for him. That's what friends are for. He was *kind* all right, kind of a serial rapist."

"I'm just telling you what we've learned."

"Sorry. Keep going."

"His wife and daughter refused to talk to us, which they have a right to do, but Leslie has them listed as character witnesses, so we know they're going to sanctify him as well. He even served as a Sunday school teacher at his church."

"That should count against him."

"How so?"

"Because he probably did it to get access to girls. Could your investigator go to Illinois to look into it? There might be something there."

"We don't have those kinds of resources."

"So that's it?"

"I'm doing the best I can, but it's true. We can't do a full investigation of the man's background. The resources literally don't exist."

"Alright," I say. I believe her. I consider telling her Ben's story, about Leslie Tierney and the baby, but decide against it. It shows what a snake Leslie is, especially since she tried the same kind of trick on me, but it's Ben's life, not mine to share.

"I'll keep looking," Paula promises and we end the conversation.

I'm relieved to see Longmont waiting when I leave the phone stall.

* * *

Back in my cell, I read *Constitutional Criminal Procedure* until my eyes bleed. The cell lighting is terrible but I save my book-light for after lights out. New batteries cost a week's salary. I'll bet anything I need glasses after this.

Rebecca is putting away her paints for the night. She makes a big production of it, using toilet paper to clean around each paint pot before tending to the care and cleaning of her three brushes. The last step is to polish the outside with a sock, which reminds me of wiping down Brooker's Lexus for fingerprints.

She sets it down and tears a sheet from her pad, flapping it in the air and blowing on it.

"You finished your painting?"

She's been working on it a long time, keeping it hidden. I assume it's the lion with the golden mane, the one I caught a glimpse of early on, a new addition for her wall menagerie.

"Yeah. I'm not sure I like it though. It could be better."

"I'll bet it's awesome. Can I see it?"

She holds it out like a serving tray. "It's for you. Be careful. It's still wet."

"For me? Omigod, it *is* me!" The golden mane is my hair. The painting is so detailed I can see Mom in my face, the way her eyes turned up at the corners. *Aw*, there's even a hump-backed bird resting on a tree branch.

I set the painting beside me and reach across the three-foot gulf between the bunks.

"Stop, stop."

"Nope. You're getting a hug whether you want one or not. I *love* this painting. It's beautiful." I pull back, still holding her shoulders. "And so are you, Becky." I lean in and kiss her forehead. "I mean, Rebecca."

Like magic, her face vanishes under a dark sheath of hair. "You're welcome," she mumbles. "It's just a picture."

I feel her muscles suddenly tighten, right before I hear heavy footsteps in the corridor. We had evening cell check an hour ago and it's too early for lights out. The steps stop outside our door. Nothing through the window. Keys rattle and the door swings open.

Twiggs again! What's he doing here? At least I have a witness now. But he doesn't even look at me, aiming a sharp head-bob at Rebecca. She stands up.

"Wait? What's happening?" I say.

Her mop of hair swirls from side to side as she moves to the door.

I follow her. "Rebecca, where are you going?"

"Nowhere," she says.

"Tell me."

She crosses the threshold and Twiggs slams the door in my face.

* * *

An hour goes by. I gave up trying to concentrate on confession law. The first time Twiggs came to get Rebecca I wondered about it, but didn't know anything about jail life. I've been here long enough now to know it's not normal. No one ever comes to get me. I also know Twiggs is dangerous. But why would she go with him?

Maybe something private, like a doctor or counselor appointment. No one's more private than Rebecca.

Five minutes before lights out, my face is mashed against the door window, searching the hall. What if she doesn't come back tonight? What should I do?

I pace until, "Lights out, lights out, ladies! Stand up for night count."

Good! They'll notice Rebecca isn't here. I stand up, waving and pointing to Rebecca's empty bunk, but the guard who peers in the window is Gonzalez. He winks and moves on.

I sit on my bunk in the dark. I never should have let her leave … quit assuming the worst.

I lie awake staring at the ceiling. Another hour passes before I hear movement in the hall. I run to the window. No voices, but I catch a glimpse of Rebecca's orange Crocs and hurry back to my bunk.

When the door opens, Twiggs' wide body blocks out most of the light. Just like the other time, neither of them speak. Rebecca comes in and goes straight to her bunk. When the door closes, it's too dark to see her face.

"You okay, Rebecca?"

"Uh-huh."

"Are you sure?"

"Uh-huh."

"What happened with Twiggs?"

"Nothing."

"Nothing at all?"

No response except rustling bedcovers. I shine my book-light on her.

She's facing the wall, sheet pulled over her head. "Goodnight," she says. "Please turn out that light."

17

I QUESTIONED her again in the morning, but she shut me down again. She was still in the cell when I left for GED.

In class, Ben and I let our knees touch under the table. Mr. Medillo was droning on about the Great Depression, but I didn't hear a word because of the electricity pulsing up my leg.

Cell 49B is empty when I return. Rebecca didn't make her bed, a rule violation. If your bed isn't made when they do cell-check, you lose privilege points.

I make it for her, still picturing the lump under the sheet from last night, like a little hiding ghost. The top sheet is twisted in knots, signs of a fitful sleep. Unraveling it, I shiver when I see the red blotch on the bottom sheet.

* * *

Rebecca refuses to look at me during dinner: mushy mixed veggies, brown apple slices and a boiled hotdog slapped on top of a bed of sticky white rice.

The only thing Rebecca even touches is the hotdog. Some mom part of me wants to say, *Eat your vegetables.* Her hair force-field is in place, split-ends fluttering with each breath. I make small talk, try to.

"What are you covering in GED?"

"Social studies. Just finished it."

"Same here. I guess we're all on the same schedule. I hope

116

English is next. That's my favorite subject, except art. Wouldn't it be great if art was on the GED? We'd kill it."

No reply. Over her shoulder I see Lola and wave. She doesn't wave back, but doesn't give me the finger either.

"Rebecca?"

"Yeah?"

"There's something I need to talk to you about tonight when we get back to the cell."

"Thanks for the warning."

"I'm telling you now because I want you to think about it. I swear I'm not doing it to be nosy. I'm just worried about you, because you're my friend and I care about you."

I search for a reaction between the slits in her downward-tilted hair and find it. She switched to zombie mode, like she leaves her body behind and travels somewhere far away. I know that place. I used to be the hiding girl.

"I'm going to ask you about Twiggs. I *swear* you can trust me. I know that's hard to believe. I have a hard time believing it about other people. But by now you either know me or never will."

Without raising her head, she picks up her tray and moves to the other empty table.

Well, that didn't go great. I go back to eating. As nasty as it is, I'm famished, like always. I'm scooping up clots of rice with my spoon when Rebecca's chair scrapes the floor.

"I'm so glad you came ba—. Lola? I mean, hi." Her eyebrow is mostly grown back.

"Medillo says they assigned me a tutor. Did you have anything to do with it?"

"Why would you ask me that?"

"Because he said you're my tutor."

"Really? Well, I did talk to him about wanting to be a tutor."

"I don't want a tutor and don't need one."

Just like I predicted. "I know, but Medillo told me if I don't do what he says, he'll deduct privilege points ... and I don't mind doing it."

"How'd you even get to be a tutor? You don't know shit. You get the answer wrong every time."

"I can help, if you'll let me."

The guards declare the end of mealtime and line us up. We march back to our cells, my hands on Rebecca's shoulders. She doesn't push them away. Maybe that's a good sign. Maybe my words got through to her.

* * *

"You can't just keep saying nothing is happening!" I say, pacing between the bunks and pulling my hair. "I don't believe you."

"I don't care if you believe me or not."

"I saw blood on your sheet this morning." I didn't want to bring it up, but ran out of ammunition. We've been arguing for twenty minutes.

"Are you spying on me?" she says, dark eyes glowing like coals. "So what if there was blood? I'm having my period."

"No, you're not. You had it two weeks ago." I point to the wastebasket. "I saw the tampon wrappers." There's no such thing as privacy in a jail cell.

She falls silent and I wait, keeping my mouth zipped tight. Maybe she sees it starting to unzip because she holds up a hand.

"Stop. Okay, I thought about your little 'friendship' speech," she says with air quotes. Rebecca loves air quotes. "You're right, I do know you, maybe better than you know yourself. Psychic, remember?" She taps her skull.

"I believe you want to be my friend. You already proved it. But if you knew *me*, you'd know how hard that is for me to accept. I haven't had a friend for a long time, maybe ever. I can't let you in."

"I totally get that. Letting someone in is dangerous, it's the only way they can truly hurt you, but you have to keep faith that someone will come along who you really can trust." I think about Lucas and swallow hard. "Someone who would never hurt you, who would do anything to help you."

"No one can help me."

"You don't know that. Please tell me."

"You're such a nag. There's nothing to even know about me because there's nothing to me. I don't even exist."

"You're suffering from trauma. That's my opinion."

A sarcastic laugh. "So now you're a lawyer *and* a psychologist?"

"Yep. Didn't you know? Next comes doctor. I plan on practicing the Heimlich maneuver on you every night in the cafeteria."

A slip of a smile, ever so tiny, but still a breakthrough. Don't squander it.

"I don't tell people this, okay? So, *private*, between you and me. Three years ago I had a list of mental disorders so long they kept me in a hospital for two months. Dissociative-this, dissociative-that, but it all came from trauma. What you told me, about what happened, I can't imagine anyone not suffering trauma from it."

She decides her hair needs brushing. When she tilts her head, she really does look like Becky, but right now, she reminds me more of me.

Don't lose her. "I know what it feels like to not exist. Look at this." I've never showed it to anyone, not even Lucas. I check the hall through the window and slip down my uniform pants, framing the scar on my thigh with my fingers.

"It's hard to read upside down, but it says *NO ONE*. I cut it with a piece of glass from a mirror I smashed when I didn't recognize myself."

She goes back to brushing her hair. After a few strokes she stops and hurls the brush. It ricochets off the lockers and lands near my feet. I pick it up and hand it to her. "Throw it again if you want. I wish I could throw everything in this place."

"So you think you have me all figured out, huh? Well, guess what? I have you figured out too. No way would anyone risk everything like you did with Lola for a stranger who wouldn't even talk to her. Only an insane person, or someone driven by something else. I say *guilt*."

"What are you talking about?"

"The way you started out calling me Becky, like you already knew me. The way you want to take care of me. The way you kissed me on the forehead and told me I'm beautiful."

I try to act all confused, but fail and give up. "I had a sister. Her name was Rebecca. We always called her Becky. She even looked a little like you. She was only eight when she died."

"Was it your fault?"

"Every day before my dad left for work he made me promise to take care of her and my mom. Then he died in an accident and it was either me or no one. Our mom was too softhearted. She couldn't hurt an ant. And Becky was just a kid. When they needed me most, I failed. I ran away."

Rebecca mashes her head into the mattress and pulls the pillow over her face. Just when it occurs to me she might be attempting suicide by suffocation, a muffled voice says, "Alright. I'll tell you. Just to shut you up."

She pulls off the pillow. "But I'm going by your swear that I can trust you and you'll never tell *anybody*. No one. *Ever.* Swear?"

"Swear."

That was my big mistake. Because as soon as she said *and then he raped me for the first time*, I knew I had to do something.

"Did you file a complaint?"

"Do you know what happens to girls who complain about things like that? They get put in 'protective custody'—that's solitary. And the people in charge? They always believe the COs, either that or they don't care."

"How long has it been going on?"

She just shakes her head.

I'm trying to keep calm, but it's not easy. "So, um, have you ever told him no?"

"No," she says fiercely, "And don't judge me. He threatened me. Said he could make up things to keep my sentence going forever. If I do what he likes, he puts five dollars in my commissary account ... that's how I bought my paint set."

"Five dollars? You're freaking kidding."

"I said don't judge me."

"I'm not judging you. I'm judging Twiggs."

"Remember, you *swore*."

18

THE LAST WEEK has been pure agony. Problems everywhere and I can't solve even one of them, which has me laboring around the track under the weight of a despairing hopelessness, the distance runner reduced to a mule in mud.

My trial starts in three weeks. Paula hasn't found anything we can use against Brooker. Every time she visits we run through my testimony and every time she trips me up. I can't even imagine what it will be like with Leslie.

I've only seen Twiggs a couple of times, killing him each time with my glare. I swore to Rebecca I wouldn't tell, but now what? I hate feeling helpless.

Meanwhile, I think about Ben even when I don't want to, which I think is the definition of obsession. I keep researching his case, but the more I read, the clearer it becomes how little I know. I've read dozens of cases about interrogation and *Miranda*, but they don't go anywhere. Paula was right. The law is complicated.

As if I don't have enough problems, I worry about her too. She sounds shakier each time we talk. The other night on the phone I made a joke about how I'll probably die in captivity and she said, "Hold on, there's someone at the door." Then I heard the toilet flush.

I stub my toe and fall on my butt in the middle of the track. Of course I do. I hear a laugh, but when I look around, no one makes a sound. Everybody knows I beat up Lola.

She comes to the library an hour a day for tutoring, still sullen and pissed off, but I think she actually wants to learn to read. She tested out at a fourth-grade level. Much to Mava's *I told you so* satisfaction, we're working with Judy Blume books.

She can make out most of the words, but has a hard time processing complete sentences. We had this conversation yesterday about *Superfudge*:

"Do you understand the sentence?"

"Yeah."

"Can you explain it?"

"Duh, his mom reached over."

"What did she do?"

She studied it again. "Something to his hair."

"Right. So the tricky part is that weird word in between. How would you pronounce it?"

"Tu-sell?"

"Close. *Tousle.* What do you think it means?"

"I don't know. Like toss?"

"I like that. Even sounds similar. Good way to remember it. So if someone's tousling-tossing someone's hair, what are they doing to it?"

"Messing it up?"

"That's it!"

It starts to rain. Just a sprinkle, but it chases the other girls under the tarps. I keep walking. I don't mind rain, especially in summer. It cools and cleanses, like even sins can be washed away. But thunder rumbles in the distance. If it brings lightning, they'll make us go inside. With all the dangers around this place, that's the kind of stupid stuff they worry about. Staging fights and raping prisoners? No problem, but heaven forbid a kid gets struck by lightning.

I'm on the far side of the track where it runs along the outside wall, twenty feet of scarred concrete blocks stained with mold. Sometimes life here is harder outside than inside because you can see, smell and taste the freedom that's always out of reach.

I watch the sky as I walk so I can pretend the wall's not there. A bird coasts into view. I love watching birds. Nothing's freer than being able to just fly away. This bird's broad wingspan lets it float like a glider.

Wait a second. ... White belly? Wingtips dipped in ink? When it takes a dive, the flash of red makes my muscles clench. It's a red-tailed hawk.

As it winds closer, I swear it's watching me, predator eyeing prey, just like the day the two men came. But this one already has prey, clutched in its talons. Something small. Looks like a mouse.

Killing machines. That's what my dad called red-tailed hawks. They'll eat anything that moves. I wonder if it's an omen.

"Hey, out of the way!"

I'm stopped dead in the middle of the track. I move aside to let some girls pass.

The hawk circles lower. I can't take my eyes off it. Is it going to attack me? Then just that like that, it lets go of the mouse and sails back over the wall.

Crazy bird. Maybe it didn't like being in a prison. If the mouse is wounded, the only humane thing to do is kill it. I ease off the track, aware that the cameras in the surveillance turrets are watching my every move. The COs get excited when people get too close to the wall.

When I locate the prey in the overgrown weeds, I quickly turn my back to it. A pimply girl jogs by on the track. I smile with a friendly wave and decide it's a good time to do stretches. Yep, that's what I need, some hamstring stretches.

I bend forward and place my hands flat on the ground, looking back between my legs, eyes locked on the hawk's cargo.

It's a mouse alright. Small, gray and still. And made of felt, with what looks like a Velcro seam running down its belly.

Keeping my hands buried in the weeds, I reach for it and tear it open.

Inside is the smallest phone I've ever seen, which means two amazing things. The red-tailed hawk was a drone, and Lucas has found me.

19

I STUFF the phone in my uniform and suppress the urge to turn it on until I get to the law library and tuck myself safely away in a far corner. The screen is the size of a postage stamp. When it comes to life, the first thing I see is a text notification from a number I don't recognize.

It occurs to me the phone might have been meant for someone else and the red-tailed hawk was just a coincidence, until I open the message.

Hey, Pit Bull.

It starts with a sniffle that dissolves into uncontrolled sobbing, for the first time since this whole mess started. *Alice the Pit Bull*. That's me, which means one hundred percent it's Lucas, and probably James. Who else could design a drone that looks like a red-tailed hawk?

Mava comes running into the law library. "What's wrong, child?"

"Nothing, Miss Mava," I say, wiping my face with my sleeve. "Everything's perfect."

"You sure about that? You don't sound too perfect."

"I'm sure."

She gives me her *There's something strange about this girl* look and goes back to her office.

The tiny keys are hard to type on.

Lucas!!! How did you find me?

Nothing comes back. I stare at the screen. One minute, two minutes. Be patient. There it is!

You okay?

Need to calm down. I keep hitting the wrong keys. It takes me forever to write, *I am now. Where are you?*

Staying on the move. Call tonight at nine. Don't use phone till then. Battery don't last.

Miss me?

Sometimes during target practice.

Har har.

I keep the phone on long enough to make sure all the sounds are turned off and tuck it in my waistband.

Re-energized, I open volume ninety-seven of the Supreme Court Reporter, ready to take another stab at finding something that could help Ben: *Brewer v. Williams*, 97 S. Ct. 1232 (1977). An interrogation case I came across last night in a footnote. Thirty pages that start out like a horror story. The defendant killed a ten-year-old girl at a YMCA on Christmas Eve.

Mava summons me to help her with a new load of donated books. I'm glad for the diversion.

"What was that crying about earlier? Hormones?"

"Oh, those were tears of joy."

"In this place?"

"God works in mysterious ways."

She gives an approving nod.

* * *

Back in the cell, I weigh what to tell Rebecca about the phone. I can't see any way to keep it from her. She'll be here when I call Lucas. My whole existence depends on keeping secrets. If one escapes, the dam might break and flood the world with them, but Rebecca's no snitch, and told me hers.

"Rebecca?"

Eye-roll. "Oh no. *Please.* No more questions."

"It is a question, but don't worry, it's not about you. I need advice."

"What kind?"

"Pochachant advice. I hear rumors about contraband, and smell the cigarettes at night, sometimes pot. Where do people hide stuff so the guards don't find it?"

Double-bunked prison cells offer limited seating options. We're eye to eye, Rebecca's head almost a foot lower than mine, scrawny elbows resting on her knobby knees.

"Why do you want to know?"

I run my fingers through my hair.

She smirks. "See how it feels to be on the other end?"

"Okay. You got me. I have something I need to hide. If the COs find it, I'm in big trouble."

"What is it?"

She's going to know in a couple hours anyway. "A phone."

Her eyes widen. "*Ni-ce.*"

I hand it to her.

"I've never seen a phone this small. It's cool." She hands it back. "Where'd you get it?" Her scrunched-up nose, dusted with cinnamon freckles, says she's loving turning the interrogation tables on me.

"A friend. I have to call him tonight."

"Ah, so that's why you're telling me."

I don't know if Rebecca's psychic, but she's hella smart.

"Ben, right? Birdman."

"Birdman?" I laugh. "No, not him. Don't call him that. Someone on the outside."

To her credit, Rebecca, unlike me, knows when to stop pressing. "Magnets," she says.

"What about them?"

"They're a good way to hide stuff. You stick them under the bottom bar of the bed frame. Since the beds are bolted to the floor the only way to see is to bend all the way down. The guards are too fat or lazy to do that."

"You think it works?"

"I know it does. I kept drugs that way for months. They never caught me, even when they tossed the cell."

"What kind drugs?"

"Opioids. Get rid of that sad look or I'm going to stop telling you anything."

"How did you get them in here?"

"Twiggs."

"That fucker. You never seem drugged."

"I'm not. He ran out right before you got here, at least that's what he told me."

"Good."

"Not when you're an addict, but it's gotten better."

"You know, it's weird, you and me being roommates and never asking each other what we're here for. I heard it was drugs for you."

She nods. "I got caught with two hundred oxy pills in my school locker. I was getting twenty bucks a piece for them. As for you, let me guess. I'd say probably ... murder."

"Wha— How did you know?"

Her head snaps back. "Seriously? I was just kidding. Interesting."

"I killed a man who tried to rape me."

"Impressive. I have to admit, you're not who I thought you were when you got here. I thought you were some kind of goody-two shoes."

"I used to be, in another life, before two men came to our house. They murdered my mom and little sister, raped them too."

A respectful silence before, "I'm not your sister, you know."

"What?"

"I said I'm not your sister. I'm not Becky."

"Duh, don't you think I know that?"

"Do you? Sometimes I wonder."

* * *

Almost time to call Lucas. I'm fidgeting, counting *one one-thousand, two one-thousand* ... I stopped checking the time on the phone because the battery's already running down. I'm cross-legged on the bunk facing the wall, facing *me*, Rebecca's painting. I just noticed a tiny ladybug on top of my pink sneaker. It's adorable.

She's painting now, humming a tune I don't recognize.

Time. I pull my blanket over me and hit the call button.

"Yeah."

"Lucas," I whisper. "It's me. Emily."

"Speak up. Can't hear you."

"It's Emily."

"I fuckin' know that, but you got to talk louder."

"You're *so* annoying!" I laugh. "There's so much to say. How much time do we have?"

"Save it for later. The batteries on them little phones don't last."

"Why didn't you include a charging cord?"

"'Cause it wouldn't fit inside the mouse and I couldn't send a fucking stuffed cat over a prison wall in broad daylight with cameras everywhere."

I can picture his neck veins twerking. "That's a good reason. How'd you find me?"

"Drone's got a video camera. Been watchin' for a couple a days, figuring out routines."

"That thing is amazing. Looks just like a red-tailed hawk. Did James make it?"

"Yeah."

"I figured. But how did you find me out here in Louisiana, in the middle of nowhere?"

"Again, later."

"Can you fly me in more supplies?"

"Like what?"

"A neck knife would be awesome. And this phone doesn't have internet. I need it to research my case. Could you get me a smart phone with data?"

"Anything else?"

"Well, I could use some pencils and an art pad, but a pad would probably be too big."

"That it?"

"All I can think of right now."

"No prom dress, maybe a new car? I ain't Amazon. You're in prison."

"Right, okay, well, I really do need internet access. I'm in here for killing Scott Brooker, the guy who picked me up hitchhiking in Louisiana. Do you remember him?"

"Hard to keep your victims straight. Yeah, I 'member him, and I know all about your case, except any recent developments."

"The latest news is I'm claiming self-defense. Which it was, but my lawyer says we need more evidence because my story has too many flaws in it. I need to find another Brooker victim to show what's called *prior similar acts*. My trial's in a few weeks. My lawyer can't do much and I can't do *anything* because I'm shut off from the world."

"Alright, a smart phone. I'll do some pokin' around too. First you got to find me a safe place to drop the merchandise, at night."

"They keep us locked in our cells at night, but I'll figure something out. Can you come visit me?"

"Not sure how. They know you Emily Calby, right?"

"The warden does."

"So they know you ain't got no family, and definitely no black father. How they been treatin' you?"

"Not so great. This place is crazy, Lucas." I peek from under the blanket at Rebecca, engrossed in applying delicate lavender brush strokes to her newest masterpiece. If she's listening, she hides it well. "Lucas, I have *a lot* to tell you."

"We cover it when we got more time and battery power. Just wanted you to know I found you."

"*Thank you.* I've thought about you every single day. I feel like I have a chance now."

A pause before, "Find me a safe place for a nighttime drop before that battery runs out."

"I will."

"Call me tomorrow, same time. Keep the phone hidden."

"I will."

He disconnects before I can say goodbye. I turn off the phone and pull the blanket off.

"You forgot to ask Lucas for a magnet," Rebecca says without looking up. "I still have mine. You can have it."

"Lucas?"

"That's something else you don't know about me. I have excellent hearing."

"Can you hear everything?

"Pretty much, *Emily*. Don't worry. I won't tell anyone."

And I know it's true.

20

"**ONE HAS CLAWS** at the end of its paws and one is a pause at the end of a clause," I recite, answering Mr. Medillo's grammar question about the difference between a cat and a comma. My fifth-grade teacher taught us the same trick. First day of English class, which is called *Reasoning through Language Arts* on the GED.

He writes it on the board. "Everyone get that?"

I friggin' hate being the class grammar expert, class anything expert, but made a deal. I talked Ben into helping take the spotlight off me by volunteering some answers, but he's not here. First day he's missed. I worry, of course. That's what I do.

Medillo writes on the board, *Let's eat Grandma.* "Lola Grimes," he calls out.

Uh-oh. I twist around.

"What?" she says, annoyed.

"Look at this sentence. Please read it for us."

Her eyes flicker to me. I send her a *You can do it* head bob. I'd better be right or she'll never trust me again.

"Let's … eat … Grand … ma."

"Good. What do you think about this sentence?"

"I think you'd have to be pretty hungry to eat your meemaw."

A blast of laughs, none louder than Medillo's guttural guffaw.

"Exactly. How do we fix the sentence so we don't have to eat poor Grandma?"

I hold my breath. *Look at the board.*

"I'd say ... it needs ... a comma."

"Yes!" I blurt. Some kids think I'm mocking her and boo. Lola agreed to the tutoring only if I promised to keep it secret.

"Where?" he says.

"... before Grandma?"

"Congratulations, Ms. Grimes. That is correct."

I don't think I've ever seen a happy look on Lola's face, but she's got one now. A couple girls pat her on the back.

I kept hoping Ben would show up late, like last time, but his seat is still empty when Mr. Medillo declares the end of class and everyone files out.

* * *

I'm in the yard, yawning my way through a set of shoulder presses with twenty-pound dumbbells.

I slept horribly last night, my mind running in circles trying to come up with a place for a safe nighttime drone drop. It has to be somewhere the drone won't be seen and the stuff will be safe until I can get to it. That's the tricky part because it won't be until the next day at the earliest.

I wasted a lot of time fixating on the cell window leading out to the roof. *If Ben could smuggle me a hacksaw blade from the shop, I could ... then I could ... then I could ...* Round and round to nowhere. I even dreamed about it. Maybe that's why roofs stuck in my head.

The weights land with a thud on the damp dirt. Roofs! The answer's staring me right in the face: the two-story, flat-roofed library building.

* * *

I burst through the door lit up like a Roman candle. "Hi, Miss Mava!"

"Good afternoon, Alice," she says, occupied opening a pile of mail.

"Anything for me?"

"Why would there be anything for you?"

"Just a joke," I say. "How are you today?"

"Fine. And you?"

"Fantastic!"

"Dear, do you drink a lot of coffee by any chance?"

"Just normal amount. Why?"

"I've just never met such a … let's say, enthusiastic detainee."

"You know the old saying. *If you aren't fired with enthusiasm, you'll get fired with enthusiasm.*"

"Who said that?"

"I don't remember exactly. I think it was somebody famous. My dad taught it to me. I love my job and definitely don't want to get fired."

"I wouldn't worry about—"

"Speaking of my job, I couldn't find enough shelf space for all those new donations." I point to the stack of boxes in the corner. "Then it came to me. Why not use the second floor?" I flip my palms like it's the most obvious idea in the history of the world. "It's not being used for anything else."

"Because it's a disaster area. We'll get rid of books we don't need. Lord knows we have plenty."

Think.

"Well, I was also thinking … we could open up a classroom, for tutoring, you know. It seems like that girl Lola, the one I'm tutoring, is actually learning. There are other kids who could be tutors too. Like that boy, Ben."

She looks at me over her glasses. "I see. So that's what this is about."

"No, no. I was just using him as an example. My cellie, Rebecca, is super-smart. I'll bet she could be a tutor. I remember what you said about Pochachant needing more teachers. Maybe we could even get outside teachers to volunteer."

She shakes her head. "The second floor isn't habitable for anything except spiders."

"I could fix it up real good."

"Honey, it would take a crew of ten to fix that place. It needs paint, carpentry, electric. There aren't any funds for things like that."

"Ben works in the shop. And I could probably get some other people to help."

"It's a very nice idea," she says. "I dreamed about something just like that when I started here as a young woman, but it turned out to be just that. Nothing but a dream."

"Could I, um, just check it out? I've never been upstairs."

She closes her eyes like she's in pain, but pulls out her keys. "Follow me, willful child."

She leads me through the main library to a door I always assumed was a closet. It takes both of us pulling on the knob to break the seal of time gone by. Behind the door is a silky curtain of webs.

"See? I wasn't lying about the spiders. You'll probably get bit."

"I'm not afraid of spiders."

"Well, ain't no way Miss Mava is going up those stairs. You're on your own. Be careful."

"Don't worry. I'll be *super*-careful."

I tunnel through the webs, picking sticky strands from my face and hair as I mount a shaky metal staircase. My footprints in the dust look like the first steps on the moon.

Mava wasn't exaggerating. It's a total disaster area. Peeling paint, piles of plaster, missing floorboards. I don't see any tutoring classes happening up here, but that's not why I came. The roof is directly above. There has to be a way to get to it.

I dodge gaping holes that risk sending me crashing through the plaster ceiling before discovering a nook on the far side of the building with three steps that end at a door. It has to go to the roof. There's nothing else out there. And it's even a regular door, not a metal prison door. How lucky is that? ... But it's painted shut. I start kicking it.

"What's going on up there?" Mava hollers.

"Just testing the structural integrity," I shout back.

I find a rusty nail and use it to cut through the painted seam. In the background, Mava announces it's time to come back down.

In a rush, the nail slips and stabs my finger. I stick it in my mouth, sucking the blood and garbling *eff eff eff.* How long does a tetanus shot last? I got one when I was six after stepping on Dad's rusty pickaxe in my bare feet.

"Young lady, get down here right now."

"Just a second."

I back up to get a running start and take off, springing from the third step and battering the door with all my weight. I land in a heap, squeezing my screaming shoulder, but I look up to see daylight peeking through a crack in the door.

It turns out to be the door to paradise. Fresh air, bright sun and a flat tar roof with HVAC units that block the view from the closest surveillance turret.

"Alice!"

I pull the door tight and retrace my path to the top of the stairs. Mava's pruney scowl pokes through the webs.

"What's the matter with you? You got a customer waiting."

Coming out of the dark stairway, blinded by the bright light, I'm surprised when Ben takes shape, but stunned into immobility when he turns his head to reveal deep bruises blotting the left side of his beautiful face.

"Ben!"

The CO, another new one, is undoing his restraints.

"What happened?"

"I already asked," Mava says. "He *says* it was a shop accident. Alice, meet CO Johnson. I think he deserves a treat and some fattening up. What do you think?"

He's plenty fat already. "Definitely. All the COs here work so hard and take such good care of us. No one deserves a treat more than they do." I give him my grandest smile of appreciation and he tips his cap.

"Come to my office, Mr. Johnson. You two have thirty minutes. No funny business. The only thing I want to hear coming out of that room are the sounds of habeas corpus."

I wait until they leave and hustle Ben into the law library, seating him at the work table and scooting my chair up close.

"So this is why you missed class. Your face ..." I reach out to touch it, but stop.

"It's not as bad as it looks."

"What happened?"

"You heard Mava. Shop accident."

I don't believe him. This is Pochachant after all. "What kind of accident? How did it happen?"

"I was using the drill press and ... okay, it wasn't an accident. Someone hit me, but it's no big deal."

"Who? Who did it?"

"Some gang dude. Everyone's in a gang over there. A lot of people join one to get protection, but it's not worth it. They make you do bad things to get initiated, then they own you. I said I didn't want to join and the guy went crazy on me."

"Did you fight back?"

"No."

"Why not?"

"No point."

"Surrounded?"

He shrugs.

"What kind of gang?"

"They're mostly divided by race. Latinos, blacks, white supremacists—guess which one picked me to join?"

"What's his name? The one who hit you."

"His name? Why does that matter?"

"He should pay."

Ben shakes his head. "You can't report stuff like this. Might as well sign your own death warrant."

The One Commandment of Pochachant: *Thou shalt not snitch.* "Don't worry. I'll think of something."

Ben closes his eyes when he laughs, eyelashes fluttering like palm fronds in a breeze. "I appreciate that, but it's not your problem. Just part of life here. You have to accept it to survive."

"Go along to get along?"

"Sounds bad, but it's the truth."

"They keep telling me that, but at some point, you can't just let people ... oh, never mind. So, just out of curiosity, what was the guy's name?"

"Has anyone ever accused you of being stubborn?"

"A few people, maybe a few dozen."

"*Corey Wilkes*. Now can we change the subject? I prefer living in denial. Life's easier that way. You still haven't told me your story."

I exhale, my shoulders sinking like they're deflatable. "I live in denial too. I guess everyone does, everyone in this place at least. Prepare yourself. It's not pretty."

Skimping on details, I outline the Day of the Two Men. It comes out robotically, devoid of feeling, which brings more guilt, but I learned a long time ago that suppressing my emotions is the only way to keep from drowning in them.

"You're not the only one who ran," I say with a catch in my throat. "I ran and left my family behind."

He reaches for my hand as I talk and I fight my reflex to pull away. He doesn't ask questions. I like that. I can see why I annoy the crap out of people.

I fast-forward to Scott Brooker, leaving out tiny details like: I'm a trained killer who was fleeing Memphis because my best friend got shot three times with an AR-15 and that my real name isn't Alice. The last part bothers me most. What if he falls in love with Alice only to find out I'm not even me?

"So anyway, I'm claiming self-defense. My trial's in a few weeks."

"Wow, what can I say? Nothing good. Saying I'm sorry sounds stupid, but I am. I really am."

"There's never anything good to say. I'm sorry for what happened to you too."

I motion to the shiny temple of law books. "I still haven't been able to find anything to help with your case, but I'm not giving up. I never give up."

He laughs. "That I believe. Don't worry about it. It gives me an excuse to come see you."

We're lost in each other's eyes. I could gaze into his forever, but he lowers his head and breaks the moment.

Sweet Mary, he's even shier than I am. We're not going to get many chances alone. *Don't think. Attack. Seize the advantage while the other motherfucker's thinkin'.* Not what Lucas had in mind, but the same principle applies.

I draw forward to kiss him, too fast, just as he's raising his chin. Our teeth clink together with an awful sound and we both pull back rubbing our mouths. I'm willing to bet my face is the color of the bright red constitutional law book open on the table beside me.

"Omigod, I'm so sorry."

Ben smiles sweetly. "Want to try again?"

When our lips meet and his eyelash brushes my cheek it feels like someone plugged me into a Christmas tree. When our tongues touch I think I might be the Christmas tree.

I pull away to catch my breath, swallowing my panting. I'm never going to forget this moment as long as I live. When I was nine, Mom took me to Atlanta to see Taylor Swift. I sang my heart out to every song. My first kiss. *Fearless.* Haha, almost.

"Maybe we should give it one more try," I say. "Practice makes perfect."

I close my eyes and purse my lips just as Mava's sonorous voice broadcasts, "And over this way is the law library." I push my chair back and pick up the constitutional law book.

"Here's one I really recommend," I say. "Written by a professor. Chemerinsky. The guy is brilliant. Oh, hi, Miss Mava! Is it thirty minutes already?"

21

I'M HEADING BACK to the cellblock from the library when my name rings out. It's Longmont, motioning from across the yard. I change course, eyes flitting to the sky for any sign of a red-tailed hawk.

"Hi CO," I say. "What's up?"

"Alice, what do you think about your cellie?"

I stiffen. "Rebecca? I like her a lot. Why?"

"Do you know much about her personally?"

"Not really. She doesn't talk very much. Is she in trouble?"

"No, nothing like that. I'm trying to help her."

So tempting to take advantage of the moment and spill my guts about Twiggs. I can't imagine Longmont knowing what's going on and not doing something. But I swore, and could be wrong. The COs protect each other. If she told Twiggs, no telling what he'd do.

"Her mother's on the visitor list tomorrow. This will be her fourth trip from New Orleans. I'm the one who has to give her the bad news each time that her daughter doesn't want to talk to her. You should see the look on her face. Any chance you could talk to Rebecca, persuade her to see her mother tomorrow?"

"I can try, but I doubt if it will work."

"See what you can do. Whatever happened in the past, her mother's trying to repair it."

"How do you know that?"

"She told me. Said she found God and gave up drugs and drinking."

"Do you believe her?"

"Not for me to say. Just pass it on to Rebecca. It could help her."

I walk away thinking about her last words. Rebecca's trapped in her own jail. She'll be a prisoner even when she gets out. *We Live as We Dream. Alone.* Her tattoo. What could be sadder than that? She'll probably end up back on drugs. She needs hope, for something. We all do.

Is it possible to forgive a mother who did what Rebecca's did to her? Not for me to decide, like Longmont said. *It could help her.* Believe that.

* * *

Beans and weenies at dinner bring back memories of sitting around the dinner table with my family. These actually aren't bad. Even better, there's cornbread.

I lugged along volume ninety-seven of the Supreme Court Reporter and open it to *Brewer v. Williams*, careful not to get food on the pristine pages. It's the case about the guy who killed the girl on Christmas Eve at the YMCA. I never got back to it.

Rebecca's picking at her dinner like it's an archeological site. The girl needs to eat more. I told her about Ben getting beat up, but her reaction was the same as his. She asked if he was in the hospital. I said no and she said, *Shit happens.*

Lola and her crew are settling in at their table. She gives me a nod. A first. Her girls notice it. With permission from the boss, Claire adjusts her eyepatch and waves. Poor girl. I heard someone stuck a sparkler in her eye when she was little.

"So I ran into Longmont today," I say casually. "She's super-nice. I like her a lot. She mentioned that, um, your mom's coming to visit tomorrow."

"Big whoop," nostrils flaring like she's going to breathe fire.

"And don't you dare give me one of your lectures about the wonderfulness of mothers. I'm not in the mood."

"I'm sorry it comes out that way. I don't mean it to."

"I don't want to talk about it. Understand? *Do not*. So just tell that 'super-nice' bitch you like so much to keep her mouth shut about my business." With air quotes.

"Okay."

I go back to *Brewer v. Williams*. I remember why I abandoned it. The facts are a nightmare. The girl disappeared when she went to the restroom. Nobody knew what happened until a boy saw the defendant carrying out a bundle with two legs sticking out. I flip back to the beginning. *Habeas corpus granted*.

No effing way. He killed a little girl and got out? Something about his confession being illegal because of a *Christian burial speech* the cops made.

"Did Longmont say anything else?" Rebecca says in a much smaller voice, parting her hair and tucking it behind her ears.

"Um, yeah, actually. She said your mom wants to repair your relationship."

A feral sound from the back of her throat. "*Repair*? That's what she said? Does she think I'm a broken meth pipe she can glue back together?"

"Those might not have been her exact words. I'm just going by what Longmont said. She also said ... was your mom religious?"

"*My* mom? The closest she ever got to religion was when she took me to church to steal money from the collection trays while she created a diversion."

"Well, she said she found God and quit drinking and using drugs."

A sarcastic laugh that doesn't eclipse the cry inside. She flips back to silent mode. I respect it and return to the case.

Two detectives were driving the defendant in a car after he invoked his *Miranda* rights. One of them started talking about how it was Christmas Eve and snowing and if they didn't find the girl's body quickly they might never find it. He said her parents deserved a Christian burial for their daughter.

It was a good speech. I would have caved. So did the defendant. He took them to the body. The Supreme Court said it was illegal interrogation even though they didn't ask any questions. The exclusionary rule barred the confession from evidence.

Huh. Now I get why that rule is controversial. Which should weigh more, following the law or convicting a child killer? If the law's not followed, is it even law? What would keep the cops from violating everyone's rights if there were no consequences? … But a ten-year-old girl. Only two years older than Becky.

"I wonder if it's true," Rebecca says, almost in a whisper. "Or even possible."

I set the book down. "How long has it been since you saw her?"

"The state took me when I was twelve and put me in foster care. She never visited."

I cannot believe she didn't even visit, but say mildly, "Three years. That seems like enough time to find religion and get cleaned up."

"She probably just wants something from me, or she'll say she's sorry and think that makes everything okay."

"Do you believe in forgiveness?" I say. "Philosophically?"

"You mean religiously? I hear your prayers every night. They go on forever. Why do you pray so much? I've got bad news. There's nothing else out there. This is it."

"You don't know that's true."

"You don't know it isn't."

"No, but I guess that's what faith is. Besides, I have to believe there's another place. If I ever let myself think it was *the end* of my family that would be the end of me too."

She nods. "Well, I don't mind them. They help me fall asleep. It's like having a TV on."

I laugh. "You are too funny, girl."

"Do I believe in forgiveness? It depends on what the person did. Can I forgive someone who stole my whole life? I doubt it. Do you forgive the men who killed your family?"

I suction my tongue against my palette. *No.* Which of course means I'm a complete hypocrite. "Those men were evil. Their only purpose was to hurt us. I'm definitely not defending her, but your mom was an addict. Do you think she's evil? In her heart?"

She blinks. "I don't know." She blinks again. "Probably." A fat tear rolls down her cheek. She shakes her hair to cover it. "Maybe not."

22

REBECCA actually visited with her mom that day. I've been dying to know what happened, but she hasn't mentioned it and I know she doesn't want me asking about it.

I'm in the library, lugging a box of books up the stairs. I didn't waste my breath trying to convince Mava the second floor is habitable, reverting instead to a plea for literacy, making an impassioned argument to store the extra books up there. "Miss Mava, no library should get rid of books. It would be like a church getting rid of bibles!" Maybe it touched her religious heart because she left the door unlocked for me.

I dump the box at the top of the stairs and make my way to the nook. I expect to see nothing when I climb the three steps and slice open the door to the roof. Lucas taught me to always expect the worst in life and be pleasantly surprised if it doesn't turn out that way. But there it is, a small package wrapped in matte black paper. Inside are a smart phone and charger.

Downstairs, I get right to work. Two weeks until trial, no time to waste. The phone's fully charged, ready to go. My first search is for *Scott Brooker.* Way too many of them. I add Champaign, Illinois and his obituary tops the results.

He was a devoted husband, father and Christian ... His hobbies included collecting old lunch boxes ... He will be remembered for his kindness and industriousness.

If I had Lucas's hacking skills, I'd rewrite it.

*He was a devoted piece of crap ... His hobbies included raping
runaway girls ... He will be remembered for his heart of pure
evil.*

I find another picture of him on his church's website, teaching his Sunday school class. Everyone's smiling except for a
blank-faced blonde girl seated next to him, younger than the
rest. The caption says, *Mr. Scott Brooker leads our Youth Group
in a discussion of the Fall of Man.*

Too many random searches for missing girls go nowhere
and make me change course, get more methodical. I tear a
fresh sheet from a legal pad and write *What I Know about Scott
Brooker* at the top.

*Assumption 1: Brooker targeted hitchhiking runaways. Basis:
"Believe me, I know runaways. I've picked up plenty." Truth
rating: Strong.*

It's also a smart strategy. No witnesses and runaways are less
likely to go to the cops.

*Assumption 2: He killed one of them and buried her body a
few months before he picked me up. Basis: "There was a girl
who said no a few months ago. You could dig her up and ask
her." Truth rating: Unknown.*

He could have said it to scare me, but there was something in
his voice, something *not* in his voice. Humanness.

*Assumption 3: His victims would be from somewhere between
Lafayette and Champaign. Basis: "I've been driving this route
for years." Truth rating: Moderate.*

Not much, but I build a plan around them because I can't
stand sitting around doing nothing. I research driving directions between Champaign and Lafayette and make an ordered
list of the cities along the two main routes. My first search is
Decatur Illinois missing girl hitchhiking dead buried body found.
Nothing.

That's the way it goes until I come to an article about a fifteen-year-old girl missing from Searcy, Arkansas, last seen hitchhiking on I-49. She even had blonde hair. My heart skips a beat until I see the date. Last year. I say a quick prayer for her. There are other Brookers out there.

That's the way the afternoon goes, tumbling down one rabbit hole after another. One girl was seen getting into a silver car when she disappeared, but they found her in Memphis with her boyfriend.

A flawed plan in too many ways to count. No way to connect a missing girl to Brooker and even connecting a body wouldn't be easy. It would take time, DNA analysis. I can hear Paula like she's sitting right next to me: *We don't have the resources for anything like that.*

When the phone battery goes dead, I give up.

* * *

Another agonizing week passes. I talk to Lucas most nights on the new phone. He told me to get rid of the mini-phone, so I smashed it to pieces and tossed it in a dumpster. I catch him up on everything from fight club to Paula's irritable bowel syndrome. I thought he'd be shocked about fight club, but all he said was *Prison's bad shit.* His main concern was whether I won the fight.

The thing I want to talk about more than anything else, I can't. *Twiggs.* Even if I was willing to break my swear, Rebecca and her bat-ears are always just a few feet away.

We're talking now, my head buried under the bed covers, trying not to disturb Rebecca. Lights went out thirty minutes ago.

Lucas is reliving what a pain in the ass I was to track down. It took a spoofed email from the judge in Arkansas to the court clerk to get ahold of my extradition order.

"So *now*," he sputters, "me and James got to go searching prisoner records in Louisiana juvenile centers. We finally found *Alice Black* at Pochachant."

"How is James?"

"My little man is good. He's killin' it at Stanford. About to start his last year. He's been in Memphis for the summer, workin' on projects, takin' care of my building."

When Lucas Ellington Jackson died, his will gave his two-story building in South Memphis to a trust managed by Kiona.

"Where are you?"

"Hotel."

"Where's the bus?"

"Sold it after you disappeared."

"Sold it?" I was tired of living on it, but that bus was our home for a long time. No one can screw things up better than me. "Lucas, I'm sorry again for saying what I said ... and for acting like such an idiot and an ingrate ... and getting you into another huge stinking mess."

"Don't worry about me. I was sicka that bus. Take a hotel room any day."

"How can you make fake documents in a hotel room?"

"Can't. Was hard enough in the bus. I sent all the gear back to Memphis, changed careers from making documents to arranging them. Not as interesting, but less work."

"What does *arranging* mean?"

"Hookin' up buyers and sellers. Made twenty thousand dollars yesterday settin' up a passport for a Russian mobster."

"Russian mobster? Isn't that dangerous?"

"He cool. Just smugglin' money outta the country."

"Oh, just that?"

"Far as I know," he says.

I ask about Kiona. "She's still in Vegas working as a boxing trainer. You know that's what she loves. Said she's worried about *The Kid*," he says. That's what she took to calling me in training. From her it was a compliment, like I had earned a title. *In this corner, The Kid.*

"Don't you miss her? You guys are married. You should be together."

"Probably kill each other if we lived together."

"Because you're both too stubborn."

"Yeah. Then you come along—the queen of stubborn. No wonder Kiona had to get off the bus, but we good. All relationships different. You learn about 'em someday."

There's my cue. I've avoided telling him. I'm not sure why.

"I'm in a relationship. Sort of. I have a boyfriend. I met him in GED class."

A long pause. "You maim 'im yet?"

"Very funny. No, but someone else did." I tell him about Ben, leaving out the hump-backed bird and the kiss, afraid he'll make fun of them.

"A gang member beat him up for not joining a gang. White supremacists, Lucas. I want to help him."

"He in the hospital?"

"No."

"Just part of prison life."

"How can everyone keep saying stuff like that? *Shit happens. Prison's bad shit.* Only going to the hospital deserves attention? That's crazy. Going to prison is the punishment. You don't go there to get punished."

"I take it you like this boy."

"A lot."

"He a nice boy?"

"Super-nice."

"Don't let him get too fuckin' nice. Boys only want one thing."

A stifled *bwah.* "It's settled once and for all. You *are* my dad."

"How come he can't fight his own battles?"

"He's not very tough. He has a gentle spirit. You can feel it when you're around him. That's why I worry. He's like a deer in a wolf pack over there on the boys' side. He didn't even fight back."

"Surprised you like a pussy like that."

"A, don't use the p-word around me, and B, please don't call him names." Of course I've wondered about it too. Ben's the opposite of me. Maybe that's why I like him, although that would be weird. "I can't figure out a way to get to the guy who hit him. His name is Corey Wilkes."

A trademark Lucas snort. "And what you plan on doin' if you *get to him?*"

"Something to keep him away from Ben."

"Like?"

"I don't know," I mutter.

"Get something straight. Only one thing matters in prison. Your own survival. Stay focused on that. What you cookin' up with that smart phone? You got a plan?"

"I had one, but already abandoned it." I explain my failed mapping strategy to track down a Brooker victim.

"I did a background check on him," he says. "Nothin' came up."

"That's what Paula said. She talked to his boss and friends. They love him like kittens."

"I'll do more digging," he says.

We say goodnight. I'm feeling under the bed for the magnet when a voice in the dark says, "Why do you think it's your job to save everyone?"

I stare into the void that consumes Rebecca.

She says, "I thought it was just me. Now I see it's some kind of complex."

"I don't know what you're talking about. I just try to help people I care about. You and Ben. What's wrong with that?"

"And Lola? You care about Lola?"

"Not the same way, obviously."

"So what's your answer? Why do you think it's your job to be the savior?"

She's right. It is a complex. A complex complex.

"Well, for one thing, like you already guessed, guilt. For letting my family down and running away. But it's more than that. I used to be a good person ... then I became a bad person. A very bad person. You don't know that part of me. I want to be a good person again. Maybe I try to make up for it."

That night I dream I'm soaring through the clouds in a white gossamer dress. Did I die? Am I an angel? It's how I always pictured it. I'm at perfect peace, lighter than the air, rising into a golden sky.

Then I feel someone watching me, someone who knows I don't belong here, and a hole opens in the clouds below, a widening tunnel of blackness that starts sucking me in. *Falling ... falling.*

I wake up in a sweat with the sheet knotted in my fists. *Just another bad dream.*

I concentrate on Rebecca's feathery breathing and still myself—until I sense movement and turn to see a face pulling away from the cell-door window. I run to the door but the hall is empty.

Did I imagine it? Was it part of the dream? What happens at Pochachant at night?

23

IN THE LAST *month, how many times did you experience disturbing memories, thoughts, or images of a stressful past experience?*

Answer: Rarely

Real answer: Ten, maybe twenty times a day.

Do you ever have violent impulses?

Answer: Never

Real answer: Ten, maybe twenty times a day. Haha. Not that many, but *Often*.

Two months in a psych-ward teaches you a lot about faking your way through personality tests. I'm in a small office at Pochachant, undergoing the psychological examination ordered by Judge Hanks. I spent the morning taking an IQ test and filling out the Minnesota Multiphasic Personality Inventory. I just finished a PTSD quiz.

The psychologist, Dr. Christy Thompson, is a traveling psychologist who assesses juveniles under a contract with the state. She's scoring my results behind a desk marred with coffee rings and cigarette burns.

She's young, with long brown hair, pretty except that one of her doe eyes sits lower than the other, making me tilt my head slightly to even her out when we talk. A purple and gold pin on her jacket lapel says she's an LSU Tiger. I know every SEC team. My dad was a huge Georgia fan.

I pick up a weekly newspaper from a side table while I wait.

It's opened to the personal ads. Meggie Tribet and I used to read them for laughs. One is circled in pen: *Attractive, fit SWF, 36, seeks SM, any race, who doesn't believe we landed on the moon.*

A man is searching for a *Missed Connection* who smiled at him in the garden department at a home improvement store. He was the bald guy holding the hedge trimmers.

The last one gets my attention:

Searching for my mother. Gray hair, overweight, short blue dress. Last seen outside Frizzell's bar. Goes by the name "Gigi." Please call if you have information.

I read it again. Interesting. Could it work?

"Okay then," Dr. Thompson says, adding my tests to a folder that's already inches thick.

"How are you feeling these days?"

"Great!"

"Really. That's surprising."

Down girl. "Well, not great, obviously. I mean, I'm in prison, so I've had better days, but I've also had worse."

"Yes, I read your history. Those were horrific things that happened to you and your family. Almost unimaginable. I'm very sorry."

"Is that whole file about me? Where did you get it?"

"They just hand them to me when I arrive."

"What's in it? Why is it so thick?"

She opens the cover and fans pages. "Looks like most of these records are from a hospital in Atlanta."

"Those are my private medical records! They're supposed to be confidential."

"Generally speaking, that's true. But I'm not a lawyer. Maybe they subpoenaed them," she says with an apologetic shrug.

The Law again. Not her fault. She's the last person I need to antagonize. She could stick it to me with a bad report.

"Have you ever taken an IQ test before today?"

"If I did, it's probably in that folder," I say sarcastically.

154 THE GIRL IN CELL 49B

"You scored very high on it."

"How high?"

"Let's just say you're a lot smarter than me. I see you've taken the MMPI before."

"I should be an expert by now."

"Yes, well, good and bad news about that. You passed with flying colors. Unfortunately, the test is designed so no one can pass with flying colors without lying."

"Maybe I'm just well-adjusted."

She lays down the file. "I'll be honest. My opinion is you faked the results on the MMPI and PTSD scales."

"You can't prove that."

"I don't want to. I want to help you."

"Yeah, right."

"You don't believe me?"

"No offense, but you're being paid by the state, the judge who ordered this examination is paid by the state and the state is trying to convict me of murder."

"Hm," she says, taking notes on a pad. "That should have showed up on your paranoia scale." She tears the page out and crumples it. "Just teasing you. I'd be careful about who I trusted around here too."

She seems alright, but you can never really tell.

"You can believe it or not, but here's the truth. After everything that has happened to you, being *well-adjusted* would be abnormal. It's obvious you've developed coping mechanisms that work for you, but that's not the same thing as being well-adjusted."

She turns pages in my file. "I see you were diagnosed with some personality disorders."

"A few." *Posttraumatic stress disorder, dissociative identity disorder, depersonalization-derealization disorder, dissociative amnesia.* "But that was three years ago. I'm fine now."

"No symptoms at all?"

She'll know I'm lying if I say no, so I say nothing.

"You know there's no shame in suffering. No reason to hide it."

"*Pfft*. No reason?"

"Sorry, that was naïve. You may have excellent reasons, but there are also good reasons to let your guard down, accept you need help. Get treatment."

A high-pitched laugh that comes out like the cry of a hawk with an arrow stuck in its side. "How long have you been doing this job? No one gets treatment here. My cellmate's a drug addict. She doesn't get treatment. A girl down the hall screams all night and bangs her head on the wall. The COs are psychopaths. As for me, I've had plenty of treatment already. Maybe that's why I'm so well-adjusted."

"Interesting," she says. "I'm looking at your answer to question eight on the PTSD scale. *How often do you get angry? Rarely.*" A smile I can't read.

"You have no idea what would happen if I let my guard down ... no idea." What she calls coping mechanisms are walls of lead ten feet thick. If they ever crack, a puddle will leak out. That's all I'll be.

"You're right. I don't," she says. "And you're right about me being new. I graduated with my Ph.D. a few months ago. They couldn't find anyone with experience to take this job."

I soften. "You're doing a good job. Sorry for losing my temper. Okay, I do still have some symptoms. Anger is one of them, obviously."

She closes my file and pushes it aside. "It probably won't surprise you that I think you would benefit from more treatment. As a court-appointed psychologist, I could probably arrange it."

"Thanks, but no."

"Here's something else to consider. Practicality. If you acknowledge suffering from mental disorders, it might result in reduced charges and penalties."

"You talked to Paula, didn't you?"

"I did. She wants to help you, so much so that it's making her ill, but she doesn't know how."

"I told her how! She's supposed to be helping me find evidence that the so-called *victim* did the same thing to other girls. What I did was self-defense, not mental illness. She said she believed me."

"She does, in her heart, but the lawyer part of her is saying there are too many holes in your story."

I sigh. "I'm working on it."

* * *

I started writing the personals ad in my head before I got to work, greeted Mava and set up camp in the law library, sheltered by stacks of books on my favorite table. It's dangerous to be carrying the phone around, but time's running out.

> *HELP! I'm searching for information about a man who sexually assaulted me three years ago. He was 43 with brown eyes, thinning brown hair and gold wire-rimmed glasses. 5'10", 190 pounds. See attached picture.*

The data came from the coroner's report on Brooker. Chalk one up for The Law. The state has to turn everything over to the defendant. Paula made me a copy.

> *He targeted runaways, especially hitchhikers. He called himself Jim, but his real name is Scott Brooker.*

I reread and delete the last sentence. Anyone searching Brooker on the internet, like Leslie Tierney, could find the post and track it back to me. Who else could it be from? He probably used different names anyway.

> *If a man like this did anything to you three or more years ago, especially if it happened anywhere between Illinois and Louisiana, please message me on WhatsApp. My life depends on it.*

I add the burner number and begin a search for websites to

post it on. The first one is a forum for runaways, but it doesn't let me attach the picture. Either does a site for abuse victims. I replace *See attached picture* with *Can send picture.*

It takes an hour to do five posts. Not much better than the old plan, but it's all I got.

* * *

After dinner, back in the cell, I do more postings, targeting free classified ads in cities between Champaign and Lafayette. I'm in the middle of one when noises in the hall freeze me. Guards yelling, doors clanking.

"Search! Search!"

Great. I attach the phone to the magnet and stuff the charging cord into a slit I cut in the mattress. I lie down with a law book and concentrate on looking bored.

As the door unlocks, Rebecca holds up a hand, fingers crossed. I do the same.

Rebecca was right. They came and went, never saying what they were looking for. They pulled everything apart, but no one bothered to get down on their knees and look under the bunk frame.

I had a song stuck in my head the whole time. Travis Tritt, one of Dad's favorites. *Livin' on borrowed time.*

24

MAVA ASKED why I was moping.

"No real reason," I said.

"It's the boy, ain't it?"

Too tired to forge another emotion, I just said, "Yeah."

I missed GED—and Ben—yesterday because of the psych evaluation, so I was excited to see him this morning, but his seat was empty and he never showed up. The last time that happened he got his face beat in. At the end of class, the girl with the bumpy nose who sits on the other side of me tapped my shoulder and said, "He missed yesterday too."

As the day crawled by, I could think of only bad reasons why Ben would miss two days in a row.

* * *

After wasting the day obsessing about the wrong thing (a boy versus a competent criminal defense), I'm in a foul mood standing in the dinner line. It gets worse when a new detainee at the front jams things up by getting into an argument with the women behind the counter for not giving her an extra slice of pizza.

I join the hooting as the COs push her to the back of the line. She makes the mistake of expressing her disagreement with several hyphenated variations on the f-word and they drag her away in restraints. Go along to get along.

I'm assessing the disgusting creamed corn—it truly looks like puke—when my radar detects Lola aggressively closing in on me from the side. She always looks ready for a fight and I'm not *un*ready for one myself.

"Hey, whatcha doing?" she says.

"Um, waiting for dinner?" Lola has never approached me for friendly chitchat. I'm wary, but not wary enough to be ready for the punch she aims at my abdomen. I almost drop my tray before her fist stops an inch from my stomach and she starts laughing.

"Ha, got you, bitch." She uncurls her tatted fingers. In her hand is a folded square of paper.

"What's this?" I say.

"A note from lover boy." She drops it in the creamed corn.

Alice is printed on top in red ink.

"Don't think anyone's missed your little romance with Bennie-boy."

My eyes flicker back and forth from Lola to the square of notebook paper sinking in the pool of vomit-corn.

"How'd you get it?"

"Some dude in GED gave it to me to give to you when you skipped class yesterday. He said Bennie-boy gave it to him. I figured, why not? Maybe he's dumping you." She stabs her finger at me and I flinch. "Gotcha again," she says and walks away.

Before my butt even hits the seat, Rebecca's telescopic eyes are dialed in on the paper cube. "What's that?"

"Lola said it's from Ben, my *lover boy,* as she calls him."

Rebecca sometimes gets this look where her lips slide in opposite directions until her bottom lip starts almost in the middle of the top one. "Interesting," she says and takes a bite of pizza, one of the few things she'll eat.

"*Allegedly* from Ben," I add. "It might be a trick, but it does kind of look like his handwriting."

"It's from Ben," she says confidently, popping the last piece of cardboard crust and tomato paste in her mouth.

I stopped asking how she knows these things. "Hey, do you want my pizza?"

"You don't want it?"

"Nah. I'm not that hungry," I lie. "I'll trade you for your corn. ... Well, I guess I should open it. Hopefully it won't explode." I pluck the wad out of the corn and dry it with my napkin. Good grief, it's folded into like a hundred squares.

I read out loud. *"I won't be in class for a few days, but I wanted you to know I miss you. Ben.* It's written inside a big heart." I hand it to her.

"Nice. Why aren't you going all gooey?"

"Why is he missing class?"

"Could be lots of reasons. You worry too much. At least you don't have to worry if he likes you anymore. First the bird, now this."

"I guess, but sometimes when I'm around him, he acts distant, like he's talking to me from another dimension."

"He's probably like us. Can't express his feelings."

"Hey, I express my feelings."

"The ones you want."

Sometimes I'm convinced Rebecca exists in a shadow universe where all of our deepest thoughts are pinned to the outside, like Christy Thompson's LSU pin.

"You should give him something," she says.

"I thought about it, but don't know what. Buying him something from the commissary seems lame."

"Draw him a picture. He'd like that."

I think about how much I love waking up to Rebecca's painting every morning. "That's actually not a bad idea. He would be perfect in a drawing, especially with those eyelashes."

Curt headshake. "You don't give a boy a picture of himself. Especially in a prison." Left off but implied is *Du-uh.*

"You're right. I'm clueless about boys. What do you think he would like? I could do a bird."

"Old news. Draw a picture of *you.*"

"Me? That's a little narcissistic, isn't it?"

"Picture the poor boy in his lonely cell." She clutches her

breast dramatically. "Pining away for his beautiful girlfriend. What could raise his spirits more than her picture to keep him company?"

"You think?"

"I *know*. Believe me, the only gift he'd like better would be a real picture of you naked."

"Haha, well that's not going to happen. I'll go with the drawing."

When we get back to our cell, Rebecca gives me another sheet from her art pad and I take a selfie. I never let anyone take pictures of me. Need to remember to delete this one.

I barely recognize myself. How could someone sixteen look so old and tired? There's a smudge on my forehead and my hair is a mess. Not a face anyone would want a drawing of. I get up and wash it, brush my hair and open the cheapie makeup kit I bought at the commissary.

"No makeup," Rebecca says. "The real you."

"That would be a demon or something."

She puckers her lips. "You're too hard on yourself, whatever you did or think you did or didn't do." She leans across the canyon between the bunks and whispers, "The *Emily Calby* I know is a good person."

I pat her pointy shoulder. "Thanks. Okay, I'll keep it real." I take another selfie.

She's unusually chatty as I work, meaning she's talking without me having to pry every word out of her. She asks how my Brooker searches are coming. I explain the new plan and ask what she thinks about it.

"Still pretty random, but better than the first plan."

"How did you know about that?"

She points to her ears and eyes.

Something's wrong with my sketch. Can you lose your ability to draw in one month? I hold the drawing next to the selfie and realize the problem isn't my art skills, but *me*. There's a mourning in my eyes, a dead sorrow I never noticed.

Rebecca says, "You never asked about my mother and 'The Big Visit.'" Air quotes, of course.

"Not because I haven't wondered. I've already pried too much."

She nods in agreement.

"How did it go?"

"I don't know." She tilts her head forward, hair tumbling over her face like a waterfall.

Take it slow. I hold up my self-portrait. "What do you think so far?"

"I like it. It's real."

"Too real. Look at my eyes. Yuck. What did you guys talk about?"

"Not much. She asked how I was doing, stuff like that. She said she was sorry about a hundred times. I didn't talk much."

"What a shock."

She makes a sound like my cat used to make when he sneezed.

"Did she look good, you know, clean?"

"She looked like a worn-out hag because that's what she is, but the wired look in her eyes that I grew up with wasn't there. I think it's *possible* she could be clean. For now."

"That's awesome. What about the religion part?"

"Well, she *says* she joined a church and goes to AA meetings every night. She works as a cashier at a grocery store. First time I ever remember her having a regular job."

I hold up the picture again. "Now look. I have a wrinkle in my forehead—in pen. Where did you leave the conversation?"

"She wanted to know if we could have a 'relationship' when I get out."

"Wow, that's big."

"No point even thinking about it. She's probably downing a bottle of vodka right now."

"Keep hope."

* * *

From *Goldibear*:

Hi! I got picked up by someone who sounds like that. He did the same thing to me. Drove me out into the woods.

Where did it happen?

I'm under the covers reading my latest messages. My personals ad post is on almost fifty sites, thanks to Lucas's help. I expected some responses, but nothing like this. I'm getting twenty messages a day.

No reply. I go to the next one. *SarahG*:

Hey, a man gave me a ride at a gas station and attacked me in his car. Maybe same?

Where did it happen?

Oregon.

Sorry. I don't think it's the same man. Thank you for reaching out. God bless you. I hope you're getting help. Don't be afraid to seek it.

Do as I say, not as I do. *Goldibear* gets back to me. Hers happened in Arizona. I send the same reply.

Lots of spam. I delete messages for *Need more sex?* and *Viagra for Women. Free Shipping.*

The last message of the day is from *Dinoslinky*. I click on it.

I'm the guy who did it. It was goooooooood. Lets do it agin!!! Rite back.

Ignore it. But of course I can't. I hammer out, *Yeah, let's get together real soon motherfucker. I can't wait to cut off your tiny dick and shove it down your throat. DIE!!*

Forces from dangerous places attack my depleted soul. I put the phone away and fall back on the flimsy pillow.

Silence in the dark except for the breathing of two scared girls. For all our armor and bravado, that's all we really are.

I turn sideways, pupils dilating until Rebecca's shrimpy form takes shape under the sheet. If it was ever about Becky, it's not anymore. I love this girl.

25

ONLY ONE WEEK before trial and I'm sitting in another boring GED class staring at Ben's empty chair. He never came back. He's been gone a whole week.

I promised Lola my next cherry cobbler dessert if she would point out who gave her Ben's note. He's a sinewy kid with a peach fuzz mustache on the far side of the classroom. As Medillo sounds his last note, I leap from my chair and climb over tables to get to him before the COs do.

"Hi!" I say.

Taken aback, "Uh, hi."

"I'm Alice. Ben's friend. I'm the one he gave you that note for. I haven't seen him all week. Is he okay?"

"If you call being in the hospital with two broken arms okay."

I grab him by the shoulders. "What happened? Did he have an accident?"

He yanks my hands away. "Yeah. He accidentally told Corey Wilkes to fuck off."

A CO barks at me to line up.

Back in my cell, pressed against the wall, I call Lucas, breaking his rule to call only at night at the scheduled time. I catch myself pulling on my hair and stop. Six rings before I'm sent to voicemail.

I hang up and text. *Call me ASAP!! It's an emergency!!!*

Ten minutes pass before the phone vibrates. "Lucas, it's me."

"Really? I thought it was some other high-strung girl who's in love with exclamation points. What's the problem this time?"

I whisper-scream the story of Ben and Corey Wilkes, pouring it out so fast I have to stop to catch my breath.

"Now he's in the hospital with two broken arms. Just because he wouldn't join a gang. White supremacists! Are you finally satisfied?"

"What's the emergency?"

"I need you to do something about it."

"Me? What can I do? You want me dress up like a nurse and go stick a thermometer up his ass?"

"I need you to take care of Corey Wilkes, so it can't ever happen again."

He laughs. "You must have a real hard-on for this boy."

"His name is Ben and I don't have a *hard-on* for him. That's gross. Please, Lucas. I really care about him."

"I'm honored you think so highly of my abilities, but even Lucas Jackson can't walk through bars and concrete walls."

"I was thinking maybe you could pressure him from the outside somehow."

"How?"

"Anything that will keep him from bothering Ben. Forever."

"Where's he from?"

"I don't know."

"That's a big help."

"Just try, please?"

* * *

I sit facing Paula at one of the folding tables in the visiting room, squinting into the afternoon sun burning through the high gym windows. She just stymied me with another mock cross-examination question. *Did you feel imminently threatened with bodily harm at the time you killed Mr. Brooker?*

"What does *imminently* mean, under the law?"

"Immediately."

"Um, yeah, I'd say so."

"*Um*? You'd *say* so? Are you not sure?"

"Yes, I'm sure."

"Did he touch you?"

"He was about to."

"How do you know that?"

"Duh, because I was there. I knew!"

"How?"

My fingers contract into fists. "*Look*, he said we were going to lunch, then he took me out to the middle of nowhere and said I had to do him a *favor* while he unbuckled his pants. Get it?"

"Did he offer to pay you?"

"Why does that matter?"

"Did he offer to pay you?"

"Yeah, so?"

"How much?"

"Ten dollars."

"What did you say in response?"

I bite my lip to throttle the rage growing in my chest. "I said make it fifty, but not because I was going to do it."

"Then why'd you say it?"

My fists slam the table hard enough to bring a threatening look from the nearest CO. "I was stalling, trying to figure out what to do. Why are you torturing me like this? You're supposed to be on my side."

"Lower your voice. I'm not trying to torture you. I'm trying to prepare you. Leslie is going to be much worse. She'll do anything she can to push your buttons and make you blow up like you just did. You have to stay calm and stick with the facts, no matter what the question. I know it's difficult."

I take a deep breath and gather myself. "Like I said, I was stalling, trying to think what to do. We were miles from anything, with water on both sides. I wanted to run but there was nowhere to go."

"What did you think he was going to do to you?"

"Rape me. He was already trying to do it. We were outside his car and he had his pants down with his ... *thing* hanging out. He wasn't going to just let me go. When I asked what would happen if I said no, he said there was another girl who said no but I'd have to dig her up to ask her."

I leave out that when I pulled the knife, I was filled with as much rage as fear, my brain flooded with images of Mom and Becky. From the second Brooker made me get down on my knees, he didn't have long to live.

"Much better," she says. "Calm and professional. That's the Emily Calby we want to see on the witness stand. Be sure to emphasize that part at the end, about digging up the girl, exactly like you just said it. It could be construed as an implied death threat."

"That's the way I heard it." I'm feeling better. My story sounds stronger each time I tell it. "So we have a pretty good case then, right?"

A twisted half-smile, her standard forced brave face. "*If* the judge believes you, but Leslie is going to fly to the moon and back to convince him you're making everything up. She has the neck knife, the car theft, the cover-up ..."

She waves her arms like the list could go on forever. "I'm sorry to be so blunt, but I want you to understand your situation."

"You don't need to apologize, Paula. It's good to be blunt. You should do it more often."

"Okay, well then, you asked for it. Your trial's a week away. We haven't found anything in Scott Brooker's past to show he was predisposed to commit such a crime."

"Are you still looking?"

"No. I ran the records check and talked to the people I told you about. That's all I could do without more to go on."

I know she's right. The proof is in my dead-end map search and going-nowhere-fast personals ad campaign.

"I guess I'll see you in court then," I say with a hollow laugh.

"Hold on. I brought you something." She scoops up a large white box with scraps of colorful paper taped to it. "Sorry. It was wrapped when I got here but the guards made me open it. Usually they leave the lawyers alone."

I pull the lid off. "*Clothes? I mean, clothes!*" The last thing in the world I need.

"For court. You don't want to testify in a prison uniform. We want Judge Hanks to see a dignified, conservative young woman."

"Instead of a runaway lunatic with a knife. Good idea." I pull out a gray suit jacket. "Ha, it's like a lawyer suit."

She blushes. "I guess you're right. I was aiming for conservative and you can't get much more conservative than lawyer attire. There's a blouse in there too."

The suit is actually really nice. I'm surprised she picked it out. A no-collar jacket with slit pockets and black ticking along both. Like something Leslie Tierney would wear. Like nothing Paula would wear.

"*Aw,* thanks, Paula. You're the best lawyer I ever had." I've only had two, but I'll take Paula over Andy the Lawyer any day.

On the way out, the CO, a woman who looks like she could squat-press two hundred pounds, searches my package. One more indignity, but it could be worse. Everyone gets stripsearched for contraband after a visit; the only exception is for lawyers.

I drop the gift box off in my cell. The CO points to the cafeteria and says, "Dinner line shuts down in five minutes and I sure as hell ain't running there with you. Go."

I'm famished. I couldn't get lunch down because I was upset about Ben. I take off running, turn the corner and run smack into Twiggs.

"They let the dogs out again? Where do you think you're going?" he says.

"Cafeteria. I just got out of a visit from my lawyer. Gotta run."

He grabs my shoulder, triggering a flashback of the last man who did it, the biker with the crushed trachea, the one who started this whole mess. *Impulse control.*

"Seein' as I got you out here in private, lemme tell you something. I see the looks you give me. Disrespectin' a CO is a violation. I could put you in solitary. No liftin' weights, no runnin' the track. No cushy job workin' for that old bitch, Mava. Yeah, I see you."

Blood simmering, "Yeah? Well now that we're out here in private, let me tell *you* something. You better leave Rebecca alone."

He snorts. "Now you're trying to tell me what to do? Here's some free advice. You do not want to get on my bad side."

Think first, act later. Not the time or place for a confrontation.

"I'm sorry, CO. I would never disrespect you. Sometimes my look comes across as an old sourpuss. My parents always told me that. Actually, I was trying to help you. I know you and Rebecca are, um, friends. The other night she told me she has a, you know ..." I whisper, "S-T-D."

"What the fuck?"

"I know. Sad, isn't it? So young. Herpes. Apparently it's the super-contagious kind. *Ick.* Honestly, I'm afraid to even be in the same cell with her. I thought you should know so you can avoid her, but *please* don't tell her I told you. She'd die of embarrassment."

He scratches his cheek.

"Sir, I only have like two minutes before the cafeteria closes. Could I go now, please?"

He steps aside and I run, heart pounding like the bass to one of Lucas's rap songs.

26

I'M ON MY BACK staring at the ceiling after lights out, contemplating my trial, which starts on Monday, three days from now. Most of Friday is already gone, so it's really only two days. There's not much to contemplate because except for my testimony, I still have zip for evidence.

Lucas hacked into the computer at Brooker's church after I told him I was suspicious about Brooker being a Sunday school teacher. He did it with a phishing email saying he wanted to make a large donation in the name of his dead father who had grown up attending the church. *Click here to see my proposal.* He always knows how to lay the perfect bait. But there was nothing there except a list of Brooker's donations and the same Sunday school picture I found on the website.

My personals ad campaign has been a ridiculous success measured by the number of replies, more than thirty a day now, but it's all been a waste of time.

I actually did make a huge legal discovery in the law library today—but for Ben, not me. He still hasn't come back to class. The only thing I could think to do to help him was keep researching his case. It finally paid off.

Look for similar cases. My legal research book has been telling me that over and over but I was missing the point, hung up on finding a case with the same facts instead of the same legal issue. It turned out to be the Christian burial speech case. No wonder I kept being drawn to it. It finally sunk in. The court said the detective's speech about the parents deserving a Christian burial for their daughter was psychological coercion, intended to get information *as surely as and perhaps more effectively* than asking questions.

That led to a case called *Rhode Island v. Innis* and there it was, in black and white. The Supreme Court said the *Miranda* protections apply not only to express questions, but to their *functional equivalent*, which includes anything *reasonably likely to elicit an incriminating response*.

Like parking a fake mother and crying baby outside the cell of a boy accused of murdering the father. Even with all my problems, I smile picturing Ben's usually impassive face lighting up when I get the chance to tell him about it.

Unable to sleep, I get out my phone to finish going through today's messages from the personals ad. Same as yesterday's and the day before. Too many stories from girls who got assaulted after taking a ride from a stranger. At first I thought it was impossible for them all to be true. Then I Googled it. More than a million runaways every year, all easy prey.

But none of the men end up being Brooker. I send each girl my form reply. Some of them want to keep writing, be friends. I'm reading a message from a girl named Shallie. *At least I got my bad luck out of the way early in life*, with a smiley face.

The supply of bad luck in life is infinite. It's a mistake to assume you've reached your limit. *Be careful ALWAYS*, I write back.

Chillin4029 is another freak saying he did it. Forefinger trembling, I make myself delete it. I also delete spam messages for diet wonders and male enhancement miracles.

Too little too late. If I could have got going on a plan sooner maybe I could have done better. The last message is from *Luv-angel88*.

Luv-angel? Gimme a break. I click on it, expecting another troll.

Hi. My name is Mary. I ran away when I was fifteen. I met a guy at a truck stop who offered me a ride. He sounds a lot like the man you described. He said his name was Dave. He took me to a deserted place and raped me. Anyway, that's it.

Here we go again.

Hi Mary. Where did it happen? Let me guess: Nova Scotia, Hawaii, Australia ...

Outside of Memphis.

I flip pages in my pad to where I traced the driving directions between Champaign and Lafayette. One of the main routes, I-55, goes right through Memphis.

When did it happen? Yesterday, last week, last year.

Four years ago. I'm nineteen now. I always hated he got away with it, but never knew what to do.

Just coincidence.

Do you remember what kind car? My test question, a fact I left out of the ad.

Not the brand, but it was silver. It was nice, super-clean inside.

I sit up too fast and get dizzy. Before I got into Brooker's silver Lexus, when I was asking through the side window if he was safe, I remember noticing the interior was immaculate.

I'm sending you a picture. I attach the headshot from Brooker's obituary. *Is this him?*

Hard to tell. Too small. Dave looked older.

So did *Jim*, the fake name Brooker used on me. His family obviously picked an old picture for the obituary.

Does it look like it could be him younger?

Could be. I blocked a lot out. Any recent pix?

Just the ones in the coroner report. Brooker's face is un-recognizable. Bloated, with a gap in his cheek where something gnawed a hole in it, a bird or maybe a nutria. Fat swamp rats. Louisiana is full of them.

No. What else? Think. *Did he talk about his daughter?*

Yes! That's like all he talked about except when he was asking questions about me.

The whole ride, all I wanted was for Brooker to quit asking

questions and shut up. *How old are you? What grade are you in? What do you want to be when you grow up? ...*

I type, *Anything else?*

Not really, except he was playing a Taylor Swift CD and singing along. I thought that was kind of weird for a man.

OMG, it *must* be him. Maybe he put Taylor on every time he picked up a girl.

I take notes under the book-light as we text back and forth. *Mary Brinson, Southaven, Mississippi.* I ask for her address.

I can't do that. Don't know you. You could be a rapist, no offense. That's smart. Anyone can be anyone online.

Rebecca's awake. I see her in the dim reaches of the circle of light from the phone, eyes glowing like moons around the last planet of the solar system, half in and half out.

Can I call you right now? I could explain everything a lot better in person.

I'm out with my friends. Why are you looking for him?

No time to hedge.

His real name is Scott Brooker. He picked me up hitchhiking three years ago and tried to rape me. I had to kill him in self-defense. I'm in prison in Louisiana. My trial is next week. I need a witness that he did the same thing to other girls.

Long wait before, *Wow.*

Do you think you could help me?

I can't swear it's him by the picture. My friends are leaving. Need to get going.

I'm losing her. *Can my lawyer call you tomorrow? She's a public defender. Paula Dunwoody. You can look her up.*

I guess. Gotta go.

My palm is sweating when I set down the phone.

"What happened?" Rebecca says.

Dazed, "It sounds crazy, but I might have actually found one of Brooker's victims. Right time-frame and location, and she knew facts I didn't put in the ad."

"You don't sound very excited."

"Because she can't identify him from the picture. It's old, but still, and she didn't exactly sound thrilled about getting involved."

"Would you?"

I stop to think. "No," I chortle. *"Hi, I'm some freak in prison you don't know. Can you be a witness at my murder trial next week?"* Saying it makes me laugh harder, causing Rebecca to crack up too.

Laugh or cry, cry and die. If I ever get a tattoo, that's what I'll put on it. I wipe my eyes.

"Sorry I woke you up," I say across the void.

"That's okay. It's more interesting than what I usually do at night," she says cryptically.

"I have to call Paula," I say. "My lawyer."

"I know Paula."

"I'm sure you do. It ought to be interesting."

She picks up on the third ring.

"Hello? Who is this? I don't recognize this number."

"Hi, Paula! It's Emily."

"Emily? It's late. How ... where are you calling from?"

"Sitting here at home at good ol' Pochachant." The laugh put me in a jaunty mood. The other possibility is I'm going crazy again.

"But calling hours are over and this number you're calling from ... how?"

"I'll tell you if you want, but you might be better off not knowing."

Silence. I picture her thinking about it under an old-fashioned lamp on a couch matted with cat hair.

"You might be right. What's going on?"

"Sorry to bother you, but something big just happened in my case."

I tell her about Mary Brinson from Southaven, Mississippi.

"How did you find her?"

"Well, again ... The important thing is I have her phone number and told her you might be calling her tomorrow."

"I have to ask. This isn't someone you're bribing or anything like that, is it?"

"Of course not, Paula. She's legit. Here's the number." I read it twice. "There is one little problem. She's not sure from his picture that it's him."

"Oh boy. That's what we call a Big, capital-B problem in the law. If she can't give positive ID, her testimony won't be admissible."

"But the silver car, on one of the two main routes between Champaign and Lafayette, and talking about his daughter and interrogating her with questions. And playing Taylor Swift? Those can't all be coincidences."

"Well, yes, they can, but I agree it's worth checking out. I'll call her ... but if she can't make an ID."

"The picture I sent her came from his obituary. It was small and taken a long time ago. If we could get some recent pictures, you know, like right before he croaked, she could probably identify him."

Her sigh comes out more like a wheeze. "Well, I could file a motion requesting some when we get to court on Monday, but I warn you, judges are not fond of last-minute surprises. First things first. I need to talk to this Mary Brinson in person. I'm not going to ask Judge Hanks to let me add a witness I never met. If she'll agree to meet, I'll drive to Southaven tomorrow."

"Thank you, Paula. I'd go if they'd let me. I could even drive. You saw Leslie's highway video." My joke falls flat. Crickets.

She says, "It's a seven-hour trip. I'd better get some sleep."

"I'm sorry, Paula. How are you feeling these days, with your IBS? I know my case has been really stressful, that *I've* been stressful."

"Nothing like the stress you're under, but it has been acting up. I have a doctor appointment on Wednesday. I've already cleared a recess with the judge. I should have mentioned it."

"No problem. Um, there is one other little thing. Mary hasn't exactly agreed to be a witness yet. She might need some persuading."

Paula says she has to go to bed.

27

IN A MILLION years, I never would have guessed my first-ever manicure would happen in a prison, but that's how I spend Sunday morning on the day before my trial.

I woke up at dawn to work on my list of questions Leslie might ask me on cross-examination. It's long. I need to be prepared, not let her surprise me. On the third run-through with Rebecca, she stopped me mid-answer and said I needed to relax, offering to do my nails. She wanted to paint them with tiny birds and flowers, but Paula's words replayed in my head. *We want Judge Hanks to see a dignified, conservative young woman.* We went with clear gloss.

She also trimmed my frayed hair, with round-tipped scissors like the kind they give first-graders, the only kind we're allowed to have.

My new clothes are laid out on top of the lockers. Lined up next to them are my toothbrush, deodorant, hairbrush, makeup and a legal pad with four pens hooked to it. I postponed my shower as long as possible so I could look fresh in the courtroom. The guards are coming to get me at six a.m.

I texted Paula when I realized my only shoes are the worn-out cross-trainers I've been wearing since I got arrested in Arkansas. They stink so bad Rebecca makes me put them in a plastic bag at night.

I'm blowing on my nails when my phone vibrates. A text

from Paula. I pull the sheet over me so no one can see from the hallway.

Is this you, Emily? It's Paula.

Hi! Where are you?

In Southaven, with Mary Brinson."

You're still there?

I had to stay overnight. Is it possible for you to talk right now?

Sure. I'll call you.

"It's Paula," I inform Rebecca and get up to check the hall. I flatten myself against the wall. She answers after a half-ring.

"Emily?" she says.

"It's me."

"I have no earthly idea how you got your hands on a phone. Please be careful. You don't need any more trouble, but I didn't think this could wait. I have news."

"What kind? Good or bad."

"A little of both."

Someday I'd like to get a call with nothing but good news, even if it's only one time. "Might as well start with the bad."

"Mary is a nice young woman who I think could make a credible witness."

"That sounds like good news."

"It would be, but she insists she can't identify the obituary picture as the man who assaulted her. I also found another picture of Brooker online."

"Teaching Sunday school?"

"Yes, how did ... never mind. She couldn't identify that one either."

No surprise. It's a side view and he's just one small face in a large group. "What's the good news?"

"Do you have your copy of the coroner's report, with the photos? I didn't bring my files."

"It's in my locker, but his face isn't recognizable."

"Get it out and—I know this will be hard—find a photo that shows his genital area, preferably a close-up. I recall there are several pictures of the ... um, lower stab wound."

"Genitals? Yuck. Where is this going?"

"Bear with me, please."

I retrieve the file and thumb through the coroner's report. "Here's one."

"Do you see a mole on his thigh?"

"Yes."

"Which thigh?"

"Right."

"What does the mole look like?"

"Nothing special. Flat and round, kind of red."

"This will sound like an odd question, but have you ever seen candy dots, the kind that come stuck to paper?"

"Of course. I love them. Pure sugar."

"Does the mole look similar in size to one of them?"

"I guess."

"Sorry to be so mysterious, but I didn't want to get your hopes up until I verified it. Mary couldn't identify the picture, but she remembered a perfectly round flat mole on Brooker's upper right thigh that she described as looking *like a red dot.* I thought she meant something tiny, like a period or a pinprick, but she meant dot candy."

"Seriously? How could she remember something like that and not his face?"

"She said she stayed focused on it so she wouldn't have to see anything else ... around there."

"Can she identify him by that in court, legally?"

"It's possible. Physical identification isn't limited to faces. It depends on whether Judge Hanks is persuaded that added to the other similarities it's competent evidence that the man could have been Brooker."

"This is great news!"

Rebecca shushes me with a finger to her lips, pointing to the door.

"Slow down. There's another problem. I haven't been able to persuade her to testify. She won't commit. I'm not sure exactly why, but it's obviously a very private matter and she just started her first semester of college in Memphis."

"Can't we make her testify?"

"We could subpoena her, but you never want to build your case around an unwilling witness. We need her on our side, I mean, your side."

"*Our* side." I look at Rebecca, fiercely guarding the cell door with her eagle eyes. I have a side again. Lucas, Rebecca and Paula. "Would she be willing to talk to me?"

"That's what I was thinking. Hold on and I'll ask."

Voices in the background before Paula comes back on. "She says yes, but not now. Can you call her later tonight?"

"I can and will."

She ends the call saying she'll bring me a pair of her shoes in the morning. Turns out we both have long feet.

* * *

Gloomy rain pelted the windows all afternoon, which I spent in the dayroom playing board games with Rebecca. Her idea after listening to me recite my direct testimony for the forty-thousandth time. She said it sounded too rehearsed and suggested I chill for the rest of the day.

First she picked out the Ouija board, but I waved it off. I wasn't taking any chances opening spirit doors on the day before my trial, not with Rebecca involved. She already seems to be in touch with some other place. We settled on Scrabble.

As we played, the back of my brain wrote and rewrote speeches to persuade Mary Brinson to testify. I asked Rebecca what she thought would work.

"You couldn't convince me to testify about my secrets in a million years."

"Great, thanks."

"Well, maybe now, but not when we were strangers. Maybe you could threaten her."

I let the suggestion pass, pretty sure she was joking. Every speech I came up with sounded fake so I gave up planning and decided to improvise.

After dinner I flip pages in the law books until my brain wears out. The lights just went off. Ten o'clock. I didn't want to call too early and miss her, risk her not calling back.

"Here goes nothing," I say. "Wish me luck." I push the call button.

A girl's voice, flat and detached, says hello.

"Hi! Is this Mary?"

"You must be Alice." It comes out like another criminal charge.

"My real name is Emily. Paula had to say Alice because of the law. It's complicated, but I want to be completely honest with you."

No reply.

"I'm calling to talk to you about testifying in my case."

"I know."

"I don't blame you for not wanting to do it, not one bit. What happened to you is the most private thing in the world. I only told one person about Brooker." Lucas.

"I never even told my parents," she says.

"Does anyone know?"

"You and your lawyer," she says sharply.

Divert, divert. "Paula's really nice, isn't she?"

"Seems like it. She's worried about you. That's obvious."

"I don't know if she told you, but the good thing about my case is it's in juvenile court. Everything is confidential, by law. So no one would have to know you testified."

"My parents will know something's up if I just disappear in the middle of the week. I'm in college. I have classes."

"Have you thought about telling them? It seems like you wanted to talk about it to someone, you know, since you contacted me."

A sound in the background. "Close the door! I'm on the phone. Sorry, my little brother."

"Wouldn't they try to help you? Mine would have, I think, although my dad would have wanted to kill Brooker."

"You *think*? You're trying to convince me and you didn't even tell your own parents?"

"They were both dead already."

Silence.

"It's alright. You don't have to say anything."

"My dad would want to kill him too," she says softly.

"That's where the good news comes in. I already took care of it!"

Nothing. Not everyone gets my sense of humor.

"There's something else," she says. "About me, that no one can know. *No one.*"

"Does it have anything to do with Brooker?"

"Nothing. Zero."

"Then I don't see why it would be anyone's business."

"You're asking a lot from me."

"I know, but your testimony could save my life. I don't have any witnesses because he took me out into the bayou."

"He took me deep in the woods."

"Our stories are almost identical. He did it to other girls too, maybe even killed one of them."

"Paula told me your story. I believe it because I lived it."

"So do you think you could help me? Paula says knowing about the mole, added to everything else, could be convincing."

No response.

Build a stronger case. "You said in your texts you hated he got away with it, but never knew what to do. This is your chance, not just for me. For all girls. Every day I hear from girls like us, victims of people like Scott Brooker."

"At least he didn't get away with it in the end," she says.

"If they convict me, he will have gotten away with it, in a way. You'd be disgusted by how many people think he's a friggin' saint. I don't know if you're religious, but I found a picture of his gravestone online, at an Illinois cemetery. It says *Devoted*

Christian. We can change it to a permanent legal record that says *Filthy Rapist.*"

"Are you sure my other thing doesn't have to come out?"

"I'm not a lawyer, but if it doesn't involve Brooker I don't see why it would. So what do you think? ... Mary?"

I turn on the speaker and hold the phone out to Rebecca so she can hear the silence. "Mary? Are you still there?"

"Okay. I'll do it."

28

SITTING ON my bunk in the predawn darkness, dressed in my suit, hair in a tight bun, face made up, I wondered about the meaning of *hope* and came to the conclusion that the whole concept is iffy because it can mean everything and nothing at the same time. I hope Mary shows up. I hope Paula does a good job. I hope Judge Hanks doesn't already hate me. But that's all it is: *hope.* Everything if it comes true. Nothing if it doesn't. Snap your fingers and it's gone.

I called Lucas before the guards came to fetch me. He hates being woken up, but sounded alert, like he was waiting.

"I don't know what's going to happen," I said. "What if they send me away and I never see you again?"

"Think positive. Glass-half-full girl. 'Member who you are."

"I'm not sure who or what I am anymore." I force a laugh. "Not like I've ever had a completely firm grasp on it."

"You know exactly who you are. Say it."

"I am Emily-the-Powerful."

"Not like a weakling, like a warrior."

"*I–Am–Emily–The–Powerful.*"

"That's better. Never forget it." He ended the conversation by saying he'd *be around.* I asked around what and he said, "Just around."

Rebecca and I are sipping instant coffee from paper cups when I hear the COs coming to escort me to the parking lot. We stand simultaneously and I wrap my arms around her. "I love you," I say.

"I can't breathe," she replies.

I let go. "Sorry. Can you do me a favor? I probably won't be back until after dinner. If you see Lola, will you ask her if Ben was back in GED today?"

"I will."

"I'll try not to wake you up if it's late."

"I won't be asleep." She stands on her toes and looks over my shoulder. "I saw you finished your drawing for Ben. It's really good."

My self-portrait. I left it spread on top of the lockers. "Thanks. I still wish I had a pencil though."

"Do you want me to give it to him if you don't come back?"

"Huh? I'm coming back."

"Just in case."

"Yeah, sure. Give it to him. But I'm coming back ... aren't I?"

"Of course," she chirps with her tightened lips sliding in opposite directions.

* * *

I'm within elbow-bumping distance of Paula at the defense counsel table. Her neat stacks of files protect us like a castle wall. Leslie's table is empty except for a legal pad and pen. There are more people in the courtroom than before, including extra guards and another assistant for Leslie.

I whisper to Paula, "Why does Leslie get two assistants and we don't get any?"

She pats my hand. "You're my assistant."

Brooker's wife and daughter sit behind the prosecutor's table, *behind the bar,* a wood barrier separating the combatants from the spectators. *Tammy* and *Dulcie.* I saw their names on the witness list. They're dressed up. Everyone is. The big event. The daughter, Dulcie, catches me looking. I expect to see hatred, but she's wearing the same vacant look as before.

"Remember what we talked about," Paula says.

"I know. Behave myself. Keep my mouth shut."

Leslie shuffles papers, looking poised and pretty in a sleek black pants suit. I look pretty good myself. Paula hardly recognized me. The shoes she brought me fit, but they're round-toed flats. I wish I had a pair of spiked heels like Leslie's. On the other hand, I've never actually worn heels. While other girls were practicing with them, I was learning how to kill people.

Paula's the only one not looking too hot. Dark circles give her raccoon eyes and sweat glistens once again on her forehead.

"Paula, are you okay?" I ask.

An unconvincing nod.

The bailiff launches into his *Oyez, Oyez* recitation, which ends with him asking God to save the State. Am I the only one who thinks that's a weird way to start a criminal trial? Who cares about saving the State? How about save the freaking Defendant?

Everyone stands as Judge Hanks enters from behind the bench wearing his black robe and quiff of thick black hair. We all wait while he gets comfortable in his royal seat.

"Good morning, everyone," he says. "Is there any business to take up before we begin this trial?"

Paula stands, leaning to her left. "Judge, there's been a late development in the defense case. The defense moves to add a new witness. I left a copy of the motion for you on the bench."

"Now?" he says. "One minute before trial?" He picks up the motion and scans it.

"I apologize, Your Honor. We—*I* just discovered her over the weekend. Her name is Mary Brinson. She will testify that a man we believe to be Mr. Brooker sexually assaulted her not long before the incident involving my client."

"Lies!"

It's Brooker's wife, on her feet. The judge admonishes her to sit down and be quiet.

Paula continues. "The Louisiana criminal code expressly provides that evidence of prior sexual acts against a minor is admissible to show predisposition."

"Response, Ms. Tierney?"

"First of all, Judge, as every lawyer in the state except apparently Ms. Dunwoody knows, that statute applies to criminal defendants, not *murder victims*."

Paula ignores the slight. "We believe the underlying principle—to alleviate the inherent difficulties of proving sexual assault cases involving minors—applies with equal force to my client's self-defense claim."

Leslie mutters something that sounds like *bullshit*. "Dredging up a girl from nowhere as a surprise witness on the day of trial? Come on, Judge. It's an obvious ruse to distract from the facts."

"How do you know that, Leslie?" Paula says. "You haven't even heard the facts."

"Please tell us," Hanks says.

Paula explains all about Mary Brinson from Southaven, Mississippi, including the mole. "She might also be able to identify photographic evidence, which is why our motion includes a request for recent photographs of the decedent."

"You want us to dig him up for a photoshoot?" Leslie says.

"Quiet," Hanks says. "You'll get your turn."

I want to bust a chair over Leslie's head, but Paula says evenly, "We're seeking the most recent photographs available prior to his death."

"How did you discover this witness, Ms. Dunwoody?"

Paula pinches her side and I feel my own gut churning. She clears her throat and swallows. "I'm afraid that's a matter of attorney-client privilege."

"If you can't even tell me how you found her, I'm not inclined to grant the motion," he says.

"With all due respect, Judge," she says, "I'm not sure the court of appeals would look fondly on denying a minor defendant her only witness in a first-degree murder trial."

Whoa! Ballsy! And it works. She has his attention.

"Is the witness here now?"

"No. She's a college student in Memphis. We intend to call her after the state rests its case."

"Ms. Tierney?"

Leslie rants about the unfairness to the state of the timing and lack of reliability of *this alleged witness.*

When she finishes and sits down, Hanks says, "I'll grant the motion—conditionally. You can proffer the testimony. If it's too flimsy, I'll exclude it. Ms. Tierney, how long do you predict the state's case will take?"

"Probably two days, but—"

"You have two days to produce the most recent photographs of Mr. Brooker before his death."

"Judge, the state doesn't possess any such pictures."

"You've listed Mr. Brooker's wife and daughter as witnesses. Work with them. Get it done," he says.

* * *

I'm perched on the edge of my chair for the opening statements, but everything is old news except the part about Mary Brinson. Predictably, Leslie paints me, too convincingly I worry, as a heartless murderer and Paula sets forth my self-defense claim in a soothing wave of air that has my eyelids fluttering.

I've been wishing for a jury, which they don't have in juvenile court, but it's just as well. Leslie would demolish Paula.

The first witness is a man who runs the highway camera system for the state. Leslie uses him to authenticate the pictures of Brooker's car on I-49, first with the blonde girl as a passenger sitting next to Brooker, then as the driver with no Brooker.

"Do you have any doubt that these pictures were taken on the date shown by the timestamp?"

"No doubt whatsoever."

"Let the record reflect that the photos bear the same date the victim was killed.

"Do you have an opinion as to whether the girl in the automobile is the same person as the defendant? For comparison, let me show you a picture of her taken closer to the time of Mr. Brooker's slaying."

She points her clicker and I appear on the screen. It's the Fourth of July picture the media stole from Mom's Facebook page after the murders, with Mom and Becky cropped out. So young and innocent, all gangly, tresses of white hair down to my elbows and teeth too big for my face.

"They look quite similar," he says, "but I can't swear it's her."

"Thank you. No more questions."

I'm waiting for Paula to stand up and rip him to shreds. He's no expert in facial identification. The highway pictures are blurry and were taken through a windshield. Might as well ask the court reporter if the pictures look like me.

Judge Hanks says, "Questions, Ms. Dunwoody?"

"No questions."

The judge tells the witness he's excused, reminding him that the proceedings are confidential by law.

I stick my face in front of Paula, pinching my lips to keep my fury from overriding my vow of silence.

She waves me off as Leslie calls the next witness, the head of security for the mall in Lafayette where I dumped Brooker's Lexus. As the video of me wiping down Brooker's car plays, he explains the parking lot camera system, including how the videos are time-stamped and stored.

"Do you have an opinion as to whether the girl in the video is the same person as the defendant?"

"It looks like the same girl."

I grab Paula's forearm. The video is grainy, low resolution. All I see is a blonde mop. She pries my hand loose and flattens it on the table.

"No more questions, Your Honor," Leslie says and returns to her chair.

"Questions, Ms. Dunwoody?"

"No, Your Honor."

WTF! Did she get stage fright? This time I practically yank her arm off. She suddenly stands. "Judge, may I please have a moment to confer with my client? In private?"

"You absolutely may. Her gyrations are distracting even from here. Take her into the hall. If you need me to put her back in restraints, just say so."

"That won't be necessary, but thank you."

I follow Paula into the hall, steaming.

She waits until the door seals, looks to make sure the hall is clear, and says, "I've had just about enough of you. What is your problem?"

"You just *sat* there. Those witnesses could have been attacked. There's no way they could say for sure that was me."

"They didn't. They said the pictures and video looked like you. They do."

"Why can't you be more like Leslie?" I say, instantly regretting it when I see the wound I inflicted.

"Leslie and I have different personalities and styles. I'm sorry you don't like mine. There's no point fighting just for the sake of fighting. I pick my battles. Remind me again, what's your defense?"

"Self-defense."

"That means that, unless you change your mind again, you're going to be taking the witness stand and testifying you killed Brooker."

Duh. "Which means there's no point arguing I wasn't in the car," I say, embarrassed. "I'm an idiot. You should punch me in the face."

"Maybe some other time. I can only be who I am, Emily. Let me ask you this. Who has the judge got annoyed with this morning—besides you, that is?"

"Leslie," I say sheepishly.

She rests a hand on my shoulder. "Ready to go back in?"

I nod.

* * *

Hanks declared a recess at noon. A guard took me and Paula to a small interview room and brought us boxed lunches and bottles of water. Each box contained a club sandwich, bag of chips and a dill pickle. The lettuce was wilted and the bacon as tough as a dog chew, but I was hungry and gobbled everything down. Paula picked at her food and ended up giving me her chips and pickle.

I apologize again for my childish behavior and tell Paula she's doing great. She says thanks, but something is off in her eyes.

"Are you sure everything is alright?"

"Well, you know me, I just worry. I hope Mary Brinson comes through."

"She will. I know she will." Of course I don't know any such thing. "Is everything okay physically?"

Another wrenched smile. "Hanging in there."

The afternoon witness is the coroner, an antsy old guy with chunky glasses wearing an oversized white lab coat. His reedy voice seems to increase in volume in proportion to the gruesomeness of his testimony. I know what happened because I was there, but as bad as it was, it sounds even worse dressed up in the language of a postmortem examination.

Leslie says, "Did you notice anything peculiar about the stab wounds inflicted on Mr. Brooker?"

He rubs his hands together like a man who enjoys his work. "Indeed I did. Most stab wounds I encounter are not very interesting."

"Meaning?"

"They bear no logic, show no forethought. They usually look like exactly what they are, the chaotic result of someone who got mad or drunk and grabbed a knife."

"What was different about Mr. Brooker's stab wounds?"

The coroner glances at me, sitting prim and proper in my suit, back straight as a board, hands folded on the table.

"They were not random. It's my opinion that whoever inflicted them knew exactly what they were doing."

"Why do you say that?"

"Let's start with the groin wound." He clicks through pictures on the screen until he finds a close-up. "See where it is? Right behind the testicular sac in the pelvic gap."

The bailiff grabs his crotch.

"It's a soft spot few people outside of physicians would even know exists. It would require skill to inflict such a wound. I've been a coroner for thirty years and have never seen anything like it."

Lucas was an awesome teacher and I practiced really hard, but Brooker put me in the perfect position to execute the move.

"Never in thirty years," Leslie echoes. "What about the neck cut?"

He switches to a picture of it. "Well, it's a slash wound, as you can see, not a puncture wound like the other one. A bit over ten centimeters in length. What stands out about it is how straight and perfectly targeted it was. Right across the carotid artery." He shoots another questioning glance my way before adding, "The carotids provide ninety percent of the blood to the brain."

Crying breaks out behind me. Brooker's wife. She stands and scoots past her daughter out of the courtroom. The coroner waits until the door closes behind her before continuing.

"The groin wound would have caused severe internal bleeding, but this neck cut is what did the trick."

"Tell us what you mean by *did the trick*."

"It killed him. He would have lost consciousness in a matter of seconds and bled to death in minutes."

* * *

The day ended with me wondering again whether I made a mistake switching from denying everything to claiming self-defense. Based on the coroner's testimony, we would have had a good argument that no thirteen-year-old girl could have possibly pulled off such mayhem. The way he kept looking at me showed he doubted it himself.

But I came to the same conclusion as always: once they found my DNA in Brooker's car, I had no choice.

As the last order of business, the judge dropped a bomb on me. He sent me to a lockup in Saint Landry for the night, an adult unit where they put me in *protective custody*, i.e., solitary. I argued, or got Paula to, that I wanted to be taken back to Pochachant, but he wasn't having it, said it would be *inefficient*.

I worked out in my cell, partly out of boredom, partly to relieve my pent-up desperation. I pressed myself to the limit, making it to sixty-three push-ups on the grimy floor before collapsing.

Then I laid in my bunk, gross and sweaty, feeling depleted and defeated. I started the morning with confidence, only to feel it drain away hour by hour.

Everything is going to depend on Mary Brinson.

29

DAY TWO of *State of Louisiana v. Emily Blair Calby aka Alice Black* begins with the testimony of the crime scene investigator, a lanky black guy with a baritone voice and thick mustache that covers his upper lip like a brush. Lieutenant Malcolm.

On the screen is a panoramic photo of a bayou, idyllic and peaceful except for the dead man floating in the water with his pants pulled down.

"So that's how you found him?" Leslie says.

"Yes."

"Lieutenant, do you have an opinion as to why his body would be in water?"

"Objection. Speculation," Paula says.

"Sustained."

"Let me ask it this way. Could you tell whether he fell into the water or was put there intentionally?"

"Put there. You can see the tracks where his body was pulled across the mud." He traces them with a laser pointer. "It would have taken quite a strong person to do it." He glances at me with the same incredulity as the coroner.

"Would putting a body in the water be consistent with an effort to hide it?"

"I can't think of any other reason."

Paula: "Move to strike. Same objection."

"Sustained."

Leslie doesn't disguise annoyance well. We're alike that way.

"You can just say yes or no, Lieutenant. In your experience, would putting a murder victim's body in the water be consistent with an effort to hide it?"

"Yes."

"Thank you. Did you detect any other efforts to conceal the body?"

He clicks on a picture of the big branch. "When we discovered the decedent, this large tree branch was parked alongside him, blocking the view from the road. You can see from this rut that it was dragged there from another place."

"Thank you. Now I'd like to turn your attention to the victim's belongings. Specifically, did he have anything of value on his person?"

"Just his clothes."

"What about in his automobile?"

"Nothing. Someone had cleaned it out. The interior and a portion of the exterior had been wiped down with a solution of sodium hypochlorite, what we typically call bleach. The swipe marks were consistent with some type of cleansing wipe."

"Did you subsequently discover any of the victim's belongings?"

"About six months after the incident, a fisherman came across a briefcase floating in the bayou, about a half-mile from where the body was found. It contained some of the victim's personal belongings, including his wallet."

"How did you know it was his wallet?"

"His driver's license and credit cards were in it, along with a photo of his wife and daughter. The photo had largely disintegrated from the water, but his family was able to identify it." He dips his head in respect to Tammy and Dulcie Brooker.

"Had efforts been made to conceal the briefcase?"

"It appeared so. Holes had been punched in it with a sharp object and it also contained rocks."

"Any fingerprint or DNA evidence?"

"No, unfortunately. Everything had deteriorated from exposure to the elements."

"Was there any cash in the wallet?"

"No."

"Nothing? Not even a dollar?"

"Not even a dollar."

"No more questions."

Paula surprises me by getting up. "Lieutenant Malcolm, has it been your experience that individuals who rob other individuals usually take their credit cards?"

"Usually."

"Let me ask you this. Were there any holes in the groin area of the decedent's pants or underpants?"

"Holes?"

"Yes. Specifically holes that could have been made by a knife?"

"I don't recall."

"Can't you check?"

"Unfortunately, the clothes were not preserved."

How convenient. I wouldn't be surprised if Leslie took them out and burned them herself. Paula spends several minutes delving into how that could have happened, but in the end, Malcolm just shrugs and says, "I'm not sure, ma'am."

"*Assuming* there were no holes in his pants or underpants, wouldn't that suggest the decedent already had his pants down when the groin wound occurred?"

Great question, Paula!

"I suppose, but again, I don't recall one way or the other."

Eyebrows stitched in frustration, "And you can't check because you failed to preserve the evidence. No more questions."

She returns to the counsel table frowning as Leslie stands up.

"Redirect, Judge. Lieutenant, you said individuals who rob others usually take their credit cards. Why not always?"

"Because some people are smart enough to know that credit cards are easily traced."

That's me.

"Thank you." She sits down and Hanks excuses Malcolm with the confidentiality reminder.

"Call your next witness," Hanks says.

"The state calls Officer William Talley of the Lafayette Parish Parks Department."

Except for his clothes, a coat and tie in place of his khaki park ranger uniform, Officer Talley hasn't changed a bit since the night he tried to take me into custody at Acadiana Park. Same tawny hair, intense brown eyes and pointy nose. Leslie starts off with questions establishing his credentials and the timeline.

"Did you have occasion during this time period to be introduced to the defendant, Emily Calby?"

"I did. Except she said her name was Alice."

"I see. Please describe the circumstances of that meeting."

Talley explains that he received a report about a young girl staying in the park alone and confronted me when I was leaving the showers. He was about to haul me in as a runaway when my *aunt* came to the rescue. Darla. I met her and Peggy at the campground that morning.

"Would it surprise you, Officer Talley, if I told you the defendant was using a false name and had no aunt?"

"It would not surprise me one little bit," he says in a tone that makes it clear he's still pissed off I tricked him.

"With what degree of confidence can you say the girl sitting at the defense table is the same girl you saw in Acadiana Park in Lafayette three years ago?"

"One-hundred percent."

I whisper to Paula. "Why is she going through all this trouble to show I was there? Like you said, I'm going to be admitting I killed him."

"She's probably worried you'll change your mind again."

"I can do that?"

She looks at me in horror. "We'll talk later."

Talley wraps up his testimony without any questions from Paula. Of course. Hanks tells Leslie to call the next witness.

"The state calls Gwendolyn Grandemeire," she announces.

Who?

The bailiff opens the door to the main hallway and hollers, "Gwendolyn Grandemeire."

A white-haired woman gripping an aluminum walker enters and wheels her way slowly to the witness box. The bailiff gives her a hand when she gets there.

OMG, it's the grandma librarian from Lafayette who told me I smelled bad when I was using the computers. The bailiff swears her in and Leslie leads her through a series of questions about her background and the time frame.

"Mrs. Grandemeire, do you remember meeting the defendant in that period during the course of your employment at the Lafayette public library."

"Oh, yes. Hello, dear," she waves with a smile.

I wave back. Leslie frowns.

"Were you able to pin down the dates when this occurred?" she says.

"Yes. I checked the computer sign-in records like you asked and found she was a frequent library visitor during the third week of July of that year."

"Please describe your interactions with her."

"Alice was in Lafayette taking care of her sick grandmother. Such a sweet girl. She would leave every day to go make her grandmother's favorite lunch. I believe it was egg salad, maybe tuna."

I'm such a friggin' liar. Hard to believe I didn't start practicing until the day everything went off the rails.

"Did you notice any change in her during this roughly one-week period?"

She lowers her voice. "I don't like to say it, but a library guest complained she had a very strong body odor. But when I mentioned it to her, she promised she would smell better when she returned, and she did. I never had another problem with her."

"Thank you, but I was referring to her physical appearance."

"I see. Well, at one point Alice dyed her hair. It was blonde, like it is now, but one day she came in as a brunette." She turns up her hands. "You know teenage girls."

"Not particularly," Leslie says. "You say her name is Alice?"

"That's right. Alice Miller. I double-checked it in the sign-in records."

"And you're sure she was staying with her grandmother, not, say, an aunt?"

"Yes, I remember it because it made me wish I had a granddaughter like her. Not to criticize my own grandchildren, of course. I adore them, but I don't see any of them ever coming over to make me lunch, if you get my drift."

Here it comes, I can tell by the gleam in Leslie's eyes and the way her hip juts out from the lectern.

"What would your reaction be if I told you the defendant is a liar, that her real name is Emily Calby, not Alice Miller, and that she never had a grandmother in Lafayette?"

"Well ... oh my."

"No more questions."

Such a bitch! That was mean to ambush her like that, embarrass her.

"Questions, Ms. Dunwoody?"

"A few."

Of all the witnesses to cross-examine, Paula picks sweet grandma. Way to go, Paula. Let's go fight a mouse next week.

"Hello, Mrs. Grandemeire. I'm Paula Dunwoody. I'm the defendant's lawyer."

"Very nice to meet you."

"I think I actually remember you from when I was a girl. I grew up in Lafayette and my mother took me to the library every week."

She chuckles. "That's quite possible. I worked there for more than thirty years. I still would be except, well ..." She points to the walker. "Osteoarthritis."

"I'm very sorry to hear that. How would you describe your course of dealing with the defendant?"

"Very pleasant."

"You liked her?"

"Oh, yes."

"If you had to pick a word to describe her, what would it be?"

"Well, let's see, I'm a librarian, so I love words. Polite, very inquisitive. She was always researching on the computers. Effervescent for sure. And a tad malodorous on that one occasion." She chuckles again.

"Accepting what the prosecutor said as true, that she made up a name and didn't really have a grandmother in Lafayette, would you trust her?"

She puts a fingertip to her double-chin and looks me over. I offer a contorted look that's half-plea, half-apology.

"I think I would. If she made those things up, she must have had a good reason."

I can't believe it. Paula played her instinct—and won. So non-Paula. All the books say to never ask a question on cross-examination that you don't already know the answer to.

Leslie looks like she wants to bury a hatchet in Mrs. Grandemeire's skull as Judge Hanks excuses her as a witness.

* * *

We break for lunch and a guard leads us to the same interview room. Today's lunchboxes hold tuna on a croissant and roast beef on a French roll. I give Paula her pick and she takes the tuna.

"Awesome job with Mrs. Grandemeire," I say, squirting a packet of mayo on the roast beef. "How do you think things are going so far?"

"About as expected."

"That bad, huh?" No response. It's impossible to get a laugh out of Paula anymore.

"The coroner and crime scene investigator raised the bar for us on a couple of things."

"I know the first one. How could a thirteen-year-old girl kill a man like a ninja assassin if she was an innocent victim?"

"You got it. Technically, it's not relevant to whether you were acting in self-defense, but it is going to take some explaining, so start thinking. Leslie's going to argue that your, um, *skillset*, fits the profile of an aggressor more than a victim."

"What's the other thing?"

"Did you take Mr. Brooker's money?" she asks point-blank.

I hesitate. "Yes. About two hundred dollars, from his wallet."

Her cringe says she doesn't like that answer.

"But that's not why I killed him. It was an afterthought. I told you, all my money got stolen with my backpack in Shreveport. ... I guess that's not a good legal excuse for stealing."

"Not optimal. Charging you with murder in the first-degree is based on the theory that you killed Brooker during the course of an armed robbery."

"I could just lie. No one knows about the money."

Vigorous headshake. "I can't let you lie under oath. That's perjury, a felony. I'd have to recuse myself as your lawyer if you did that. And keep in mind they already have a fairly good case without the money because you stole his car."

"I only did that to get away. Isn't it obvious? I dumped it as soon as I got to Lafayette. I didn't try to sell it or anything. ... Do you think I should have stuck with denying everything instead of switching to self-defense?"

"Believe me, I've pondered that question many times. The pictures and video look like you, but not beyond a reasonable doubt. But if your DNA is in Brooker's car ... well, that's different."

"Exactly. That's why I changed my mind when Leslie said it at the discovery conference."

"We should have talked about it first. Blurting out in court that you killed him was a bad move."

A bleak nod. "Bad moves are my specialty. Who's the DNA expert? She said back then she didn't have a specific person yet."

She shuffles papers. "Dr. Riley Carson, a geneticist at the University of Texas."

"Is she any good?"

"Never heard of her, or him. Could be a him. We'll find out after lunch. It's Leslie's last witness except for rebuttal."

"What's rebuttal?"

"After we put on your case, Leslie's going to be able to bring in her character witnesses to testify about what a wonderful person Brooker supposedly was."

"That's where the mother and daughter come in, huh?"

"And the reverend from his church."

"Do I stand a chance? Just be honest."

Her shoulders sink like I just lowered the moon onto them. "Let's call Mary Brinson."

"Okay. Before we do I forgot to tell you something about her." She closes her eyes. "Go ahead."

"It's nothing bad. Mary told me she had a secret that no one could know about. That's part of what was holding her back from testifying. I asked if it had anything to do with Brooker and she said no, so I told her it couldn't come out in court."

"You really shouldn't be giving legal advice."

"Was I wrong?"

"I know you get tired of hearing this answer, but it depends. Personal matters outside the scope of the case are usually inadmissible because they're not considered relevant, but the rules of evidence are filled with exceptions."

"Big surprise."

She unlocks her phone and holds it up like she's making a toast. "Here's to hope."

Hope. Everything if it comes true. Nothing if it doesn't.

Mary answers and Paula puts her on speaker, explaining she's with me. We exchange hellos. Mary says she's eating a late lunch in the student center before her last class and can't talk long.

It's not until I hear "I'm leaving for Louisiana after class" that I realize I've been holding my breath. My relief is audible. Paula holds up a *shhh* finger.

Paula offers to let Mary stay at her house but she says she's spending the night in Lafayette with a friend from high school. I guess she didn't tell her parents. They'd be driving her, wouldn't they? She promises to be at the courthouse by eight.

"Thank you again, Mary," I say. "I appreciate it *so* much. More than anything in the universe."

"Well, I have some reading to do before class. I'll see you in the morning," she says and disconnects before we can say goodbye.

Paula turns off her phone and we sit looking at each other.

"She doesn't sound too thrilled about it," I say, breaking the silence.

"No, but she said she's coming."

"Yep. That's what she said."

* * *

"Ms. Tierney, call the state's next witness," Hanks says as the afternoon session commences.

Here goes. The final nail in my coffin. It *has* to be the drop of blood on the floorboard carpet from when I cut myself. I took my time cleaning that car. Leslie stands and I wait to hear, "The state calls Dr. Riley Carson," but those aren't the words.

"No more witnesses," she says. "The state rests."

I turn to Paula and whisper, "What about the DNA expert?" She shrugs.

Hanks says, "You have one more witness listed. A Dr. Riley Carson."

"Given that the defendant is going to testify she was present at the scene and did indeed kill Mr. Brooker, we decided not to waste the court's time or the state's money with Dr. Carson's testimony."

"Very well. Is the defense ready to proceed with its case?"

Paula stands. "Your Honor, we weren't expecting to begin to-day, based on Ms. Tierney's estimate of two days for the state's case. We only have two witnesses. My client and Mary Brinson, who won't be here until tomorrow. Would it be possible to recess until morning?"

"Sounds reasonable to me. Ms. Tierney?"

I expect her to object, but she says, "That's fine, Judge."

Hanks allows me to meet with Paula before they ship me back to the Saint Landry jail for the night. I never thought I'd miss Pochachant, but I do. I wonder what Rebecca's doing, and Ben. Is he still in the hospital? Where's Lucas? I need my phone!

I wait in the interview room while Paula takes a bathroom break. She returns with two bottles of water from the vending machine.

"Alright," she says. "This is actually good for us. Gives us one more chance to go through your testimony."

"Don't you think it's a little weird that Leslie called off her DNA witness?"

"She's probably satisfied she has you boxed in to testify. And she might have been telling the truth about saving the state money. We're all under budget pressure. Expert witnesses charge hundreds of dollars an hour."

"Why would Leslie go all the way to Texas to get an expert anyway?"

"Enough about Leslie. Let's go through your testimony from beginning to end—direct and cross. Fair warning, I'm going to probe much harder about your *self-defense skills*. That's how you should refer to them tomorrow. Leslie is going to be all over it. Be careful about your word choices."

I spend two hours answering Paula's questions, her stopping to correct me the whole way through. "Don't say, *That's when I had to stab him.* Say, *That's when I had to exercise my right of self-defense.*"

She finally sets down her pad, looking spent. "That about wraps it up. One last question. I think I know your answer, but it's my job to ask. Christy Thompson submitted her psychological report last night."

"Did she say I lied on my tests?"

"No, but she gave her opinion you're still suffering from PTSD. She devoted most of the report to the disorders you were diagnosed with three years ago ... I didn't know about those. I'm so sorry."

Her shoulders slouch another inch. Paula apologizes too much, but it's never just words. It's like she takes on other people's pain as her own. I even saw it in court when Mrs. Grandemeire said she couldn't work anymore because of her osteoarthritis.

"What's the question?" I say.

"I just wanted to raise the possibility of me approaching Leslie about a plea deal due to ..."

"Diminished capacity? No thanks. Makes me sound like a cripple. Besides, you heard Leslie at the probable cause hearing. She's going to prosecute me to the max."

"Maybe she'll change her mind after reading the psychological report. It's so heartbreaking."

"You think Leslie has a heart? It doesn't matter anyway. I'm innocent. Even if no one believes me," I say.

With a flicker of hurt in her eyes, "I believe you, but I also know that innocent people sometimes get convicted. Like I said, it was my job to ask."

The guard knocks on the door and says it's time to take me to the jail.

Paula gathers up her files. "I'll see you in the morning. Mary said she'll be here at eight. That will give me time to speak with her before court starts. Try to get some good rest. It's going to be a long hard day." She pulls a tissue from her purse and dabs her forehead.

"You too, Paula. Take care of yourself. Seriously."

30

DAY THREE. I'm in the back of the van on the way to the courthouse. My new suit is damp and rumpled. Sweat rings stain the underarms of my blouse and a smear of mayonnaise from yesterday's lunch defaces the front. I haven't had a shower since I left Pochachant because there are no juvie facilities at the jail. I tried to wash my hair in the cell sink, but the water pressure is bad and I couldn't get all the soap out. It looks even worse, oily and stringy.

It was so important to me to look good on the witness stand, not like the *gutter rat* Leslie called me. A small thing compared to all my other problems, but it makes me want to cry.

We pull into the alley behind the courthouse. "Could you tell me the time?" I ask through the cage that separates the animal in the back from the humans in front.

"A little past eight," the driver says.

I repeat a prayer that became a mantra last night. *Please let Mary Brinson be here.*

When they take me into the courtroom and I see Paula sitting alone, head resting on her folded arms, I feel sick. I scan the room as the guards undo my restraints. Same people as before. No new college-age girl. They lead me to the defense table.

"Hi, Paula," I say quietly.

She bolts upright. "Oh, hi Emily."

"She's not here is she?" I say.

"Well, she's only fifteen minutes late. She's probably on her way."

"Yeah, probably," I say. "Are you okay?" Her eyes look like they're filled with glue and the sweat on her forehead has spread to her neck.

"Honestly, I've been better. I'm sure it's just stress."

"You still have your doctor appointment today, right?"

"I do, but if it looks like it's going to interrupt your testimony, I'll call and reschedule it."

"No! I mean, that's not necessary. If that happens ... it will give me a break and time to regroup. Go to the doctor."

I look at the wall clock. Eight-twenty and my defense is dead before it even started.

"Did you call her?" I say.

"I did. Twice. No answer."

"Have you tried texting? You know, sometimes we don't answer the phone," *we* meaning everyone in the universe except old people like Paula.

"Good idea." She fumbles with her phone with trembly hands.

"Do you mind if I try it?"

"That might be better."

I find Mary in her contacts.

Hi Mary. It's me. Emily. I'm at the courthouse with Paula. Where in the world are you?

I back up and replace the last sentence with *Are you getting close?*

No reply. She probably chickened out. A part of me always thought she would. I set the phone on the table and sit next to Paula in silence.

"All rise," the bailiff bellows when the clock hits eight-thirty. Judge Hanks enters with his usual steely poker-face. The bailiff waits until he gets situated before *oyez*-ing court back into session.

"Is the defense ready to proceed?" Hanks says.

Paula uses the table to push herself out of her chair and slowly makes her way to the lectern. "Your Honor—"

"Louder," Hanks says. "I can't hear you."

She leans into the microphone. "Your Honor, we've run into a bit of a problem. Our witness, Mary Brinson, has not yet arrived. We're in the process of trying to locate her."

"Is she on her way?"

"We honestly don't know. We spoke to her yesterday and she said she would be here at eight. We've been unable to reach her this morning."

"Can't you begin with your client's testimony?"

"We were hoping to have a chance to talk with Ms. Brinson before we started, since she's our only outside witness."

"Are you suggesting we sit around and wait?"

"If we could have a short recess, it's possible she might still show up."

"*Possible*," Leslie scoffs.

"Leslie," Paula says with forced calm. "I'm asking you as a colleague and officer of the court to please join my request for a short recess. I know you want to win, but my client's life is on the line here."

"All I want is *justice*. As for your little psychopath, get out the world's smallest violin."

Right eyebrow jittering madly, "How *dare* you call her that. She's an amazingly strong young woman who's survived a thousand times more pain and hardship than you ever could."

Leslie launches at her like she's ready to fight. "You don't know a damn thing about me or my hardships."

"Show some heart," Paula pleads.

"Like she showed when she butchered Scott Brooker?"

The only time I've seen Paula even close to angry was when she snapped at me in the hall at the beginning of the trial, but right now her eyes are bulging, fists clenched and shaking.

"Your Honor, please, I'm only asking for ... for ..." Her face goes ashen as she grabs for her side and lets out a cry. Her eyes roll back and she falls on the floor.

"Paula!" I scramble over the table and grab her hand. Her

skin is cold and clammy, pulse galloping a hundred miles an hour.

Hanks: "Bailiff! Call an ambulance!"

Paula's gurgling like she's trying to vomit. A cop elbows me out of the way and turns her on her side. I wait and watch help-lessly until a man and woman in white shirts and dark pants burst through the double-doors wheeling in a bright yellow gurney.

"What happened?" the woman asks as they lower the plat-form and lift Paula onto a thin mattress.

"Something's wrong in her gut," I say. "She has irritable bow-el syndrome. She was supposed to go to the doctor today. Right before she fell out, she grabbed right here." I pinch my left side.

The man talks into a radio as the woman tightens restraint belts around Paula. "Subject appears to be in shock," he says. "Possible bowel rupture. Have a surgeon standing by."

They pull up the side rails and roll Paula down the aisle. I trot along behind until a guard blocks me at the door. The gurney cuts the sharp corner into the hallway and disappears.

Everyone's on their feet, even Judge Hanks. "This court will be in recess for thirty minutes. Bailiff, take the defendant to the interview room."

* * *

Sitting alone at the wide counsel table when we reassemble, I feel like I'm stranded on an island. Paula's protective embank-ment of files has been swept clean, along with every other trace of her. Purse, phone, pads, pens. Like she never existed. Judge Hanks just announced he has bad news.

"I have received a report from the hospital regarding Ms. Dunwoody's condition. She did indeed suffer a ruptured intes-tine and is being operated on as I speak. It's a very serious sit-uation. I know you will all join me in sending her our prayers."

I bow my head with my hands clasped. I don't dare look at

Leslie because if I detected even a hint of her usual smirk, I'd stab her in the face with my pen.

Hanks says, "We are now faced with what to do about Ms. Calby's case. The only options are to declare a mistrial or appoint another public defender to continue."

"I favor option number two," Leslie says. "The state has already expended a great deal of time and energy in this case."

I raise my hand.

"Ms. Calby?"

"What's a mistrial?"

"It means we start over."

"When?"

"I'm not sure. It could take several weeks to find this much open time on the docket."

I'm never going to be more ready to testify than I am right now. "Your Honor, several weeks might not seem like a long time to you, but I'm stuck in a prison. I agree with Ms. Tierney. I want to continue."

"You realize that appointing a new lawyer midtrial could put you at a severe disadvantage compared to someone like Ms. Dunwoody, who's worked on your case since the start."

"Oh, I realize it a lot. That's why I don't want a new lawyer. I make a motion to represent myself."

Even though I expected Leslie's sarcastic laugh, it still grates on my nerves. She says, "Judge, as entertaining as that would be to watch, the state objects to risking reversal of this case on appeal because the defendant wants to play lawyer in her dress-up clothes."

"It would be a sight to behold," Hanks agrees.

I clear my throat. "With all due respect, Judge, could we please discuss the relevant law?"

Chastened, Hanks says, "Court reporter, strike my last comment."

"The Supreme Court says I have a constitutional right to represent myself. I believe it was in *Farena v. California*." I can't believe I pulled that out of my … I read about it in the criminal procedure treatise. I guess the idea appealed to me even then.

Hanks tilts his head. "It's *Faretta*. Did Ms. Dunwoody tell you about that?"

"I looked it up myself. I've been studying the law, every day, in the law library at Pochachant."

"Ms. Calby, I appreciate your pluck or courage or whatever you want to call it, but that would be a serious mistake. There's an old saying in the law. *A lawyer who represents himself has a fool for a client.* Have you ever heard it?"

"I haven't heard that one, Judge, but if you're calling me a fool, I ask that the record reflect it."

He shakes his head at the court reporter. "Folks, this has been a trying day for everyone. Ms. Calby, I will take your request under advisement. We will recess until Monday morning, at which time we will resume with a *Faretta* hearing."

Huh, even has a name. I have a lot of research to do.

Leslie says, "Is it really worth waiting that long to deny her ridiculous motion?"

"This will give everyone time to study the issue and we'll also know more about Ms. Dunwoody's condition."

"One more thing, Your Honor," I say. "I request to be taken back to Pochachant. They have me locked up in protective custody in an adult unit. I can't even take a shower. I believe that's called cruel and unusual punishment under the law."

"No, it's not. You see, that is the difference between knowing some legal jargon and understanding the law. However, I do agree it would be more appropriate given the lack of juvenile facilities here. Over the recess, I want you to think long and hard about your request. Your life is at stake."

Exactly. *My* life.

31

MY RIDE BACK to Pochachant got delayed for hours because no van was available. I couldn't get out of that courthouse fast enough. It's just another prison with nicer furniture, and without Paula, enemies all around me.

The CO who takes me to my cell is new, a woman with reddish-brown kewpie curls. COs come and go at Pochachant almost as fast as prisoners. She says her last job was at a Wendy's.

It's already lights out and the halls are quiet and eerie. I can hear my footsteps for the first time.

Worn out. I can't wait to get back to my own bunk. Funny how everything in life is relative to your circumstances. Dirt can be gold if it's all you got.

I tell the CO my cellie's asleep and ask her to let me in quietly. I tiptoe through the dark, yanking off the dirty suit. The lump in Rebecca's bunk doesn't stir. I wish she were awake but I feel better just being near her.

My nightshirt is where I left it, folded under my pillow. I press it to my face, glad it still smells like me. I got it in a trade for two bags of Skittles I bought at the commissary for a girl with a sugar addiction. It has a fat cat on the front saying, *I'm CLAWSOME*. Kind of juvenile, but I like it.

Too tired even to call Lucas. I'll do it in the morning. He must have figured out they've been keeping me in Saint Landry. I slip under the covers, adjust my pillow and try to unwind.

"Welcome back," Rebecca says.

"Augh, faker!" I leap from my bunk and land on top of her, planting kisses as she faux resists. I start tickling her, like I used to do to Becky.

Cackling, "Stop, stop." I finally discovered how to make her laugh.

I roll off. We barely fit side by side on the narrow mattress. "It's crazy, but it feels good to be back. Hard to believe I was only gone three days. Seemed like forever ... so much happened."

I know she's dying to know what, but *State v. Calby* is the last thing I want to talk about right now. "What's been going on here? Any news about Ben?"

"He's out of the hospital and back in GED."

"Great! Did Lola tell you?"

"She didn't have to. Everyone knows. You know how the girls love drama, anything to spice up the boredom. So first dreamy Ben disappears from GED, then *you* disappear, then Ben shows back up with both of his arms in casts, then—"

I groan. "How'd he look otherwise?"

"They say his eyelashes are still there."

"Come on, for real."

"The girls in your GED class say he's fine. They fawn all over him because he looks so pitiful trying to carry his book in his cast-arms."

"Bitches! Nobody can love him like I do."

We collapse in a giggle fit before reality sobers me up. "Poor Ben." I don't remember if I ever formally added Corey Wilkes to the deserves-to-die list. I put him on top. "Did you give him my drawing?"

She points to the lockers. "It's still there. I was going to wait until Monday, a full week, to make sure you weren't coming back."

Except for Lucas, I've never met anyone as brutally honest and practical as Rebecca. I laugh again as my tight-rope nerves begin to loosen and muscles relax. "I should go back to my bunk. I'm so tired I can barely keep my eyes open."

"Oh no you don't. Tell me what happened or I won't be able to sleep."

I recount the past two days, stammering when I get to the end, "Then Paula ..." It starts as a hiccup and escalates to a complete meltdown. All the feelings I've kept caged inside, my own little Pochachant of imprisoned emotions. The despair, fear, loneliness ... They all bust free.

I don't know how much time passes before I'm aware that Rebecca's cradling me like a baby, my tears soaking her nightshirt. We fall asleep like that.

Sister love.

32

SEEING THE BACK of Ben's head as I enter the class-room sets my heart fluttering like hummingbird wings. His hair looks longer. Is that possible in a week and a half? I love the way he tucks it behind his ears and wish I could touch it. Unfortunately, the girls' line is jammed up and I'm stuck at the back of the room. Medillo is already talking by the time I make it to my seat.

The first thing I notice are Ben's delicate fingers sticking out the ends of his bulky casts, which start at his elbows and run to his knuckles. He's dangling his pencil awkwardly over his open workbook. A few people have written on the casts, including a red heart that irks me. He better have saved a big space for me.

Medillo is telling us to get ready for a reading comprehension test. I sit down and smile at Ben as I open my workbook. He smiles back, but it's not what I wanted. Mine is all toothy excitement, Ben's a brittle curl of ambivalence, same as always. The boy needs more effervescence.

Medillo says, "You have thirty minutes by that clock, starting … now."

I write in the margin of my workbook, *I can't believe that happened to you. I've been so worried.* I draw a fractured heart at the end.

Thanks, he scribbles. *I've been worried about you too.*

We both have crazy lives.

Hey, we have to work this test. Talk later?

Can you come to the library today?

Doctor. Tomorrow?

It's a date!!! I have great news for you.

He gives me a perplexed look and goes back to work. I absolutely cannot wait to tell him all about functional interrogation. If anyone ever needed good news besides me, it's Ben. He'll probably just start kissing and hugging me with his casts. I think I'll let him!

I need to sweet-talk Mava into giving us some extra time alone. I missed her too. My peeps.

The first test problem is a business letter with some unfinished sentences we're supposed to complete. Easy, but made harder by watching Ben struggle to write out of the corner of my eye.

Class ends and Ben turns to me, melting me with his soulful eyes. His lashes look like chocolate awnings.

I say, "I got your note, with the heart. It was so sweet. I wanted to write back, but didn't know how to reach you in the hospital and ... I've been sort of occupied."

"I know. I've been thinking about your trial a lot. How's it going?"

"Could be better. I'll tell you about it tomorrow at the library."

I reach for his arm, but he pulls it away, which hurts my feelings until I hear the CO coming up from behind. "No contact, no contact. You know the rules."

Ben gives me a fingertip hand-puppet wave as they take him away. *Prisoners of Love.* I could see it as a movie.

* * *

"Miss Mava! Miss Mava!" I'm just inside the door of the library.

She's clomping down the hall in her wide square heels, thudding bullets.

"Mercy me, look who's here." She leans in for a hug and I

almost pull her on top of me. I can't believe I've turned into such a hugger. The first time Paula touched me I reacted like she was a rattlesnake. I wish I could hug her now.

"Did you miss me?" I say.

"Well, it was nice and quiet around here for a change."

"Oh."

"I'm jokin' you, child. Course I missed you. Ain't easy runnin' this place without the Law Library Director around."

"Aw, you're just being nice."

"How were your court proceedings?"

Ben and Rebecca are the only ones I told about my trial. To everyone else, I just said I had *court proceedings* in Opelousas. "Oh, fine. I have to go back next week. Do you have any work for me?"

"Just the usual things. Some boxes of those supplements came in for your law books."

"I'll get right on them. Can I ask a favor? It's really important or I wouldn't ask."

"What is it?"

"My friend Ben's coming to visit the law library tomorrow. We have so much to talk about. Someone hurt him again in the boys unit. This time he had to go to the hospital."

"I'm sorry to hear that. Pochachant's a dangerous place. No place for kids, that's for sure."

"Is there any way you could maybe distract the CO a little longer than usual, so we could have more time? I really need to talk to him about his case. I found law that might set him free. I'm not making it up. I swear."

"Far be it from Miss Mava to stand in the way of love or justice. I'll get to cooking tonight. Nothing charms those good old boys like food. I'll make a whole picnic if need be."

"Thanks, Miss Mava. You're the best."

The supplements are updates called *pocket parts* because they slide into an envelope built into the back cover of law books. I race through them and stack the empty boxes in the corner.

I set up a work space with a fresh legal pad and new pen. It could take an hour to find *Faretta v. California* in the books. It takes ten seconds on my phone.

The defendant got arrested for grand theft and wanted to represent himself. The judge agreed, but changed his mind after questioning him about his legal knowledge. The guy did okay until the judge tripped him up with something called the hearsay rule.

The case holding is as clear as day: *The Sixth Amendment, when naturally read, thus implies a right of self-representation.* I just need to convince Judge Hanks my decision to waive counsel is knowing and intelligent. Since I haven't done anything intelligent this entire case, it's going to be an uphill battle.

I compile a small stack of books to check out: *Louisiana Criminal Code (Abridged), Criminal Rules of Evidence, Juvenile Justice* and *Trial Advocacy.*

A red-lettered spine catches my attention. *Win Your Case.* Haha, perfect. It's by a guy named Gerry Spence. *America's Winningest Trial Lawyer,* the cover says.

I start with it, keeping my phone beside me. I've struck out all day trying to reach people. I called Lucas the minute I woke up and got sent to voicemail. I've texted Mary Brinson four times with no response. I called the hospital in Opelousas, but the woman said Paula got transferred somewhere and she couldn't tell me where. Apparently, the law is that everybody's medical records are confidential except mine.

Win Your Case draws me in like a magnet. Not a typical law book, that's for sure. Full of passion and power. I take notes as I read. *Be authentic. Know yourself. Admit fear. Connect emotionally.*

The opposite of everything I've been fighting to suppress. The key is to control emotions, channel them into a strategy, not use them to make things worse. The book says to always remember the *three Cs* of a good witness: calm, courteous and considerate. I feel like he's talking directly to me. My focus is so intense I almost miss my phone lighting up. *Lucas!*

I run to the restroom and lock the door. "Lucas," I whisper.

"Where you been? What's goin' on?"

"They kept me in Saint Landry at night. I'm back at Pochachant now."

"So what happened? Is the trial over?"

"*Well*, there were a couple of glitches."

I fill him in on everything and everyone: Paula, Mary Brinson, Brooker's wife and daughter. "So anyway, now I don't have a witness or a lawyer. I go back on Monday and ... oh, one little part I left out."

"Here we go."

"With Paula gone, I thought I might just ..." My voice drifts off.

"Can't hear you. You thought what?"

"I thought ... I'd go ahead and represent myself."

"Say what?"

"Represent myself. Be my own lawyer."

Rapping on the bathroom door. I mute the phone speaker, smothering Lucas's string of profanity.

"Alice?"

"Um, yes, Miss Mava."

"I've been looking for you everywhere. Now I hear talking. Is somebody in there with you?" she says accusingly.

"No, ma'am. Just me. I talk to myself a lot when I'm in the bathroom."

"Oh, well, excuse me then."

I wait for her thudding steps to fade away.

"Lucas, please don't tell me how *fucking stupid* I am. I need your support right now. I'm close to the breaking point. I can feel it. And I've already made up my mind. If I go down, I'm doing it on my terms."

I turn on the faucet while I wait for a reply.

"I can respect that," he finally says. "I'd probably wanna do the same thing. Be just as fucking stupid though."

* * *

"Might as well try her again," Rebecca says. "Nothing to lose."

She's talking about Mary Brinson. We just got back to our cell from dinner, which was bizarro-world because people stared at me the whole time. The competing rumors are:

Number 1. Ben and I tried to escape Pochachant together, but got caught and the COs broke Ben's arms while he was trying to protect me.

Number 2. I've been in solitary for breaking Ben's arms because he cheated on me.

Lola came over to taunt me about it, I thought, but she just wanted to talk about tutoring. I apologized for being so lame lately and promised to be better starting next week, trying, mostly just pretending, to adjust to the idea of being stuck here for a long time.

"She's not going to answer," I say. "I've already sent her six texts."

"Were they mean?"

I open my phone and scan the messages. The lights are still on, but I figured out that if I put my folded pillow on top of the lockers and press against the wall, no one looking in can see me. "They're not that bad, well, maybe a little."

"Like?"

"Here's one that says, *I can't believe you abandoned me!! Thanks a lot!!!* Five exclamation points."

Another cat-sneeze laugh. "I guess it could be worse."

"Actually, that's the nicest one."

"You should learn to meditate. You need to calm your brain."

"Do you meditate?"

"I don't have to. It's built into my head. Send one more text, but make it nice, and apologize for the other ones."

I read out loud as I type. "*Mary, I'm sorry for my other messages. That was very wrong of me. I was just really pissed off.*"

Rebecca hiccups. "Not *pissed off. Disappointed.*"

"I was just really disappointed. I don't blame you for not coming. It's not your fight. Anything else?"

"Tell her Paula's in the hospital. Play on her guilt."

"Yeah, that's good. *It was a bad day. Paula had a ruptured intestine and is in the hospital.*"

"You need something nice at the end."

"I agree." I type it. "How about this? *Whatever else, we will always be sisters because of what happened to us. Peace and love, Emily.*"

Rebecca gives me the okay and I send it.

"What does Rebecca the Seer think will happen? Tell my fortune. Predict my future."

I'm only joking, but with an ominous, unblinking look, she says quickly, "No. I don't want to. I mean, I can't."

The hair on my neck stands up, but before I can react, she points at my phone. The screen is lit up with *Mary Brinson*. I motion Rebecca to come sit with me so she can hear.

"Hi, Mary," I say.

"Um, hi."

"What's up?"

"I'm sorry for ignoring you. I felt bad about not showing up and didn't know what to say."

"I'm sorry for the mean texts. I knew you were never really sure about testifying. I just had my hopes so high because ..." My entire freaking life depended on it. "Well, just because. I wish you could have told us in advance though. It was a pretty big surprise." I picture Paula hitting the floor.

"It was too late. I didn't make up my mind to come back from Lafayette until court started."

"Huh? You were in Lafayette? I thought you never left home."

"I came, like I said I would. I spent the night with my friend from high school, like I told you and Paula. I even had my clothes laid out for court before I went to bed."

"What happened?"

"In the morning, my phone rang. It was a woman. She said she was the prosecutor."

"Leslie Tierney?"

"I think that was it."

"What did she want?"

"She said it was a routine witness interview. I said I didn't feel comfortable talking about something so personal on the phone with someone I didn't know. She asked if you had subpoenaed me. Did you?"

"I don't think so."

"She said if I wasn't subpoenaed I didn't have to show up. Then she said it was her duty to inform me she would be asking me a lot of personal questions in the interest of truth. I remember those words, *in the interest of truth*. Remember when I said I had a secret that no one can know about?"

"Yeah, but you said it didn't involve Brooker. Besides, she won't even know about it if you don't tell her."

"She already knew. I had an abortion when I was eighteen. I never told a soul. My parents are evangelicals. They think all abortions are murder. They'd disown me if they knew. She said she had a record of it."

Rebecca leans her head on my shoulder.

"Leslie's so *effing* sneaky," I say. "I don't know how she got that, but I doubt it can be used as evidence. It's not relevant to anything. And even if she could, juvenile court records are confidential."

"I asked about that. She said something like, *Well, you know, in today's world, nothing stays secret forever*. It sounded like a threat."

Rebecca's cheek rubs my shoulder bone in agreement.

"I couldn't risk it. I'm sorry."

"Is there any possible way I can change your mind?"

Silence before, "I'll be praying for you."

"Okay ... take care."

"You too. Good luck. I hope Paula's okay."

33

ON FRIDAY, I fake a stomach ache to skip GED class and hit the law books. I'll miss seeing Ben, but we never get to talk in class anyway. I'm counting on him showing up at the library. We made a date.

Win Your Case gave me a boost, but it was all strategy, no law. I pour down lukewarm instant coffee and pick up *Criminal Rules of Evidence*. That's how the trial judge tripped up the defendant in *Faretta*, asking what he knew about the hearsay rule of evidence.

I go to the table of contents, my already downgraded ability to concentrate further impaired by the alarm check shrieking through the cellblock. Just as distracting is the alarm bell in my head named Leslie Tierney. Scaring away a witness? That *has* to be illegal. I'll research it at the library. Maybe I can use it against her.

Something else has been nagging at me too, a small shape in a dark corner of my brain I can't make out.

Focus girl. I start with the hearsay rule. Doesn't seem that hard. You can't use out-of-court statements in court if the person who said them isn't there to back them up. Makes sense. Then why is the chapter more than a hundred pages long? ... Because there are twenty-nine exceptions. How can a rule even be called a rule if it has twenty-nine exceptions? That makes the rule the exception.

An out-of-court statement is hearsay only if it is offered to prove the truth of the statement.

What? Why else would it be offered?

The complexities of the hearsay rule are many ...

The bells have stopped ringing outside, but Leslie is still blocking my brain paths. No way am I going to master the hearsay rule in time for trial. I give up and fan pages, my thumb stopping on *Expert Witnesses*.

Expert witnesses are frequently called upon in criminal trials to testify regarding forensic evidence such as DNA. DNA is found in saliva, hair, semen, and blood.

That's it! The dark shape in my brain is named Dr. Riley Carson, the DNA expert who never showed up. I open a browser on my phone and key in the name.

A professional headshot pops up alongside a bio. It's a woman, older than I thought with a first name like Riley. I scroll through her bio. Impressive. Harvard, Yale. She's published four books on genetics. One of them won a prize: *DNA in the Modern Criminal Justice System*.

Dang, I thought maybe Leslie made her up. I go back to the evidence book.

The procedure for "qualifying" an expert to testify involves questioning the witness in court to establish his or her credentials.

Wouldn't take long to qualify Dr. Riley Carson because ... she's beyond qualified. Huh. Why would Leslie need the world's greatest DNA expert for my piddling case? I check over my shoulder for Mava and bury my head behind the mounds of books I set up as a shield. I find Riley Carson's profile again. Her office phone number is at the top. I'm surprised when she answers.

"Riley Carson."

"Oh, hi." Throatier, "This is Leslie Tierney."

"Who?"

"Leslie Tierney, with the prosecutor's office in Saint Landry Parish, Louisiana. I'm calling to talk about the case."

"What case?"

"You know, *the* case."

"No, I'm afraid I don't know."

"The Emily Calby case." No response. "I may have referred to it as the Alice Black case. That's the defendant's alias. ... Blood in the front seat of a Lexus?"

"Who did you say you are?"

I end the call.

Leslie, you lying slut.

She never even talked to Riley Carson, which means she probably never found my DNA in the car. Which means she tricked me into confessing. Me and my big fat impulsive mouth.

I enter a search for *Leslie Tierney*. I did a quick one when I first got the phone, surprised by the lack of information. Except for her picture, the only information on her prosecutor profile was where she went to college and law school, both in Indiana. This time I keep digging until I come to a newspaper interview: *The Prosecutor Defendants Love to Hate.*

> *District Attorney Leslie Tierney doesn't mince words when it comes to what she sees as her primary job duty: "Keeping the creeps away from the rest of us."*
>
> *She's good at it. Tierney, 34, is undefeated with a trial record of 41 and 0, along with hundreds of guilty pleas. Rumor has it she's sent more violent juveniles to adult prison than any prosecutor in the state.*
>
> *Now she's running for district court judge ...*

The thought of Leslie with all the power of a judge is scary.

> *Asked about her reputation for being overly aggressive in prosecuting juveniles, Tierney said, "I'm proud of it. Trust me, we're not talking about truants and shoplifters. The juveniles I focus on are the worst of humanity."*

That's a lie. Ben is definitely not the worst of humanity. I might be a closer call, but not Ben.

Tierney shies away from questions about her personal life, declining to discuss her childhood years or family. "I don't live in the past," she said.

Told that a criminal defense attorney described her as "vengeful," she said, "I don't seek revenge. I only seek justice."

I reread the last lines. Like reading my own words—well, Lucas's. *Justice. Always comes too late, but it's still justice.* He said it the night we met. Getting justice became my purpose for continuing to exist. I even debated the difference between revenge and justice with a preacher in Lafayette.

But I'm nothing like Leslie ... am I?

*   *   *

No yard time today, a rule if you miss GED. I forced in a cell workout before shower time and curled my hair using twisted strips of damp toilet paper, a trick one of the girls taught me.

I'm staring into the stainless steel mirror bolted to the concrete wall, putting on makeup. Even with mascara, my eyelashes aren't as thick as Ben's. I apply a lipstick called *Paramour Pink*, taking extra time to get the lines straight. Lucas would die laughing if he saw me turning into such a priss.

I hear the CO in the hallway, coming to release me to the library. I hold up my self-portrait. I could have done so much better with a pencil. The sad look in my eyes still startles me, somehow more real than even my mirror reflection. I sandwich the drawing between pieces of cardboard I fished out of a trashcan so it doesn't get bent. I hope Rebecca was right about this whole idea and Ben doesn't think I'm stuck-up for giving him a picture of myself.

Crossing the yard, some girls jumping rope hoot and holler at my bouncing curls. I'm practically bouncing myself when I enter the library.

"Hi, Miss Mava!"

"Who are you, stranger?"

"Oh, this?" I fan my burning face. "Just thought I'd spruce up a little. You know, for a change. A little change is always good."

"That young man better appreciate you."

"Oh, he does," I say quickly and head for the law library.

I don't even pretend to work. The library's closed on weekends so today is my last chance to check out books I might need before Monday's *Faretta* hearing.

The first thing I do is pull out a criminal defense treatise and find *Prosecutorial Misconduct* in the table of contents. I study the subheadings. *Witness tampering.* Yep. *Deceit.* That should be Leslie's middle name. *Fraud upon the court.* Yes, yes, yes.

But the first sentence of the chapter squashes my excitement. *The burden of proving prosecutorial misconduct is high and faces many hurdles.* Why do you always have to *prove* everything when you *know* it's true? Drives me crazy. There's no way Mary Brinson is going to be willing to testify against Leslie.

The front bell jangles and I sprint out of the law library, but it's not Ben, just a girl looking for a book about dogs. I help her find one and check it out. I ask if she has a dog. She says she did, but her mom's boyfriend shot it, so she's hoping to get another one.

The wall clock doesn't make a sound, but I hear it ticking in my head. Almost three. If Ben doesn't come, I won't see him again until after my trial, or maybe never. If I'm convicted, they might haul me away to some other place.

The door opens again and this time I know it's Ben from the scrape of his ankle shackles and a man's deep voice. I run out to greet him as Mava's flats tap down the hallway.

"Hi, Ben!" Bless his heart. The stupid guard put the shackles right over his casts.

Mava says, "Welcome, CO ... Delacorte," reading his name tag. "Let's get this poor boy's chains off. These two have legal work to do and I have something special just for you. You like homemade fried chicken? How about fresh apple pie?"

The CO takes off the shackles and follows Mava to her office like a happy puppy.

I hurry Ben into the library and seat him at my work table. My drawing is face down in front of us. I *so* hope he likes it.

No time to waste. "I cannot believe how much I have to tell you," I say. "First, I have a surprise. It's big. Ready?"

"I guess," he says, expressionless.

"*Ta da!* I found *binding* precedent from the United States Supreme Court that Leslie Tierney and her detective friend violated your right to counsel when they tricked you into confessing. It's called *functional interrogation.*"

I ramble on, explaining all about the Christian burial speech case and *Rhode Island v. Innis* and the exclusionary rule. Why isn't he smiling? He hasn't smiled since he got here. No reaction at all.

"You realize what this means, right? There's a good chance you can file a petition for habeas corpus and get your conviction overturned. Get out of here. Be free, like an Arctic Tern!"

He stares at me like I just said *Hello, did you lose an umbrella?* in Chinese.

"Corey Wilkes," he says.

"Pardon?"

"Corey Wilkes. Do you remember his name?"

"Of course. He's the one who did this," I say, pointing with my eyes at his casts.

"He's dead."

It takes a couple of seconds to process. "Really? Yay!"

"Yay? Tell me you didn't just say that."

"Well, he won't be able to hurt you anymore. Who did it?"

"People are saying the Crips. They're a black gang."

I know all about the Crips from Lucas. "Well, he was a white supremacist and they are a black gang, so it kind of makes perfect sense."

"I want to know the truth," he says. "Did you have anything to do with this?"

"Me? How could you ask me something like that? That really hurts my feelings."

His eyes soften and he takes my hands. "I'm sorry. I had to ask because it's been weighing on me. When I first told you about Wilkes you pressed me for his name and said he should have to pay. There's a rumor someone from the outside put a price on his head."

I cough. "Really. That's, um, interesting."

"You wouldn't lie to me, would you?"

My first true relationship test. I have to do something right in my life. Might as well be this. I will not lie to my first true love, starting right now.

"I mean, it's possible, maybe accidentally. I have a friend outside. I asked for his help. I asked if he could stop Corey Wilkes from hurting you."

His look turns dark and he lets go of my hands. "Why? I told you I didn't need your help."

"I know, but I just couldn't stand seeing you getting hurt like this. But I definitely didn't say to kill anyone and it probably didn't even have anything to do with that. I shouldn't have even mentioned it."

He lowers his chin. "So you're saying you should have lied?"

"That's not what I meant. I just meant ..." FUCK. *I do not know how to do love. How is it even supposed to work?*

Seconds tick away.

"Look," he says. "I know you were trying to help, but we just don't think the same way. My mom's a college professor. She's been a peace activist since I can remember. She raised me to be a pacifist."

"What does that mean? You don't fight back?"

"Honestly, no. I was taught that violence isn't the answer. It only leads to more violence, like what happened here."

"So you feel bad for the guy who punched you in the face and broke your arms?"

His lips tighten, then relax. "Alice, you are without a doubt the most unique girl I have ever met. I think you're awesome and I really care about you."

I spew relief. "I'm so glad. I care about you too. I really was only trying to help. I brought you something." I pick up my portrait, but before I can turn it over he holds up a hand.

"I wasn't finished. I care about you, but you had no right to interfere with my life. I don't know exactly how to say it, but I don't think we should, um, hang out anymore. We're just too different."

"Huh?" I stare in shock, mouth hanging open as the words grudgingly sink in. "Well, excuse me for *interfering* with your repeatedly getting the shit beat out of you." *Not good relationship talk, not good relationship talk.*

I expect him to get mad, want him to be, but his tranquil, soulful look stays the same. I back off, slumping in the chair.

"So you're breaking up with me? Just like that? This is just our first fight. It's normal for couples." *Isn't it?* I swallow hard. *I will not cry.*

"Well, we're not exactly a couple." He says it gently, but the words slice like a razor.

"But we kissed."

"I know. Again, we're just too different."

I sit mute, no clue what to do or say. I realize I'm still holding the drawing. *What a stupid girl.* "Here. I made this for you."

"Whoa, this is, um, really good," he says awkwardly. "It looks exactly like you. You're an amazing artist."

"You can have it if you want." *It's not like I have any other use for it.*

"I–I couldn't take it. It wouldn't be right. I'm sorry, Alice. I really am."

I capture a snapshot of his long-lashed empathy that I'll hold onto forever, then proceed to completely lose my mind. "You're sorry, alright. A sorry excuse for a man. A pus—"

I attempted to inhale the words as they came out, but it was too late. Maybe I needed to get the last word in or maybe it was just a different kind of self-harm. It could have been as simple as needing to escape the encounter as quickly as possible.

He stood and walked out, leaving me holding the picture. I heard him call down the hall to the guard.

I waited until he left the library then began tearing my drawing into strips, which I made into a neat pile and tore into squares, which I tore into smaller squares. I kept going until my sad-eyed face was a pile of confetti. Then I started pulling my hair out.

34

MY FIRST thought when I woke up Saturday was I needed to get to work on my case. My second thought was Ben. After he walked out, I sat in silence, on my hands to keep from yanking my hair, until Mava came in.

"Why'd the boy leave so soon?" she said. "I never even broke out the apple pie. You had another good half hour."

"Well, we kind of broke up."

"That's a surprise. I thought you liked him."

"Not really. I mean, I sort of did, but ... it's complicated. You know how relationships are."

"How about a slice of apple pie to cheer you up? Baked it just last night."

"Thanks, but I'm not very hungry right now."

Actually, I thought I might puke any second. She must have felt sorry for me because I plodded back to my cell carrying the entire apple pie.

Paranormal Rebecca saw through me right away. I never even mentioned Ben was coming to the library, yet with all of the things going wrong in my life, her first words as I set down the pie were, "*Ben*. What happened?"

I didn't cry like I thought I might. As I talked, Rebecca got that look where her lips slide in opposite directions. I've never been sure what it means, but the more I explained, the farther her lips slipped.

I walked to the window ledge and picked up Ben's

hump-backed bird. "My bird has flown," I said. "What should I do with this?"

She held out her hands. "Let me see it."

I tossed it to her. She raised it in the air as if admiring it and for a moment I thought she was going to tell me to save it as a memento. Then she slam-dunked it into the trashcan. "The sky is full of birds. You're a hawk, he was just a sparrow."

* * *

We ate Mava's apple pie for breakfast. I should have gone straight to the law books, but went back to sleep instead and didn't wake again until Rebecca shook me for lunch. Depression or exhaustion, maybe both.

The food and extra sleep helped me bounce back. Every thought of Ben felt like a needle being stuck in my heart, so I locked them in a black box. No time to grieve. What else is new? I didn't have even a second to grieve for Mom and Becky before I was on the run.

The first thing I do with my new energy is call Lucas—*furious.* Like he's trying to avoid me, it take five rings before he picks up.

"You ain't supposed to call in the daytime," he says.

"Corey Wilkes is dead."

"Who dat?"

"You *know.* The guy who beat up Ben."

"The white supremacist?"

"Yeah, him."

"That's good."

"You did it? I can't believe it. You ruined my life."

"Hey, jailbird, which one of us lives in the land of the free? How does Lucas kill a man in prison?"

"So you didn't have anything do to with it?"

"Didn't say that. I said I didn't kill 'im."

He proceeds to explain he was trying to help, *just like you fuckin' asked.* The only way he saw to pressure Wilkes from the outside was to hurt his family and even Lucas couldn't do that, not after what happened to Jarrett and Shondra, his little brother and sister who were gunned down in a drive-by.

He says there was a gang guy who owed him a big favor for not killing him one night a long time ago. The guy had a gang friend who had a gang cousin at Pochachant, two of them in fact.

"Once they found out who he was, it didn't take much convincing. But I didn't say nothin' about killin'. I asked them to *deter* him from beating the hell out of your chicken-ass boyfriend and it worked. Ain't much better deterrence than death."

My first instinct is to defend Ben, but I can't. I also can't stay mad at Lucas. He did what I begged him to do. Whether Ben ever appreciates it, I'll bet people will think twice before picking on him again.

"Thanks," I say, deflating. "I'm just sad because Ben broke up with me over it, said he was raised as a *pacifist* and we're too different. And please don't badmouth him right now because I know you're about to."

In a soft voice I rarely hear, "I'm sorry that happened. I know you liked Ben."

I appreciate him acknowledging Ben as a person I cared about, thought I loved even.

"You gonna be alright?" he says.

"You know me. I'm always alright. I don't have any other choice."

We end the call and I go to work on my case. Pen in hand, I map out Monday on a legal pad. A CO will collect me before dawn to take me to the van. I'll already have been up for an hour getting ready. I'm determined to look good in my final hours. Rebecca cleaned and ironed my clothes at the laundry.

When we get to Opelousas, all I have to do is convince Judge Hanks I'm competent to represent myself while Leslie snickers and the judge tries not to. Me, *Outburst Girl*, with the five thousand-page psyche file. If by some miracle I win that battle, I'll take the witness stand and Leslie will try to shred me into as many pieces as my self-portrait.

No biggie. Haha. *Laugh or cry, cry and die.*

I dive back into the books, finishing *Trial Advocacy* and picking up *Juvenile Justice.* The hours tick by quickly. The tissue paper stuffed in my ears to help me concentrate keeps me from hearing the steps in the hallway before the cell door unlocks. I turn with a start, but it's only Longmont.

The only times she's come to our cell have been to tell Rebecca her mom's here for visiting hours, so I'm surprised when she points at me and says, "Alice, you have a visitor."

"Me? Who is it?"

"I don't know. It wasn't on the schedule. A suit. Something official."

I shrug at Rebecca and follow Longmont.

Maybe it's a new public defender. I could picture Hanks not taking me seriously and appointing a new one before I even got a chance to make my *Faretta* argument. Or it could be someone from the prosecutor's office, but I don't think they're allowed to talk to me without my lawyer present ... except now I don't have a lawyer. Another trick?

I drink in the soggy, late afternoon air as we make the short walk between buildings. A pencil-necked CO stands outside the visiting room with a clipboard. Longmont tells him she brought Alice Black. "She wants to know who her visitor is," she says. "It wasn't scheduled."

He looks at the clipboard. "Just says *Official,* but I heard a rumor it's FBI."

Great. *Could I get you anything else to go with your disaster du jour, madam?* There's no good reason why the FBI would want to talk to me. Maybe they've been looking for me the whole time and just found out I'm here. After all, it wasn't the FBI that let me run away from the foster home, just Agent Forster.

Wait a minute. FBI? Unscheduled visit? It probably is Agent Forster! He probably got word of the trial, maybe when they subpoenaed my medical records.

I enter the visiting room searching for his butter-smooth face and close-cropped salt and pepper hair. The gym is packed. Weekends always are. But I don't see Agent Forster and my spirits take a nosedive until ...

Oh. My. God. He's tucked away in the farthest corner, but Lucas Jackson can't hide even in a gym filled with a hundred people.

Longmont motions for me to go ahead of her. "Slow down," she says. My heart is punching through my chest and I'm having a hard time not grinning as we get close.

He's wearing a suit. I've never seen him in one. His head is shaved. Thick rectangular glasses cover his contact-tinted green eyes. He totally looks like the FBI.

When he stands, Longmont flares back to avoid his muscle-bound chest. "Agent Peterson. FBI," he says, towering over her, holding out a photo ID and shiny gold badge.

"Nice to meet you," Longmont says. "This is Alice Black. I'll leave you two alone." She gives me a good luck nod and walks away.

"*Loo*-cas," I whisper.

"Quit lookin' around like you just robbed a bank. Be cool. I'm an FBI agent here to discuss a criminal investigation."

"But what in the world? Isn't this a big risk?"

"We need to have a heart-to-heart no one can overhear. Can't trust electronic communications."

He knows. He was in signal intelligence in the army, *sig-int* as he calls it.

"Or cellmates."

"Oh, we can trust Rebecca."

"How do you know that? What if someone offered her a million dollars to sell you out?"

"Well, no one's going to offer her a million dollars."

"So you just admitted she can't be trusted."

"No I didn't. I'll bet she wouldn't do it even for a million dollars."

"Whatever. I'm here to talk about what comes after."

"After what? ... Oh, the trial? I haven't really thought about it much, honestly." Haven't been able to face it.

"I figured. I have. Let's face facts. You ain't got no lawyer. You got no witnesses. You got no *case*."

"I have me. Emily-the-Powerful. You said it yourself." I don't feel very powerful right now. I want to climb into one of his pockets and go to sleep and have him walk out of here with me. "And I have you. Seeing you in person makes me feel stronger."

"Hold onto them feelings. You is powerful, but in case you get racked up for murder-one, we need a backup plan, a way out."

I sag. "I don't think there is any way out. I'll appeal, just because why not? I'm pretty sure they have to let me out when I'm twenty-one. I got lucky, one year too young at the time of the crime to get transferred to adult court where the sentence for first-degree murder is automatic life in adult prison."

"You sixteen. Five years is hard time, long enough to kill any spirit, even one as strong as yours, 'specially in a shithole like this. I got a different plan. I'm instructin' you to stay calm right now with every molecule of your body. Don't react. You hear?"

I nod.

"The plan is I bust you loose and we take off."

I bow my head and cough. Talking into my hand, "That's crazy. You can't bust someone out of Pochachant."

"We ain't doin' it at Pochachant. We do it in the alley behind the courthouse while the guards are transferrin' you to the van."

"How do you know about the alley?"

"I told you I'd be around."

"Are you serious? Lucas, we can't do that. If you kill a cop, they always get you. You told me that."

"No one's gettin' hurt. They gonna hand you over on a silver platter."

I try to study his eyes, but the light reflecting off his fake glasses keeps me out. "Tell the truth," I whisper. "Are you high?"

He shakes his head.

"So they're just going to hand me over to you. Howdy do, nice to meet you, here's our star defendant, Emily Calby. Y'all drive safely now."

"Nope. They gonna hand you over to Agent Peterson of the FBI."

"Ah."

"You thirsty? Watch this." He waves to the nearest CO, beckoning with a hand as big as a dinner plate.

A twitchy white guy comes over with an annoyed look. "Yeah."

"Get this detainee a bottle of water."

"This ain't no restaurant."

Lucas leaps up, a mountain erupting out of the sea. The startled CO shrinks away.

"Agent Peterson," Lucas says, showing the badge. "FBI. What'd you say your name was, son?"

"Um, Jaeger, sir. Sorry. I didn't know you was FBI. I'll be right back with the water."

Right in the middle of Pochachant. "That was amazing," I say under my breath.

"Ain't nothin' better than bein' in the FBI," he says with genuine pride. "This badge is like a magic wand. Wave it and people will do whatever you want, especially these losers. They spend their entire lives dreamin' of being in real law enforcement. FBI's like superheroes to 'em."

I don't have to ask where he got the badge. He has a drawer full of them in the document room back in Memphis. "Well, that was a nifty trick, but you just drew attention. *Never draw attention to yourself.* You taught me that at the beginning."

"It's a good rule, but all rules got exceptions."

I laugh.

"What's funny?"

"Nothing."

"See, now word's gonna spread the FBI's interested in you, which means when I show up in that alley with my badge and a phony court order from a federal judge to turn you over, they won't be surprised."

"Hm, I could see it working, but even if it does, they'll be looking for us everywhere. That's been one of the secrets of our success. No one's ever been looking for the two of us together. We're kind of easy to spot. Why did you cook this up?"

The CO comes back with the bottle of water. "Here you go, sir."

"Thank you, Jaeger," Lucas says. "I'll put in a good word for you."

He bows and quickly walks away.

"So why, Lucas? I thought you were joking. It's not worth it. I can survive five years." I think, I hope.

He gazes at the ceiling. I haven't seen him do it in forever and missed it. I always imagine what he sees up there. Stars, unicorns, could be anything. He rubs his cheek, as butter-smooth as Agent Forster's. Yet one more lesson he taught me: *Attention to detail. Separates winners from losers.*

He leans in, elbows like tree trunks planted on the table, his shadow swallowing me, eyes just inches from mine.

"Emily, listen. I've had a ... let's call it an excitin' life. And through luck or maybe the grace of that god you believe in, I got a lot to show for it. Plenty of money, my health—that's a miracle right there—got Kiona and my little man James. But I ain't been able to enjoy even one minute of it since you got picked up. What you said in the bus that day before you walked out—"

"I want to apologize again. I was just acting out ... and I wrecked everything." The enormity of that truth makes me heartsick. I pick up the bottle of water and twist off the cap.

"Don't talk. Just listen. You ever notice how I'm always cussin' and bitchin' at you?"

I snort water out my nose and disguise it as a sneeze. "Now that you mention it, but I know you do it because you care about me."

"Good. Glad you know it." He hangs his head. This is the

weirdest conversation I've ever had with Lucas. He seems ... depressed.

"Lucas, no matter what happens, I won't let this place or anything else kill my spirit. You know me, *one tough little motherfucker.*"

I thought the memory would make him smile, but he remains stone-faced.

"Hear me now," he says. "What you said that day was true. I ain't your daddy. I know I act that way sometimes. Lotsa times probably. Hell, I ain't even your real adoptive daddy. Just a bunch of forged documents, like you said. I ain't good at saying I'm sorry, but I am for that."

"You hear me," I say. "Real or not, you will always be my dad and I will always be your daughter, and proud of it."

35

"**CAN YOU** define the hearsay rule for me?" Judge Hanks says.

Judges must be in love with that rule. I spent Sunday holed up in my cell cramming. I only left for meals.

"The hearsay rule is that you can't use out-of-court statements in court." I move on quickly to preempt questions about the twenty-nine exceptions. "Of course, as you know, Judge, the rules of evidence do not strictly apply in juvenile proceedings." Got that from the *Juvenile Justice* book.

He nods approvingly.

The *Faretta* hearing has been hit and miss. Each time I screw up I remind Judge Hanks that the Supreme Court specifically said *technical legal knowledge* isn't relevant to whether someone can knowingly and intelligently waive their right to counsel.

It's a weird feeling, a sad one, standing at Paula's podium and talking into her microphone. Hanks started the day with more bad news. She developed sepsis—blood poisoning—when her intestine burst. She's in intensive care in critical condition at a hospital in Baton Rouge. I'll try to reach her tonight if I can get back to Pochachant.

"I've reviewed your psychological report," Hanks says. "Dr. Thompson concluded you're still suffering PTSD from the terrible things that happened to you and your family. That's certainly understandable."

"Why is that important?"

"Because I need to be convinced you're competent."

"She also said I passed the tests and am very intelligent."

"I don't doubt that, Ms. Calby, but even though this is juvenile court, if you're adjudicated guilty of murder you will face a substantial period of incarceration and never be able to escape the consequences of that determination. Never. Your life is on the line here."

"That's the point I've been trying to make, Judge. It's my life, not yours or Ms. Tierney's or the State's. If you'll bear with me, I'd like to read you something I wrote down from *Faretta*." Leslie says that a lot, *If you'll bear with me.*

I try to hold my pad like Leslie, a light saber of logic, useful for stabbing the air to make a point, kept close enough to read from, but never blocking my face or seeming like a crutch.

"The Supreme Court said the right to counsel under the Sixth Amendment is for counsel to be an *assistant*, not, and I quote, *an organ of the State imposed on an unwilling defendant.*"

Resounding in open court, the words sound powerful, undeniable.

"It went on to say that to force a lawyer on a person against their will makes the lawyer a master, not an assistant. A master, Judge. That's not right."

Hanks squeezes his forehead like he has a migraine.

"Thank you. I understand the law. I'm more interested in your personal situation. Your behavior has been erratic in this case on more than one occasion. Your spontaneous decision to confess to the crime at the discovery conference, albeit with a defense, shows a lack of judgment at odds, to say the least, with competent self-representation."

"You are so super-right about that, but I have good news. I fixed that problem. I decided to exercise only good judgment from now on, in everything I say and do." I cross my heart.

The court reporter giggles and the judge shushes her. "I'm not sure it's as easy to control as simply *deciding*," he says.

"That's because you don't know me. I have a very strong will."

"We're aware," he says.

I'm not lying about the decision. Last night while I couldn't sleep I took stock of my life, at what I've become—a joke that makes even court reporters laugh—compared to what I could be if only I used better judgment. If I hadn't stormed out of the bus with the gun—horrible judgment—I wouldn't be here in the first place. Everyone, even Darla, gives me an easy out by blaming it on the PTSD, but like Lucas says, we always have a choice: A or B.

People get scared or lazy, think, "Poor me. I ain't got no choice." But you always got a choice. How should I react? A or B. What should I do next? A or B. Sometimes you get lucky and got choices all the way to fuckin' Z. But you always got at least A or B.

"I *have* good judgment, Judge. I just haven't used it. But I'm going to from now on."

A snarky laugh from Leslie.

"Ms. Calby, as I've been explaining since the beginning, the hazards of self-representation are extreme. I need to understand why you so badly want to risk them."

I set my pad down, smooth my blouse and step in front of the lectern, like Leslie does. Paula clung to it like a life preserver. I don't blame her. It feels naked out here.

Be authentic.

"Judge Hanks, everyone in this room knows what happened to me and my family. Since the day the two men came to our house my entire life has been out of my control. I don't even feel like a human sometimes, more like a puppet. Someone or something else is always pulling the strings. Like right now, no offense.

"I don't have anyone to rely on but myself. I don't have a family, don't have my friends." I point to Paula's empty chair, which I arranged close to mine. "I don't have Paula—Ms. Dunwoody. No one but *Emily Blair Calby.*"

As it comes out, syllable by syllable, the floor shakes and the walls rumble and I feel my center of gravity shifting. I know it's in my head, which is good because hitting the floor and yelling *Earthquake!* would no doubt hurt my competency argument.

I just reclaimed myself, for the first time since the end of everything.

With more confidence, "*Faretta* said it's not inconceivable someone could represent herself better than a lawyer. I know you don't believe that's possible for me. None of you do. Everyone just wants to laugh at me and that's fine. I'm getting used to it."

The court reporter dips her head in apology. Even the judge's tight lips speak of atonement.

"It is my right under the constitution of the United States of America to control my destiny. I make this decision knowingly and intelligently. I am not incompetent. Am I little weird? Probably, but that shouldn't disqualify me."

*   *   *

Leslie went on a tirade about how I'm an impudent, impulsive child who would make a mockery of the proceedings and risk getting the judge reversed, after which Hanks declared a thirty-minute recess.

Sitting alone in the usual interview room brings home how much I miss Paula. I've prayed for her, but feel guilty I haven't spent more time thinking about her, especially since the stress of my case probably pushed her over the edge. There's just no room in my head.

Same with Lucas's proposal to bust me out. I can't even take it seriously. I asked where we'd go and he said, *Maybe South America*. Crazy.

When we get back to the courtroom, the judge surprises everyone.

"I'm going to grant Ms. Calby's motion," he announces, holding up a hand to silence Leslie. "Conditionally. I have grave concerns about it and warn you, Ms. Calby, that I will revoke my decision if you demonstrate the slightest bit of questionable behavior. Do you understand?"

"Yes, Your Honor."

"Stand when you address the court."

I stand. "Yes, Your Honor. Thank you."

He offers to appoint *standby counsel*, but I decline after he explains it to me, afraid a standby lawyer would try to take over and be a stand-in lawyer.

We recess again, this time for lunch. I'm as prepared as I can be with what I have, so I sit still and try to clear my mind, wishing I had a window to look out of while chewing on a mushy chicken salad sandwich.

* * *

"Is the prosecution ready to proceed?" Hanks says.

Leslie stands. "We are, but repeat our objection to allowing the defendant to represent herself."

"I've already heard and rejected it—for now. Is the defense ready to proceed?"

I follow Leslie's lead and stand. My knees are trembling. *You're a hawk. You're a hawk.* "We are."

"Do you have a witness to call?"

"We do. The defense calls Emily Calby."

I walk to the witness box, chin up, focusing on the state seal of the pelican and her babies above the word CONFIDENCE. I can do this.

The bailiff tells me to raise my right hand.

"Do you swear to tell the truth and nothing but the truth, so help you God?"

"I do." I sit down and fold my hands on my lap, careful not to slouch.

Such a different view from up here. I'm used to looking at Judge Hanks. Now I'm right in front of Leslie and her assistants and, behind them, Tammy and Dulcie Brooker.

Dulcie's a cute name. I wonder who gave it to her. Her mother's thoughts are easy to read. Venomous rage and hatred.

Dulcie remains inscrutable. Maybe she's just numb. I get that. Sometimes numbness is the only place to go. It's when you stay too long that trouble starts.

I've never been able to study her. She has her father's ski-slope nose and thin lips and her mother's hazel eyes. Her thick wavy hair is the color of maple syrup and pulled back in a ponytail. She's wearing a simple black shift with a high-scooped neck, like something I might wear if I ever owned a dress.

When I was in the car with Brooker, he said his daughter was seventeen and applying to college. She must be more than halfway through by now.

Hanks says, "We're ready when you are, Ms. Calby."

I stand and clear my throat. "Could you state your full name for the record?"

I sit down. "Emily Blair Calby."

I stand up. "Did you have occasion three years ago to meet the decedent in this case, Scott—"

"Hold it, hold it," Hanks says. "You don't need to ask yourself questions. Just explain what happened in detail. But I remind you again that you are not required to testify and you may very well incriminate yourself by doing so."

I nod and try again to clear the lump from my throat. "Could I possibly have a drink of water?"

"Bailiff."

The bailiff fills a paper cup from a water cooler and brings it to me.

"Thank you. Well, what happened was I was hitchhiking from Shreveport to Lafayette. I had a bus ticket, but it got stolen, along with my money, by a guy who snatched my backpack off the sidewalk in Shreveport. He took off running and just when I caught up to him, he threw my backpack into the Red River, so I—"

Judge Hanks is holding up a stop-sign hand.

"What's wrong now, Judge?"

"We don't need that much information."

I freeze my eyeballs to keep them from rolling. "Okay, Judge, but you just said to explain in detail, so I was trying to follow your instructions."

"Appreciated, but you can move ahead to how you met Mr. Brooker."

"Like I said, I was hitching from Shreveport to Lafayette on I-49. I spent the night in Alexandria. I have witnesses for that," I note. *I don't see how it's relevant, but it's only thing I have witnesses for. Alex and Alice and their Amazing Adventure to Alexandria.*

"The next morning I hitchhiked to Lafayette or tried to. That's when I met the sex predator."

"Objection!" Leslie is on her feet.

"Sustained. Do not refer to the victim by that term. That is a legal conclusion."

I start to object that if they can call him a victim, I should be able to call him a sex predator, but take a slow breath instead. "That's how I met the decedent."

I describe how he pestered me with personal questions. "He went on and on, talking about his daughter and comparing me to her." My eyes flit reflexively to Dulcie, but her head is bent forward and all I see is the crooked part in her hair.

"After we drove for a while, he asked if I was hungry. He said he knew a family restaurant in the next town with real home cooking, said he spent his life on the road and couldn't eat fast-food anymore." Tammy Brooker nods.

In my head, I'm still reciting questions to help me stay on track. *How did you feel about that suggestion, Ms. Calby?*

"I didn't want to go off the interstate with a stranger, but we were in the middle of nowhere and he was giving me a ride, so I felt pressured to go along. When I hesitated, he said, *Homemade apple pie to die for.* I remember those words exactly."

I explain how we left the interstate and passed through two towns without stopping. "When we passed the second town I said we must be lost and should go back to the interstate. That's when he changed completely, from a normal person into a monster."

Leslie is on her feet again. "Objection. Opinion."

"Sustained."

"I'm not allowed to have an opinion, Judge?"

"Only experts are permitted to offer opinions in court, not lay witnesses."

"With all due respect, I read in a book about evidence that a lay witness can give an opinion if it's rationally based on personal perception. I wasn't saying, like, literally, he was a monster, like Frankenstein or Dracula."

Hanks opens his mouth, pauses, looks to Leslie, and says, "On reconsideration, the objection is overruled."

"As I started to say, his voice changed and his eyes turned cold. It was all very sudden. Before that he was acting all dad-like. He turned off the highway, down a rocky road and took us into the bayou."

And what were you thinking at this time, Ms. Calby?

"I knew something was wrong, but didn't know what to do. We were isolated, with bayou on both sides of the road. I wanted to run but there was no place to go."

I reach for the water cup before realizing it's already crumpled into a ball in my other hand.

"The decedent kept accusing me of being a runaway, said he had picked up plenty of them and we were all sluts who needed money. He told me he'd give me some money, but said I had to do him a favor. I just turned thirteen. I didn't even know what he meant. Then he undid his pants."

The courtroom is quiet except for the whir of the air conditioning.

"For some reason I remember hearing a barred owl howling when we got out of the car and thinking it sounded like a wolf," I say absently. "He made me get down on my knees."

Like I'm being interviewed for a documentary twenty years after the fact, I lapse into a monotone and relate the story of the knifing and aftermath. It was dream-like when it happened and still feels unreal. I follow Paula's advice and hammer on what Brooker said when I asked him what would happen if I refused.

"He said something like, *Another girl said no a few months ago, but you'd have to dig her up to ask her.* I took that as a threat he would kill me if I refused. I think any reasonable person would have felt the same way."

Leslie is up again. "Objection. Move to strike that last comment. It's a legal and factual conclusion."

"Sustained."

I've been avoiding eye contact with her. She unnerves me, sucks away my confidence. I can sense her motor revving up, straining to break loose and steamroll me on cross-examination.

"When it was over, I was scared. I didn't know what to do, so I took his car and abandoned it in Lafayette. I never intended to keep it. I sunk his luggage in the bayou, with his wallet in it, like the crime scene investigator said."

I look up at Hanks and shrug. "That's about it, Judge."

"Very well," he says, subdued. "This is your only opportunity to offer direct testimony. Is there anything you've left out? Anything you'd like to add?"

"Not really. Just that, right before I stab— ... exercised my right of self-defense, I asked the decedent if he really had a daughter. He wanted to know why I asked. I said I felt sorry for her ... and that was the end."

Dulcie Brooker sucks in her bottom lip.

Connect emotionally. Do emotion and good judgment go together or are they mutually exclusive?

"I'd like to say one more thing, Judge. I'd like to tell Dulcie that I am very sorry she lost her father. I lost my dad and know it's something a person never gets over."

Tammy Brooker leaps up. "Don't you dare talk to my daughter like you know her. She lost her father because you murdered him, you little witch."

"Sit down," Hanks orders harshly.

Leslie waves her down. "I apologize, Judge, but we echo her objection and request that you instruct the defendant to not speak directly to Mr. Brooker's family. They are not interested in her phony sentiments."

"Sustained. You are so instructed, Ms. Calby."

"Yes sir, but I wasn't being phony—just for the record."

Crying again. Not from the mom. It's Dulcie, face buried in her hands.

36

DURING THE thirty-minute recess between direct and cross-examination, I eat an apple left over from lunch, feeling pretty good about myself. I started the day winning the *Faretta* hearing. I avoided any fatal tactical blunders in my direct testimony. I testified from the heart, but controlled my emotions. I didn't even have to lie, a miracle in itself. Everything came out better than anyone could have predicted, me most of all.

Dealing with Leslie will be a different story. She's going to try to get my goat, just like Paula said. Try to make me lose it, look like a rabid killer. I have to not let her. *Take control. Own the situation.*

I return to the courtroom feeling strong and powerful. This lasts for the first five seconds of my cross-examination, the time it takes Leslie to ask her first question.

"Do you understand you took a sworn oath to God to tell the truth?"

I wasn't expecting it. I twitch. She sees it. I think. Does she know I'm religious? She must, but how? *Stop.*

"Yes."

"I'm glad to hear that. In that case, please tell the court why you've been hiding under a false identity for three years?"

I didn't think of that question either. I focused all my preparation on Brooker.

"Um, excuse me, Judge," I say. "Am I allowed to object, like a regular lawyer?"

Hanks gazes down from his perch with a face etched in consternation, maybe pity. "You can object to any question, *provided* proper grounds exist."

"I read in a book that cross-examination has to be limited to what's asked on direct examination. I didn't testify about my earlier life."

Nodding, "That's actually a very reasonable objection, but I'm going to overrule it until I see where she's going. Please answer the question."

Know yourself. "Well, it's a big, complicated question. At first I was just running for my life. The men who killed my family were still on the loose. One of them threatened to chop me into pieces."

Admit fear. "I was afraid every minute of the day and night, even when I was asleep."

Leslie purses her lips. "What happened to your family was an absolute tragedy and I completely understand that reaction."

Seriously? Could Leslie possibly be not *all* bad?

"What I *don't* understand is why you maintained a false identity for three years *after* you knew the perpetrators were deceased and no longer a threat."

Nope. Not possible. It's the hardest question of all. There was Lucas, of course, but it was bigger than that.

Be yourself. "That's where it gets complicated," I say, cheeks inflating like a pufferfish. "I didn't want to be Emily Calby anymore. She was the girl who failed her family and ran away, the girl who lived. I feel guilty every single day just for being alive."

I expect Leslie to mock me, but she breaks eye contact and looks down at her notes.

I've never admitted it so clearly and undeniably, definitely not to myself. Darla figured it out, Lucas too. Rebecca guessed right away. Every night, like a leaky ceiling, one drip of guilt at a time that smacks me right on the forehead, no matter which way I turn, even when I'm lying face down, penetrating my brain and heart and soul. What a strange place to come to terms.

I reach for my hair, forgetting it's wrapped in a bun. "I also didn't want the attention, especially from the media. I just wanted to be left alone. I still do. And there was no life to go back to. Everything was gone. I couldn't face living in foster care ... so there were a lot of reasons."

Hanks is rapping his knuckles on the bench. The hollow below amplifies the sound like a bass drum. "Ms. Tierney, how is this testimony relevant to what happened to Mr. Brooker?"

"I'm laying the groundwork to show that nothing that comes out of her mouth can be believed because her very existence is a lie."

She's got me on that one.

"Since it's her word against a dead man's, her credibility is the central issue in the case."

Two more knuckle raps. "Proceed, but you are on a short rope."

"Ms. Calby, three years is a long time for a teenager to survive on her own. You must have had some help."

I stare at her.

"Well?" she says.

"Well, what?" I say.

"What's your answer?"

"What's your question? That was a conclusion."

Hanks stifles what sounds like a laugh. "I'll construe that as an objection. Sustained."

"Very well," Leslie snips. "Allow me to rephrase. Did you have any help?"

"Yes."

"From whom?"

"Several people."

"Were they men?"

"Men and women."

"Was there one man in particular?"

Does Leslie know about Lucas? She could be fishing, like with the DNA. I don't want to take the bait again, but don't have a choice. She might have proof.

"Yes."

"Did you do favors for him?"

"Favors? Sure, I guess. We were friends."

"Did they include sexual favors?"

I don't have a chance to react before Judge Hanks' gavel explodes in my right ear. "Stop right there, Ms. Tierney. That is so far beyond the scope of direct it's outside the solar system."

"I'm simply trying to understand how Ms. Calby managed to live for three years with no visible means of support. She testified Mr. Brooker offered her money to perform a sexual act. What if it was her idea?"

I grip the arms of the chair and start to rise but Hanks keeps me in place with his palm pressing against air.

"Do you have a factual basis for the question, Ms. Tierney?" he says.

She throws up her hands. "Unfortunately, Your Honor, the only other witness is dead, so we're left to speculate."

"You've already established she used a false identity. Move on to Mr. Brooker. Now."

"I will be happy to do that, Judge," she says, words dipped in artificial sweetener.

"Ms. Calby, besides stealing Mr. Brooker's car, did you take anything else from him?"

"I didn't steal his car … just borrowed it."

"Did you *borrow* anything else?" she says.

Paula said if I lied under oath about taking the cash from his wallet, I'd be committing perjury and she'd have to recuse herself. But Paula's not here. On the other hand, so far I've managed to tell the truth and it's made keeping my story straight a lot easier.

"Okay, so I could lie and say no and you could never prove otherwise, but because I want my testimony to be believed, yes, I took some cash from his wallet. About two hundred dollars. But it never occurred to me to do it until after I had already acted in self-defense. All I wanted from Brooker was a ride to Lafayette. Stealing was never my intent."

My studies have taught me there's no word more important to criminal law than *intent*.

"So you just thought, oh well, I killed the man, might as well take his money while I'm at it?"

"No. I did it because I was broke and afraid and stranded in the middle of nowhere. All my money was in the backpack that got stolen in Shreveport. I didn't take anything else."

"What happened to his other belongings? He was a traveling sales executive. Surely he had a phone and computer."

"He did. I sunk them in the bayou with his other stuff."

"And why did you do that?"

"Um."

"To destroy evidence?"

"Well ..."

"Destruction of evidence is also a serious crime. So you admit to more guilt?"

I should have lied. Of course I should have! What was I thinking? Since when have I cared about lying? Not since I was twelve years old and still Emily Calby. Maybe it's a consequence of my reclamation, but swearing to God weighs on me too.

"Yes. I admit I stole his money and sunk his property in the water. But that's it. And borrowed his car. But that's it."

"And killed him."

I pull my suit jacket around me. "Only out of necessity in self-defense."

"How did you feel about it afterwards? Killing a man."

"How did I *feel*? How would you feel if a man took you out into the woods and tried to rape you and the only way out was by killing him?" *Keep it together.* Softer, "I was in shock. I didn't really feel anything. I was numb."

I suppose I could explain about the three girls who were competing for space in my dissociating head, relate how the hiding girl—me—stayed in the corner the whole time and blame everything on the calm girl and scary girl who made all the decisions, but I'm not going to be *that* authentic.

"How do you feel about it now?"

She is *really* getting on my nerves. Hanks saves me.

"Ms. Tierney, how are her present feelings relevant to whether she acted in self-defense three years ago? Stick to the facts."

Close call, but I dodged having to either lie or admit I could care less about Brooker. He deserved to die. Simple as that. I thought it then and think it now.

I do feel bad for Dulcie though, and even her mom, who has given up on her death-ray vision, or maybe her eyes got tired and she's just taking a break.

Leslie steps out from the lectern. "May I approach, Judge?"

"You may."

She walks casually to within a few feet and slips her hands in the pockets of her black pants. "I grew up playing tennis," she says. "I got to be quite good. I even played in college."

What am I supposed to say to that? Congratulations?

"It took a lot of practice though," she says. "A lot of time and patience. Skill only comes with practice. Would you agree with that?"

I stay silent.

"The point?" Hanks says.

I know the point now.

"Ms. Calby, I couldn't help but notice you omitted from your direct testimony any discussion regarding the manner in which you killed Mr. Brooker."

"I said I used a knife."

"Ah, but you were being too modest. You didn't just *use* it. We all heard the coroner's testimony. He said it would take great skill to inflict the wounds you did. Skill only comes with practice. High-level skill only comes with practice and dedication combined."

I take a chance on breaking her focus. Smiling, "Are you testifying or am I? I'll be glad to trade places with you."

"Sustained. Stick to questions, Ms. Tierney."

I pissed her off this time, that's for sure. She yanks her hands from her pockets and grips the rail around the witness box, leaning in. "The coroner testified he had never seen a groin wound like Mr. Brooker's in thirty years. To what do you attribute that remarkable success?"

My shoulders heave. "Actually, it was kind of lucky. It only happened because of the position he put me in."

"Is that your testimony, that the wounds you inflicted were the result of luck?"

"Not, like, *good* luck. It was all horrible, but, yeah, mostly. It's not like I'm some kind of professional killer if that's what you're suggesting."

Effing mistake! This is why the books say to keep your answers as short as possible on cross-examination. It's debatable whether I'm truly a *professional,* but it was stupid to *open the door* to the issue, as the books call it.

"So you didn't have any training of any kind?"

"Well, I train a lot physically. I like to stay in good shape."

"Did you have any training in how to use weapons? Specifically, a knife. In fact that reminds me, I believe you were wearing a ... what's it called? A *neck knife?*"

She knows what it's called. "Yes."

"Please tell the court what a *neck knife* is," she says like it's a dirty word.

"Just what it sounds like. It's a knife you wear around your neck."

"And it's designed to be concealed under one's clothes, is that correct?"

"Um, you can wear them in or out."

"But you chose to wear your neck knife hidden, correct?"

"Yes."

"Can you tell the court why were you wearing a concealed neck knife?"

Honestly, the more time that's gone by, the more I believe all girls should wear them ... okay, maybe not all, but any girl or boy who doesn't have other protection from predators. Her question is number five on my list of possible questions she would ask, so I'm ready for it.

"Because being alone and a young girl, I was afraid I might run into a rapist like Scott Brooker." *Zing.*

She doesn't flinch. "Did you ever train to use weapons to kill people?"

"Judge?" I say. "When I testified you made me stick to the facts about the decedent."

Leslie puffs up. "Your Honor, it's obvious you've been trying to protect the defendant from her foolish decision to waive her right to counsel."

"Watch your step, counselor," he says. "It's my responsibility to look out for everyone who comes before this court."

"And admirable that is, but here the evidence speaks for itself. The coroner testified—in seeming amazement—about the defendant's skill in killing Mr. Brooker. Whether she was an innocent victim, like she claims, or someone trained to use deadly weapons is directly relevant to her credibility regarding self-defense."

Hanks scratches his cheek, already stubbled from the long day. Gray. I knew he dyed his hair. "Go ahead. Repeat the question."

"Ms. Calby, did you ever train to use deadly weapons to kill human beings? Yes or no."

If I lie, I'm breaking my sworn oath and not being authentic. If I tell the truth, I risk looking like an assassin and exposing Lucas. Easy choice. *Sorry God*, again.

"Of course not. That's crazy." I wish Dulcie didn't have to hear this. "I took out the knife when he made me get down on my knees. He was standing right in front of me with his pants pulled down, so it makes sense the knife would go up, right?"

"What about the precision neck wound across his carotid artery?"

"I–I was just … it all happened so fast. I didn't even have time to think about it. I just slashed."

"I see. Lucky again, that's your testimony?"

"Like I said, I'm very physically fit. Ask anyone at Pochachant. I'm obsessed with working out. And I grew up playing softball, which requires a lot of hand-eye coordination. Maybe that had something to do with it."

"So you're just a naturally gifted killer?"

I don't have time to object before Hanks reprimands her and tells her to reframe the question.

She continues to berate me, challenging almost every word of my testimony. It rattles me inside, but I manage to keep my cool.

Nearly an hour passes before Hanks looks at the wall clock and says, "Are you about through, Ms. Tierney? This is getting repetitive."

"Almost, Judge. Ms. Calby, at the end of your direct testimony, you recounted a conversation with Mr. Brooker. Do you recall that?"

"Yes."

"Could you describe it one more time?"

"I asked if he really had a daughter."

"Why did you ask that?"

My eyes dart to Dulcie. "I knew what was about to happen and I really did feel bad for Dul— ... for his daughter."

The emotion, genuine as it is, passes Leslie right by. She's already asking the next question.

"And you indicated he answered affirmatively and asked why you had raised the question, is that correct?"

"Yes."

"What exactly did you say after that?"

She's on a mission, but I can't figure out what it is. "Um, I don't remember my exact words."

"Allow me to refresh your memory." She picks up a sheaf of paper. "You then testified, and I quote, *I said I felt sorry for her and that was the end.* What did you mean by *the end*?"

"That's when I, you know, exercised my right to self-defense."

"To be clear, that's when you stabbed him in the groin and slashed his throat, is that correct?"

I mumble, "Mm-hm."

"I'm sorry, I'm not sure the court reporter got that. Could you repeat your answer?"

"Yes."

"And just now you said *I knew what was about to happen.* So you admit you knew in advance you were going to kill him?"

Too late I realize the trap she laid, and how I fell into it head-first. The mock cross-examination with Paula replays in my brain. *"Did you feel imminently threatened with bodily harm at the time you killed Mr. Brooker?" "What does imminently mean?" "Immediately."*

My flushing skin betrays me. "No, not in advance. It happened, like, all at the same time."

"But you had enough time to have a conversation about it beforehand, right? Does that sound like someone in imminent fear of being attacked?"

"I was stalling for time."

"Until you could get your neck knife out? Is that your testimony?"

"No, I mean, at that point, yes, but—"

"Thank you. No more questions," she says. She takes two steps and stops.

"Sorry, Judge, almost forgot. Ms. Calby, isn't it true that before you were extradited to Louisiana, you were arrested in Arkansas for carrying an illegal handgun?"

With pleading eyes, "Judge?"

Hanks looks at me like a man who just changed his mind. All he does is shake his head.

"I'll repeat the question. Were you arrested for carrying an illegal handgun?"

"It wasn't loaded."

"Yes or no."

"I was never convicted."

"Answer the question."

"Yes."

"Thank you. And bear with me, Your Honor, just one more. Ms. Calby, were you angry after those two men hurt your family like that?"

"Of course I was."

"Angry enough to kill?"

I don't answer.

Leslie says, "Now I'm finished, Judge."

37

TOMORROW IS my *denouement*, one of Mom's look-up words from the fourth grade. My sentence was, *Sleeping is the denouement of my day*. Mom laughed and stuck it to the refrigerator. All that's left are the rebuttal witnesses and closing arguments. Then my fate will rest with The Law.

The sky is dusky by the time I make it back to Pochachant. Hanks wanted to keep me in Opelousas for the night, but I argued it would be a denial of my right to the effective assistance of counsel because I need my law books. Either he bought it or was sick of arguing with me because he didn't put up a fuss.

I spent the ride back consumed by the question of whether I killed Brooker purely out of self-defense, like I've been telling myself for three years. Was there another way out, another ending to the story in which Brooker lived?

I could have pulled out the knife and threatened him. He wasn't carrying a weapon. But then what? We were miles from anywhere and he was a lot bigger than me. I would have lost the element of surprise, my most powerful weapon according to Lucas. If it happened today I could probably take him without a weapon, but I was small, weaker then. And he could have had a gun in his car. How could I know?

I needed to act fast … but I also knew he needed to die. Can something be self-defense and murder at the same time?

No Rebecca when I get back to my cell, a disappointment and new worry. Having missed dinner, I tear open a pack of peanut butter crackers from the commissary and get out my phone. I find the number for the hospital in Baton Rouge, but get transferred to an ICU nurse who says Paula's resting and can't talk.

"How's she doing?"

"I'm not permitted to say." She starts to explain about patient confidentiality and I cut her off.

"Could you please tell her Emily called and that I'm praying for her?"

Just as well I didn't get through. I would have had to lie. I know Paula. If I told her I'm representing myself, she'd feel even worse, blame herself.

I polish off the crackers and call Lucas, outlining the day's events: the *Faretta* hearing, my direct examination and disastrous performance on cross.

"Leslie started bragging about how she was a good enough tennis player to play in college. I was like, what in the world? Then she said you can only get good at something through practice and dedication and I knew I was being set up. She tried to make me out to be some kind of an expert killer because of the way I stabbed Brooker."

"Bottom line?" he says.

"I really thought I had a shot until things fell apart at the end. She made it sound like Brooker and I were just sitting around chatting when I decided to pull out a knife and stab him. And omigod, you should have seen the look on that judge's face when he heard I got arrested in Arkansas for carrying the Sig. Tomorrow's going to make it all worse. Leslie gets to bring in character witnesses to testify that Brooker was an angel."

"You remember our conversation."

"Hard to forget."

"I'll be ready."

"Lucas, I don't know."

"Give me a thumbs-up if the result's good, thumbs-down if it ain't."

"Where will you be?"

"Around."

"I'm just not sure. I don't want to live in South America."

"We'll figure it out."

Someone's unlocking the cell. "Gotta go." I hang up and stuff the phone under my pillow.

It's Longmont with Rebecca in tow. A relief.

"You're back," Longmont says cheerfully. "Rebecca here just had a nice long visit with her mother."

Rebecca rolls her eyes.

"Alice, I know you've been in court and have to go back in the morning. You up for a shower? We could also stop by the cafeteria and pick up some leftovers."

"Really? That'd be awesome. Thank you."

I gather my shower stuff while she talks to Rebecca. "Your mother sure looked happy today. I've never seen her like that."

Rebecca's hair-shield falls into place.

"I hope you'll see her again soon."

"I'm ready," I say quickly. I know Rebecca. She does not want to talk about it.

On the way to the showers, "CO, can I ask you something? Why are you so different from the other guards?"

"Different how?"

"Not being a butthead." That's the mildest way I can think to say it.

She laughs. "I just try to do my job."

"You actually seem to care about the girls. No one else does."

"There are a few of us. People take these jobs for lots of different reasons. Sometimes the wrong ones."

"What do you think of, you know, the other COs?"

We come to a set of double-doors. She stretches out the wire attached to the keyring on her belt and selects a key. "Depends which one," she says, unlocking the doors.

"Twiggs."

"What about him?"

I can't decipher her tone and can't see her eyes. *The eyes tell all*, Mom always said. "Just wondering what you think of him."

"There are some rumors, but there are rumors about every-one in this place. Depending who you ask, I'm either a lesbian or sleeping with the warden."

We reach the showers. "I'll wait for you out here," she says.

"I'll be quick."

The cafeteria crew is cleaning up for the night, but she persuades them to assemble a take-out bag for me. Leftover beef stroganoff, steamed carrots and a piece of bread. They ran out of dessert, but throw in an extra carton of milk.

I thank her again as we approach the cell. She wishes me good luck in court. I can't tell if she knows about the trial. She's pulling on the cell door when I block it with my foot.

"CO, about Twiggs. Just so you know, they're not just rumors."

* * *

I lick my finger and turn to a clean page in one of my legal pads. I'm ready to go to work on a list of questions for the rebuttal witnesses but realize I don't know anything about any of them. Guilt kept me from ever looking up Dulcie or her mother and I never paid attention to the preacher. I open my phone and do a search for Tammy Brooker. Nothing relevant comes up except Brooker's obituary.

I search for Dulcie. Her Facebook page is the top link. She goes to college in Illinois. Her cover photo is a golden Labrador. Not a very active user. Her last post was several months ago, a picture of the college volleyball team. I recognize her in the back row. That's really cool. I didn't know she was so tall.

I scroll down, wondering if she knows her profile is set on public. A beach trip, flowers in a meadow, more pictures of her dog. Usual Facebook fare, but then I come to a meme, white text over a picture of treetops shrouded in fog.

That is all I want in life: for this pain to seem purposeful.
— Elizabeth Wurtzel

It's dated not long after I killed her father. I caused that pain. I quickly close the window and do a search for Brooker's preacher. His name is on the witness list: Reverend Georgie Dykes. *Georgie*. What is he, like five?

His picture pops up on the church website. Deep tan, coiffed hair, plastic smile, like a TV evangelist. My pastor back in Georgia was like family. I grew up with him. But after the incident where the preacher kicked Lucas and me out of church for being a *mixed family*, I'm wary of them all.

I skim past links to church events and blog posts about spirituality, ending up in the ads. I'm about to close the page when I see *More Results*.

No friggin' way. At the top of the next page: *Wife Accuses Local Pastor of Domestic Violence*. It's good ol' Georgie boy, from five years ago. I take notes as I read. They were getting divorced and she accused him of *slapping her in the face and locking her in the bathroom on more than one occasion*.

That's all there is.

I toss the legal pad aside and flip my pillow, wet from my freshly shampooed hair, so squeaky clean I keep sniffing it. I call Lucas to finish the conversation that got cut off when Longmont brought Rebecca back.

No answer. Just as well. I'm wasted.

Rebecca has been unusually quiet tonight, even for her. She's been polishing her paint box for half an hour.

"Any word about Ben today?" I say.

"Nope."

"I miss him. Is that pathetic, to miss someone who rejected you?"

"Probably, but that's the way people are. The more someone rejects us, the more we miss them."

I wonder if she's talking about herself. "How was your visit today with your mom?"

"Not bad."

"Do you want to talk about it?"

"No."

"Okay. Let me know if you change your mind."

Something's not right with her. She turns away when I try to look at her, lips caulked together. I watch as her face turns redder and redder, like a balloon about to pop.

I'm about to ask what's wrong when she blurts, "Emily," and slaps a hand to her mouth, eyes riveted on the cell door. "Emily," she repeats in a whisper. "Is it okay if I call you that when there's no one around?"

"Of course. You should. That's my name."

Can a name make a difference? I wouldn't have thought so until today. Maybe it took being my own lawyer, responsible for the fate of my client, but the judgment Emily Calby showed in court today kicked the crap out of how Alice Black would have behaved.

"I have to tell you something," she says, one hand pinching her lips as she speaks, like she's in a fight with a conjoined twin. "I don't want to ... but I have to. It's about ... oh, never mind."

"What? No never mind. You can't leave me in suspense like that. What is it?"

"It's just that, well, do you remember the night you asked me to predict your future and I said I couldn't?"

I laugh. "Actually, I do. I was just joking, but the way you reacted kind of creeped me out."

"I had a bad feeling that day." She squeezes her eyes shut. "I still have it. I can't make it go away." Her eyes pop back open, wider than I've ever seen, brown buttons on eggshells.

"Feeling about what?"

"Something bad happening—to you."

"Don't worry. I already know. I'm going to get convicted for killing Scott Brooker."

"Maybe ... but I'm not sure that's it."

"It must be. Even if it's not, nothing could be worse than that."

"I guess that's true," she says. "And I'm not always right. So there's probably nothing to worry about."

It's obvious she doesn't believe that. The closer we've become, the better I can read her, as if every day she raises the shades behind her eyes one more notch.

Right now, I see something in them much darker than worry. *Dread.*

38

"**THE BEST**," Tammy Brooker says from her round-back chair in the witness box, dabbing at her eyes with a tissue. She got her hair done and is wearing a modest floral print sleeveless dress. No accessories except for her wedding ring and a pair of pearl earrings. She's answering Leslie's question, *Was Scott a good husband?*

Leslie coached her up good. Gone are the perpetual scowl and nasty edge in her voice, replaced by a calm, credible woman talking with deep sadness about how she lost her husband in a brutal killing. I started the morning objecting to the whole process:

"Judge, am I allowed to call character witnesses to testify about what a great person I am?"

"No," he said firmly.

"Then how come Ms. Tierney gets to?"

"Because you have accused the decedent of a terrible crime and he is not here to defend himself due to the fact that, according to your testimony, you killed him."

"Alright."

In an hour, Tammy Brooker has testified that Scott Brooker was a good everything, even a cook.

"He was all the things a person could want in a husband. Faithful, honest, loving, you name it."

I shuffle my feet, but manage to keep the rage-tiger caged.

"How about as a father? Was he a good father?" Leslie says.

"He was a wonderful father. To be truthful, I think he loved Dulcie even more than me. She was everything to him."

Soft weeping behind me.

"Did you hear the defendant's testimony yesterday about your husband?"

Return of the scowl. "Yes."

"I apologize for asking you to relive it, but did the acts the defendant described sound like acts your husband would or could have done?"

"Absolutely not. You have to understand, Scott wasn't capable of cruelty. It wasn't in his DNA. We're talking about a man who spent his Christmas Eves working at the church soup kitchen."

"Would he ever pick up a hitchhiker?"

Smothering a *harrumph*, "Probably the defendant. She testified Scott compared her to Dulcie. I don't doubt that. His compassion would make it impossible for him to pass by a girl stranded on the interstate, especially one near Dulcie's age."

"Thank you, Mrs. Brooker. No more questions, Judge."

Hanks locks and unlocks his long fingers. "Very well," he says. "We have a bit of a predicament here. Mrs. Brooker, despite my earlier ruling, I'm afraid the defendant, acting as her own counsel, has a legal right to address you personally."

The crevices in her forehead deepen, but she nods.

With a warning built into his tone, "Ms. Calby, do you have any questions for Mrs. Brooker?"

"Um, just a couple." I go to the lectern and adjust the microphone. "Mrs. Brooker, I don't mean to be disrespectful, but did you usually accompany your husband on his business trips?"

"His business trips? Of course not."

"So you don't really know what he did when he was away, do you? I mean, you can't be sure."

"I *know* my husband," she says. "Or I did, until you murdered him."

"Judge?" I say, wincing.

"Mrs. Brooker, please avoid legal conclusions."

Silence ticks by before Hanks says, "Ms. Calby, what are you waiting for?"

"She hasn't answered my question. Should I ask it again?"

"You could," he says.

"Mrs. Brooker, did you know what your husband was doing when he was away on business trips? That's all I'm asking."

"Not every minute of the day or night. How could I possibly know that?"

"Thank you. No more questions, Judge." I return to my seat.

* * *

The Reverend Georgie Dykes looks nothing like his glamour shot on the church website. It must have been taken twenty years ago. He's tried but failed to hide the years with plastic surgery and hair transplants, leaving behind a skull-like face stretched tight as a drum with rows of hair plugs sprouting like carrot tops from his head.

He speaks in an irritatingly sanctimonious tone, as if his every word should be taken as gospel. Leslie has led him through a similar litany of the sex predator's wonderfulness.

"*Upright*. That's the best word I could use to describe Scott. He was one of the only parishioners I allowed alone in the church office where we kept the collection money because I knew he would never steal a red cent."

"Do you believe he would ever physically harm anyone? Specifically, would he hurt a young girl?"

"Oh, Lord, no. Scott was a man who worshipped the figure of Eve."

I swallow a laugh. I'll bet he did.

"His respect for women was exceeded only by his respect for God."

"And you traveled here all the way from Illinois to stake your professional reputation on Mr. Brooker's good character, isn't that right?"

"Yes. All of God's children are broken in some way. There are no perfect ones among us, but Scott was as close as it gets."

Give me an effing break. *God, you need a new man down here. This one's a complete idiot.*

"That's all the questions I have, Judge," Leslie says.

"Very well."

Dykes stands to exit before Hanks holds up a hand. "Ms. Calby, do you have any questions for this witness?"

"As a matter of fact I do." I return to the microphone and put on my brightest, blondest smile. "Good morning, Reverend!"

Taken aback, "Well, good morning, young lady."

"I'm the defendant in this case. I have a few questions. You said you trusted the decedent alone with the collection money."

"That's right."

"Did you trust him alone with the Sunday school class he taught?"

"Well, of course."

"Reverend, isn't it true that all of the students were minors?"

"That's usually the case with a *Youth Group*," he says sarcastically.

"Isn't it true that churches are rampant with child sexual abuse?"

Leslie stands. "Objection. Irrelevant."

"Sustained."

"Allow me to rephrase," I say. Throughout the trial, I've compiled a list of Leslie's courtroom sayings. "Reverend, isn't it a proven fact that pedophiles sometimes take jobs at churches to gain access to children?"

"Judge!" Leslie bellows.

"Sustained. Ms. Calby, the rules of evidence do not permit questions based on unfounded innuendo. They must have a *factual* predicate relevant to your case."

"Okay, sorry." I study my legal pad. "Reverend, how can you afford plastic surgery on a preacher's salary?"

Leslie's up again. "Objection. Judge, this is getting ridiculous. *Please* make her sit down."

"Sustained. Ms. Calby, this witness is not on trial."

"I'm trying to impeach him. And the factual predicate is right in front of us. I don't mean to be rude, but look at his face."

Hanks picks up his gavel like he wants to reach out and knock me in the head with it, sets it back down and flexes his fingers. "The question is *not relevant*. Move on. Reverend, I apologize."

"Mr. Dykes—"

"*Reverend* Dykes."

"Excuse me. *Reverend* Dykes." You pompous ass. "You said in your direct testimony that the decedent's respect for women was exceeded only by his respect for God. Is that accurate?"

"Yes," he says curtly. Nobody's trying to hide their irritation anymore.

"How are you able to judge that? A person's respect for women."

"I do not judge. I am a man of the cloth."

I roll my eyes. "How are you able to *measure* a person's respect for women?"

"Because, young lady, I have eyes and ears. I am an observer of life. I know what I hear and see."

"Did you hear and see it when you were slapping your wife in the face and locking her in the bathroom?"

His mouth gapes as Leslie catapults toward the bench. I plug my ears to protect them from Hanks' gavel thundering through the sound system.

"There you go, Judge," Leslie says, flipping her hands up. "Are you satisfied? This is what you get for letting her represent herself."

Hanks' sigh into the mic sounds like rushing wind. "Ms. Calby, until this cross-examination your demeanor and performance have been a pleasant surprise. I'm very disappointed you would ask such a slanderous question after what we just got done discussing."

"But I have a factual predicate, Judge. I found an article online where his wife accused him of the exact same facts I said.

Unfortunately, because I'm locked in a prison and don't have a printer, I couldn't bring you a copy, but all you have to do is Google him."

Oh, brother. You have to be so careful what you say in court. I read the confused look on Hanks' face and jump in before he can speak. "And now you'll probably ask me how I found something online when I'm locked in detention."

"I am curious."

"Well, the honest answer is there's a girl at Pochachant with a contraband phone."

"More than one from what I hear," he says and looks over at the reverend, a bit less reverently.

"It was my ex-wife," Dykes sputters. "She was lying, trying to extort alimony from me. We reached a settlement. No court ever said it was true."

Hanks gets his *I wish I could be playing golf* look. "Ms. Calby, even if the allegations are true, they aren't relevant to this case."

"With all due respect, Judge, the witness opened the door to the question by claiming to be an expert on measuring people's respect for women—including the decedent's."

"Fine, you've made your point. Do you have any other questions?"

"No, sir."

"Then sit down. Reverend, you are excused."

* * *

Lunch is a cold chicken panini on stale ciabatta bread. Not great, but a step up from the usual fare. It even came with a side of pasta and a pepperoncini.

Another "mom"-guard, you can always spot them, brought me some coffee. Muddy and barely warm, but caffeine is caffeine. I sip it as I assess my morning performance. I did okay with Tammy Brooker, but screwed up with the preacher, started to revert.

Need to dial it way back down for Dulcie, the last rebuttal witness. I read about the dangers of cross-examining a *sympathetic witness*. You risk looking cruel and turning everyone against you. Witnesses don't come any more sympathetic than poor Dulcie. I can't attack her, not tactically, not decently, even by the low standards of my dark heart. So what do I do?

I'm still thinking about the question when court resumes and Leslie summons Dulcie to the witness stand. She passes me wearing the same black shift as yesterday. Maybe she ran out of clothes. They're probably staying at a hotel. Her hair is twisted in a messy knot at the back.

"Good afternoon, Dulcie," Leslie says like they're old pals. "How are you today?"

"Okay." Her face is drawn. She skipped makeup today.

"I know this is all very hard on you, so I'm going to keep my questioning short. Could you begin by describing your father?"

In a barely audible voice that sounds younger than her age, "Um … what do you want me to describe? There's a lot to describe about a person."

"I'll be more specific. Did you have a close relationship with him?"

"Yes."

"How close was it?"

"Very close."

"Could you please describe it for the court?" Leslie prods.

"It was more than a typical father-daughter relationship."

"Alright, then. Having a close relationship with your father, could you ever imagine him doing the acts alleged by the defendant in her testimony?"

Dulcie avoids making eye contact with me, but she's not really looking at Leslie either, more like gazing right through her.

"What do you think? You already heard my mother and Reverend Dykes. They both said my father was perfect."

"So he was a good father?"

Voice breaking, "He taught me everything I know about life."

Leslie says, "No more questions."

Judge Hanks holds out a box of tissues to Dulcie and turns to me. "Ms. Calby, do you have any questions?" It comes out like a dare.

I stand up and hesitate, still trying to catch Dulcie's eyes without success. "Um, I guess not, Judge."

With palpable relief, "You may step down, Ms. Brooker. Thank you for coming today."

"Thank you," she says in a daze. "I mean, you're welcome."

She passes the defense table looking at the floor, looking lost.

"The state rests," Leslie announces.

Hanks nods. "Very well. What about the defense? Any surrebuttal?"

"What's that, Judge?"

"Witnesses to rebut the rebuttal witnesses."

I almost make a joke and say, *I wish.* "No, sir."

"Are both sides ready for closing argument?"

"The state is ready," Leslie says.

"Ms. Calby?"

"Would it be possible to recess until the morning to give me a little more time?" I'm ready to argue that Leslie has two assistants and I don't even have a computer, but it's not necessary.

"Objection, Ms. Tierney?"

"No objection."

"Then court will be in recess until eight-thirty tomorrow morning at which time I will hear closing arguments. I spoke with Ms. Dunwoody during the noon hour. I am pleased to report she is out of danger, although still in intensive care. She asked me to give you her best, Ms. Calby."

I nod, happy she's out of danger, but still feeling guilty that I helped put her there.

They keep me in the interview room until the van is ready. When the guards lead me out the back door into the alley, I pretend to stretch while flashing two thumbs-up, just in case Lucas is watching. If I do decide to go with his crazy plan, I'm at least waiting until the trial is over.

39

I ENTER cell 49B to find Rebecca rocking back and forth on the edge of her bunk, gripping the iron frame with white knuckles. Lines of anticipation or apprehension, maybe both, etch her usually baby-smooth skin.

I wait until the CO leaves. "Don't worry," I say. "Nothing bad happened. I mean, nothing worse than usual. Looks like your premonition was off this time."

She lets go of the bar and flops on her back. "Well, I didn't guarantee it would happen today."

I laugh. "It wasn't a criticism. It's not like I'm disappointed."

"Oh, right. So what did happen?"

"Leslie presented her rebuttal witnesses."

"I know that. What did they say?"

"Good grief. You're turning into me. Can I get out of this suit and relax first?"

I change into a uniform and unwrap the tight bun in my hair, brushing it out while massaging my scalp, aware of Rebecca studying my every move. I wash up with cold water and plop down on my bunk, drying my face with a towel as rough as canvas. All the comforts of home.

"So?" Rebecca says.

"Well, there's really not that much to tell ..."

I summarize the testimony of Tammy Brooker and the Reverend Georgie Dykes. Shocking Rebecca isn't easy, but she practically chokes on her laugh as I describe my cross-examination of Dykes.

"You said it just like that, him slapping his wife and locking her in the bathroom?"

"Yep."

"That's *aww-some*."

"Not really. I got in big trouble for it. It wasn't 'relevant' according to the judge," borrowing Rebecca's air quotes.

"What about Dulcie?"

"Hm, what about Dulcie? Good question. She said all the right things, but something seemed weird about her testimony. I wish you could have been there to see if you got the same vibe."

"What kind vibe?"

"I can't put my finger on it. She wouldn't look at me, not even a glance, and she kept her answers super-short. If someone killed my father, I'd want to testify all day long about how great he was."

"Everybody's not you. It sounds like she's depressed."

"I think you're right. She wore the same dress as yesterday and didn't even bother to do her hair or makeup."

"And it's kind of obvious why she wouldn't want to look at the person who mutilated her father with a knife."

"Mutilated? You don't have to put it like that."

"How would you put it?"

"Well ... probably something like that if I was being honest."

"Tell me exactly what she said."

"She said she had a very close relationship with her father and that it was more than a typical father-daughter relationship. Then Leslie asked if she could ever picture him doing something like I said and she said he was perfect."

Her eyebrows arch. "Perfect? She actually used that word?"

"Mm-hm."

"Anything else?"

"Leslie's last question was whether Brooker was a good father. Dulcie said he taught her everything she knows about life and started crying."

"Sounds to me like she dug your grave pretty deep. She just did it without a lot of wasted words."

"Thanks, Rebecca. Thank you so much for that opinion."

*　*　*

I spend a couple of hours after dinner working on my closing argument. The words burble with anger and I have to cross out and rewrite each sentence.

My phone vibrates with a text saying it's Lucas, but I don't recognize the number. Paranoid, I write back, *How do I know this is really you?* He provides verification with, *Who the fuck else would it be?*

I call him and he explains he ditched the other burner because he got a couple of calls from unknown numbers that spooked him. That's why I couldn't reach him last night. It spooks me too.

He saw my thumbs-up when I left the courthouse and thought I won. When I tell him I still have another day of trial, he complains, "You know how hard it is to hang around that place incognito?"

"I don't exactly have a lot of control over the schedule."

I catch him up on the day's events, the rebuttal witnesses. He laughed about Georgie Dykes before saying he had work to do and disconnecting me.

I try the Baton Rouge hospital again and finally get through to Paula.

"Paula! It's Emily. How are you?"

"Emily," she says, weakly but warmly. "So good to hear from you. I'm making it. How are you? I've been worrying about you."

That's Paula, in critical condition for a week and worried about me.

"I'm sorry, Paula. I probably caused the whole thing."

"No, no. It was a problem waiting to happen. It had been

getting worse for a while. I should have gone to a specialist a lot sooner. Please forgive me for not being there for you at trial."

She out-apologizes me as usual.

"Tell me what's happening," she says. "I spoke with Judge Hanks, but he wouldn't say anything except that your trial is still going on. I'm surprised he didn't declare a mistrial. How do you like your new public defender? Who did they assign to you? Is it Steve? He handles a lot of serious juvenile cases. Tanisha's good too."

"Er, well, you see, the thing about that is ..."

40

THE CELL is dark and still when my eyes snap open. There's no foggy, half-asleep moment wondering where I am or why I woke up. I fell asleep thinking about Dulcie, dreamed about her and she's still here.

I punch the thin pillow into shape and try to get her out of my head. Think about something else, something happy. *Puppies.* I love puppies, especially Rocky, the black lab I grew up with. We got him when he was only eight weeks old ...

Dulcie has a golden lab. I saw it on her Facebook page. I squirm and sit up. There's no way I'm falling back asleep. I reach under the bed for the phone. *4:20 AM.*

Why is she stuck in my brain? Obvious. She's suffering and *I caused it.* Me, a girl who lost her own dad and suffers for it every day.

I open the browser and go back to her Facebook page. There's her dog. I study the page more carefully. She's majoring in biology. Her best friends are Amelia and Haley. They're together in almost every picture. Tall like Dulcie, probably on the volleyball team with her.

Nothing new, but I didn't expect there to be.

I scroll down to where I left off last time, the meme about wanting her pain to have a purpose. The tree tops in the background poke through the fog like heads fighting to stay above water. I skate past images of a volleyball tournament and a girls' night out before landing on another sad meme. June 15. Yellow words superimposed on a black heart blocking out the moon:

Everyone bears a hidden pain.
It may not show, but every person has a secret burden.

I did so much damage that day I never saw or even thought about. I remember Lucas talking about his time in Iraq. *We could deliver a missile on top of a man's head from a thousand miles away, obliterate his whole family and never see nothin' but a puff of smoke on a screen.*

I'm sorry, Dulcie. I really am. For the very first time, I truly wish I didn't kill Scott Brooker.

The words burn my eyes and I hurry to the next post. ... Wait a second. What did I just see? I scroll back up to the meme.

June 15 ... three years ago? That was *before* I killed Brooker. Can't be right. I do the math again. Huh. Exactly thirty-one days before Brooker picked me up hitchhiking.

I assumed all her pain was about losing her dad.

Below the meme she gets noticeably younger. A few pictures with friends or her mom, but none of Brooker.

I come to a picture of her holding a cake, surrounded by her mother and girlfriends, everyone bursting with Facebook smiles. *Happy Birthday to Me! Fifteen!* There's Brooker, in the background, stretched out on a recliner under the light of a floor lamp, gazing at the backs of the girls with a crooked smile.

I land at the bottom of her page. Her very first post, another meme. Gray letters over a black background:

Don't ask why someone keeps hurting you.
Ask why you keep letting them.

She was only thirteen.

I try to reconstruct Dulcie's testimony word by word. I told Rebecca that when Leslie asked if she could imagine her father doing something like I said, she said he was perfect, but that wasn't exactly it. She said her mom and the preacher said he was perfect.

Then Leslie asked if he was a good father and she said he taught her everything she knows about life. But there are good and bad things to learn about life. I get gooseflesh when I think about her answer to Leslie's question about their relationship. *It was more than a typical father-daughter relationship.*

Is it possible?

I reach for a legal pad and clip my light to it. *Dear Dulcie ...*

I tear off the sheet, fold it in a square and slide it into the lapel pocket of my suit jacket. Five o'clock. Time to get ready.

41

THE BREAKING sun washes the morning sky in creamy orange as I exit Pochachant walking alongside Longmont. I was surprised when she showed up at the cell to retrieve me, first time it's happened. A front must have passed through overnight. The bomb crater potholes in the parking lot are filled with water and the air's cooler. Hard to believe it's already October.

I look for the van, but there isn't one. Instead I see two guys in crisp blue uniforms and Mountie hats standing next to a red-on-white state trooper car with the motor running and headlights on. Longmont tells me to wait behind while she does some paperwork.

"What happened to the van?" I ask when she comes back. "And why the state troopers?"

She shrugs. "Those things are above my pay grade."

A trooper comes over and double-checks my transport restraints before guiding me to the car. He opens the back door and tells me to be careful getting in. I have one foot on the floorboard and the trooper's hand grazing the top of my head when I twist back to Longmont.

"CO, if I don't come back for some reason, will you please look out for Rebecca?"

She nods with a quizzical look.

Rebecca's sense of foreboding followed me to the parking lot. I'd worry more, except there really isn't anything worse that could happen than being found guilty, which I'm already expecting, unless I die in an accident on the way to the court-house. Even that would have its advantages.

Everything about the ride feels different. The car, for one thing. I'm used to having privacy in the back of a van. And the state troopers aren't like the regular drivers. They don't talk, not even to each other. The only sounds are the rushing mo-tor, thumping wheels and intermittent squawks from a radio mounted below the dashboard.

The scenery is mostly bayou with a few farms. We're in the fast lane and everyone gets out of our way. I poke my head up to see the speedometer. We're doing eighty. So much for The Law. Cops break it whenever they want.

I study the occupants of the cars we whiz past. Just regular people on their way to work or taking kids to school. Normal life. I hardly remember it.

Pulling off the Opelousas exit, squealing tires from behind make me turn my head. It's another cop car with blue lights flashing. Are we getting pulled over for speeding? That would be too funny.

The radio erupts. "Three four niner, are you with me?"

The passenger pushes a button. "Roger that."

"This is your detour ..."

Detour? For what? "Excuse me, sir."

He shushes me. "Copy," he says. "We will be there in five."

"Excuse me," I repeat in my politest voice. The Alice Black in me wants to bite his ear off for shushing me. "Could you please tell me why we're taking a detour?"

He ignores me, talking to the driver and pointing.

I sink back into the seat. Just as it occurs to me they might be hijacking me to another place, the back of the courthouse comes into view and the radio belches again. "You will be ap-proaching the alley from the west. Barricades are in place."

"Copy."

Barricades? *Oh, jeez.* They must have found out about Lucas's plan. Maybe that was Rebecca's premonition. *Lord, please let him be safe.*

Closing in on the courthouse, I see the barricades, blocking off the side streets. We swing into the alley and grind to a halt at the back door, same as always except that the troopers rush to extract me from the backseat like a meteor is about to land on the car.

A shriek at the end of the alley. "It's her, it's her!"

They hustle me inside, down the hall and into the elevator, carrying me by the armpits when I trip over my ankle restraints. We get off at the courtroom level and head straight for Judge Hanks' chambers.

When we enter, Hanks is sitting alone at the end of the conference table holding a coffee mug and looking at a large computer monitor set up in the middle of the table. He picks up a remote and turns it off.

"Thank you, officers," he says. "You can remove her restraints and leave us."

"Are you sure, Judge?"

"We'll be fine. Please shut the door behind you."

They follow his instructions.

"Good morning, Ms. Calby," he says casually when they're gone.

"Nice to see you, Your Honor."

He takes a swig from his steaming mug. "Would you like some coffee?"

"Yeah, um, sure."

He fills a ceramic mug with the state seal on the side. "I have some sweetener, but no creamer."

"That's okay. I like it black."

He hands me the cup, leans back and stares at the wall of golf pictures.

I slurp the coffee, hot and fresh. It would be awesome to start every morning of trial like this, drinking coffee and chatting with the judge. I don't understand what's happening, but a little bird in my ear says, *Don't ask.*

I say, "Would you rather be playing golf, Judge?"

His laugh is a *humphf*. "You caught me. So you know what this is about."

I shake my head. "No idea. I've just seen you looking at your golf pictures before."

"Oh, come now. You're not under oath, but I would appreciate honest answers."

"I'm not trying to be a smart-ass, Judge, but what's the question?"

Exasperated, "The question is are you or are you not responsible for this?"

I'm lost. "Brooker?" Is he allowed to ask me that out of court? I already testified. Where's the court reporter? Where's Leslie?

"Not Brooker," he says impatiently. "*This*." He points the remote at the monitor and it lights up.

It takes a moment for me to recognize the courthouse from the outside. The sound is off but words crawl across the bottom of the screen: *CNN LIVE: BREAKING NEWS. Missing Home Invasion Victim on Trial for Murder in Louisiana ... Emily Calby Disappeared at Age 12 ... Horrific Crime Captured Nation's Attention ...*

"Oh, shit. I mean ..."

"I share the sentiment. So you didn't leak information about your case to the media?"

"Absolutely not."

"Do you give me your word?"

I gawk at the screen. The street in front of the courthouse is swarming with news trucks. "Trust me. *That* is the last thing in the world I want. Like Ms. Tierney said, I've been hiding for three years."

Rebecca's premonition. It came true.

"Some people—including someone in particular whom we both know well—are likely to assert you leaked the information to gain sympathy."

A prematurely gray man in glasses is talking as a video of me getting out of the state trooper car a few minutes ago plays in a corner of the screen. "Never, Judge. I'll swear on a bible right now."

"Well, someone did and I'm going to do my best to find out."

"Did you think about Ms. Tierney? She's running for judge. Her whole campaign is to clean the streets of *gutter rats* like me."

His telephone rings. He ignores it. It rings again. Then again. He unplugs it.

"She was the second person I thought about."

* * *

"Ms. Tierney, I'm asking you as an officer of this court, are you responsible for this mess?" Hanks says.

"Of course not. I think we all know who the most likely leaker is." She stabs an accusing finger at me. "It seems obvious. She's losing her case, so she resorts to a sympathy ploy."

"Ms. Calby has denied it, as has everyone else in this room. Everyone be aware that an investigation to determine the leaker's identity is already underway. In the meantime, we will all be subject to enhanced security."

He goes on to impose a gag order to not talk about the case to *anyone and that includes your dog,* saying violators will be held in contempt of court. "Ms. Calby, are you paying attention?"

I'm seated sideways at the defense table, trying to spy on Dulcie. On the way in, as I got even with her table, I pointed at the window and said, "Look! There's someone out there with a camera." Everyone turned and I dropped my note in front of her. She had to have seen it.

"Are we finally ready to get on with closing arguments?" Hanks says, clearly irritated.

"The state has been ready," Leslie says.

I stand up. "Judge, the defense is not quite ready because we would like to call one more witness in … what did you call it?"

"Surrebuttal?"

"Correct."

"Here we go again," Leslie says. "Objection. There are no more witnesses on the witness list."

Hanks says, "You can't add new witnesses at this point, Ms. Calby."

"She's not a new witness. I'd like to call Dulcie Brooker."

"Your request is denied," he says flatly. "You had the opportunity to cross-examine her yesterday and declined."

"But I have new evidence."

He looks doubtful. "And just how did you find new evidence overnight while locked in a cell?"

"Remember I mentioned that girl with the contraband phone? I found it on the internet."

Leslie stands and practically spits at me. "Are you incapable of doing even one decent thing? Just one? Your Honor, the state refuses to be a party to the defendant inflicting more pain on these victims."

"It's okay."

Everyone looks at Dulcie, still wearing the black shift, no makeup again and hair even messier than yesterday.

"It's okay," she repeats.

"Are you sure, Ms. Brooker?" Hanks says. "I've already denied her request."

"I'm sure."

He clicks his fingernails against the bench in staccato bursts that sound like a Georgia woodpecker. "Very well," he says, throwing his hands up. "Come forward, Ms. Brooker."

For the first time, I'm standing when she passes me. She's at least five-ten, maybe taller. She angles around the side and settles into the witness box. Hanks reminds her that she's still under oath.

I say, "May I approach the witness, Your Honor?"

"No."

"You let Ms. Tierney do it."

He scowls and motions me forward.

I stop before I invade her space. *Be authentic. Admit your fear. Connect emotionally.*

"Dulcie. Is it okay if I call you Dulcie? I know your mom doesn't like it, but I feel weird calling you Ms. Brooker."

She nods.

"First, I'll tell you that I'm scared to death right now. I've been scared for three years, honestly. Every day. I hide it pretty well most of the time, but it takes so much work to hide the truth. It's exhausting."

She looks me in the eyes for the first time, but her face is unreadable.

"Judge?" Leslie says impatiently.

"Get on with it, Ms. Calby," Hanks says.

"Dulcie, I looked at your Facebook page last night. I apologize for violating your privacy, but it's set on public. I'm not sure if you know that."

A frown, at me or Mark Zuckerberg I'm not sure.

"I saw you have a golden lab," I stall.

"I do."

"I used to have a black lab, well, my family did. They're really good dogs. I don't think there's a more loyal kind of dog anywhere."

Leslie erupts. "Now we're talking about dogs, Judge?"

Dulcie ignores her. "I agree."

"I'm going to ask you some personal questions and I won't blame you if you don't want to answer them. Just say so. I won't try to get the judge to make you or anything."

"Okay."

"So, yeah, I kind of saw some sad memes on your Facebook page. I thought they were because of … what I did, but then I noticed some of them came before your father's, um, death."

Leslie says, "Can we please get to a question, Judge?"

"Ms. Calby?"

"I'm getting there."

A helicopter is clattering outside, maybe the state police, or a TV station getting an overhead view of the breaking news. To have any chance of keeping it together, I tell myself that nothing outside of this courtroom exists.

"Ms. Calby," Hanks says more harshly.

More harshly back, "I said I'm getting there. Dulcie ..."

But I'm not. I have no freaking idea what to ask or how to ask it. Should I ask what her hidden pain is? Should I ask who was hurting her when she was thirteen and why she kept letting them? If she says her seventh-grade boyfriend broke up with her, if I'm wrong about this whole thing ...

Might as well cut to the chase. Do or die. I've made some terrible decisions in my life. I hope this isn't another one.

Be delicate. "I really hate to ask you this question, but did your father ..."

Alarm bells go off everywhere. The guards and bailiff run out the main door. Hanks closes his eyes and lowers his head.

They come back a minute later. "Everything's okay, Judge," the bailiff says. "A reporter tried to come in through the rear delivery door. That door has been secured and the reporter escorted from the building."

"Get out there and tell them to secure every door and every window. And if there's another alarm, don't *everyone* run out. Your job is to guard this courtroom. Where were we? Ms. Calby?"

"I was in the middle of a question."

"Go on."

"Dulcie." I pause, my throat dry and tight. During the time-out, I almost changed my mind. "I was asking ... did your father ever, um, touch you inappropriately?"

From behind me, "Judge!"

"Sit down, Ms. Tierney. I'll handle this. Ms. Calby, we are not going to engage in another fishing expedition, certainly not one as offensive as that. You should be ashamed of yourself."

I open my mouth, but Dulcie talks first.

"I'll answer it," she says. "I have two answers. The first one, *Emily,* if I can call you by *your* first name, is that you didn't just kill my father, you slaughtered him. Those pictures will haunt me every day for the rest of my life. I think you must be a very sick person."

I almost nod in agreement.

"You handed me a note earlier. She opens my sheet of legal paper and reads. *"Dear Dulcie: The truth can set you free. John 8:32. Emily Calby."*

Leslie rushes the bench. "Did you hear that, Judge? She communicated with the victim in direct violation of your no-contact order. I move to hold the defendant in contempt of court and terminate this examination."

"Would you please just be quiet?" Dulcie.

I've been wanting to say that for three months. Leslie's eyes burn like torches, but she can't fight with her own victim.

"You want the truth? Here's the truth, Emily," Dulcie says. "I hate you. I always will."

Judge Hanks says, "Thank you, Ms. Brooker. That's enough. You may step down."

"I'm not finished. Do you understand why I will always hate you?"

"Of course," I say. "I'd be shocked if you didn't. I'd hate me too."

"You mentioned loyalty. Do you understand the meaning of true loyalty?"

"I think I do." Standing by someone at any cost, no matter what, even when they're wrong.

Hanks says gingerly, "Ms. Brooker, you're not supposed to be asking the defendant questions."

I say, "I deserve them, Judge. She can ask me whatever she wants."

"Have you ever for even one single second felt bad about what you did to my father?"

"Honestly? Not until last night, after you testified. I know it sounds bad, but I hated him for what he tried to do to me, and for how he bragged about doing it to other girls."

"And for what happened to your family?"

Hanks is waving his arms. "Hold on, hold on. Ms. Brooker, please, I can only handle one unlicensed lawyer at a time."

"It's okay, Your Honor," I say. "Yes, probably. I had a lot of anger inside me. I still do. And at that moment I'm not sure I could have separated what your father was doing to me from what the two men did to my mother and sister. But that doesn't change what happened. Everything I said was true."

Hanks pounds his gavel. "Okay, that's enough. Ms. Brooker, you are excused."

"Judge, I said I had two answers to her question. I'm finished with the first one. May I continue?"

With a grudging look, "If you really think it's necessary."

"You asked if my father ever touched me inappropriately. The simple answer is yes."

A gasp, more than one, followed by stunned silence, as if all air was suddenly vacuumed from the room. Then Tammy Brooker wails, "Don't let her do this to you, sweetheart. Oh, dear God, please."

"It's true, Mom," Dulcie says, tears breaking free. "It started when I was twelve."

42

LISTENING TO Dulcie's testimony broke my heart. Once she got going, I stepped aside to let her talk straight to her mom. No one interrupted, not even Leslie. She said there was another girl too, at the church, who was younger. I wondered if it was the blonde girl in the Sunday school picture, the one who wasn't smiling.

When she finished, Hanks said he didn't need closing arguments and declared a one-hour recess. A guard took me to my same little room to wait. Everyone we encountered on the way, the same court people I see every day, fell silent as I approached. We passed an office where three deputies were huddled around a blaring television: *We are now getting unconfirmed word that Emily Calby has admitted under oath that she stabbed—* One of them spotted me and muted the sound.

For the first time, I'm glad the interview room has no window. I pace back and forth, three steps each way from wall to wall. Lucas must know the news by now, especially if he's been *around*, as he calls it. At least I don't have to worry about him trying to bust me out, not with all the cops and cameras. Darla and Peggy have probably heard it. Peggy keeps the TV on all day.

Everyone in Dilfer County will know. Gossip spreads like wildfire in that place. I wonder what Meggie Tribet will think. We used to fantasize about being famous someday. Haha. Not exactly what I had in mind. And my preacher. What will he think about the choir girl he baptized as a baby?

A guard knocks and opens the door. "It's time," he says, inscrutable.

* * *

We're waiting for Judge Hanks, me at my table and Leslie at hers. Her assistants are gone. Tammy and Dulcie aren't here either. The only people left are the bailiff and court reporter. Leslie seems oddly absent, hands folded on the table, gazing ahead at the empty witness box.

Hanks enters from behind the bench.

"*Oyez, Oyez—*"

"Skip it," Hanks says. He sits down, holding a piece of paper. "I'm going to get straight to the point. The court has reached a decision in this case. I will read it into the record.

"*In the matter of State of Louisiana v. Emily Blair Calby aka Alice Black, Case No. 21-9835, this court hereby finds that, by her own admission, said Emily Blair Calby caused the death of Scott Brooker on the date and in the manner alleged in the petition.*"

Not exactly the opening I was hoping for.

"*However, the court also finds that Emily Blair Calby was acting in lawful self-defense at such time and is therefore not legally responsible for said death.*"

I close my eyes and bow my head.

"*The court reaches this conclusion based upon the defendant's testimony, which the court found credible, bolstered by evidence that the decedent showed a propensity for committing similar acts against minors.*"

It's good Dulcie and her mom aren't here.

"*Accordingly, Emily Blair Calby is hereby adjudicated non-delinquent and all charges against her are dismissed.*"

I want to cheer and cry at the same time. I want to throw my legal pad in the air and dance on the table. I want to hug someone, but the only candidate is Judge Hanks. I expect Leslie's claws to be out, ready to tear into Hanks with a torrent of objections, but she shows no emotion at all.

"Are there any questions from the defendant, or counsel for the defendant, or defendant-counsel? Ms. Calby, I have no idea what to call you now."

"How about *Emily*, Judge? Anything you want. I'm just so happy! May it please the court, I have a question. Oops, forgot." I stand up. "What does it mean? Can I just walk out of here?"

"Not quite. First, trust me, you wouldn't want to walk into that mess outside. Your paperwork needs to be properly processed. With all the attention, I hope you can appreciate the need for us to be extra careful to get everything exactly right."

"Sure, Judge, that makes perfect sense," I say almost jovially.

"You'll be kept overnight and released sometime tomorrow morning."

"Can I go back to Pochachant?"

"Actually, I've arranged to have you transported to a guarded hotel room. You are no longer charged with a crime. You will be comfortable and secure there."

"I don't want special treatment and really need to go back to Pochachant."

"You realize that the news of your case has most likely already reached there."

"I know, but my stuff is there and I have people I need to say goodbye to." There's no way I can just disappear on Rebecca.

Hanks shakes his head. "Another first, someone who wants to go back to Pochachant. I will have you placed in protective custody."

"Thanks, but that's not necessary. I'm safe there."

* * *

Ho-lee crappola. Outside is madness. The alley is blocked at both ends by barricades holding back swarms of people, including a girl about my age waving a big sign:

#FreeEmilyCalby

"There they are!" someone shouts and cameras go up everywhere.

One spectator stands out. He always does. Lucas, towering above the horde in his FBI suit and fake glasses, arms folded. I give him an enthusiastic double thumbs-up, but the crowd thinks it's for them and cheers.

"How is your trial going, Emily?" comes a shout.

I guess the verdict hasn't leaked yet, but it probably won't take long.

From the other end of the alley, "Emily, did you really kill someone?"

A woman pushes to the front, almost falling over the barricade. "Is it true you're acting as your own lawyer?"

The same two state troopers from this morning hurry me into the car. No restraints except my seatbelt. I've finally made it in life. Haha.

The driver turns on flashing lights, triggering a chain reaction, and a caravan of law enforcement vehicles creeps forward.

Cameras are everywhere when we reach the street. Cops on foot clear a path. One guy jams a huge lens in my face, so close it smacks the window. I almost flip him the finger, but force myself to stare resolutely at my lap, aware my life has once again been flipped upside down.

* * *

"Surprise!" Rebecca says when Longmont pulls open the cell door. She was waiting for me in the parking lot when the state trooper car pulled in.

Rebecca's holding out Gerry Spence's *Win Your Case* like a serving tray. Perched on top is a lumpy chocolate cake with a single burning candle. Her gleaming brown eyes sweep me with a warmth I haven't felt since I used to give goodnight hugs to Becky, powerful enough to knock you over, fill your heart and break it at the same time for fear of losing it.

"*Aw*, thank you. This is awesome," I say.

"Blow out that fire hazard before I get fired," Longmont says.

"Make a wish," Rebecca says.

I laugh. "Those are for birthdays."

"Wishes are for everything," she says seriously. "Even if they never come true."

I make a wish and blow out the candles. My wish is that Rebecca could come with me tomorrow. Lurking under the celebration is the knowledge that I'm getting out in the morning and she'll be stuck here all alone.

"Congratulations, *Emily*," Longmont says. "I still think you look like an Alice."

"You're in on this too? How did you guys hear?"

Rebecca lets loose a chain of cat-sneeze laughs. "The '*Missing Calby Girl on Trial for Murder*' news is everywhere."

I'm going to miss those air quotes so much.

"Lots of girls skipped yard time to watch it on TV in the day-room. Someone said *FreeEmilyCalby* is trending on Twitter. But the verdict only came out a little while ago, which is why your cake is three mushed-up cupcakes left over from lunch. I'll bet Birdman is kicking himself in the ass now," she cackles wickedly.

I love Rebecca's loyalty. When Dulcie asked if I knew the meaning of true loyalty, I wasn't sure why. I think I figured it out. She was trying to tell me how hard it was going to be for her to testify against her dad, to be disloyal, even after what he did.

Maybe Rebecca is right. Maybe Ben *has* heard and is thinking he made a mistake. It's possible. I shouldn't care, but of course I do.

My adrenaline has drained away by the time Longmont says goodbye. Rebecca and I sit on the bunks finishing off the cake.

She says through frosted lips, "I wonder whatever happened to my premonition."

"What are you talking about? The news leak! You nailed it."

She shakes her head. "I don't think that was it. It was something really bad."

"That was bad, believe me. It *is* bad. My whole life is going to change. I'm sure that was it."

She wordlessly slides her lips in opposite directions.

* * *

We're waiting for dinner. The line is backed up halfway down the hallway. On my right, not two feet away, is the metal door leading to the basement, to fight club. A fitting conclusion to my life at Pochachant, I suppose. I rap my knuckles on it, listening to the sounds reverberate in the empty cavern below.

Everyone knows about my case. Some girls congratulate me and shake my hand. Most just stare.

I checked my phone before we left for the cafeteria. The headlines were insane:

Three-Year Search for Emily Calby Is Over: She's in Prison

SHOCKER: Lone Home Invasion Survivor Turns Killer

Missing Victim Represents Herself in Secret Murder Trial— And Wins!

Most of the articles have the same assortment of photos: me giving two thumbs-up coming out of the courthouse, me in the back of the police car on our way out and twelve-year-old me on the Fourth of July with Mom and Becky. The media freaking loves that picture.

A detainee who I never paid attention to, well-fed with lots of ink and a southern-fried accent, steps directly in front of me. I reflexively stick my hand out. She knocks it away.

"You think you're so special, bitch? I hope you fucking die. That's how special you are."

"Nice to meet you," I say as she walks away. I'm not letting anyone ruin this day, not even the misogynist trolls posting sick comments on social media about how I deserve to be raped and killed.

The line finally starts moving again. When we cross the threshold into the cafeteria, talking stops and all eyes fall on me.

"This is so messed up," I whisper.

"You're a celebrity," Rebecca says. "The Beyoncé of Pochachant."

I laugh through my nose.

Normal chatter resumes by the time we collect our utensils and head for our usual table, me feeling self-conscious in the extreme. Rebecca mutters something about the white navy beans looking too much like baby teeth as we approach Lola's table. She gets up and steps into the aisle, blocking my path. I have no choice but to stop.

"Ever'body, lemme have your attention," she commands.

What now? Holding the tray, I'm wary of being exposed on all sides.

"You see this bitch right here? I almost killed her one night."

I roll my eyes.

"But I want to say right now, *Alice Calby* or whatever the fuck your name is." She pauses for a well-timed laugh from the crowd. "You ain't been here long, but you made Pochachant a better place. Y'all don't know it, but this girl's been tutorin' me. She's smarter than the dumbass she acts like in class. One of these days, I'm gettin' that GED."

She starts clapping for me, which makes people feel compelled to join in. My face burns red as a beet. "Say something," Rebecca whispers.

"Um, hi girls! Thank you so much. I will miss all of you." In the corner I spot Twiggs with his arms crossed. Gonzalez is next to him, stroking his mustache. "Most of you," I add to laughs.

I hurry to my seat and suffer through a meal of stuffed cabbage and girls wanting me to autograph their napkins.

I call Lucas when I get back to the cell.

"Lucas! I did it! I'm free, well, almost. Can you pick me up in the morning?"

"I gotta drive all the way back out to that place?" he says.

"Oh, well …"

"I'm kiddin'. I ain't only gonna be there, I'll be waitin' out front in a brand new Cadillac. Just leased it."

"Sweet! I like literally can't wait to see you."

"You be safe tonight, you hear?"

"Don't worry. I will."

43

"**WHAT A CRAZY** couple of weeks," I say, sorting through my worldly possessions: pink shower slippers with torn straps, cheap makeup kit, a cache of pens and legal pads, some hygiene stuff, a few snacks and, of course, the phone.

"Crazy, but good," Rebecca says. "Except for Paula ... and the media ... and Birdman. Are you still upset about him?"

"I probably will be once I have time to think about it."

"Do you hate him? I would. You helped him and he paid you back by dumping you."

"Nah. I think he was just being true to who he is. I respect that, even if I don't respect him not standing up for himself. He was right. We're totally different. It never would have worked out."

I toss a half-empty bag of stale Doritos into the trashcan.

"I'd still like to help him. He was so upset about Corey Wilkes I don't think he even heard what I was explaining about functional interrogation." I wave to my meager belongings spread across my mattress pad. "You want any of this stuff?"

"Can I have your nightshirt? I mean, you know, when you're done wearing it tonight."

"Of course. You can have everything, except I'm not sure about the phone. Lucas made me swear I'd get rid of it so no one could ever trace it back to us."

"That's okay. I don't have anyone to call."

Awkward silence.

"Rebecca," I finally say.

She puts up her hand. "Don't."

"You don't even know what I'm going to say."

"Yes I do. You're going to tell me how much you're going to miss me and how you want to stay in touch, blah blah blah."

"Okay, so you do know what I'm going to say. Why can't I say it? It's all true."

"It's true in your head, but not in real life. Things never work out that way."

"They will this time. You'll see. I'll write you letters and come visit you. Then when you get out ... Where do you think you'll go?"

She hunches her shoulders.

"Maybe things will work out with your mom and you can go live with her. If not, maybe I could talk Lucas into letting—"

"Stop. Can we just pretend it's another night?"

"Okay." I spy the stack of law books on the lockers. "Hey, would you mind taking those back to the library for me?"

"No problem."

"You know, Mava's going to need a replacement. It's a cushy job, much better than working in the laundry. Interested?"

"I doubt they'd let me transfer."

"I bet they will if Mava requests it. She gets what she wants. I'll recommend you. I'm not sure how though. I want to say goodbye to her in person, but no one's told me what time I'm getting out."

"Count, count," reverberates down the hall. I recognize Longmont's voice. She never does count for our cellblock. Usually the COs just peer in the window and move on, but Longmont stops and unlocks the door.

"Hey-hey, girls."

"Hi CO," I say. "How come you're doing count tonight?"

"Just wanted to see what life's like over in this neck of the woods. You guys doing alright?"

"Fine," I say.

"How about you, Rebecca? Everything okay?"

She answers with a blink.

"Talkative as always," Longmont says with a smile. "So how does it feel to be spending your last night at Pochachant, Emily?"

"Not bad."

"Come on, it's gotta be better than not bad. You're going free in the morning."

I tilt my head toward Rebecca, pajama legs tucked beneath her, hair-drape in place.

Longmont's eyes shoot an apology. "Well, you two have a good night," she says and leaves. "Count, count."

Thirty minutes later, it's lights out. I send a quick text to Lucas saying I'll see him in the morning, but don't know exactly what time. To avoid accidentally leaving the phone behind, I stash it under my pillow. Surely they won't search me on the way *out* of prison.

"Night-night, cellie," I say. I want to hug her so bad, tell her again I love her and that everything will be alright, to just keep hope. But I know she doesn't want to hear any of it.

"Goodnight, Emily," she says.

My prayers are full of thanks and apologies, but mostly I pray for Rebecca. I'm in the middle of them, soothed by her whispery breathing. It's like one of those meditation apps of the ocean lapping the shore, steady and reliable. Then it suddenly stops, like the power just went out.

"Rebecca?" Silence.

I sit up. "Rebecca, are you okay?"

"This is it," says a tremulous voice.

"What? What are you talking about?"

"My premonition. *This* is what it was about." To herself, "I don't understand though. It was about you. I'm sure of it."

Noises outside the cell, heavy feet and clanking keys. Twiggs' fat grin pops into view behind the window.

Rebecca repeats in a murmur, "I just don't understand. This is only about me."

Not anymore.

The door swings open and I'm blinded by a flashlight.

"Hey girls," Twiggs says. *Girls* comes out *grills.* He's been drinking again.

"So, blondie, didn't know you was a celebrity." He sweeps the light to Rebecca. "Let's go," he says. She doesn't move.

"I said let's go. Now."

She swings her bare feet onto the floor.

"Stop," I say. "You don't want to do this. Trust me."

He shifts the beam back to me. "You trying to tell me what to do again?"

Clutching the bed covers to my neck, "Remember what I told you that day? She's going to kill me for saying this, but her herpes is super-active right now. She's got blisters seeping pus all over the place. It's so gross. No offense, Rebecca."

I can't see her in the dark. She might be fuming, but she's smart enough to figure out what I'm trying to do.

"Aren't you tired of her anyway?" I say. "This place is full of girls. I would think a man like you would have lots of choices." I could puke for real right now.

"Choices, huh? Alright, how 'bout you?" he says. "I had my eye on you since the day you got here."

When Rebecca told me about Twiggs I decided I had to do something about it. I haven't and this is my last chance. Even if I could talk him away tonight, he'll be back and Rebecca won't have anyone to protect her. I cannot—*will not*—leave her behind at Twiggs' mercy.

"Alright, but only if you agree to leave Rebecca alone after I'm gone."

"What?" Rebecca says. "Uh-uh. No way."

Twiggs pounces on it. "You serious? No tricks?"

"No tricks ... just treats." *Gawd.* "But you have to go slow and be gentle. I–I've never done anything before."

Even in the dim light from the hall, I see his eyes sparkle.

"Shore, shore. I'll be gentle as can be."

"Okay. I have to change clothes first. Wait outside. I'll just be a minute."

He eyes me suspiciously, but backs out.

As soon as the door closes, Rebecca says, "You are out of your mind. Enough with your savior complex. It's not worth it. You going with him tonight isn't going to help me or fix anything."

"Don't bet on that," I say as I change out of my nightshirt into my uniform, making sure Twiggs isn't spying through the window. "Believe me, I have no intention of letting that fuckwad lay one finger on me. There's no time to argue. I need to know *exactly* what happens when he takes you. I have a plan."

"We go to the basement. He knows a way to get there without cameras. In the basement there's a door leading outside to the parking lot where the COs park their cars. He has a blue van … with a mattress in back. What's your plan?"

Twiggs is knocking on the door.

I pull my phone from under my pillow and hold it up. "Evidence," I say. It's more of a broad concept than a plan, but I feign confidence. I stuff the phone inside my underwear and tug my top down.

Twiggs cracks the door open. "You ready?"

"Almost."

"You cannot do this," Rebecca whispers. "He's dangerous."

"So am I. Listen to me. No matter what happens, don't call for help, even if I don't come back tonight. You have to swear— like I swore to you. Not telling anyone about Twiggs was the hardest promise I've ever kept."

"But—"

"Swear."

She showers me with spit when she finally breathes. "Alright. I swear."

The door swings wide open. "Let's go. I ain't got all night."

"Ready! Bye, Rebecca."

* * *

We move silently through the dank basement, Twiggs navigating by flashlight. Entering from the other end of the compound, we travel almost the entire length of Pochachant underground before arriving at a familiar place.

Straight ahead is the corridor to the fight club vault. On my left are the stairs leading to the cafeteria hallway. At the top is the same door I rapped my knuckles against earlier.

But Twiggs takes us to the opposite side, where another stairway materializes. I didn't notice it that night, maybe because the steps are so blackened by mold I can barely see them even now. At the top is another metal door.

He motions with the flashlight for me to climb them. Never let yourself get trapped. Lucas taught me that the first week I knew him. The back of a van is not a good place to be.

"Um, maybe we could do it down here," I say.

"On the dirt? Hell no. My van's got all the comforts of home. Go on," he says.

"I'll follow you."

"Hell no. They say you killed a man."

"Fake news."

"Go."

I grasp a rusty iron railing and climb the steps. Twiggs stays close behind, too effing close, pressing against me when we reach the top as he unspools the wire on his keyring.

In the old days, the hiding girl would be in the corner praying while the calm girl took charge, trying to fend off the scary girl's violent commands from the fringe. It's a sign of my improved mental health that we're all merged back into one crazy self now.

So tempting to jab an elbow in his stomach and try to knock him down the stairs, but it wouldn't advance any goal other than the joy of watching him fall. Even if it worked, with a dirt floor I'd probably succeed only in enraging him. Instead I focus on the key he's inserting in the lock. T-14, according to a plastic tag. Attention to detail.

Directly outside, backed up to the curb, is a windowless blue van. Behind it, a hundred feet away, cypress and pine trees rise above the prison wall, razor-wire shimmering like Christmas tinsel in the moonlight. We're at the back of the prison. The boggy night air is still. The rumbling HVACs on the roof drown out any night sounds.

Twiggs unlocks the van with a remote and pulls open one of the rear doors.

"Get in," he says.

"It's dark in there. Don't you want to be able to see?"

"There's a dome light. I'll turn it on when we're inside."

"Could you turn it on now? I know it sounds silly, but I'm afraid of the dark."

Not to mention that it absolutely kills video quality. My "plan" is to somehow record our conversation, then somehow stop the action before things get too far, then somehow get out alive with the phone—then blackmail him. If he ever lays a finger on another girl at Pochachant, I'll stream the video everywhere. Once I know Rebecca is safely separated from him, I'll probably do it anyway.

He laughs. "Whatever your highness desires."

He climbs in and switches on the light. It's a cargo van. No backseats, just a lumpy gray mattress. A Confederate flag hanging from the roof curtains off the front seats.

It occurs to me this might not have been the world's greatest decision. In fact, it bears all the hallmarks of my very worst decisions: reckless, impulsive and incredibly risky. But I didn't know what else to do on the spot. I couldn't let Twiggs take Rebecca from the cell again.

Not even a weapon. I asked Lucas to fly me in a neck knife with the drone, but he said it would only make things worse. *Imagine if a girl on trial for killin' a man with a neck knife gets caught with another one.* I should have pressed him harder.

I scan the interior. A cooler, some rags, a McDonald's bag. When my eyes land on a roll of gray duct tape, my throat constricts. Sweaty palpitations presage a panic attack. There I am, bound on Mom's bed, tape over my mouth, hyperventilating. But there's just no time for it. I clench my teeth, repeating in my head: *Rage beats fear, rage beats fear.* Another Lucas lesson.

Think two steps ahead. Three if possible. More Lucas. The roll of tape. I reimagine it, converting it from an instrument of terror into a problem solver.

"There," Twiggs says, backing out of the van, boots crunching the crumbling asphalt. "Happy?"

"Not quite. I want my first time to be romantic. Remember, slow and gentle. You promised. Could you turn on some music?"

He laughs. "I can do that."

He goes around to the front. I pull out the phone, find the video camera and start it running.

The ignition clicks and the radio blasts, *Running with the devil, Ahhhhhh.*

Nice! "Um, I don't like hard rock. Could you put on something else?" I grab the duct tape.

"You're high maintenance. What kind music you like?"

"Country."

I tear off a piece of the tape as the radio jumps from rock to hip-hop to an agricultural pesticide commercial to a preacher declaiming, *The prudent sees danger and hides himself, but the simple go on and suffer for it.* I remember the Proverb from Sunday school. What have I gotten myself into?

I loop the tape and stick it to the back of the phone, keeping one eye on Twiggs, silhouetted by the moonlight through the Confederate flag. I attach the phone to the bottom of the closed rear door. The interior's black, like the phone. Blends in okay, but I need to keep his focus in a different direction.

"How's this?" Twiggs says.

Shania Twain is singing *I'm Gonna Getcha Good.* I almost laugh until it occurs to me Twiggs is probably thinking the same thing.

"Fine," I say.

"Fuckin' finally." He exits the front, comes back around and sidles up next to me. "Now get in."

The opening looks like a gateway to hell. A rancid smell from inside singes my nostrils, like something died in there.

"You know, don't you just love the moonlight and night air? They're so, uh, sensual. How about we stay outside?"

"Get in."

I do, saying a quick prayer. Stains on the mattress immediately evoke images of Rebecca. *Rage beats fear.* I stake out a seat on the right wheel well. If he sits facing me he should be directly in the camera frame. He'll also be within arms' reach of grabbing me.

Twiggs boosts his fat backside up and in with a grunt. My eyes stay glued on the phone. His left foot comes within an inch of kicking it. When he slams the door, the phone shakes but holds firm.

He stretches across the interior to the cooler, pulling out a drippy beer bottle. Too big to fit on the wheel well, he stuffs a dirty bed pillow behind him, leans back and sinks into the mattress. He wrenches the top off the beer bottle and drains half of it.

"Well, that was a fuck bunch of work," he says. "You better be worth it. Come 'ere," he says, reaching for me.

I jerk away, too fast, slamming my head against the hull of the van. "Hold on, hold on. You said you'd go slow," I say, rubbing my scalp.

He pulls back. "My o-pology." He empties his beer bottle and reaches into the cooler, pulling out two more. "How 'bout a beer?"

"Um, okay."

He hands me an icy bottle. "Cheers," he says.

I've never opened a beer in my life. Except for the lying, stealing and killing, I'm still the good girl from Dilfer County, Georgia. I twist the top off slow and ladylike—*hissss*—and take a fake sip.

"Come on. You gotta drink it down, like this."

He's getting drunker, which is good and bad. Slows coordination but can also heighten aggression and unpredictable behavior.

"I like to sip it," I say. Need to hurry things up but keep them under control at the same time, not an easy balance. "So how old are you anyway? I mean, I know you're a lot older than me."

"How old you think I am?"

"Thirty?"

"Close enough. How 'bout you?"

"*Sixteen*," I say toward the camera while looking at the ceiling. "Wow, that's like double."

"Keep your voice down."

"Sorry," I whisper, then louder again, "What do you like to do with girls like me?"

"You know. Usual things."

"No, I really don't know. Like I said, I'm very inexperienced. Could you be more specific?"

I'm almost sorry I asked as he slurs his way through a disgusting narrative of sex acts. I suppose it's inevitable I'll have sex someday, but it won't be for a long time. The day the two men came, sex and violence became the same thing to me.

I mimic another sip of beer, prompting him to guzzle another half a bottle. "So the girls at Pochachant like to do those things with you?"

"Most. Some need persuadin'."

The radio switches to Garth Brooks, *Friends in Low Places*.

"How do you persuade them?"

"Why the fuck you ask so many questions?"

"Just curious how things work. Like, for example, how did you persuade Rebecca?" Like a jungle cat, which I basically am, I sense his alertness. *Slow down.*

He empties the second beer bottle and tosses it aside. "Didn't take no persuading. Your roommate's a slut."

He *so* should not have said that about Rebecca.

"Really? I totally did not know that. She said you raped her," I enunciate. "She said you threatened to report her for things that would lengthen her sentence if she didn't do what you wanted."

He leans in. "The fuck you talkin' about? Better watch what you say."

"Sorry. I'm super-awkward when it comes to talking to boys, er, grown men. It was the only thing I could think to talk about that we have in common."

He settles back, resting his beer bottle on his gut like it's a coffee table. "What's that?"

"You know, that I'm a detainee at Pochachant and you like to rape detainees at Pochachant."

That should be enough video. Talk your way out and be sure to grab the camera.

But it's too late. I pushed too far. He reaches out and grips my uniform top in both hands, red-faced and puffed up. "You know what you are? A tease. And guess what? I fucking *hate* teases. Game playing is over."

He rips my uniform top straight down the V-neck. "Haha. Now we're talkin'. That's what I like to see."

Think, then act. Just a bra, just a bra. Let him stare, keep his attention while I flip my grip on the beer bottle and grab the neck. *Stupido.* He gifted me the best weapon in the entire van.

"Enjoy!" I say, ablaze with fury. "Because it's the last thing you're ever going to see."

I smash the bottle against his skull. It doesn't break, but stuns him long enough for me to grab the sides of his head and plunge my thumbs into his eyes.

Just like the up-the-intestine knife move I used on Brooker, I never thought I'd have to use eye-gouging. It's a street-fighting trick from the old South, Lucas explained as I practiced on melons with faces I drew on them. He called it *a fuckin' Triple Crown winner.* Painful, disabling and terrifying all at the same time.

Twiggs panics, grabbing at my wrists. I squeeze harder, but

he's too strong and rips my hands away, bloody thumbs and all. When he realizes he can't see, he begins shrieking like a wounded animal.

"*Shhh, shhh.*" He's not listening. "Shut up!" I hit him again with the bottle. This time it breaks, but his skull must be thick as a rock. He's up on his knees, throwing wild punches. One catches my ribcage and sucks my breath away. I fall sideways just in time. His next punch leaves a dent in the van right where my head was.

Twiggs suddenly freezes, going completely still. I'm baffled before I realize he's going by sound. I slide right, stretch out my left arm and click my fingers. He lunges for the sound and I circle behind him, snatching the keyring from his belt.

Unspooling the wire, I pray. *If it's at all possible, Lord, please forgive me—again.*

I lasso his neck and plant my foot between his shoulder blades for leverage. Lucas and I only spent a couple of hours practicing garroting, but it's not rocket science. Twiggs paws at the wire, but it's already deeply embedded in his skin. Voices from the past haunt me. Mom's scream. Becky's silence. I pull harder.

His shouts diminish to gurgles, but he keeps kicking like a mule. Just when I think my muscles are going to give out, he goes still. I relax my grip, blinking from the sweat running in my eyes.

Silence except for the radio. My dad loved Johnny Cash. He's singing *Ring of Fire.*

I glance at the camera. I didn't want quite that much evidence.

44

I SIT in the dark pouring beer on my hands to wash off the blood. The first thing I did was grab the phone. The video was still running. Then I turned off the radio and dome light.

I dry my hands with an oil-stained rag and call Lucas.

"Thought you'd be in bed for the night?" he says with a yawn.

"Yeah, well."

"Too excited to sleep?"

"Excited would be one word for it."

"Go back to bed. We'll talk in the morning. You woke me up."

"I'd really love to do that. Unfortunately, I have a little problem."

"Tell me 'bout it tomorrow. I need my beauty rest."

"It really can't wait until then. Lucas, don't kill me, but I need your help. Bad. I'm in big trouble."

"Already? You ain't even out yet."

"And I'm not going to be getting out any time soon if I don't do something quick."

I hear a noise outside the van. Footsteps. "Hold on," I whisper and huddle behind the front seat. A flashlight beam sweeps the Confederate flag.

"What's goin' on?"

"*Shhh.*"

I peek out. A CO passes. Looks like a regular patrol. I wait until he disappears.

"Lucas, first let me warn you that you are not going to believe this ..."

"Ironic, ain't it?" he says after my summary. "You get acquitted of killin' a man in self-defense in the morning, then kill another man in self-defense in the evening."

"Crazy, I know."

"Fuckin' ironic. Probably ain't ever even happened before."

"I know, I know. Listen, please. I need to get Twiggs and his van out of here."

"You said you got everything on video. You got proof this time. Self-defense."

"A, they aren't letting me out of here tomorrow if they find out I killed a CO tonight. There'll be another trial, this time with the whole world knowing about it. B ... the video could *possibly* show it as murder."

"Murder? No way. A correctional officer sexually assaults a minor prisoner in the back of his van? That's grounds for lethal self-defense."

I know everything there is to know about self-defense law after being immersed in it for two months. "Unfortunately, the law says once the threat terminates, you can't use any more force. At that point you become the aggressor. Someone, like Leslie Tierney, could possibly argue it wasn't necessary to strangle him after I gouged his eyes out."

"Even if he attacked you first? That law's bullshit. By the way, for your information, this is exactly the kind of conversation you ain't supposed to be having over electronic communications. You just admitted you might be guilty of murder."

"No, I didn't. I said it was *possible* someone could argue that. Could we have this discussion later? Did I mention I'm still sitting in the back of the van with the body inside the prison compound? I'm calling because I have an idea, but it would put you in a lot of danger."

"*Pfft.* Like that'd be somethin' new. What is it?"

"You find a tow truck and come pick up the van and the body and get rid of them—forever. No evidence left behind that can come back to haunt me, like with Brooker. I know it's a big favor to ask, a *huge* favor."

If anyone ever does kill me, I really hope it's Lucas. He's the only one with just cause. I can picture his trademark half-shoulder roll that accompanies his snort.

"A *big* favor is pickin' someone up at the airport. A *huge* favor is lettin' 'em stay at your house. That's your idea? In addition to a long list of other flaws, they ain't gonna let me drive into a prison and take a CO's car without some kind of authorization."

"That's true ... wait! I just thought of something."

I pat down Twiggs' pockets and find his phone. It's locked. *Please let him use Touch ID.* I fish for one of his hands in the dark. It's still warm. I press a wide thumb on the button. Nothing. I find his other thumb. The phone lights up.

"What's going on? You stop for a coffee break?" Lucas says.

"Hold on. Working on something." I search his contacts. *Gonzalez.*

Whos handing fronte gate tonight? I send the text. I figure Twiggs can't spell.

"Almost there, Lucas. This could work."

A reply comes up. *Marlboro, same as always. You must be shitfaced.* Round yellow face in tears emoji at the end.

Just testing to see if your awake. I add the same emoji and hit send.

"One more step," I say. I hold my breath as I search his contacts. There it is. *Marlboro.* "Okay, what do you think about this plan?"

* * *

Getting Twiggs off of and under the mattress wasn't easy, especially bent over in the dark while trying to be quiet and avoid the broken glass from the beer bottle. I smashed my head against the roof twice. There's a big lump, but at least if someone shines a light in they won't see a dead body.

A car motor freezes me. It can't be Lucas. He warned me it would be a few hours, best case. Not only does he have to find a tow truck, he has to YouTube how to operate it and drive all the way out here. I crack the flag curtain and watch a pickup truck pass by and disappear.

Marlboro answered my text asking him to let the tow truck in to pick up my broken-down van. *No problem*, he wrote. *You need to replace that shit-can.*

I think I'm ready to go. I do a final run-through of my checklist:

My phone. Tucked in my pants.

Shirt. Front taped back together from the inside with the duct tape.

Vehicle. In neutral with the emergency brake off.

Twiggs' keys and phone. Keyring in my hand, ignition fob and phone in my pocket with all the sounds turned off.

Maybe I really am a professional killer. The girl who killed Brooker and the two men was someone I didn't know. I watched her from a different place. I never thought Emily Calby could do such a thing.

I take a last look around. I didn't even try to clean the van. My marks are everywhere. Saliva on the beer bottle, probably hair strands, fingerprints all over the place.

An impossible plan, but I *have* to believe. Lucas will find a tow truck, one way or another—because he's Lucas. He always carries fake IDs, so he'll be covered if Marlboro asks for one. He'll probably wear a disguise, maybe the fro wig. I love it and keep telling him he should let his hair grow out.

The plan *will* work ... it could work ... it might possibly not fail.

I pinch key T-14 from Twiggs' keyring and slice open the rear door of the van. No sounds except the HVACs. I hop out and lock the doors, stashing the remote and Twiggs' phone behind the left front wheel like Lucas told me to do.

I wanted to keep the phone in case Marlboro or Gonzalez try to text Twiggs, but it kept auto-locking and wouldn't let me change the settings without the password. Scary girl popped out of nowhere to offer a suggestion: *Just cut off his thumb and take it with you.* I chased her away. Besides, Lucas said he needed the phone for the *after planning.* Always thinking of next steps.

The clank when I unlock the basement seems to echo into the stratosphere, making me look up into the starry sky. I say hi to Mom and Dad and Becky and tell them not to worry. I'd like to spend more time talking to them, anything to keep from descending into the pit of blackness inside the basement. I'm having a hard time making my legs go until I see car lights coming down the parking lot.

I tiptoe down the stairs and plant myself on the bottom step, checking my phone. One minute after midnight. Of course. It's always turning midnight in my life.

One itsy-bitsy part of the plan I didn't have time to figure out was how to get back to my cell. Twiggs led me through a maze of passageways I'd never seen before. Even assuming I could retrace the path and do it without encountering a CO, both of which seem unlikely, I don't know which key opens the cell door and can't be standing around in the corridor in the middle of the night trying Twiggs' keys in the lock.

In front of me, on the other side of the basement, are the stairs leading to the cafeteria hallway. I know my way back from there. I've been making the trip three times a day for more than two months, but there are cameras all along the way.

I'm stuck. Pure and simple.

One a.m. finds me on my knees praying.

Two arrives as I'm watching the video for the first time. The camera angle is perfect, right on Twiggs. His voice is muddled in a couple places, but mine rings loud and clear.

The video presents an open and shut case on my behalf—until the garroting starts. At one point I'm yanking on the wire and we're both looking at the camera like we're posing for a picture … except Twiggs' eyes are gone so he's not exactly *looking.*

Three o'clock and I'm pacing the dirt floor, wondering and worrying about Lucas. He cut off communication after our first call.

My phone vibrates. *Finally.*

Almost there.

Roger that. What the state trooper said when we were taking the detour to the courthouse.

Lucas being almost in reach makes me second-guess my plan. Maybe I should try to hide in the tow truck and drive out with him. But I'd be a fugitive again, and probably a suspect in Twiggs' disappearance.

Ten minutes ... twenty minutes ... a half hour. What does *almost there* mean to him? Ten years? What if he couldn't get in? But then I hear a motor. Loud, a truck not a car. He's here.

The truck stops and idles outside the door. A lift grinds, chains clank. I grip the step to restrain myself from running out to see him. He might kill me for real, throw me in the back of the van with Twiggs and drive us both away.

He must have studied up good because it only takes ten minutes before I hear the groaning motor drag the van out of the parking space. *Thud, chink, jangle,* and he's gone.

I wait, staring at the phone. I can't stand it.

Then it comes, a thumbs-up. *Ya-ay!* I throw my head back and fan my sweaty neck with my hair. It's probably a sin to thank God for things like this, but I do it anyway.

* * *

It's looping in my head and I can't get rid of it. A nursery rhyme song. *Tick tock, says the clock, good morning, morrr-ning.* I'm at the top of the stairs, clinging to a key tagged L-11. I had to try almost all of them before the lock to the cafeteria hallway finally turned. The rest of the keys, including the keyring with its bloody wire, are buried in a far corner of the basement, soaking in sulfuric acid. I found a shovel and the jug of acid in a utility closet.

At exactly seven-thirty a.m., I press my ear to the cold metal door and listen for an army of girls marching to breakfast.

The plan? Solid as a wing and a prayer, as usual. Play a game of *Blindly Guess Which Girl Is on the Other Side of the Door and Go*. I calculated my odds of winning—meaning coming out where I'm supposed to be, behind Rebecca—at twenty-five to one.

How? There are about two hundred girls in four cellblocks. To avoid food riots, they switch the cafeteria order every week. Our cellblock, B, is third this week. Rebecca and I line up somewhere in the middle of our block, meaning I need to exit after approximately 125 girls have passed the door. Practicing our slow shuffle with the stopwatch on my phone, I estimate one girl should pass the door every five seconds.

That's assuming everything goes smoothly, which it usually doesn't. Sometimes the line gets jammed up and sometimes the cellblock order gets switched when a group shows up late. The real odds are probably more like a thousand to one, higher even, but I need hope to hold onto and twenty-five to one is already stretching it.

Then there's the even bigger problem. The COs are going to know I'm missing before anyone sets foot in the cafeteria when morning count finds only one girl in cell 49B.

Have to at least try.

Here they come, clomp, clomp, clomping, COs barking commands. I hope Rebecca kept her swear when I didn't come back, another possible snag. I'm sure she spent all night worrying.

I start the timer on my phone when the first footsteps pass. *125 girls x 5 seconds each = 10.42 minutes*. Maybe Mr. Medillo could use it as a problem in GED. The kids would find it much more interesting than racing snails.

Emily is a juvenile detainee who recently garroted and de-eyed a correctional officer. She's hiding behind a basement door, waiting to sneak into a cafeteria line of 200 other detainees. Emily needs to enter the line after 62.5% of the girls have passed the door. Assume one detainee passes the door every 5 seconds. How long should Emily wait before she opens the door?

Ten minutes seem like an hour. Patience is not my strength, obviously. What if I'm way off and the line passes me by completely? I keep my ear to the door, trying to keep count, but it's impossible.

The timer runs out. *Go.* I turn the key and crack open the door. The first face I see is one-eyed, red-headed Claire. Jaw dropping, she pokes Lola.

Lola scowls and there's a moment when I think all is lost, but she scans the corridor and moves her thick body into a blocking position. She may not have book smarts, but her street smarts are lightning-quick. She nods and I slip in front of her.

When I turn to say thank you, she licks her finger and smudges my cheek, showing me a spot of blood just as I hear, "What the fuck are you doing up here?"

Gonzalez.

"What the fuck does it look like she's doing?" Lola says. "She's saying goodbye to her friends. Haven't you heard? This bitch is gettin' out today. Leave her alone."

"Don't backtalk me, Grimes. I'll write you up." He sticks his finger in my face. "You. Get back in your place. Ain't no special privileges here."

I'd *love* to get back in my place but have no idea where it is. Lola jerks her head toward the back of the line. I missed it by a mile. Our cellblock must have arrived late, which would make a lot of sense if they discovered a detainee missing during count. But if that happened, wouldn't Gonzalez be rounding me up instead of sending me back in line?

Lola crushes me in a too-hard hug and pounds my back with her fist. "*Now* we're square," she says. "You take care, blondie."

Rebecca is distilled practically to jelly when I stroll up, like she's seeing a ghost. I casually slide into line.

"Twiggs?" she whispers.

"Gone."

We don't speak as we move into the cafeteria and pick up our breakfast trays. My last meal at Pochachant consists of runny eggs, undercooked bacon and burnt hashed browns.

"What happened?" she says as we settle in our seats.

"Best you don't know."

"I was worried about you."

"I know. I thought about that all night. I couldn't get back. I'm so sorry."

"Well, I didn't worry *that* much."

A motorboat sputter-laugh. "Gee, thanks."

"I didn't mean it like that. I didn't worry more because you're a superhero."

I start to laugh again, but realize she's serious.

I survey the room as I eat. All around me, talking, laughing, shouting. COs stand in the corners shooting the breeze. Same ol', same ol'. It doesn't make any sense.

"So, Ms. Seyere. Do tell. Why is everything normal? Why wasn't everyone looking for me after count?"

"Your favorite CO."

"Longmont?"

"She came to do count and collect us for breakfast, said she'd been keeping 'an eye on us' after something you told her." Her eyes narrow.

"I didn't break my swear," I say. "I wanted to, believe me. She told me there were rumors about Twiggs and all I said was they weren't just rumors. What happened?"

"First, I played dumb, said they probably came to get you while I was asleep to let you go, but she didn't believe me, didn't believe I would have slept through it."

"So what did you do?"

With a tormented face that looks even younger than usual, "I begged."

"Really? I cannot picture you begging for anything."

"It's the only time I remember, honestly. Even when I ran out of drugs, even when I ... was a child. I didn't know what else to do."

"What did you say?"

"I begged her to trust you, told her you wouldn't let her down, would never let any friend down. She wasn't convinced until

I started crying. I think that shocked her. Me too, actually. I can't remember the last time I cried. Maybe it helped."

So much to unpack in her words, but I just say, "I guess that makes two of us now."

"Two what?"

"Two girls who would never let a friend down."

She tilts her head and I'm prepared for her face to disappear, but she catches her silky bangs and tucks them behind her ears.

"Anyway, she said you had exactly thirty minutes to show up before she reported you missing. You made it by forty-five seconds. I was watching the clock when you walked up and practically gave me a heart attack. And, uh-oh, I think she's on her way here right now."

"Another premonition?"

She shakes her head.

From behind me, "Hello, Emily."

I turn. All sparkly, "Oh, hi, CO!"

Her face is definitely not the same happy one that greeted me yesterday when I got back from court. After all it took to get here, this is where everything falls apart. Even my lie factory can't manufacture a plausible explanation for why I wasn't in my cell.

"Did you have a nice last night at Pochachant?" she says, studying my face.

I can't decode her voice. "It was okay. You know, just a regular night, except kind of sad because I'm leaving my friends, like Rebecca and, um, you."

Rebecca is drinking from her milk carton, dark eyes wide over the edge of the waxy box.

"You look tired."

I haven't slept in more than twenty-four hours. I must look terrible. "Yeah, now that you mention it, I guess it wasn't exactly a *regular* night. I had a hard time sleeping, what with all the excitement and knowing I was getting out this morning. You know how it is."

Control yourself. One of the surest signs of lying is over-explaining.

Grim-faced, she makes her way around the table. "I'm sorry that the time has come," she says.

I hold up my wrists, expecting her to wrap them in shackles.

"Good luck, Emily. It's been nice knowing you." She sticks out her hand.

I shake it with a firm grip. "Um, you too, CO. Thanks for everything."

As she strolls away, Rebecca says, "Whoa, she's my favorite too."

45

I COULDN'T have picked a nicer day to get out of prison. The sun is shining and the air tastes fresh and cool. A plump grayish-brown bird resting on a spiral of razor wire sings *pup-poo, pup-poo.*

I'm standing inside the compound with my caretakers, two state troopers I just met. The solid metal gates slowly creak open, revealing the boundless possibilities of freedom ... and a mob of news trucks with arrays of satellite dishes mounted on top. They're parked just outside the perimeter fence. Reporters are already shouting questions I can't make out.

I groan, then smile because smack in the middle of the chaos sits a shiny black Cadillac with dark windows.

"I can take it from here," I say. "I'm free, right?"

The troopers look at each other, shrug and let me walk on alone. I'm wearing the jeans and double tees they arrested me in back in Arkansas. The jeans are loose. I lost weight. I carry Rebecca's rolled-up painting like a baton.

I left everything else behind, except for the phone, which is stuffed in my pants. I agonized over whether to destroy it, finally deciding I couldn't risk letting go of the Twiggs video, just in case. I trimmed off the end and deleted my texts and call records but I know everything's easily recoverable. I had a big Fourth Amendment speech prepared in case anyone tried to search me on the way out, but no one did.

I concentrate on keeping my chin up and posture straight as I strut down the walkway. The din grows louder with each step. A muddle of voices high and low, indistinct, except for one that lands smack in the center, like a smooth middle harmony. A simple *Emily,* with a question mark at the end. I hear it again. *Emily?*

Squinting into the sun, I see Ben, standing alone behind the fences separating the boys from the girls, holding a paintbrush. Parked next to him on the sunbaked leaves is a five-gallon bucket.

And just like that, I'm back in GED class, tingling from the touch of his knee against mine, and in the library, his serene spirit washing over me, soothing the pandemonium in my head. Whatever else Ben is or isn't, he'll always be my first love. No kiss will ever mean as much as that one in the library when his beautiful eyelashes tickled my face.

He raises his fingers in a peace sign.

Peace. There are worse philosophies of life. I flash one back with a smile as crooked as my conflicted feelings. *Goodbye, Ben.*

The questions get louder as I draw near the Cadillac.

"Emily, what do you have to say to the world?"

Um, nothing.

"Emily, what did you learn from this experience?"

Always destroy the evidence.

A gaggle of cheering girls wave #FreeEmilyCalby signs. I blow them a kiss. The last question I hear as I climb into the Caddy sticks in my head. "Where do you go from here, Emily?"

"Good morning, Lucas," I say calmly.

"Mornin', Em," he says.

"Can we please get out of here?"

He puts the car in neutral and floors the accelerator. The media vultures jump back like a train is coming down the tracks. He eases the car in gear and we cruise away.

"Shoot," I say. "They're getting pictures of the license plate."

He reaches between the seat and console and pulls out a Louisiana plate. Two steps ahead.

I take a long last look at Pochachant as it shrinks behind us. *You wait*, I said to Rebecca when they came for me. *You'll be hearing from me real soon.* She mumbled something in a voice so thin and whispery that, for the first time, it matched the fragile physical self of the strongest girl I ever knew. I had to ask her to repeat it, but still couldn't make it out. The third time I studied her mouth like a lip-reader. *I'll miss you*, she said. I pulled her close to hide my tears.

"So?" I say when the road bends and Pochachant disappears from view.

"So what?"

"You know what?"

"So is you ain't got to worry about that man or his van comin' back to git you."

"Seriously? *Thank you thank you thank you.* What a relief! I knew you could do it. How did you?"

"Better off not knowing." Same thing I told Rebecca.

"What happens when they come looking for him, realize he's missing?"

"Got it covered. We talk about it later. I got one thing I want to say to you right now. So stop that roulette wheel spinnin' in your head and focus. This is important."

"Okay."

"You focused?"

"One-hundred percent." Is he going to say *I love you*? Don't expect too much. Probably something more like *Glad you're back*.

"What *the fuck* is wrong with you?"

Stunned, I manage only, "Huh?"

"This killin'. You got to stop. Take up another hobby. I'm gettin' too old for this shit."

"It was self-defense. And justice! I was never allowed to tell you, but he was raping Rebecca."

"Who?"

I slap my forehead. "My cellie. I told you about her a million times."

"They better ways to get justice."

"*You* taught me *that* way. *Deserves to die.*"

"Them was special circumstances. There's millions of fuckers out there who deserve to die. You can't kill 'em all."

"It wasn't my fault," voice clipping. "He attacked me. I'll show you the video."

"Answer me this. Did you absolutely have to put yourself in that dangerous situation?"

A bobble-headed nod. "Yes! I couldn't leave Rebecca behind and let him keep preying on her. She's tiny, Lucas, like a child. She *is* a child. She's only fifteen."

He sighs. "I know you think you doin' good, but it ain't your job to save the world and you ain't Supergirl. Your chances are running out. Think what you just went through. You know how lucky you was to get outta that place?"

I unclamp my fingers from the death-grip they have on the creamy tan leather seat and fall back. "I know. It was lucky. I couldn't have done it without you, obviously."

"I ain't even talkin' about that fat fuck. That's a whole story by itself. I'm talkin' about your trial."

"Hey, that wasn't luck. That was hard work, and brainpower ... okay, and some luck."

"And you got your justice."

"I did." It's still sinking in. I'm free. *I'm free.*

"And you didn't have to kill no one to do it. No knives, no guns, no strangling devices."

"*The Law* was my weapon." Several seconds pass before I add, "I see your point."

"You got to promise me. No more violence."

"Mm-hm."

"No, *mm-hm.* Gimme your word. Right now. No more violence."

"I said okay."

"Gimme your word. Say it."

"Alright already!" I raise my right hand. "I give you my word. No more violence ... except in self-defense, right?"

* * *

When he's sure we're not being followed, he lets me pick a place for lunch. I opt for a roadside dive made of cypress planks with a sign advertising *Best Cheeseburgers in the Bayou.* My return to quinoa and kale can wait.

He grabs me by the back of my shirts as I start to exit and shoves a pair of oversized sunglasses and a Memphis Grizzlies cap into my hands. "You got no idea how much your face has been on the news."

I put on the glasses and tuck my hair under the cap. I almost look like a boy.

People stare when we enter, but not because they recognize me. We always get looks: the giant black man and the skinny white girl. Lucas insists on facing the door, the most comforting person in the entire world to have watching your back.

I order a cheeseburger, onion rings and a chocolate milkshake. The pictures on the laminated menu make my mouth water.

"Got a surprise for you," Lucas says when the waitress walks away. "Call it a gift."

"A gift? You didn't have to do that. What is it? Another handgun?"

"I'm gonna pretend that was a bad joke. I got you the best gift of all. Information. First, tell me again 'bout your adversary, why you hate her so much."

"Leslie? You know why. Every reason under the sun."

"Summarize."

I'm still cataloging her inventory of misdeeds when the food arrives. Greasy cheese drips from the steaming burger. The onion rings are thick and crispy. Oh, man. The milkshake even has whipped cream and a cherry on top, with sprinkles!

...Wiping mustard from my chin, "*And* on top of all that she mocked me, the whole time. Called me a *gutter rat* right in court."

"Ever wonder why she hated you so bad?"

"Pure evilness. No other explanation. I never did anything to her."

"Maybe she hated what you represent."

"What's that supposed to mean?"

"Know anyone else she hated?"

"Do we have to play this game right now? I'm tired."

"Answer the question. Who else did she hate?"

"Probably everyone. She obviously hated Ben to pull such a dirty trick on him, sending him to adult prison for life."

"You and Ben got anything in common?"

A strained laugh. "Obviously not, according to him. He said, *We're just too different.*" I make his voice sound whiny, which isn't fair. It was always calm, tranquil, like him.

"Think harder."

I draw a blank and shrug, drenching an onion ring in so much ketchup it looks like a bloody organ. *Nice thought, Emily. Very nice.* "So are you going to tell me what this big 'information' surprise is?" Air quotes. It's only been an hour and I already miss Rebecca.

"You ever take time to think why people is the way they is?"

Oh, brother. Soon he'll be staring at the ceiling. Easier to just go along at times like this.

"Sometimes," I say. "I did it with the girls at Pochachant."

"Ever wish people didn't judge you when they don't know you?"

"Like, every day. Have you seen the horrible comments people are making about me on social media? Come on, what's the information?"

"*Leslie Donahue.*" He spells the last name. "Check it out sometime. Not now. I wanna enjoy this artery-cloggin' meal."

I wolf down my food and excuse myself to the restroom. He knows why.

Like every name you look up on the internet, there are a lot of them. Locked in a stall, it takes until the fourth page of search results before I come to a headline:

Man Killed at Shadow Lake Protecting Daughter

It's from an Indiana newspaper, dated twenty years ago:

> *Local lawyer Mark Donahue, 41, was fatally shot at Shadow Lake Park yesterday when he intervened to stop three men from harassing his twelve-year-old daughter, Leslie.*
>
> *Witnesses say an altercation ensued in which one of the men pulled out a gun and shot Donahue twice in the chest. He died at the scene.*
>
> *The suspects, all juveniles, 14, 15 and 16, were arrested this morning.*
>
> *"It's a sickening, senseless crime," said police spokesperson Lt. Roberta Alvarez. "A father and daughter were simply enjoying a nice afternoon at the park when the three young men approached and began making inappropriate comments to the girl. Mr. Donahue stepped in to object and was gunned down directly in front of her."*
>
> *She announced that public defenders had been appointed to represent the suspects. Ironically, Donahue spent his entire legal career as a public defender representing indigent criminal defendants.*

All the things that passed me by. Leslie's overreaction at the beginning when I said she knew nothing about victims, and again when Paula said I'd survived more pain and hardship than she ever could. *You don't know a damn thing about me or my hardships.*

I locate the interview with Leslie I came across back at Pochachant. *The Prosecutor Defendants Love to Hate.*

> *Tierney shies away from questions about her personal life,*

declining to discuss her childhood years or family. "I don't live in the past," she said.

But we all do, stuck in the memory graveyard of dead dreams and broken hearts, their threads woven into our souls. There is no escaping. Never.

Told that a criminal defense attorney described her as "vengeful," she said, "I don't seek revenge. I only seek justice."

Those words again. My words.

Ben was wrong. We're not completely different. We have one thing in common. We were both juveniles who killed men with daughters.

I return to the table. "Can we drive to Opelousas?"

46

"**HOW DID** you figure it out?" I asked on the way.

"'Cause I hate sittin' on my ass doin' nothin'."

From the outside, there might not be two more different people on the planet. Inside, we're practically twins.

He sometimes pretends he isn't paying attention to me, just to annoy me, I think, but he absorbs every word. He remembered me telling him how Leslie tried to set me up as a professional killer with her little story about being good enough to play tennis in college. Her alma mater was one of the only bits of background info on her D.A. profile, along with her picture.

He searched everything—college newspapers, alumni magazines, website archives—until he found a picture of the school's tennis team from fourteen years ago. There she was, middle row, third from left: *Leslie Donahue*. A public records search showed she got married and divorced after law school, keeping her married name, *Tierney*.

We pull up to the St. Landry courthouse. The news trucks are gone. "Good luck," Lucas says.

"Thanks." I hand him my phone. "This has the Twiggs video on it if you want to see what happened."

The courthouse people are surprised to see me when I stroll in the front door, smiling and waving. I sign in and go through the metal detector. A directory says the District Attorney's Office is on the fourth floor. I take the stairs.

A secretary with wild curly hair, painting her nails with silver glitter, snaps to attention as I enter.

"Hi, I'm Emily Calby! I'm here to see Ms. Tierney." Centered on an open door behind the reception area is a brown piece of plastic with a white beveled edge: *Leslie Tierney, Assistant District Attorney.*

"Do you have an appointment?"

"Nope."

"She can't see you without—"

Leslie appears in the doorway, hand on her hip. "It's okay, Lila."

She waves me in, closes the door and points to a dingy vinyl armchair across from her metal desk. Not what I imagined. I expected something fancier.

"Surprised to see you here," she says.

The office is bare as a bone. Nothing on the walls. No plants or desk tchotchkes. The only clue as to the occupant's identity is a stained coffee mug on the credenza. *Lawyer—Because Bad-Ass Isn't a Job Title.*

Then I see it, half hidden by the desk phone, a photograph in an oval frame that was once gold. Most of the paint has flaked off, leaving a dull, leaded finish. It's a young girl leaning against a man with the same piercing green eyes and celestial, turned-up nose. He has his arm around her. She's wearing a goofy grin and I realize I've never seen Leslie smile before.

"What's this about?" she says brusquely.

"Well, *we-ee* need to talk. And since we've already wasted a lot of time talking while you tried to falsely convict me of murder, I'll get to the point. I could destroy you and part of me really wants to."

"Excuse me?"

"I read a lot about the law during my case. One topic I found very interesting was *prosecutorial misconduct*."

"What are you insinuating?" Eyes slitting, a cobra prepared to strike.

The time for defense is long past. *Attack. Seize the advantage.* "I'm not *insinuating* anything. I'm *accusing* you of gross prosecutorial misconduct, including, let me see," I tick them off on my fingers, "obtaining illegal confessions, witness tampering and committing fraud upon the court."

"Ooh, the little lawyer is riding high, learning new words every day. I'm scared."

Maybe because the law's on my side, an almost preternatural calmness lifts me up. "You should be. Let me be more specific. Two years ago you obtained an illegal confession from a boy named Ben Breyer and sent him away for life in adult prison."

A mocking peak of her shoulders. "No clue who that is. I handle hundreds of cases."

"I guess he didn't mean much to you. He was just a sweet boy whose life you ended. Allow me to refresh your memory, a phrase I learned from you, by the way. After Ben—Mr. Breyer—invoked his *Miranda* rights, you brought in a crying baby and stood outside his cell. He thought you were the baby's mother and confessed."

"Even assuming I did that, which I'm not conceding, I can't control what people think or do. I never claimed to be the baby's mother. It wasn't even the victim's baby."

"Oh, I see. You just decided to go borrow a baby and stand outside a jail cell for no reason. Yeah, that makes perfect sense. Get real. It was *functional interrogation* and you know it."

I have her attention now.

"You tried the same thing on me when you blocked me in the hall after the probable cause hearing and gave me your little speech about Dulcie. No offense, but it was a weak effort, not anywhere close to the Christian burial speech in *Brewer v. Williams*. Now *that* was a masterpiece."

In the stillness of her glare, I see her brain processing, analyzing.

"Let's move to the present. You intimidated my only witness, Mary Brinson, to not show up by threatening to expose her abortion, which had zero relevance to my case. I'll have to research the law, but I don't see how you even got that record legally."

She rolls her head, not just her eyes, but her whole head. "My tolerance for you is running out quickly. It's malpractice for a lawyer to not interview witnesses before a trial. I simply advised her, like any good prosecutor would do, that given the nature of the allegations, I'd be asking her some personal questions."

"And telling her that if she wasn't subpoenaed, she didn't have to show up for trial? Is that what any good prosecutor would do?"

"Are we done?" she says.

"Not quite. I also think you lied to the court, to Judge Hanks, about finding my DNA in Brooker's car. I called your DNA expert, Dr. Riley Carson. She never heard of you."

"That doesn't prove anything. Like I told the judge, a DNA expert was unnecessary at that point and there was no need to spend the state's money on her. You have no proof of anything."

"Well, you know, one thing I'm learning is that there's legal court and public court. You may have noticed I'm famous now. You're probably the one who made me that way, but if you're the leaker, it backfired."

I wave to the window. "There are a hundred reporters out there wanting to interview me. The way I figure it, once I tell the story about how you tried to railroad poor victimized Emily Calby, it's going to be up to you to *dis*prove it. For the DNA, it should be easy. You either have it or don't. If you don't, you're screwed."

She's a master of keeping a straight face, but that one zinged her.

"What do you want from me?"

"This whole time all I wanted to know was *why*. Why would a prosecutor lie and cheat to send kids to prison, why did you hate me so much? Lucky for you, I figured it out."

"Oh, really."

"Yep, really. But before I tell you, here are my demands."

Forced laugh. "*You* have demands. On *me*." She stabs a finger into her chest hard enough to hurt. "That's rich."

"Three of them. First, you will withdraw from your campaign to be a judge."

I hold up a hand to shut her about-to-explode mouth.

"Second, you will resign as a prosecutor. You are not fit for either job. Third, before you resign, you will take whatever actions are necessary to free Ben Breyer from prison. He made a stupid mistake, but he didn't have a gun, didn't even know about any gun, and didn't shoot anyone. Two years at Pochachant is enough punishment, especially since his conviction came from an illegal confession that was the only evidence against him."

A chirping laugh. "You really are insane."

"Possibly, but let's stay focused on the issues. If you do those three things, in return, I will not ruin your life forever—like you effing tried to do to mine. It's a simple deal, and more than fair."

She pushes her chair back from the desk. "Extortion is a serious felony. Would you prefer to be arrested now or later?"

"Nice try, but you need to pay attention to me. I'm here to do you a favor. Do what I say and I won't expose you. You'll still be able to go on and make a life. If I go public, those same things are going to happen anyway, don't you think? You might also be criminally prosecuted and lose your bar license. In the absolute best case, you'll be an un-erasable internet supervillain for eternity."

"And to what do I owe this great act of kindness?"

Poised and smug even now, my role model and most hated enemy. I glance again at the picture, back when the lives of young girls were still full of fathers and mothers and sisters who couldn't be taken away.

"Because I know what happened to twelve-year-old Leslie Donahue and her father ... and it breaks my heart."

Her desk phone starts buzzing, but she doesn't pick up. When it stops, the seconds pass in silence. She picks up the photo and cleans the glass with a tissue.

Like she's talking to herself, "I thought you were guilty. I would never try to convict an innocent person. I was just *so convinced.*" She massages the photo like she's trying to revive the captured moment. When she looks at me again, her bully bravado is gone.

"You probably won't believe this," she says. "But I wasn't always a terrible person. My father used to say I was as sweet as pie. *Lee-Lee*—that's what he called me—*you are the apple of my eye and sweet as pie.*"

I say, "Then the boys killed him and something snapped. I totally get it. That's why I'm here. We have way more in common than you think."

Justice or *revenge*, whatever you want to call it. We just used different tools.

A knock and the door opens. It's the assistant.

"Ms. Tierney, just a reminder that you're due in court in ten minutes."

"Thank you, Lila."

Lila gives me a dirty look and pulls the door shut.

"You're a great lawyer," I say. "Strong and powerful. I learned so much from watching you, tried to imitate you. There's so much real injustice in the world. You don't need to invent any. Think about your dad. What would he want for you? He was a public defender."

The moment, if there was one, is broken. Her face hardens, like soft clay flash-baked into stone.

"Well, that's all I have to say." I stand to leave.

"Ms. Cal— ... Emily. You said something in your testimony. *I feel guilty every single day just for being alive.*" The slightest nod of affirmation.

"Maybe it's time we both stop feeling that way. There's nothing we could have done to save them." People have been telling me that for three years, but I never truly acknowledged it.

I turn for the door.

"One more thing," she says. "What you did in there, in that courtroom? Girl, you seriously need to go to law school."

* * *

I stroll out of the courthouse feeling light as a feather, greedily filling my lungs with the fresh air. *Free* air. My already wide smile practically swallows my face when I see Lucas waiting in the Cadillac. My rock, as solid as the earth itself.

Law school. It does kind of make sense. The courtroom part was exciting, to put it mildly, but I also loved digging in the books for the clues to the infinite puzzles that seem to make up *The Law*. My parents always said I was good at arguing, although I don't think they meant it as a compliment. Most important, like I figured out at the beginning, the law always wins—but only if you have the knowledge and skill. Otherwise, it will crush you.

And the craziest part about law is it's actually *legal*.

Lucas was right. My chances are running out. Violence isn't the only path to justice, not even the best one. And now I gave him my word. *When a man got nothin' left, he got his word.*

I'm crossing a red-brick plaza, lost in these revelations, when a tall man with a bald pate and long sideburns wearing a blue baseball jacket startles me from the side.

"Hey there," he points. "I know you. You're that Calby girl."

"Sorry, don't know her." I fake smile and keep walking, but he keeps pace with me.

"Ah, come on. I know it's you. I saw you on TV."

"Okay, well, have a nice day." I speed past him.

"Damn, your ass looks as good as your face. Can't blame the man for trying."

I turn, eyes aflame. *Deserves to die.*

Epilogue

SAM COOKE is in an awful way, singing about another Saturday night where he ain't got nobody. Lucas's musical tastes are definitely mellowing. Less hardcore rap, more old school R & B. That's probably what happens when you get old. He turns thirty-six next week.

I sing along. It is another Saturday night, but I got somebody—Lucas—and I'm thankful for it every minute, except when he annoys the crap out of me. Haha.

We're home in Memphis, in the building where we met. I'm sitting at the same kitchen table where I asked him to teach me how to kill, writing a letter to Rebecca.

Joseph Black is no more. Lucas is once again officially *Lucas Ellington Jackson*. After I reverted to being me, he decided he might as well go back to being him too. No point trying to hide anymore. Three months have passed and the media hounds are still around.

"Public loves missin' blonde girls," Lucas explained. "Can't get enough of 'em. If you was a black girl, no one would've ever heard of you."

Turns out it's not a crime to fake your death unless you do it for fraud or to evade the law. I researched it. Lucas did it to avoid breaking the law. Staying would have necessitated killing *grill-man* for the assault weapon attack three years ago. Retaliation. Code of the street. The good news is someone else killed him while we were away.

Lucas and I are actually legal now. We got a lawyer and filed a guardianship proceeding. It didn't look like it would go through until FBI Special Agent Jeffrey Forster showed up and testified on our behalf. He didn't get word of my case until the news broke. It was awesome to see him. He told the judge he spent six months studying me and the only time he ever saw me happy was when I talked about Lucas.

Lucas loves reminding me that he's my legal guardian, calling me his *custodial charge*, as in, *Hey, custodial charge, gimme that remote.*

The only people still looking for Twiggs are the cops. That same long night Lucas borrowed the tow truck and cleaned up my mess, he hacked Twiggs' phone password (the brilliant *1-2-3-4*) and sent a text to Gonzalez.

Heat's on. Words out what we been doing to the girls. I'm taking off and ain't never coming back. You might want to do the same. The law's coming.

Gonzalez stayed, which was a mistake. They arrested him not long after Longmont went to the authorities and the Justice Department launched an investigation. Seven COs and the warden have been fired and the state terminated its contract with the private prison corporation.

A text pops up. It's Paula, with an update on Ben. She's been representing him in his post-conviction relief proceedings. She sounds like a different person since they removed a diseased part of her colon while she was in the hospital. I can hear it in her voice, even her texts. This one has an exclamation point. I love it!

Leslie upheld her end of the deal. A week after Paula filed Ben's habeas petition, she submitted an affidavit admitting what she did, calling it an *error of professional judgment* she made to obtain what she believed to be *essential justice* for a terrible crime. She resigned the same day.

Paula says Ben's hearing is next week. *He wanted me to tell you thanks and to say again that he's sorry. Don't know what that last part means.*

Sometimes I still daydream about him.

Tonight is my big coming-out party. My one-hour interview on national television. The media weren't going to let it go—let me go—so I decided to take control of my story. A one million-dollar *honorarium*, the result of a bidding war, provided extra incentive. We filmed it last week at a studio in Los Angeles.

We're having a watch party tonight. Darla and Peggy are driving over from Little Rock. James is still in classes at Stanford, his last semester, but Kiona's flying in from Vegas later this afternoon.

The money goes to the *Mava Dixon Learning & Counseling Center* at Pochachant. They've already started renovating the second floor of the library. I wanted to keep some of it, at least enough to buy a car since I just got my driver's license, but my conscience wouldn't let me. Blood money. The main reason I'm famous is because Mom and Becky died and I lived.

When word of the donation got out, my fans adored me even more and the trolls called me a media whore. You really can't win.

Hi Rebecca!

How are you, sweetie? I don't have much new to tell you that wasn't in my last letter, except—get this—Leslie Tierney moved back to Indiana and is taking a job as a public defender! How switched-up crazy is that?

I just got the news. I set up a *Leslie Donahue Tierney* alert on my computer and a link showed up in my inbox yesterday to a story from Leslie's hometown newspaper in Indiana. It recounted her past, including her rise and fall as a prosecutor, quoting her saying she was grateful to have a second chance to make her father proud.

Tonight's my big TV interview!! I wonder if they'll let the girls watch it. It was fun in a way. I even had a professional makeup artist and hair stylist—too funny, right?

Don't forget, I'm coming to visit again in exactly two weeks. I had to wait until Lucas could find time. He still won't let me drive there alone. With all the weirdos who come looking for me, he's like a freaking helicopter parent. I can't wait until everything dies down.

I love getting your letters so keep writing! I was SO glad to hear you saw your mom again and she's still clean. That's awesome!!!

Tell Mava I said hi! I told you working in the library was a great job. I'm hoping they'll let me visit her this time when I come.

I'll close same as always. If I'm not there to hug you when you walk out of Pochachant in two months and nine days, it's because the world ended, which you probably would have predicted in advance anyway. :)

Hugs and kisses from your favorite exclamation point lover,

Emily

p.s. To the CO reading my private mail, treat those girls right or The Law will be coming for you next.

Lucas lumbers into the kitchen and slaps a stack of envelopes on the glossy black table.

"Your latest fan mail," he says and goes to the refrigerator. The *I Love Dogs, It's the People that Annoy Me* magnet, scratched and chipped from all its travels, is back where it started the day I bought it for him at the Oak Court Mall. It's holding up my GED certificate.

Lucas drinks mixed veggies from a blender as I sift through the mail. Usual stuff. Love letters, hate letters, book agents. Here's one I haven't seen.

"Hey, Lucas. What do you think about me being a model? I just got an offer from a modeling agency."

"For what, combat accessories?"

"Har har. I'm serious."

"Fuck no. Stupidest thing I ever heard."

I toss it in the shredder basket. Last week Lucas threatened to shoot a paparazzi going through our trash.

"Well, what do you think I should do?"

I've been trying to figure out a next step since the day I walked out of Pochachant, the reporter's shouted question still nagging at me. *Where do you go from here, Emily?* My old life, the anonymity, living on the run, is gone forever. I miss it, but it is nice to have a home that's not on wheels, even one with bars and plywood on all the windows.

"Ain't it obvious?"

I know what he's talking about. The New York Times even wrote an article about my case and how I represented myself. No one ever did track down who leaked the information.

"The lawyer thing? That's what everyone says, but seven years of college? I don't know about that. Sounds like forever. And I researched it. The only lawyers who make real money represent big corporations. Lawyers who help people, public defenders like Paula, make practically nothing."

"You figure it out. No hurry," he says and heads for what used to be the document room, but is now the finance center.

With all the attention, he reluctantly gave up his career as a forger. He and James are taking on the financial world. James developed an algorithm that can predict the rise and fall of stock prices with remarkable accuracy, although it currently depends on hacking into corporate computers to obtain inside information. Lucas said the system needs *tweaking*.

I come to an envelope with what looks like a kid's handwriting in green ink. I tear it open and unfold a sheet of lined notebook paper.

Dear Mrs. Calby:

OMG, too funny. *Mrs.* It's written in loopy, exceptionally neat cursive. All the lines are perfectly straight, even the right margin.

My name is Margaret. I am nine years old and in the fourth grade and you are my hero. All my friends heroes are from the movies, but you are real.

I want to grow up to be a lawyer just like you. My mom said you are not a real lawyer, but I think she is wrong because you won your case.

My daddy died two years ago and the hospital sued my mom because we couldn't pay the bills. A free lawyer helped us. Lawyers help people when no one else can. I hope you will always be a good lawyer.

Sincerely (and love),
Margaret Kennan

Aw, sweet kid. I add it to the shredder basket. The next letter doesn't have a return address.

It's from another sexual assault victim. I hear from a lot of them. This one's a boy. Says a rich guy hired him as a personal assistant and raped him, but the police don't believe him. He wants to know if there's anything he can do. Yep. Sue the bastard in civil court for battery and the tort of outrage. But he can't do it by himself.

I pick Margaret Kennan's letter from the shredder basket and reread it. *Lawyers help people when no one else can.* I take the letter to the refrigerator and stick it under the *I Love Dogs* magnet, return to the table and open my laptop.

Filling out the SAT application, I laugh when I get to the question about *Activities.*

What did you think of
The Girl in Cell 49B?

THANK YOU for reading *The Girl in Cell 49B*, book two in the *Emily Calby Series*. We know you have lots of reading and other entertainment choices, so we really appreciate it. If you liked the book, please consider posting a review on **Amazon** and **Goodreads** to help spread the word. And thanks again!

Have you read *The Hiding Girl*?

EMILY'S PERILS began in *The Hiding Girl*, book one in the Emily Calby Series:

Twelve-year-old Emily Calby was a good girl from rural Georgia until the day two men came and murdered her family.

Only the killers know she survived. Now's she's on the run, hanging by a thread, overwhelmed by trauma. In Memphis, she makes an unlikely ally in an ex-gang member who takes her in and trains her in "self-defense." When more tragedy strikes, Emily sets out alone on a terrifying journey for justice. Nothing will stop her—not cops or creeps, not even her own splintering mind.

Dark and gritty, but filled with heart and hope, *The Hiding Girl* is a twisty, fast-paced thriller and a testament to the boundless limits of human love, sacrifice and the will to survive.

Praise for *The Hiding Girl*

"Dark and gritty ... an exceptional, heart-pounding story full of raw emotion, deep-seated fear, and an undercurrent of hope and innocence. Deeply atmospheric ... without peer in contemporary mysteries/thrillers." — *Publishers Weekly* BookLife Prize Semifinalist

"In Emily, Author Dorian Box has created a rarity—a teenage protagonist that is at once sympathetic, vulnerable and largely fearless. ... This sharp characterization within a fast-paced work of suspense makes The Hiding Girl one of the year's most exciting series openers." — *BestThrillers.com* (named a 2020 Best Thriller of the Year)

"The story that author Dorian Box has created for Emily Calby is nothing short of thrilling, but it's The Hiding Girl's masterful interplay of character, setting, and theme, along with its fast-pace and high emotional stakes that makes it a real page-turner." — *IndieReader* (starred review, Official Seal of Approval)

"[A] unique mix of hope, shattered innocence, pain, fear, and vulnerability ... a great, suspenseful read." — *Readers' Favorite Award for Suspense Fiction*

"Stunning, captivating, heartbreaking but also heartwarming. ... [T]he characters were so alive, believable, with heart and warmth, humor and love. ... This book is certainly on my 'best ever books' list." — *NetGalley*

"A fantastic book that completely demolished my expectations. ... This novel is fast-paced and action-packed but it has a profound human element that sets it apart from other novels in its genre." — *BookishFirst*

"Author Dorian Box keeps his audience on the edges of their seats with the gripping first installment in his new Emily Calby Series." — *FeatheredQuill.com*

Also by Dorian Box
Psycho-Tropics

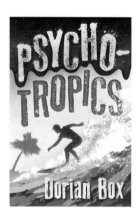

Writer's Digest Award Winner in Genre Fiction

A HIGH SCHOOL reunion in a South Florida beach town unburies the past (literally) in this dark mystery of revenge and redemption. Lottery-winning surfer Danny Teakwell seems to be living the life, but he's been hiding a terrible secret, punishing himself for two decades.

Now he's hit rock bottom. So he thinks. The ghosts from his past show up at the reunion, launching him on a mayhem-filled race through the Sunshine State to save a missing woman, and his soul.

The odds aren't good. He only has three days and his main allies are a pill-popping lawyer, crusty barkeep, and seven-year-old embalming expert. Heart and dark humor combine with page-turning action and a twisty plot that will keep you guessing until the end.

Psycho-Tropics Editorial Reviews

"An engaging thriller with plenty of humor, good characterization, and a memorable villain ...." — *Kirkus Reviews*

"Marrying humor with suspense is not easy, but it comes across masterfully .... A truly enjoyable read." — *Judge, 23rd Annual Writer's Digest Self-Published Book Awards* (Award Winner in Genre Fiction)

"Clues are tossed out like bait, twisting and turning the storyline along .... The characters are brilliantly constructed .... The dark humor serves to lessen the tension in all the right ways before it heightens again .... Effortlessly captures the wonderful eccentricities of life in South Florida ...." — *IndieReader* (Official Seal of Approval)

"A genuinely creepy sadist is the high point of Box's dark thriller set in Florida in 1995." — *Publishers Weekly*

"*Psycho-Tropics* is like riding Pipeline with a hangover. It's jaw dropping, heart thumping and addictively exhilarating, but with a hint of disorientation, dizziness and an unsettled stomach. But by the end you'll be smiling ear to ear and bursting to tell your mates how good it was." — *Surfer Dad UK*

Order it on Amazon

Notes about Louisiana
Locations and Law

REGARDING LOCATIONS, they are all fictional. There is no Pochachant Detention Center for Juveniles in Louisiana, although notorious examples of inhumane juvenile detention centers do exist. One of the most infamous was the Walnut Grove Youth Correctional Facility in Mississippi, which a federal judge described in a 2012 settlement order arising from a class action lawsuit as "a cesspool of unconstitutional and inhuman acts." Allegations included that prison guards sexually assaulted detainees, encouraged violence and smuggled drugs into the facility.

Nor is there a juvenile court in St. Landry Parish. I purposely chose a location without a juvenile court to avoid any unintentional parallels to real courts or real people. While there is a St. Landry courthouse and jail, they bear no resemblance to those described in the book.

As someone who has blogged about the benefits of maintaining factual accuracy in fiction, I researched and made an effort to remain reasonably faithful to the law and procedure of juvenile court proceedings in Louisiana, although I took some liberties to facilitate the story-telling.

The most significant departure involves Emily's self-representation. As explained in the book, in *Faretta v. California* (1975), the U.S. Supreme Court held that criminal defendants have a Sixth Amendment right to represent themselves, provided they waive their right to counsel knowingly and intelligently. The Supreme Court has never ruled on whether this right extends to juveniles, but not surprisingly, states are more wary of allowing juveniles to engage in self-representation. The Louisiana Children's Code permits minors to waive their right to counsel, but with limitations, including that they cannot do so in cases involving a "felony-grade delinquent act."

Acknowledgments

I'M INDEBTED to my daughter, Caitlin, law professors Mary Pat Treuthart and DeLeith Gossett, author Andrew Diamond, and graphic designer Gary Wayne Golden for their tremendous help in making *The Girl in Cell 49B* a better book.

About the Author

"**DORIAN BOX**" is a former law professor whose eight nonfiction books include an Amazon Editors' Favorite Book of the Year. *The Girl in Cell 49B* is his third novel, the second in the *Emily Calby Series*.

In his academic life, Box received numerous awards for both teaching and research and wrote thousands, possibly millions, of scholarly footnotes. He's been interviewed as a legal expert by National Public Radio, the *PBS Newshour, New York Times*, and many other sources.

Dorian lives out his childhood rock star fantasies singing and playing in cover bands that earn tens of dollars sweating it out in smoky dive bars until two a.m.

**Follow Dorian at dorianbox.com
and on Facebook and Goodreads.**

Made in United States
North Haven, CT
22 April 2025

68242406R00212